MW00463691

THE STANDOFF

A JACK WIDOW THRILLER

SCOTT BLADE

Black Lion Media

Black Lion Media

COPYRIGHT © 2019.

SCOTT BLADE.

A BLACK LION MEDIA PUBLICATION.

ALL RIGHTS RESERVED.

AVAILABLE IN EBOOK, PAPERBACK, AND HARDBACK.

KINDLE ASIN: B07WDDZT1Q

PAPERBACK ISBN-13: 978-1-955924-21-4

HARDBACK ISBN-13: 978-1-955924-20-7

(ORIGINAL KDP ISBN-13: 978-1686892370)

VISIT THE AUTHOR'S WEBSITE: SCOTTBLADE.COM.

THIS BOOK IS COPYRIGHTED AND REGISTERED WITH THE US COPYRIGHT OFFICE UNDER THE ORIGINAL ISBN. ALL *NEW* AND *ALTERNATE* EDITIONS ARE PROTECTED UNDER THIS COPYRIGHT.

THE *JACK WIDOW* BOOK SERIES AND *THE STANDOFF* ARE WORKS OF FICTION PRODUCED FROM THE AUTHOR'S IMAGINATION. NAMES, CHARACTERS, PLACES, AND INCIDENTS EITHER ARE THE PRODUCT OF THE AUTHOR'S IMAGINATION AND/OR ARE TAKEN WITH PERMISSION FROM THE SOURCE AND/OR ARE USED FICTITIOUSLY, AND ANY RESEMBLANCE TO ACTUAL PERSONS, LIVING OR DEAD, OR FICTITIOUS CHARACTERS, BUSINESS ESTABLISHMENTS, EVENTS, OR LOCALES IS ENTIRELY COINCIDENTAL.

THIS SERIES IS NOT ASSOCIATED WITH/OR REPRESENTS ANY PART OF ANY OTHER BOOK OR SERIES.

FOR MORE INFORMATION ON COPYRIGHT AND PERMISSIONS, VISIT SCOTTBLADE.COM.

THE PUBLISHER AND/OR AUTHOR DO NOT CONTROL AND DO NOT ASSUME ANY RESPONSIBILITY FOR AUTHOR OR THIRD-PARTY WEBSITES OR THEIR CONTENT.

NO PART OF THIS BOOK MAY BE REPRODUCED, SCANNED, OR DISTRIBUTED IN ANY PRINTED OR ELECTRONIC FORM WITHOUT EXPRESS WRITTEN PERMISSION FROM THE PUBLISHER. THE SCANNING, UPLOADING, AND DISTRIBUTION OF THIS BOOK VIA THE INTERNET OR ANY OTHER MEANS WITHOUT THE PERMISSION OF THE PUBLISHER IS ILLEGAL AND PUNISHABLE BY LAW. PLEASE DO NOT TAKE PART IN OR ENCOURAGE PIRACY OF COPYRIGHTED MATERIALS IN VIOLATION OF THE AUTHOR'S RIGHTS. PURCHASE ONLY AUTHORIZED EDITIONS.

PUBLISHED BY BLACK LION MEDIA.

ALSO BY SCOTT BLADE

1

JOSEPH ABEL PALMED A HEAVY, jagged rock in one hand and followed behind the guy he intended to bludgeon over the head with it, staying five feet back, giving the guy enough space to tempt him to make a run for it, but staying close enough to taunt him.

The guy wasn't young, wasn't old, but was right at the cusp of forty, which he considered the peak of his athletic lifespan. He played baseball in high school, which got him into college on a scholarship. But it didn't get him into the major leagues. It didn't get him into any leagues. He didn't play anymore. He made a different occupational choice.

His hair was fair, cut short. It was up off his ears, but coiffed and swirled like nature had decided that he would need no hairbrush other than his own fingers to style it.

In regular life, he was a good-looking man, almost to a fault. His peers often referred to him as "Pretty Boy."

However, he wasn't that pretty anymore, not now. There was dried blood in his hair mixed in with the swirls. His nose wasn't broken, but it was swollen. He was certain that they could've broken it easily enough. But they didn't. Not so far. That could change.

Abel said things to tease the guy.

"Think if you run, you can make it to the trees?"

The guy stayed quiet.

"I dare you. Go for it."

The guy did nothing. Abel continued taunting him.

"You sure? Just take off. Go for it. Who knows? Maybe you'll get lucky."

Silence.

"We could give you a head start?"

Nothing.

"Would you like that? I can have my guys close their eyes and count to ten, like hide-and-seek. Think that's enough time for you to make it to the trees?"

The guy did nothing.

What Abel said or did to the guy depended on what the guy said or did.

So far, the guy said nothing and did what Abel told him to do. No protest. No planning to run. No plotting to fight back.

The guy knew it didn't really matter what he did. Abel was never going to give him a head start. Not really. If he took off running, he'd get a bullet in the back.

Either way, Abel was going to smash that rock over his head. There was no stopping it. An unstoppable force meets an immovable object. The rock was the unstoppable force, but his head was no immovable object. It was just an object, like pottery —very easy to smash with a big rock.

The guy was Abel's prisoner. He had been for eighteen long hours, ever since they set a trap for him, a trap he walked right into like a rookie cop, like it had been his first time.

The trap involved a two-way radio that the guy thought hid in one of several abandoned structures that stood on the compound grounds. The structures were all there when they moved in.

They came with the property, sort of as-is kind of deal, like buying a house and having to take an old car that came with it.

The prisoner chose an old shed to hide the radio in. He had chosen it before he had ever even been there. He had seen it from aerial photographs taken by drone. It was part of his preparation before coming to the compound.

The radio was a thin thing, black rubber with a hard plastic case.

The same remote-controlled law enforcement drone that took the recon photographs flew over the compound overnight and dropped the radio from less than a hundred feet in the air. It flew in quietly, emitting no more sound than a hum. It flew just over the tree line in order to avoid being seen.

Pretty Boy snuck out on his second night, while everyone else was asleep, and waited for it to show up overhead at a preset of approximate coordinates he had memorized before going undercover.

The drone flew overhead right on time and dropped the radio. It landed in the snow, between trees. Not exactly where Pretty Boy had rehearsed where it would land with his handler and agent-in-charge, but these things never went exactly according to plan, almost never. In fact, whenever something went as planned, he usually questioned it as too good to be true. In undercover situations, when something's too good to be true, it doesn't just mean that it probably isn't true. It also means that it is probably a trap. Things didn't go off exactly how he planned, but they were close enough.

He stumbled right into the radio on his way to the shed. He should've taken it as an omen.

He should've known better.

Everything seemed fine for a while until one of the children caught him sneaking out on another night. He had been heading out to make one of his nightly radio checks. He couldn't make the radio check from inside the compound. At night, he slept in a huge room on a cot with twenty other cult initiates, all on cots like military boot camp.

At first, he thought his cover was intact because the children weren't supposed to be out after curfew, either. He and the children had converged accidentally, a stroke of bad luck. They met on the same exit point in the main building.

They all stopped dead in their tracks. The children too. They thought their parents had sent him out to find them, like a search party. And he thought he was dead in the water, busted right there. They were all concerned with covering their own butts.

Like a good undercover cop, he struck a deal with them. He made them promise not to say anything, and he would say nothing. Silence for silence. It was a good trade. They had feared punishment from their parents if he turned them in. And he feared death. So they agreed. He thought it was a solid agreement—a verbal contract. But children were the worst assets to have in an undercover situation because they're unpredictable and unreliable. Plus, kids don't keep secrets very well. He should've known, but he thought he was in the clear. He thought that if he could trust anyone, it would be the children. They wouldn't turn him in. He thought they would keep their end of the bargain. And they did…for almost one whole twenty-four-hour period—almost.

He was busted the next night.

The compound crowned the top of a thick forest in the middle of nowhere in northern South Carolina, twenty miles south of the border with North Carolina. It was nestled between a town called Carbine and a small county with miles and miles of half-abandoned farmland, dirt roads, and long stretches of unprotected forestland called Spartan County.

Spartan County met all of Abel's needs when he was picking out locations for his militant cult, which originally didn't start with the purpose of raising an army, but it evolved that way. Abel didn't start out with an ironclad purpose. He just started the cult and people came—unexplainably, the way cults often go. Families came. The lost came and joined—willingly, happily.

Over the years, he grew more and more ambitious. Leading a cult was supposed to be part of his retirement, a new chapter of life, but the longer time passed since his days in the Army, the more militant he grew.

Pretty Boy knew this. He had read the files over and over. He had memorized them. The good thing about the Army for law enforcement was that they kept impeccable records. They had files on Abel the size of the Oxford Dictionary. This included comprehensive psychological records and tests. Apparently, the Army had thought it prudent to force him to meet with a psychologist for a period of months, during his tenure in the military. Perhaps it was because his unit had the highest body count in Baghdad during Operation Iraqi Freedom. Perhaps because they had the highest number of allegations of cruel misconduct of any other security team during the long transition from the old Iraq to the new democratic version, post-Saddam Hussein.

No one knows the whole story, the whole picture, of why they had enough of him. It was a where-there's-smoke-there's-fire kind of situation. Something about him rattled the brass because they assigned him and his team members to psychological observations.

Either way, none of it mattered now. None of the records he read, none of the preparation he did, made any difference. He was caught now. He was Abel's prisoner.

Both Pretty Boy's hands were zip-tied tight behind his back. He knew the attack was coming. He knew Abel wasn't marching him battered and broken just to set him free.

He was a condemned man.

To have hope at this point would almost be a blatant betrayal to himself, but he couldn't help it. Hope clawed at him. A human brain is a problem-solving machine, and self-preservation is the brain's number one priority. As he marched to his death, his brain continued to work out ways to survive. It calculated and assessed every option to get away that came along.

Hope is a tricky thing. It's hard-wired deep in the brain like roots. It can't be shaken loose. It's too deep, too intrinsic. Even though he knew that hoping was futile, his brain latched onto that hope like a bad drug that can't be beaten—once hooked, always hooked.

Pretty Boy couldn't make a run for it. But that was what he kept thinking about over and over.

Go! Run! His brain shouted to him. It taunted him as much as Abel had done, as if they were working together, partners in torturing him. But he kept thinking it all out, calculating the odds.

If he ran flat-out as fast as he could, could he make the tree line? Could he make it to safety?

His instincts kept telling him to go for it—pushing him, but it would be pointless, and he knew it.

He would never make it—not in the snow, not in the cold temperatures, not in his weakened state, and not with his shattered morale. That was the biggest gut-punch. They had broken him the night before. Abel and his guys had stomped out most of the hope he had of being rescued. They literally stomped on him until he had nothing left.

Making a run for it wouldn't work.

They would shoot him in the back.

No way could he outrun a bullet, and Abel and the six guys who followed behind him had plenty of bullets.

Pretty Boy didn't count all the bullets present, but he counted four fully automatic weapons and two shotguns, and that didn't cover all the guns on them.

He knew Abel had a holstered Glock, which told him that the six guards also had sidearms. Altogether, there must've been thirteen firearms among them. That meant possibly hundreds of loaded rounds with four of the weapons firing full auto—if they so wanted.

Not to mention the shotguns, which he figured were loaded with buckshot, most likely.

Buckshot is deadly at close range and often still deadly at mid-range and can even be deadly at the mid-to-long range. The guys with the shotguns behind him were close enough in range to cut him down before he ran to mid-range.

They would shoot him dead without having to reload.

There was no running away, not this time. His only hope was his backup swooping in at the last minute, like the cavalry does to save the day in a movie.

But real life never works out like the movies.

He had no chance to run and no chance of fighting back.

Pretty Boy wore the same thick garb as the rest of the cult's newcomers: brown tunic-like clothes, somewhere between robes and medieval peasant gear. From the looks of it, the clothes they all wore were picked straight out of a cult catalog.

The cult's winter fashion line. He remembered joking with Adonis when he first saw the clothes that he would be wearing.

The cult's garb came in tiers, like military uniforms, each specifying one's status in the chain of command.

He was dressed in the lowest level of clothing offered to the cult's newest members, which meant that his outfit screamed to everyone that he was a newbie.

Even with the right garbs, Pretty Boy stuck out like a sore thumb to Abel.

Abel suspected him almost straight away, which was sad for Pretty Boy because he had been an undercover agent for five years.

Ten days ago, he showed up at the gate with a group of outsiders, all wanting to get in, all wanting to join the cult.

Newbies showed up several times a month in small groups wanting to join. Many of them were militia rejects, the kind of people too extreme for typical militia groups.

Most militia groups walked a fine line between extremism and simply having a fear of government. Most were in the business of knowing weapons, learning survival skills, and engaging in an overall sense of family. They tried to avoid extremists because they weren't in the business of terrorism. They only wanted to live their lives in the tradition of the American revolutionaries. Despite their political slants, they tended to live and let live. They kicked out extremists.

Therefore, extremists were the people who showed up at Abel's gates. They were lost souls looking to belong, but lost souls with extreme views.

Abel didn't take on everyone who showed up. Unlike most militia groups, he sought the extreme-minded as well as those who would die for their beliefs. Nothing's more dangerous than crazed martyr-like followers seeking someone to follow.

Many of those who sought Abel were turned down. They didn't believe enough or didn't pass the smell test.

Pretty Boy wasn't the first undercover cop to attempt to infiltrate Abel's group, but he was the first to succeed.

When newbies showed up, the cult performed tests on them to make sure they were who they claimed to be. They wanted to make sure that newbies were earnest about their intent. They wanted to make sure there were no narcs.

The cult accompanied the tests with an unofficial background check. Pretty Boy was the first undercover agent to pass. He passed the background check and all their smell tests. No problem. He was in.

One of the tests was a series of questions. And one of the questions was how he had found out about the cult. The second was how he had gained entry to the testing phase.

Pretty Boy had learned the answers back during the briefing phase, preparing to go undercover.

Newbies heard of Abel and his followers in all kinds of different ways: the internet, the dark web, social media groups, and good old-fashioned word of mouth.

Word of mouth came from outside militia groups who were like-minded. Often people who joined militia groups were kicked out because they were too extreme or unhinged, or they were searching for a religious element.

That was when someone in the group would take them aside and tell them about this place in South Carolina.

Someone would ask, "Have you heard of Joseph Abel?"

It was the story of Abel that interested people, but it was his unexplainable, undeniable charismatic persona that captured them.

Abel was a legend among the militant, among the conspiracy theorists, among the backwoods survivalists.

New recruits came from all over. Most of them were lost souls with nowhere to go. Some of them felt misunderstood in their own lives. Some of them knew of the anti-government positions of Abel, and they wanted to join for those reasons. They shared the same sentiments.

Whatever the reasons for joining up, everyone who came turned into a true believer before long—all but one. And now he was caught, beaten, zip-tied, and marching to his own death.

The undercover agent had ridden in with a small group from fifty miles north of Atlanta at a designated recruitment center, which was an old, run-down church with a pastor who favored the extremist side of religion.

A building attached to the back of the church existed as a halfway house, used by the state for battered and abused women, as well as former junkies and other lost souls.

As soon as Pretty Boy got there, they tested him.

It all went down like the swirling water in a draining bathtub. Before he knew it, he was sucked down the drain with the rest of them.

First, he passed their tests. Next, they took all his earthly possessions.

"Shake loose your mortal ways," Abel preached the newbies. "This is a fine day for you. You're no longer lost. We're your family now."

Once Pretty Boy was sucked down the drain, they tore off his clothes and shoved him into brown garb, like a new inmate joining the general population of a maximum-security prison for the first time.

He believed they made all their own clothes. Later, he confirmed this when he saw the women cutting and sewing various fabrics.

The fabric and many other goods were picked up by two of Abel's guys who went to Carbine, he guessed. They must've had several large P.O. boxes designated for deliveries and shipments of materials they needed.

The guys who went never came back empty-handed. There were always shipments of something—grains, ingredients, supplies, and fabrics.

After they clothed him, Abel's men asked him to do two things.

First, they gave him back his old clothes and his wallet and his cheap burner phone; he had bought it at a gas station. It was packed with fake contacts, and phone calls made to numbers that correlated with his fake undercover identity—in case they went far enough to check all that out, which they didn't.

Over a roaring backyard fire, they made him toss his old things into the fire, including the burner phone, which the agency he worked for had anticipated. That's why the agency gave him general coordinates of where he could expect the tiny radio to be airdropped in during the night.

The radio was all he thought about as he watched his fake stuff burn.

The second thing they made him do—over the fire and over his burning possessions—was pledge his undying allegiance to Joseph Abel and to the Athenian cause. All of that done in some weird half-religious, half-militant ceremony.

He wished he could go back and turn down this assignment. But hindsight was always twenty-twenty.

Wasn't it?

Pretty Boy started at the lowest level and, therefore, wore brown, representing the muck and the dirt.

The Athenians considered all newcomers to come from the muck. All those from off the street, all those who were newly pledged, were the uninitiated, the unenlightened, commoners, the filth.

Joseph Abel, however, wore all-pristine, all-white garb—white pullover under a white winter coat and white pants with newly washed white underwear underneath. He wore all white everywhere, all the way down to the laces on his boots and the yarn in the socks on his feet.

His uniform signified that he was the highest-ranking member of his cult, higher than a bishop in a church. He was the pope. Therefore, his uniform had to be the cleanest and most immaculate and the whitest of all the dress of all the members—always.

Everything reminded his followers of their lower station.

Abel did as the kings and clergies of old history did by making their followers kneel or stand below them when conversing. Only he did it with clothing. He showed them who they were, which was nothing. And he was everything.

It was all about status.

Abel's dress and mannerisms and stature were to be held above all others.

He was their leader, their king, their savior.

Cleanliness is next to godliness. That was one motto he lived by. He exemplified it to them not just by making himself always appear cleaner than they were, but also by putting them to work every day so that their own clothes and bodies remained dirty and sweaty and beneath him.

"You serve the Lord, and the Lord will provide," he preached to them.

Abel's clothes were always clean. Theirs were not. It was that simple.

His laundry was done every single day. One of his wives made sure of that. It was her job to make sure that it was so. And she did a fine job. They all did fine jobs.

He would miss them—in a way—after the thing he planned to happen happened.

The discovery of the undercover agent ruined his plans somewhat. He wanted to linger longer and enjoy his five wives, but the discovery of the undercover agent moved up the timetable. No big deal. He was ready. They were ready. It was time to act. The thing he planned would happen soon, at least the first part.

His followers knew of the first part. They were part of the first part. They didn't know the exact plans of the second act. They thought both acts went together like a one-two punch. They didn't know that their sacrifice wasn't the main act. It was only the distraction, the announcement.

The second part would come as a major attack on members of the US government - the real terrorists, in Abel's opinion. The Deep State was his enemy. They were the real enemy of the people, as he saw it.

He promised his followers that the attack would send terror tremors across the United States and the world. It would echo through the halls of power. It would be worth their sacrifice.

Abel tracked behind Pretty Boy through a field of snow, with the tops of dead wheatgrass, half-leafless trees, and white-misted sky.

He slowed and stopped.

He knew it wasn't their final stop, but he had a flair for the theatrical, the drama of forcing the guy to walk to his own death, finding the right spot, and then pushing onward to a different stop, teasing him, taunting him—predator and prey.

It amused him, but this was nearing the end of the line for Pretty Boy.

Abel couldn't keep this up forever. Things needed to be done. Preparations needed to be made. And explosives needed to be checked and rechecked.

Plus, it was no fun anymore. Boredom had set in and displaced the joy he had known.

Pretty Boy lost all hope—mostly. Therefore, he lost his fear, and no fear meant acceptance, and acceptance meant no fun for Abel.

A man at the end of his rope was no fun to torment with the theatrics of hope in his last moments of life, because he has no hope. He has nothing left to lose.

* * *

BEFORE THE MILITARY, before Abel rose through the ranks in the Army to the title of general, before he was a revered cult leader, he had been a hunter.

He was a natural-born hunter. That was what he was good at.

As a boy, he'd hunted with his father, deep in the Tennessee woods. That was back fifty-plus years by now.

For Abel, the fun in hunting wasn't about the ritual or the cycle of life or any of that nonsense. The fun came from the savoring, the relishing of the kill. That was what he loved.

Abel liked to hunt, and he liked to kill, and he liked to taunt—as simple as that.

He saw war the same way. That's what made him so good at it.

In war, you win by defeating the enemy. That's where Abel and ninety-nine percent of the military disagreed.

Simply winning never works, not in the long-term. Simply winning doesn't work because enemies come back. They evolve.

Victories last only until the enemy's ranks replenish.

Abel often preached in his sermons about defeating the enemy.

Every Sunday, he preached to his followers from the grand, white steps of the compound's main building. He used to preach in the church that was off closer to the main driveway, but the population of his cult had grown too big.

Now, he did his preaching outside, and he did it almost every day at the same time.

Pretty Boy had witnessed one of these sermons. He remembered it.

Abel stood on the steps as usual and preached.

"You can't just defeat the enemy. You must do more. You must take the extra step. You can't just crush the enemy. You must crush the enemy's spirit. You must crush their hopes. You must dash all sense of who they are from the history books. You must beat them into unquestionable submission. That's the only true way to win a war."

As Abel finished this sermon, he stared down at the undercover agent. Chills ran down Pretty Boy's spine as if Abel were threatening him directly. This was the sermon he had heard before they set a trap for him. He should've known. He should've escaped then, but he didn't.

Abel used to be in charge of a special Army unit. They were assigned to clean up the insurgents in Baghdad. They were good at it. They had been dubbed the Baghdad Cleaners by their peers. Abel and his crew got a reputation as "shoot first, ask questions later" types. They killed a lot of bad guys, which explained why the Army hadn't interfered with their unsavory methods.

Back then, Abel had a motto that he preached to his guys.

"Leave no enemy behind," a twist on "leave no man behind."

Abel believed this principle down to his core. It was the same as "win at all costs." That was why he was so good at war. At least, he thought so, and so did the Army—apparently—because they kept promoting him. They kept protecting him from allegations of war crimes. They kept burying the truth as long as it suited their goals.

He was good at his job. His team delivered results—no question. If they were given an Iraqi target to prosecute, they found him, and they killed him—period, point-blank.

During his tenure in Iraq, the Army gave him freedom of action. They called it all Black Ops and turned a blind eye while he and his crew did their thing.

Abel spent years in the US Special Forces, which let him do the things he loved to do—hunt and kill.

He hunted the enemy, he killed the enemy, and they paid him to do it.

As the war wound down, they couldn't look the other way anymore, not with journalists having more and more access to company units within the military. When the dust settled, people noticed things. Questions came up, too many for the Army to ignore.

They took away his job.

They had to put the muzzle on him, but they didn't want to fire him. You don't fire your broadsword. You sheath it and hope for the best. In the end, they didn't fire him. They didn't demote him. They promoted him.

They made him a one-star general and gave him a medal and assigned him to his very own command. Essentially, they made him into a glorified desk jockey. They assigned him to one of the worst commands a general can get, a place with a bad reputation —bad because it was notoriously boring, which was spirit-crushing for a guy like Abel.

They sent him to Fort Polk in Louisiana, which was nicknamed Fort Puke by those who served there.

To other generals, there was no bad place to get a command, but that was because they were on a career path only, and Abel wasn't. He didn't join the army so he could advance his career and retire, not after having tasted what it was like to hunt and kill in the Middle East. Especially not after it took him over a decade to meet like-minded soldiers and Marines and a couple of sailors.

By this time in his career, Abel had assembled a like-minded group, a group that would follow him to the ends of the earth —blindly.

He had found a core group of guys, of killers just like him. They all left their posts shortly after he did—all honorable discharges. Each of them waited out the remaining time on his contract.

Then they left their respective military homes and joined up with him, becoming Athenians.

By the time Jargo, the most recent addition, joined him, Abel was already established as the leader of a cult, right there in South Carolina.

* * *

PRETTY BOY'S REAL NAME, with his official title, was ATF Agent Tommy Dorsch.

Abel knew his name. They all did. They knew everything about him that needed knowing. He couldn't keep secrets from them. They had ways of seeing to that.

Dorsch's hands hurt from the zip ties. His face hurt from the fists he had endured the night before. His body ached. His mind ached.

"Keep moving," Abel barked.

Abel shoved him with a quick left jab. He had grown tired of his prey, and Dorsch knew it.

Dorsch looked forward and to the right and saw old playground equipment covered by blankets of snow. Old metal pieces from a merry-go-round stuck up and out of the snow and dead grass. One end of a seesaw punched almost straight up and tilted a certain way, as if it had been forever stuck in that position.

The cult had lived on the compound for so long by this point that the latest generation of children had been born there and raised there. All of them were young, under six years of age. Older children were brought in by members from the outside but were sent away, off to boarding schools.

Before six, they were trained and brainwashed into the ways of the Athenians so that when they went off to school, they would maintain their core beliefs and question everything else they were taught. But it was decided that they needed to be sent to boarding school every year for two reasons. The first was to meet the state's requirements for education for any child. The Athenians got tax breaks and all kinds of benefits for operating as a religion and church. And the second reason was that Abel wanted them to learn the evil ways of the outside world in order to cement the community's mistrust in it.

It all worked in tandem like he was setting up the perfect biosphere of people who lived and breathed as he saw fit.

In school, the kids would learn about evolution, but it was already instilled in them how false and fake the outside world was.

In the far distance, a train horn blasted for a long moment, breaking the silence, giving Dorsch a newfound, but brief, hope. This was a reminder of the civilized world; he had almost forgotten the outside world existed.

Dorsch knew the train was far away because there were no sounds of singing tracks or train cars rushing by or a bell from street crossings.

Still, he listened raptly, feeling his blood rush through him with the fury of a river. His heart pounded in his chest as if his body were gearing up for one last attempt to save his own ass, but he did nothing. He didn't run. He didn't fight back. He didn't resist. Nothing changed.

The horn blared once more. Then it died away like an echo lost at sea. With the vanishing train horn, he was left with one image of the outside world. It vanished completely a long second later.

"Move," Abel barked again, not ultra-aggressively, not authoritatively, not forcefully, just low and calm and commanding, like a doctor soothing a sick patient. Only a gleam of joy sparked across his face as if he enjoyed it, which he did.

They walked on, continuing past the snow-buried playground equipment, past more leafless trees, far from the compound, far from the road, and far from the eyes of others in the community.

They walked beyond the center of Abel's farm-sized property, beyond more empty fields of snow, past more trees until they came to another open field—the last one.

They stood two-thirds of the way across the compound's entire property.

Now, there was no chance that anyone Abel didn't want to see, would see what was going to happen next. Unless they shot Dorsch, no one would hear anything either.

Dorsch felt the last remaining ounce of hope that he had left deflated from him like air from a balloon. He shouldn't have had any hope left, anyway. He knew that because he was all alone.

The only people there were the people who lived on the property and him—the outsider.

His own people weren't coming for him. He knew that now. His backup wasn't coming. They were in the dark. They didn't know he was about to die.

His boss and friend, Agent Adonis, wasn't coming for him.

He wasn't going anywhere. He was Abel's prisoner till the day he died—today.

The sky above became overcast and turned gloomy and gray, like a painter's used up mixing pallet.

South Carolina was in a polar vortex that swept across the nation, lasting a long time, turning the temperatures in the US down to record-low levels. Snow and violent winds bombarded states that normally never saw snow.

Abel was grateful for the momentary release in the weather. In a sick way, he believed the slowing of the snow was a sign from God. And he'd told this to his followers that very morning.

Since the train horn, the surrounding air filled with sounds of whooshing wind and distant noises of cracking branches and swaying trees and dead silence and nothing else.

Despite the hopelessness, despite the dead silence, Dorsch listened hard. He closed his eyes and slowed his walk to a shuffle.

At first, Abel thought Dorsch was praying. He couldn't fault the guy for doing that. He was a man of God himself. So he said nothing, but Dorsch wasn't praying. He was listening, trying to make out another sound that he thought he had heard.

He heard a distant buzzing sound break through the rustling wind. It was far off and faint. It was somewhere in that realm, of maybe it was there, or maybe his mind was playing tricks on him.

At first, he wasn't sure.

Dorsch ceased his forward shuffling and stopped and stared up at the sky, his eyes darting left, darting right, desperately searching. Frantic.

He needed to find what he was looking for. He needed to see it. He needed it to be the ATF's spy drone. He needed to know that they had sent it to find him—to save him. He needed to know that Adonis hadn't forsaken him, that his service to his country had meant something.

He needed these things to happen, to see it above them, but there was nothing. He saw nothing in the sky, no drone, no backup—nothing.

Abel stopped behind Dorsch and looked to the sky with him. He looked left, looked right, and mockingly followed Dorsch's gaze.

The six armed men who patrolled behind them also stopped, just like a group of highly trained bodyguards for a Middle Eastern dictator.

Each of the armed guards slowly scattered around Abel and Dorsch, forming a wide circle.

Abel asked, "What're you looking for?"

Dorsch stayed quiet.

"Are you looking for one of those drones?"

Dorsch stayed quiet.

"You think it's out there?"

Dorsch stared up at the sky.

"You think it can see you?"

Abel stepped forward, and with his free hand, he snatched Dorsch by the collar and spun him around so that they were face-to-face so that he could see into the agent's eyes.

Abel pulled in close and whispered to him.

"There's no drone. No one's coming for you. No one."

Abel breathed in and breathed out, slowly and jeeringly.

Dorsch could smell his breath.

"They wouldn't see us. They'd have to send the drone down to see. Too much cloud cover, you see? Too much winter grey."

Dorsch breathed again.

Abel said, "Well, not unless they had infrared lenses strapped on it. Like we had in the Army, which they don't. Not for you. They won't waste that on you. I'm surprised they even bothered using a drone for you. Does the ATF even have infrared lenses on their drones?"

Dorsch stayed quiet.

"We did."

Abel breathed once more. Then he shoved Dorsch hard in the chest, forcing him to stumble backward, almost falling over, but he didn't.

Dorsch stayed standing and stayed quiet, and stayed defeated.

Abel saw in Dorsch's eyes a single shred of hope, of resistance, possibly.

They hadn't broken him completely, not as Abel had thought, but enough was enough. He had things to do, things to prepare. He had an operation to oversee. He couldn't be out here all day, tormenting this guy, despite how much fun he was having.

They were surrounded by acres and acres of rolling snow-covered hills and dark trees. The sounds of stillness echoed across the sky, killing off any notion left in Dorsch's mind that he had heard a drone buzzing overhead.

In fact, the buzzing hadn't been there at all. It was his mind playing tricks on him, giving him a delusion of hope, like a mirage in the desert.

Abel breathed again, coldly and calmly like before. He could see his own breath. He could see Dorsch's breath. He could see the thick air around them.

Without a command from Abel, Dorsch assumed they were moving on; he turned and stumbled forward, again, weak, barely able to walk straight, partially from external bruises, partially from internal bruises, and partially from sleep deprivation.

Blood was near-frozen on his face after being pummeled all night by six sets of hardened fists, fists that had pummeled many people over the course of their existence. They were the kinds of fists that knew how to hold back and how not to. For him, they hadn't held back.

Dorsch had one black eye, and his nose was broken. Plus, he was pretty sure that he had at least two cracked ribs. Possibly, he had internal injuries other than cracked bones, but he wasn't sure of that. Most of the pain was merged into one overshadowing, continuously throbbing pain by this point.

The six armed men who surrounded him and Abel had the sets of fists that had pounded him into hopelessness the night before. He stopped stumbling and stood up as straight as he could and looked at them.

It was the first time that he noticed they were no longer following behind him. Now, they were staying back, but flanking him and Abel in a wide circle. Then they all stopped and stood guard.

Dorsch noted their weapons again.

The six men were armed with serious weapons: assault rifles, a couple of shotguns, and one sniper rifle slung behind a guy's back by a shoulder strap, as if it were the most important thing to him in the entire world.

They were all big guys, probably spent enough time in the gym to compete in all the Olympic Strong Man competitions and come away with the gold.

Two of them were above average height, while three circled around six feet, and one was short and stocky.

The tallest one was a black guy armed with an M4 assault rifle. He stood a hair over six-foot-five.

The sniper was the next one down. He was over six feet tall. If he hadn't been that tall, the stock of the sniper rifle on his back would've been dragging behind him in the snow. It was a massive rifle.

Dorsch recognized it as a fifty-caliber, a deadly rifle that fired a bullet that could punch a fist-sized hole through an engine block.

They were all former soldiers who used to swear their allegiance to their country, but now they swore it to Abel.

Dorsch looked at Abel. He saw the rock. He looked past it and saw a Glock burrowed down in a holster on Abel's left hip, under the white winter coat. The holster stuck out like a sore thumb because it was the only thing he wore that wasn't all white.

Abel didn't brandish his weapon, not the Glock; instead, he squeezed his hand around the heavy stone, plucked from a rock quarry in the trees at the back end of the compound where a river zigzagged through the corner of the property.

He held the rock, gripping it tightly, keeping it down at his side, but visible. Every time Dorsch looked at Abel, he saw the rock, as if an unseen spotlight were trained on it.

Abel stood still. He watched Dorsch for a moment, studying him.

Abel had a look in his eyes unlike any that Dorsch had ever seen before. In the academy, in his last five years working for the ATF, he took a lot of courses and read a lot of books and attended a lot of seminars about criminal psychosis and criminal behavior. A theme that always struck him in those courses was that criminals are often good people gone bad, as if there were some kind of redeeming quality about them, always lingering under the surface, as if they could be saved.

He saw none of that in Abel's eyes. There was no good left in him—no hope of redemption. There was pure evil.

Even though Dorsch had stopped moving, Abel barked an order at him.

"Stop right there."

Dorsch froze and stared at Abel. He looked down at the heavy rock again.

Abel said, "Face away."

Dorsch paused at first. Then he turned back to face away from Abel. He locked eyes with the tall black guy, who stared back and smiled, just a slow, demented grin. But its presence there was big and obvious.

"On your knees."

Dorsch didn't argue. He had no arguing left. He dropped to his knees. They slammed and sank down deep in the snow like two heavy cement blocks.

Abel saw Dorsch's breath again; only this time it was heavy and frantic.

Abel stayed back for a moment, watching, enjoying, almost salivating. Then he spoke, asking a question that seemed way off in left field.

"Do you know your Bible?"

Dorsch stayed quiet at first, and then he nodded.

"That's not a very reassuring answer, but okay. It's not a sin to not know it. It's not one of the Ten Commandments to memorize the Bible."

Dorsch didn't answer.

"Do you know the story of Cain and Abel?"

"Of course."

His speech was a little battered, a little irregular, which happens when a trained, retired Special Forces operator slams the butt of an M4 into your jaw twice, followed by his crew using their fists to pummel your face and torso.

Dorsch felt shame that he hadn't lasted longer through their beating him, but he was no soldier. He hadn't been trained by the military or ever seen any combat, not like these guys. What was he supposed to do? He was terrified for his life.

Abel saw the guy thinking. He didn't wait for him to finish his thought. Abel spoke anyway.

"Cain said unto Abel, 'Abel, let's go out into the fields.'"

Abel paused at the end and looked down at Dorsch.

"And Abel followed."

Dorsch stayed quiet. Fear overtook his face.

"We're out in the fields now. You can't tell because it's winter. Because of the polar vortex, we've got all this snow. But we are. During the warm seasons, these fields grow things for us. We live off what God provides. You see?"

Abel looked around, waved his stoneless hand out in front of him, and brushed it over the vastness of hills and trees and snow and silence as if he were giving a sermon to a crowd of followers who weren't there.

"You hear that?"

Dorsch looked over the same vastness and listened.

"No. I hear nothing."

"Exactly. Nothing. No flapping helicopter blades. No pitter-patter of SWAT boots on the ground. No ATF reinforcements. No FBI. No police. Not even a single drone. Where're your people now?"

Dorsch didn't answer.

"You've been forsaken, my son."

Dorsch stayed quiet.

"I'll tell you where they are. They're regrouping. They're huddled up someplace, planning, talking, scheming. That's what people who work for your government do. They sit in their offices and make their career off your backs. They scheme. They're all about schemes and plans and asking permission. They don't live. They're not free. Not like us. Here."

Dorsch thought about his wife. He thought about the woman he loved. It wasn't his wife. He thought about his lover. He thought about how he wanted to leave his wife for her. Then he thought about guilt.

He looked over the horizon, past the trees and overcast sky. A dark object darted out in front of the clouds, igniting his hope once again, like gasoline on a single flame. He thought, for one second, that it might be the drone after all, but it wasn't. It was a bird, just a blackbird, probably separated from its flock.

Abel saw Dorsch looking once again. He glanced back fast and saw the same blackbird. He knew the thoughts that Dorsch was having. It was written across his face. There was another sudden burst of hope, which, like before, took a sudden nosedive into despair.

"Ah, a lost bird. A bird lost from its flock. Like you."

A fresh, single tear formed Dorsch's face. He said nothing.

Abel asked, "You know what that is?"

"A crow?"

"Know what they call a group of crows, don't ya?"

Dorsch didn't answer, but he knew. Everyone knew.

"They don't call it a flock. They call it a murder of crows. But that's a lone bird. He's not in a group."

Abel paused a beat and said, "That's a bird looking for a murder."

Suddenly, Dorsch burst into a pleading tantrum—uncontrollable and compulsory, which put a smile on Abel's face. They had broken him.

"Don't kill me! Please! They'll trade for me!"

"What'll they trade?"

"Your freedom! All of you! They'll negotiate! You can go free! Your people can go free!"

Silence.

Dorsch took a long breath. He spoke again in that battered voice.

"They'll come for me. They'll come to take you-all out if you kill me. People will die. Is that what you want? Your people are at risk. Don't you want them to live? They follow you. They trust in you. You can save them."

Abel held the heavy stone out in front of Dorsch. He raised it to his waist. Then he bent down and showed it to him. He clutched it in his boney hands like a pro ball pitcher clutches a baseball.

Dorsch said, "They'll come for me! Soon! They'll come with a hundred agents! They'll come with more firepower than you've got! Everyone will die!"

In a cold whisper, Abel said, "I'm counting on it."

With a sudden explosion of violence and force and power and rage like a berserker, Abel leaped up on the balls of his feet, raised the heavy stone, one-handed, and thumped it down on top of Dorsch's head in the dead center of the agent's fair-haired swirls.

The stone cracked his skull.

Abel heard it. The men circling him heard it. Animals not hibernating in the surrounding trees heard it.

The murderless crow heard it.

The guy's skull *cracked* like cheap pottery versus a sledgehammer.

Blood splattered out and sprayed all over the snow and covered the front of Abel's pristine, all-white garb that his wife had worked so hard to clean. And he thought nothing of it. He had other outfits in his wardrobe.

One fatal blow was all it took.

Dorsch slumped forward. Abel stepped back and watched the guy's body fall and hit the snow.

The guy's eyes stayed open—lifeless. His fingers twitched behind him.

Blood continued to percolate out of the huge crack in Dorsch's head and skull.

Abel stopped moving away. He crouched on his haunches to avoid getting more blood on his clothes or on his boots and stared closely at Dorsch, watching him die.

Abel didn't hit him a second time, although the temptation was there. He just stared at the gouge in the top of the man's head.

He watched the cherry-red blood seep out like a slow-erupting volcano.

After a long minute, Abel stood up and dropped the rock. One side of it was soaked in blood; the other was clean. The rock thudded on the snowy ground.

He turned to his men and shot each of them a glance and a smile, one by one.

"They'll be coming."

"When?" one of them asked.

"By morning. We can count on it. He missed at least one radio check. Get to the tunnel. Make sure it's not compromised and double-check the van. The engine. The weapons. The bombs. All of it. No mistakes."

One of his other guys nodded because that meant him.

Another asked, "What about the body?"

"Leave it. They'll probably see him with one of those drones they've been flying around us. A visual confirmation that their inside agent is dead will speed things up. Or not. Won't make no difference."

Abel looked at his watch and noted the time.

"They'll be setting up around us by morning. Don't you boys worry. The federal government is punctual, if nothing else."

All seven men walked away, back to the compound.

They left the dead ATF agent sprawled out on the snow in his own blood.

Eight hundred and fourteen miles north and west. Hours before Abel murdered an ATF agent in cold blood with a rock, Jack Widow turned the wheel of a stolen Lexus LS 500 to the left and merged onto a busy Chicago street early in the morning. He quickly merged again onto Interstate Sixty-Five South, where he headed southeast to the Atlantic coast of the United States, to warmer climates, like the birds of winter. He hoped he could avoid the brunt of a historic polar vortex that the newspapers had been saying would bring the snowstorms of the century.

Widow's life went like this: He came to a crossroads. He decided on the spot, and he followed through with that decision, for good or bad, better or worse.

Widow wasn't stuck up. He wasn't set in his ways. He didn't have a problem with pride. He had no pride. He had no disgrace, either. He just was. Simple. Decisions could be altered. Travel plans could be mended. Courses could be corrected. Minds can change, including his, and it probably should have—right there. But how was he supposed to know what he would get himself into? Widow wasn't a fortune-teller. He was both lucky and unlucky. Some people always seemed to win at sports. Some people always seemed to win at opportunities. Some win with money. Others win with love. Widow seemed to win at getting himself both into and out of trouble.

Seconds before he made that turn, on a whim, he headed south to spend the rest of winter in warmer climates, maybe the southern part of South Carolina or maybe Georgia or maybe Florida. Maybe he would drive down to the Florida Keys.

Widow liked the random, the spontaneous. Like a wild animal, he lived one second at a time. He lived in the no man's land of life plans.

Widow was a violent nomad.

Normally, it didn't matter where he was going all that much as long as he was moving and not standing still. Being still was for the dead.

This year things were different because far to the north, an unprecedented polar vortex swept over the earth, veering farther south than ever before, shattering world records.

Polar vortices circle over the planet every year, but ninety-nine years out of a hundred, they stay pretty close to the arctic poles, leaving the rest of the world unaffected—not this year. This year, North America was going to experience record freezing temperatures all over the map. The polar vortex would see to that.

Widow was only at the beginning of it. He was on the outer edge. He suspected the worst was yet to come. He noticed a mention of it in a newspaper, somewhere, on some park bench or bus depot, more than a week earlier and tonight he heard about it on the radio.

From what he heard, he figured that South Carolina would have snow, and maybe Georgia, but he thought Florida wouldn't. Therefore, Florida was most likely where he would end up.

It was the end of November. It shouldn't have felt like the Christmas holiday season, not yet, but what else was there on a calendar to look forward to before the New Year?

Thanksgiving had passed. His birthday had passed.

Christmas season was upon him, just as it was for everyone all over the world.

On the long, but gratifying drive out of Chicago and Illinois down to Indianapolis, where he changed course onto Seventy-Four and headed southeast, Widow listened to the FM stations on the car's radio. They played nothing but Christmas music. He listened to original classics, and then country versions, and then pop Christmas songs. Most were the same songs, just repackaged or rebooted or whatever people called it these days.

Some songs he had never heard before, while others he had heard done to death.

When he got bored with all those versions, he clicked to a hip-hop station and listened to hip-hop versions of Christmas songs. He flipped through the various stations until one song sounded familiar. He wasn't much for music that was highly commercialized, but this one was catchy and familiar. He didn't know the title, but he was sure the artist was a rap group called Run DMC. He had heard them before, probably on a battle carrier somewhere in ancient history. He recognized the song because it was from one of his favorite Christmas movies, Die Hard.

He left the station on and listened to the song from start to finish and hummed along with it as if he was back in high school.

The song did exactly what it was designed to do. It reminded him of John McClane, an average cop just trying to reconcile with his family by flying out to Los Angeles to visit with them, but instead of good cheer and family reconnection, McClane is forced to run around a building all night fighting terrorists.

Widow looked in the rearview and mouthed a line from the movie to himself. Then he smiled.

Happy trails, Hans.

At the end of November, the front part of December had been his favorite time of year, long ago when he was a kid. It wasn't anymore. It hadn't been for a long time, and with good reason. He was all alone, which normally he liked, but being alone in December often made him feel lonely.

Once, December had been a time he spent with the only family that he knew, his mother. It was usually just the two of them.

Sometimes they would go spend the day at the home of one of her deputies. It was all a good time.

Now, it was different for him. His mother had long been dead. Some asshole had betrayed and murdered her way back when she was a sheriff of a small Mississippi town. All that felt like ancient history now.

Years before that—even more ancient history—after an argument over sharing who his father was, a teenaged Widow ran away from home. He never spoke to her again, not until the day she died—a fact that he would regret for the rest of his life. It remained one of his deepest regrets.

After he ran away from home at eighteen, Widow joined the Navy, the NCIS, and then became an undercover agent for Unit Ten, a secret unit with the NCIS that investigated the kinds of crimes that no one wanted. They operated in the shadows, investigating Black Op crimes, mostly. They investigated crimes that were hidden behind top-secret levels of security clearance, the kind of things that there were no filings of.

They were black on black.

Widow was the first and only undercover agent to be embedded with the Navy SEALs. He had the scars, the tattoos, the memories, and even bullet wounds to prove it.

Most of his Christmases had been spent with one of his two families. In childhood, they were spent with his mother. As an adult, they were spent at sea with his SEAL family.

Those memories were behind him now.

Now, Widow was a loner, a nomad, a drifter like his father before him.

The biggest drawback of being a loner, a drifter, and an orphan all in one was this time of year. The holiday season was a downer, especially Christmas Eve and Christmas Day. On Christmas Day, it seemed like everyone else spent their time with family and friends, and almost every business in the country was closed. And Widow was out there, alone.

Early on, he formed a yearly ritual, a way of having his own Christmas.

Every year, he sought a twenty-four-hour roadside diner, the kind of place that doesn't close no matter what day of the year it is. It was the kind of place that would stay open during a nuclear fallout over the risk of losing one dollar in revenue.

Normally, these diners were the corporate kind, like a Waffle House or an IHOP or a Denny's.

Widow liked to spend Christmas drinking coffee, eating eggs and bacon, and chatting with the waitress who was unfortunate enough to spend Christmas where she didn't want to be.

So, every year, Widow found himself alone in an empty diner with only the waitress and a cook and, sometimes, a busboy.

Widow was there because he had no one left. She was there because she had drawn the short straw.

The waitresses were always different, but the story was usually the same.

She needed the job, needed the money, had to work, had to buy presents for her kids, had bills to pay. Hers was a story as old as capitalism.

Sometimes, there were other customers, mostly truckers stuck out, or a local beat cop who had to work. But it was usually just him and her.

Widow was there because he had no place to go. Truckers would be there because they had to eat. Cops were there because police departments don't close.

The only living relative that Widow had left was his father, maybe, if the guy wasn't dead in a ditch somewhere, but Widow had never met him, didn't know him, and cared nothing about him.

Widow's father had been an army vet turned drifter, not unlike himself. The guy had come into the town where Widow was born thirty-seven years ago, met his mother, and left them both behind. His time there was like signing a guest check-in book in a hotel. Signed, book closed, and forgotten.

Widow didn't hold any grudges, not against the father he'd never known. The guy never even knew he existed, anyway. Maybe he was still alive. Maybe he was out there, spending his Christmases all alone, too.

There was no way to be sure. Widow didn't have a Facebook account. No Twitter. Widow didn't do social media.

Widow changed the radio station in the Lexus and found the same Run DMC Die Hard Christmas song playing on another station all over again. It started from the beginning. He cranked up the volume, turned up the heat on the heater, and cruised on to the southeast.

He felt the warm engine air blast out of the vents and smash across his face and neck and chest. It felt good.

He continued down the same road, singing along as loud as he pleased inside the car. He imagined old John McClane running around a building on Christmas fighting bad guys, and he wondered whose holiday was worse.

The one thing that they had in common, he figured, was that McClane threw a terrorist off a building, and Widow had just thrown a bad guy off a penthouse balcony.

Ironic.

UNDER THE GROUND, an acre into the woods and hills, in an uncharted cavern, carved out of basalt and rhyolite rocks by millions of years of underground water flow that no longer ran, Abel's men checked and double-checked that their panel van was clean and gassed up and working properly. There's nothing like planning an escape, and having a mechanical issue ruin it all later. That kind of thing happened in life all the time, every day, but not in Abel's company; it didn't. Mistakes in a military Op were unacceptable.

Under normal circumstances, it was a one-man job, but two of his guys were down there anyway, an over-precaution to an onlooker, but necessary when dealing with crude explosives.

One man checked over the van, making sure it was mechanically sound. At least he did the best he could. When dealing with machines, anything could go wrong at any point. There's no such thing as preventing mechanical failure to a perfect one-hundred percent guarantee. But there was no reason to share that fact with Abel or the others. They had all served together overseas long enough to understand that bad luck was the great enemy of preparation.

The second man didn't bother with the van's mechanics. He was charged with weapons detail. He checked the crew's weapons and the supply inventory, as well as the explosives they were carrying.

The back doors to the van were wide open. The guy checking the weapons had laid out five M4 assault rifles, all fully loaded, all ready to go.

There were two combat shotguns, loaded with Magnum slugs, the kind that could blow the head off the shoulders of anything that ever had a head and shoulders, and at a good range if used by a skilled shooter. And they were all skilled shooters—no question.

The guy charged with weapons detail counted them up again, slowly, like he was just learning to count for the first time. He did this not because he was slow, but because certain things in warfare required painstaking, methodical attention, like knowing the number of firearms in your company, and knowing that they were all working properly and armed with enough firepower to kill cops.

Finally, after a second double-check, he spoke with chewing tobacco stuffed between his cheek and gums. He spat once and spoke.

"Weapons're locked, loaded, and accounted for."

The mechanic, named Dobson, stayed under the hood and said nothing.

"Any problems with the engine?"

"Not sure."

"We can't have no issues. Not now."

"I know."

"So, what is it?"

"It could be nothing. Just got a weird electrical read from the diagnostic machine."

"Isn't that what the diagnosis does? It gives you readings?"

"I didn't like this one. It was weird."

"What's weird about it?"

"It was fast, like an electrical surge."

"A surge?"

"It went a little haywire for a second. It started to lose power."

"Started to lose power? Or it did lose power?"

"It only lasted for a second, but it was there."

"What does that mean?"

Dobson shrugged and adjusted his eyeglasses.

"Could mean nothing."

"What else could it mean?"

Dobson paused a beat, took off his cap, and scratched his bald head as if he had wanted to do it for ages. His head reflected and glistened from steel-framed lights mounted on the cavern's ceiling.

"It could be nothing."

"Or?"

"Or it could mean that a sensor or a module isn't firing correctly."

"How do we fix it?"

"Maybe the system needs a re-flash."

"Refrag?"

"A re-flash. Modern vehicles are all electronic. Even the cheapest ones run an electronic computerized system. There's a bunch of systems working together, firing together. Might mean that one thing isn't working properly, and it's firing back at the other systems like a pinball."

"What does that mean?"

"Probably nothing."

"Can it wait?"

"Yeah. I don't see why not."

They both looked at each other. They had no time left. The ATF was coming, and they knew it. Everything had been planned and put in place. The wheels were already turning. The ship wasn't stopping now. Therefore, the van had better do what it was built to do—drive and carry.

The weapons handler, whose name was Flack, said, "Better keep this to ourselves."

"Of course. It's nothing."

Hopefully, Dobson thought.

"Agreed. We can't be throwing a wrench in this whole thing if it's for nothing. Not now. The general won't be happy about it."

"I think we're on the same page. No use in reporting something that's not a thing."

Dobson disconnected the diagnostic machine and then waited thirty seconds, counting them out loud. At the end of his count, he reconnected the diagnostic machine and checked the screen for readings again.

"There. Nothing happened that time."

"See, it's nothin'."

The two men looked at each other. Both were having the same two conflicting thoughts at the same time.

The first was mistrust. That was automatic, like an instinct. Doubt was something every man experienced, whether he had served in the same military unit as his friend or not, which these two men had.

The second thought was forced faith. Trust blindly that the other man would die with the secret—blind faith.

Faith is a soldier's unspoken requirement to do his job. Soldiers have to have faith in their orders, faith in their guys, and faith in the intel they're given. "Never question" was a military requirement—never question orders, never question loyalty, always keep the faith.

Abel's men didn't differ from every other military operator. They were also required to have blind faith, more so than other units. They had all rolled out of their military lives, given up promising careers, abandoned the chance for family life, just to join his cause.

They all had faith.

They believed in what he stood for. They believed in his solutions, in his causes.

Dobson unhooked the diagnostic machine and removed it and lowered the van's hood. He dropped it and listened to the heavy metal sound of the American-made van's hood dropping to the frame and the latches locking in place, securing the hood closed.

Dobson rolled the diagnostic machine away and left it on the side of the garage area. He stepped back to the rear of the van, the back doors still opened.

He stood next to Flack.

"M4s look good."

"Everything's good."

"What about the packages?"

Dobson pointed to two double racks that took up most of one side of the back of the van. The racks were metal, painted black. They were drilled into the bed and the wall of the van with two cage doors that closed and locked to prevent theft, as well as securing the contents so they wouldn't bump around during transport.

Flack stared at the racks and the contents.

"They're stable."

"Will they work?"

"No one can say that with any certainty. You know that. Especially when they were packed by idiots that we tricked into thinking we're some kind of religious cult."

"We're the ones who taught them how to pack the explosives."

Dobson said nothing to that. He knew it was true. If the van didn't break down en route, and the explosives didn't blow them up in transport, there was still a chance that the bombs wouldn't even go off because many of them weren't packed by either Dobson or Flack. Nor were they overseen by either man. Packing, engineering, and encasing a bomb wasn't easy, especially this many.

If just one of them didn't explode as planned, Abel would blame one or both of them for it, even if they weren't hands-on responsible. That's how military life went. The man down the chain of command got the blame, and so on—a pecking order.

"They'll explode. Probably."

"What about the C4s in the house?"

"Those will go off; I'm sure."

"Why so sure? You think the C4 was packed better than our explosives?"

"The C4's military-grade. And I saw to them each personally. Much easier when they're already assembled."

"True. They'll go off, then."

Dobson replaced his ball cap on his head.

He asked, "Will these go off? You know, on their own? Like an accident?"

"No. I don't think so."

"You told us how to pack them."

"I know. But I can't help it if one of you was asleep when I was giving instructions."

Dobson asked, "Think they'll explode if we get into a high-speed chase with the cops?"

"Think the van will hold up if we get into a high-speed chase with the cops?"

They looked at each other and then back at the racks.

"It'll all be fine. Gotta have faith, right?"

"Right."

"They'll all know soon enough."

Flack smiled and said, "Semper fi."

They looked at the heavy rack and the tight stacks of exactly forty-one pipe bombs. Each was carefully built and packed with crude explosive materials of gunpowder or match heads or some with chlorate mixtures. The packages surrounding the outer cases were packed with small nails and shards of broken glass, making for extra-deadly shrapnel.

They were all tightly packaged into priority shipping boxes from the US Postal Service. Each was sealed and stamped properly and addressed with a different name and address. All the addresses were in the US, including two in Hawaii and one in Alaska.

There were forty-one packages with forty-one names and forty-one addresses. Each was carefully handwritten so it wouldn't fall prey to being misread by the post office.

AT THREE A.M., Widow cruised along on a quarter tank of gas and listened to Chuck Berry on guitar, on what might be considered a slow station by today's radio standards, but was heaven to Widow's ears.

The guitar strings, the melodies, all of it buzzed in his brain like a honeybee. Chuck was a master. Thanks to him, Widow got away from Christmas music, and he forgot all about John McClane's problems.

Widow liked all kinds of music. It depended on his mood, depended on the setting, and depended on the company he kept. Late night, open road, quiet, just him and the stars, then rock and roll was the right call, the right fit.

If he had been cruising along with a woman by his side, then he would've made a different call—maybe. It depended on the woman.

To ask Widow if he had a type, he might think on the question for a moment, but in the end, his answer would be: *My type of woman is the tough kind.*

Widow left the heater on. It blasted and warmed his face. It warmed his arms with every exhalation of hot breath pulled off the engine.

It had been a long time since he had driven a great distance by car, all alone. He enjoyed it as if it were a brand-new experience. Plus, there was the bonus that this car had belonged to bad guys who were no longer breathing at all, which they deserved.

Widow pictured a warm, sandy Florida beach in the winter and smiled. That was his destination, he figured. Warm Florida weather, a sandy beach, and surfing all sounded great.

A few moments later, he yawned, the first time during the entire trip so far. He could stop and check into a motel, but he didn't.

He just passed the first exit to a small town with a funny-sounding name—Fancy Gap, Virginia.

He had never heard of it, and he had been down this way before, but never paid attention to that exit sign. He never noticed it. If he had, then he was certain he would've remembered it.

Not much farther, he saw a second exit to the same town. This one was more like a pit stop, with a single gas station in view from the interstate.

He stopped and filled up the car's tank, and at the counter grabbed a doughnut that was supposedly fresh, and a cup of coffee, which was also claimed to be fresh. He bought the doughnut and the coffee to fill up his body's tank.

From the drive down the exit ramp to the short distance to the gas station, Fancy Gap hadn't struck him as much of a place to stop and hang out. Nothing he saw was very appealing, and he didn't want to dig deeper to discover its treasures.

After he filled the car's tank, he leaned on the hood and ate the doughnut, and drank the coffee.

At the last sip of coffee, he yawned again, which he attributed to the long drive and the doughnut.

He looked around, gazing up the road and down, looking for any sign of a motel. He saw nothing.

After putting the paper, the doughnut came in into a trashcan; Widow went back into the station to get a refill on coffee and an answer to a question.

He had to pay for the refill. It was a dollar. Actually, it was ninety-five cents, but what's the difference? The nickel he got back went straight into one of those charity coin slots to help starving kids from somewhere else.

The answer he sought was free.

He asked the gas station attendant where to find the closest motel. The guy told him it was back at the exit he had already passed.

Widow didn't want to go back; he never did. He told the guy this very thing. The guy got a little irritated, a little protective of his small town. He replied Charlotte was to the south in the direction Widow was headed. Then the guy said that Widow might be more comfortable in a big city. And then he added it was only a hundred more miles on down the road.

At that point, Widow politely but aggressively noted that it was a hundred seven miles on down the road.

The gas station attendant said nothing to that.

Widow yawned again, rudely, and thanked the guy and took his fresh refill of coffee and hit the road. The coffee sat in a cup holder, and Widow's ears tuned back into the Chuck Berry station and the guitar sounds.

One hundred and seven miles later, Widow didn't stop. He didn't get a motel in Charlotte because, during the drive, the caffeine from the coffee had kicked in. He felt awake. He felt alert. And he went forward to see what lay ahead. He should've stopped. He should've turned back, but Widow never turns back.

THIRTY-NINE MINUTES AFTER FOUR A.M., two black, unmarked helicopters hovered over the perimeter of Abel's compound. They kept a wide enough berth and spread and altitude to remain hidden.

The sounds of rotors could be heard on the ground, but they didn't care about that. Sounds might raise suspicion, but they would confirm nothing.

At one gate into the compound, ATF agents wearing body armor were torching through two sets of thick, bolted locks on a metal gate. Getting through the gate was important. It meant the difference between raiding the compound by driveway or choppering in, which would've required an entirely new plan.

As the ATF agents burned clear through both locks, they stopped and retreated to the back of one of three black SUVs. Then the first SUV burst through the gates, followed by the other SUVs and South Carolina State Police cruisers.

The three SUVs blasted blue flashing lights embedded in the vehicles' grilles. Ten police cars followed behind them tight, all loaded with more ATF agents, heavily armed with assault rifles, sidearms, and riot guns loaded with tear gas.

The ATF and police stormed the compound.

The helicopters closed in overhead, circling, covering vast snowy areas outside the main building. The sounds of the rotor blades echoed over the treetops.

WHOMP! WHOMP!

Remaining leaves on trees scuttled off the branches. The branches and trees swayed heavily under the helicopters' rotor wash, kicking up loose snow. Snow washed and spiraled up into the air like slow-moving white twisters as the helicopters lowered to the ground. First one, then the other. Multiple ATF agents hopped out of the helicopters and scattered into their unit formations.

The helicopters rose back into the air, resuming their circling patterns.

On the ground, gravel and snow kicked up violently under speeding tires. The SUVs' tires tracked over a long snow-shoveled driveway, and then broke off their course to head in separate directions, covering all likely escape points from the compound.

The leader of the raid, and Dorsch's boss, was in the front SUV, on the passenger side.

The driver skidded the SUV to a stop, one hundred feet from the compound's main building, where everyone should have been sleeping.

The ATF agent-in-charge was a woman, but the leader of the SRT team was a man. The ATF's SRT stands for Standard Response Team, which is a team of tactical operators with SWAT skills, training, and duties.

Officially, the show belonged to the agent-in-charge, but only after the raid was over, and arrests had been made—her investigation, his operation. But the raid was the SRT's turf. The SRT's leader was a typical former military hard-ass, like many guys she knew.

She jumped out of her SUV, left the door open, and switched her rifle's fire selector to single-shot, a precaution because her intel had reported that the compound was loaded with children and elderly people. They didn't know for sure how many were living there, but they estimated it was near a hundred.

The team leader made the call to move in and stand by at tactical positions surrounding the main building.

The helicopters sprang to life, and huge beams of light flashed out of spotlights attached to their underbellies.

The helicopter spotlights washed over the compound: the grounds, the trees, the snow, the buildings, the barn, and the front and rear entrances of the main building. The light shone over a little church off to the farthest distance of the cluster of buildings to the east. It washed over a large barn, over outer and inner fences that housed goats and sheep.

The chicken pen lit up and then went dark.

The chickens made no noise because they weren't there. They had been moved into the barn because of the cold weather. So had the goats and the sheep.

The state police cars and ATF SUVs drove around the yards, circling the compound like a group of outlaw bandits circling a wagon train of weary travelers.

Several police cars pulled up at the rear and drove over snowy hills to get as close to the sides and back as they could.

One of the helicopters circled around to the back and washed its spotlight over the windows and the back doors.

Police lights spiraled—fast, washing blue light over everything.

The agent-in-charge stood by her SUV. She was short, barely five feet tall. She wore business casual attire—black pants, black boots, black button-down top—underneath a Kevlar vest which read: *ATF.*

Over that, she wore a black winter coat with a hood and wool lining.

She stayed back behind the hood of the SUV. One of her agents handed her a megaphone. She took it and spoke into the radio.

"Joseph Abel. Athenians. This is Agent-in-Charge Adonis of the Alcohol, Tobacco, and Firearms Agency. With me are the South Carolina State Police. We have warrants to arrest you and to search the premises. We want you to step out here. Slowly and with your hands visible. We want this to be a peaceful exchange. Please comply with this demand. You got sixty seconds. If you refuse to obey, we will enter with force."

Most of the Athenians were farmers. She didn't want to use force, but she had to find her guy. The Athenians were a part of a crazy, anti-government cult, but they were still farmers, no match for nearly a hundred ATF agents and police armed with assault rifles, shotguns, three SUVs made with reinforced steel, and ten police cruisers, not to mention two federal tactical helicopters.

The people inside would need at least sixty seconds to wake up in the dead of night, put on their clothes, and shuffle outside to see what was going on.

Abel would have to get out of whatever silk-sheeted, king-sized bed he spent his nights in. She imagined he was not alone, either. He probably had two young girls in bed with him. At least, that's what she pictured when she was learning about him. She tried not to let things cloud her judgment. But Abel's file told of a man who was as despicable as they come.

She had done the research on him. She had read stories about the Athenians, too. They were hard to peg because, like many crazy religious cults, they were armed with crazy ideas and guns, and led by a sexual predator.

Abel might not even be asleep. He might've been in the throes of passion with two under-aged girls, or one of his wives, or whatever young girl was the victim today. She had no proof of this, but it was the first thing that she imagined. She couldn't help it.

One thing that made Adonis a good agent was her ability to imagine the worst in people. It was a curse, really, but useful in law enforcement. She saw her negativity as a power that heightened her suspicion in people. Profiling is a useful tool, even if it is frowned upon by the public. But it only works for those who are gifted and well-trained. Profiling is skewed by the user's prejudices. If you have a prejudice against criminals, then it works fine. If you've got prejudices against short people, then it's a corrupted tool.

The other reason she gave them sixty seconds was that she didn't.

It was a lie. They weren't giving them sixty seconds. They were going to wait for forty-five, no longer. At forty-five seconds, it wasn't her show anymore. It belonged to the SRT team leader. Normally, he'd give the order to fire tear gas into the compound, forcing them to run out. But they couldn't use tear gas. The windows to the main building were barred. There was too much risk of the canisters just bouncing outside.

Before the team leader took over, she had instructed him to give a shoot-to-kill order on Abel if the man resisted even a little.

They were not to shoot any of the followers.

It had been more than twenty-five years since Waco, Texas, and the standoff with David Koresh and his followers. It was still a black mark on the ATF's history. They had learned their lesson back then the hard way.

Adonis had no intention of repeating it.

She lowered the megaphone's receiver and set it on the hood of the SUV. She raised her rifle and stared down the sights and waited.

The team leader gave a command over the radio, feeding into the agents' earpieces. The SRT agents moved in and surrounded the main building. Boots shuffled through the snow to tactical positions over corners and against brick walls. Some were prede-termined, others were chosen on the fly.

Trigger fingers slid into trigger housings, ready to shoot to kill. The ATF agents and the South Carolina State Police in rear positions stayed low, stayed behind the cover of thick metal SUVs and police cars.

Snipers set up their rifles from back near the busted gate and from two adjacent snowy hills.

Both helicopters had marksman shooters aiming from open side doors.

Three agents sported riot guns, loaded them with the tear gas canisters, and waited.

Assault rifles took aim at the points of escape. Eyes accessed the different escape routes from the main building, but also factored in the other structures as well, in case of an ambush, even though they knew the Athenians were inside the main building.

Still, they had to plan for unknown variables. The only intel they could go on was what happened outside and not indoors. They could only go on what they could see and not what they couldn't. They didn't know if the Athenians had built underground tunnels, which would mean a whole different set of rules of engagement.

The SRT agents looked organized and strategic as if they were prepared for anything, but the truth was this whole operation had been assembled the afternoon before. That didn't hinder the SRT too much because they practiced entry and capture every single day in various ATF-owned properties. These guys lived for this.

Adonis knew that. She had faith in them. Still, it was a last-minute Op, which happened a lot. Criminal enterprises usually run on tight schedules, just like businesses. The ATF had to maintain the ability to turn on a dime. They had to be adaptable.

The official green light for the raid had come hours ago, followed by the team leader being brought up to speed, followed by a briefing of the intel with his guys on the compound's layout. And then a plan was put into place. Now they were executing it.

Agent Adonis could've been angry with the agency for not taking her more seriously before. She was the one who had been pushing hard that Abel was bad news.

Now, with a missing undercover agent, they took her seriously. She just hoped they weren't too late. She hoped Dorsch was still alive. For her, it was more than camaraderie. It was more than doing the right thing. It was personal. She was involved with him. They were more than friends. They were having an affair. She hadn't felt guilty about it. But if he died, that would be a different story altogether. If she couldn't get him out alive, it would be her fault.

It took the potential death of an undercover agent to get the ATF to listen to her.

The green-lit raid made that apparent because with official backing came more manpower, more guns, and more money than the tiny five-man team she had been given to investigate two weeks earlier.

She had sent Agent Dorsch in undercover and kept four agents working support, but there wasn't much they could do without blowing his cover.

Agent Adonis stayed calm, stayed alert. She looked at her watch, a clunky but reliable Timex piece. It had a simple digital face with multiple functioning buttons and a black rubber wristband. It was the same watch she had used as a teenager. It was the same watch she had back in the Marine Corps, and it was the same one she still trusted. It was almost superstitious, like a ballplayer's lucky pair of socks.

Adonis looked back down the rifle and waited.

The helicopters swooped around slowly, hovering like giant buzzards.

6

INSIDE THE COMPOUND, no one was asleep. Everyone was fully clothed and fully awake, as if they had been waiting for the ATF. They had already prayed, but that didn't stop them from being stone-cold nervous. Some of them were more nervous than others, which was understandable. The more nervous Athenians had an important task, which gave them a sense of pride but also nearly paralyzed them with fear, both at the same time.

Many of them shook and trembled and shuddered. They couldn't help it. It was only natural. They were afraid. Some of them hid it. Some didn't, but they all shared it.

That's why Abel had instructed some of them to stuff a slug of raw opium paste between their gums and cheeks. It helped calm them. It made them euphoric and more likely to follow through with their assignments. Belief would only take them so far.

By the time the ATF showed up, they were high as kites, which was all a part Abel's plan.

They waited until Adonis made her plea over the megaphone. They waited for the beams of helicopter searchlights to wash over the barred windows before they made their moves.

They all wore white: white slip-on shoes, white pants with no pockets, white tops, white vests, white cotton jackets, and white skullcaps.

Their clothes were all starched and pressed and neat as if they were gearing up for an event that would be the defining religious experience of their lives, something biblical, like the next great flood.

In their minds, this was the rapture they had been promised. The dead would rise to plague the earth, and they would ascend to heaven. It was all right there in scripture and Abel's sermons.

The children were spread out along the walls, holding hands, standing in lines—single file, waiting to head out to the grounds, waiting to meet with the "bad men."

They had been taught that outsiders were bad until they were initiated.

The children thought they were going to go out and be brave little warriors. They were taught that they were fighters for Abel's teachings—for the ways of their saviors.

They shivered from fear and confusion. The children weren't given the benefits of the opium. They were fully aware. They were present.

The older ones were more scared than the younger ones because they had a better comprehension of the events unfolding, more grasp of reality.

Fear hit them hardest.

They were also more steadfast because they had been preparing for this day for most of their lives.

The younger ones were convinced that the whole thing was a game.

Half the Athenians stood at the front entrance and the other half at the rear.

Adults stood in front of children like protectors from the "bad men."

In each group of Athenians, there stood one who wore all the same white garb, did all the same things, blending in with the rest, but was different.

The different ones among them were the ones with the opium in their gums. But that wasn't all that was different about them.

On their persons, they possessed two additional items that made them stand out. They wore exploding suicide vests. In one hand, each held a small remote, like for a television, but with only a single button.

The vests were suicide bomber vests. The devices in their hands were detonators.

7

Adonis looked at her Timex.

It ticked away.

Time was almost up.

She stared up at the compound over her rifle's ACOG scope, through the gloom, through the white-blackness of a late snowy night, and saw no movement. No lights flickered on. No eyes peeked out of windows. No curtains flapped like someone was hiding behind them—no sign of life.

Suddenly, a bad feeling wafted over her like Spidey sense or women's intuition or a good old-fashioned cop's gut feeling. Something didn't feel right. It wasn't just that no one was coming out of the building; it was that no one was even turning on the lights to look out.

A heavily armed convoy of a hundred ATF agents and police would scare anyone out of his or her home in the middle of the night. Never in her wildest dreams would she have imagined that no one would come out or respond at all. It was weird.

She set down her rifle and got on her radio again.

"Clip, come in."

Clip was short for Clemens, the team leader for the SRT. In Adonis's opinion, of all the guys who do the door-bashing and the entry and the tear gas launching and all that stuff, he was one of the more reasonable ones the ATF employed.

Clip came back over the radio with one simple response.

"Go."

"Clip, something's not right here."

There was silence over the radio, as if Clip was accessing the compound to see if he could spot what she was warning him about.

"It seems good to me. Time to move in."

"I don't think we should."

"What's on your mind? Be quick."

"Look at it. No one's coming outside. No one's looking through the windows at us. There's not one light on in the entire damn building. Isn't that weird?"

"It's four-thirty in the morning."

"Yeah, but there are a hundred armed cops out here. No one's moving around in there."

Silence.

Adonis said, "If we were outside your house, wouldn't you wake up at least?"

"They don't need to come out to see us. They got cameras at the corners of the buildings. They're probably watching us right now."

Adonis looked up at the corners. She couldn't see any cameras. She clicked the button on the radio to talk.

"Maybe you're right. I still think we should back off. Reevaluate."

Clip said, "I say we go. Over."

"I don't know."

More silence.

"No disrespect, Adonis, but it's my call. Not yours. I handle the tactical side of this Op. I say we go. We won't get another shot. We got them by surprise. We need to take it. Your guy is in there. And I don't want another Waco. Let's not give them the chance to arm themselves. We go now."

"I don't want that either. That's why I think we should hang back."

"No. We're going."

The radio went dead.

A moment later, on a general channel that fed into everyone's radios, Clip's voice came on.

"Everyone, go on my mark."

Seconds passed.

The snipers lined up their shots as best they could. The agents in the helicopters readied their weapons. Everyone trained their guns on windows and doors.

The men on the ground got ready to move in.

Just then, before Clip could give the order to move in, everyone but the guys in the helicopters paused and listened. They heard something in the distance, behind them, back toward the entrance and the busted gate and the snow-shoveled drive.

Adonis turned, pinned her back to the SUV tire well, and watched above her as a single helicopter approached from the darkness. It wasn't one of theirs. She waited till it was in a better view.

She heard the blades and saw the helicopter clearly. It was mostly white, with the tail painted blue.

It was hard to miss, with the night sky behind it.

The helicopter was on a downward trajectory as if it were coming in for a sweep of the compound.

Clip came over the radio before Adonis could.

"Ramirez."

The voice of one of the pilots of one of the ATF helicopters came back on and responded.

He said, "I'm on it."

The helicopter that Ramirez piloted perked up and circled over the back of the compound. It tilted and yawed and ascended toward the sky, and then it swooped up at high speed toward the oncoming unknown helicopter.

The ATF helicopter intercepted the unknown helicopter back over the busted gate.

The unknown helicopter stopped and hovered a hundred feet in the air, seeming to study the events unfolding.

After a full thirty seconds of silence, Ramirez spoke over the radio.

"Clip."

"Go."

"It's Channel Thirteen News."

Both Adonis and Clip said the same word only Clip said it over the radio, over the main channel.

"Shit."

Clip paused a beat, and then he ordered, "Go now!"

Adonis froze, but the SRT agents rose like football players right as the quarterback barked the go order at them. They took off, running toward the main building.

From the air, the whole thing looked like an army of soldiers converging on a target city all at once, like a violent siege was about to occur.

The agents made the run in seconds and stopped at both entrances and at the windows that were designated as their zones.

At the steps to the front door and at the steps to the back, the agents all froze and dropped to crouched shooting positions, readied for whatever would happen next.

Everyone stopped because the doors to the main building jerked open suddenly and violently. Dozens of groups of people stampeded out of the building like it was on fire.

Clip barked an order over the radio.

"Don't shoot! Hold your fire! Hold your fire!"

The agents on the ground heard the order buzz over their earpieces.

They stayed where they were. No one opened fire.

Adonis was still back behind the SUV. She watched over the hood. She stared on in horror at what she saw.

All the Athenians running out were children.

They were in the front. Every one of them was dressed in stark white clothing from head to toe like they were about to take part in something special.

The ATF and her team hadn't known an exact number of children present in the Athenian compound, but they had estimates, mostly from Dorsch's radio messages. The first thing an undercover agent does when they can get a message out to their team is to give intel—headcounts, weapon counts, the number of children, and any signs they see of criminal activities, and, especially, notes on whoever their target was. Here, Dorsch had provided a guesstimate of the number of children and a detailed report of everything else he could share about what he knew of Abel until his last radio check.

The information he provided on Abel was nothing more than they already had in his profile. But the number of children she saw running from the compound's main building was close to the number he estimated to live there.

She stared on.

After the children made their way out and ran past the agents on the ground and away from the buildings, she saw adults of all ages—men and women. They were all holding hands. The women were out in front, and the men filled in the gaps. They ran tightly in a circular pattern. She saw some teenagers, few, but some. They all started breaking off as if they were terrified of something.

Why were they in circles like that? she thought.

It was only a moment later that her question was answered.

She watched as the hordes of children and teenagers and some adults ran at the agents.

Agents raised their rifles and aimed. No one fired.

She heard the agents on the ground ordering the running white-clothed masses to stop, to freeze, to stay where they were, but no one listened.

Clip barked the same order from before, only louder.

"HOLD YOUR FIRE!"

The Athenians numbered about a hundred. They were coming out of the building fast and spilling out into the snow, into the yard, and into the gloom.

The agents on the ground saw no visible weapons. So, no one fired, but they continued to bark orders and warnings at the cult.

Adonis raised her rifle again and maxed out the magnification on her ACOG scope to see them.

That feeling of uneasiness, of intuition she had, seemed to get louder in her head like a silent warning system.

Something's not right, it whispered. It grew louder and louder.

Not right.

NOT right!

NOT Right!

NOT RIGHT!

Suddenly, Adonis froze in horror. She knew what it was. She saw it. She saw them, the adults in the middle of the circles, eyes closed, running behind the children toward the ATF agents.

Their lips moved fast. They whispered to themselves—fast, as if they were speaking in tongues, like they were praying.

She saw something else. She saw the detonators in their hands. She saw the vests on their bodies, under open coats.

She saw the crude explosives.

Adonis jumped back off the SUV's hood and reached for her radio. She clicked the talk button and shouted into the receiver.

"SUICIDE VESTS!"

The warning came too late.

The Athenians, the circles of people in white, stopped dead in front of the ATF agents at the front of the building.

The Athenians in the rear stopped underneath one of the helicopters. It was low to the ground so that the shooter could provide cover fire for the agents on the ground.

The Athenians threw their hands up to the sky, spread out wide as if they were praising the ATF agents as gods. All of them raised their hands that way except for the ones in suicide vests. The ones in the suicide vests squeezed the triggers on their detonators.

Suddenly, in a violent, terrifying second that seemed to slow down time, the quiet calm, the gloom that surrounded the compound erupted into several huge, devastating fireballs as the suicide vests and their wearers exploded almost at the same time.

The pressure waves ripped limb from limb, followed by fire, followed by heat, all in the same second, all in the same collision of destruction.

Smoke and fire and immense heat ripped through the air as if they followed behind missiles launching from the ground. The fire roared and burned and raged. The heat seared the skin of everyone who felt it. Multiple blast waves shocked and exploded and tore up from the bombers' torsos and ripped into the air. The main building's windows exploded and shattered. The glass shattered inward in a massive wave of millions of smaller pieces. The bars on the windows rattled on their hinges. The wood and the brick heated, catching fire almost instantaneously. The porch went up in a spheroid of flames.

The compound was hit with a firestorm.

The explosions rocked the main building and echoed through the others. Body parts tore through the air and the smoke like a macabre firework show.

Adonis was thrown back off her feet from the multiple blasts.

Her body slammed down into the snow so deep that she felt stuck instantly.

She stared up at the dark sky for what felt like a long, long moment, but was really just magnified by the slow-motion feeling of the whole moment. She couldn't move. The wind had been knocked out of her.

She could no longer see her agents or the explosions, but she could hear them. She could still see the smoke.

The explosions paused for a long moment, and then they picked up again, almost as if a new set of explosions had begun. They continued to roar. The first wave wasn't the only wave. She figured there was a second wave. The second wave was different. It was worse than the first, more powerful, louder.

It seemed like everything was exploding. The whole thing seemed to be a coordinated effort, meant to be a horrifying trigger of exploding dominoes.

After several minutes of explosions and fire and smoke, the explosions stopped. Adonis was left with only the sounds of the screams of agony of the agents and the few Athenians left alive.

Adonis stared up to the sky and watched more black smoke fill the air and cover any sign of stars in the sky.

8

ELEVEN DAYS BEFORE THE EXPLOSION, the fire, and the near-hundred dead in a brick and wood multi-building compound painted all white, in the unusually snowy woods in Carbine, South Carolina, ATF Lead Agent Toni Adonis had taken the lead on a new investigation that began from a tip, originating from a mailman out of Augusta, Georgia. The tip led her and her team straight to the Athenians. Which she thought was about as generic a name to call a cult as possible. Why not just call themselves the Romans or the Spartans or just plainly call themselves the Jedi?

The Athenians became a joke among agents involved in the tree of communications from the agent who first took the call about the tip to Adonis's boss.

Not much was known about the Athenians on a federal level. When she first got the case, she had to start at the state level just to get info about them. But the state level had little on them. She had to move to the local level and inquire about them with the Carbine Police Department, who sent her to the Spartan County Sheriff's office. No one had much.

It wasn't until she got the registered name of their leader and the CEO of Athenian, Inc., a registered company in the state of South Carolina, that she learned something interesting.

Athenian, Inc. was basically both a registered business and a certified religious entity. But the leader of both things was a man named Joseph Abel.

Abel had quite an interesting history. Once a one-star general in the US Army, Abel was now seen as a militant religious fanatic. He wasn't on the FBI's Most Wanted List or anything. His name wasn't on any official terrorist watch lists that Adonis could find. But after a long morning and afternoon of piecing together the man's documented history and current whereabouts, she put together a terrifying profile of a man who was dangerous and at worst could be a terrorist leader in the making.

The Spartan County Sheriff's office and the Carbine police had nothing negative to report about the Athenians. They kept to themselves and didn't break any laws that the various police departments were aware of.

Abel's Athenians were a quiet, religious sect—common enough people, mostly simple-minded, ignorant—the kind of people you would expect to find in a religious cult. They were the kind of people who follow and never question. Doubts never crossed their minds, but that wasn't just because they were ignorant and naïve. It was also because of Abel.

Abel was a kind of anti-government, anti-society, anarchist, David Koresh-type, but with ten times the charisma and ten times the know-how.

Certainly, his military background gave him a commanding presence.

The Augusta mailman informed his supervisor, who told the postmaster, who told the postmaster general, who contacted the ATF and the FBI about a tightly packed box that snagged open from connecting with a loose rack in an off-freeway Postal Service depot.

A forklift driver had been moving pallets. He sped up a little too hard, a little too fast, and bumped into a pallet, which started a chain reaction of boxes falling over and knocking over the next box, like dominoes, where the final shipping box was busted open. The whole thing was a total accident, an entire piece of bad luck for the senders and receivers of the shipment.

The box contained nothing illegal. At first, they thought the accident had busted the contents because they found thousands of crushed, burned-out light bulbs and shards of glass. They thought they had accidentally broken open a shipment of bulbs or something else made of glass. Upon further inspection, they realized that the light bulbs were already crushed and broken.

The box was marked: *For Recycling Purposes.*

The part that was strange, other than wondering why any company would ship broken glass to be recycled, was that the box of crushed, burned-out light bulbs had a return address from a fake company owned by a notorious militia group called the Two Percent, which was already flagged by the FBI for radical behavior and anti-government activities, including promoting domestic terrorism and especially acts of violence using pipe bombs against large crowds.

The Two Percent had blogs on the dark web, with lists of targets and instructions on making pipe bombs and many other things that kept the FBI monitoring them.

A flag was triggered after the mailman saw the contents of broken glass and after the postmaster general was notified. The triggered flag alerted the FBI, who investigated further.

The Two Percent owned no company or manufacturing business or recycling business. The only things they manufactured were propaganda and hate. The only thing they recycled was the steady stream of the same conspiracy theory claims.

The FBI found four more pallets loaded with the same broken glass, the same recyclable markings, and the same "Ship To" address, with the same recipient.

Coupling the broken glass with an armed robbery in South Carolina of a large plant nursery where the robbers stole dozens of bags of fertilizer, the FBI agents involved raised their eyebrows along with their suspicions.

The broken glass could be what it claimed—possibly—but broken light bulbs are often used to pack pipe bombs. Not a red flag but that combined with the false recycling claim and the origin of the shipping and the stolen fertilizer out of South Carolina and the direct connection to the Two Percent militia group meant the FBI was inclined to notify the ATF.

The ATF took the case. It turned out that they were already tracking numerous shipments of weapons and bullets and piping to a religious group in Carbine—the Athenians.

It all seemed to connect on paper.

The ATF began monitoring them. They assigned Adonis to lead the case. Within one day, she had a team in place and was planning to infiltrate them with an undercover agent. She had enough to warrant infiltration; when it came to bomb-making materials in the hands of crazed anti-government cults, the ATF didn't drag its feet. They had no time to waste.

Adonis was certain that if they dug enough, they would find an internet connection and communication between the two militant groups, and they did. Then they got more than they bargained for when they tapped the Army to provide records of Abel. Their requests were met with resistance at first. That was until she explained the bomb-making materials and militia group connections that the ATF and the FBI already had.

The Army cooperated, reluctantly, but with enough to paint quite a terrifying picture of the guy.

Whoever Abel used to be had long been buried. He was a ghost. It turned out that he had the kind of past with titles like Black Ops and acronyms like USSFs, United States Special Forces.

Before sending Dorsch in, they set up an external surveillance team close to the compound. They used drones and watched them for five days. They studied them. They heard gunfire every morning from eight a.m. till noon; target practice they surmised, or shooting classes, taught by Abel's right-hand guys.

They got plenty of video of it happening from two surveillance drones.

The property was twenty-five acres on either side of their compound and covered with huge, thick trees and snow.

If it weren't for one small break, a break that Adonis couldn't use in court, she would've been told to move on.

One of her drones captured the license plate of a black panel van parked in the back lot of the compound, with a bunch of other vehicles, which was weird because the driveway headed in the other direction. No matter, it was the plate that they could identify as one caught on camera near the nursery and the stolen fertilizer.

It wasn't enough to get the proper authorization from a judge for a raid of the compound, but it was enough to convince her boss to authorize an undercover operation.

In her early life, Adonis had gotten a lot of flak because when asked what Toni was short for, she would say that her first name wasn't short for Antonio or Antonia or Antoinette. It was short for Anthony, a boy's name, given to her by her dead father. He was African, but not in the African-American way. He was actually from Africa. He was born in the former French colony of Morocco. So was her mother. They were both originally Moroccan. They spoke French and English. They grew up around post-colonial francophone traditions. They kept Toni in the same traditions, even after they moved to the American South. Adonis was born and partially raised in Atlanta.

One tradition, shared by both the French and Moroccan people, once upon a time, was a strong patriarchal hierarchy—prehistoric, olden, and outdated now, but it had been there.

Because of this patriarchy, Adonis was given her grandfather's name, Anthony William Adonis. Whether it was popular at the time to do so or not, it was what it was.

As an adult, Toni Adonis kept the Toni part, but never ever revealed to anyone that her first name was Anthony or that her middle name was William. If her team had ever found out, they would call her Willie for sure. No getting around it. It would've been with love, but it would've been annoying and embarrassing and a wrecking ball that would undermine her in her new leadership position.

She would take the male names with her to the grave.

9

ADONIS'S PARENTS were both dead now, cancer for one and a car crash involving a drunk bus driver, the bus he was driving, and a head-on collision at a stoplight, for the other.

Her father would've been upset with her for choosing to be an ATF agent—such a male-dominated profession as law enforcement was the last thing he would've wanted for her—but her mother would've been proud.

Adonis knew that, but neither parent lived to see it.

She was the first in her family to go to college, to get a degree, and to advance in a career field like law enforcement.

She was an only child. She had no connection to her extended family back in the old world. Somewhere, she had an email address and the name of her mother's sister, but she had never had contact with her. Why start now?

She remembered she had emailed once, after her mother died, but never investigated to see if anyone ever received her note or emailed her back. It's possible that her mother's sister read the email and responded, but it went to her spam folder.

Adonis just never searched for it.

She loved working for the ATF. Mostly they tracked and busted illegal firearms sales and illegal stockpiles of military-grade weapons. Arms dealing and gun smuggling was a big trade in North America, a trade that got little media attention, if any. These days it was Homeland Security or ICE or that got all the media attention. There was still a lot of coverage of the war on drugs as well. The DEA benefitted from those stories. And the FBI always got top-billed in the media, while her agency was the forgotten child.

On top of having a male name in a mostly male field, Adonis was black, a fact that some of her colleagues resented when she started, thinking that she had been included as a token black. Many of the higher-ups gave her grief about it. So did the men on the ground, in training, in the field. But once she continued to show up every day, putting her all into the job, she earned respect and was given it. The negative comments stopped, and, over time, she fell into their brotherhood like any man, black or not.

Adonis's rise through the ranks seemed pretty fast to her male counterparts, but to her, it had not been fast at all. To her, it was because she doubled her efforts over her male counterparts. She worked twice as hard as they did. She was always the first to show up and the last to leave. Some affectionately called her The Pit Bull because she possessed toughness and determination and stubbornness, and she had a small frame.

She had put in the work, and now she was in command of her first major operation.

They called the operation: *Cherokee Hill*, after a nearby location with miles of rolling hills to the east with the same name. Carbine was a border town in South Carolina, twenty miles south of the North Carolina state line. Despite the opportunity for a command, despite her pit bull nature, despite wanting to prove that a black woman was just as good as or better than any man in the ATF, Adonis would come to dread ever hearing the name Cherokee Hill.

10

TOWARD THE BACK of the Athenian compound, and under the snow and the hills and the dirt, Joseph Abel sat in the front passenger seat of a black panel van.

Dobson sat in the driver's seat, and the rest of the crew huddled in the back between assault rifles stored up along the wall on one side of the cabin and the forty-one packaged, addressed, and stamped pipe bombs secured to another.

They moved ahead slowly along the driving trail paved on the floor of the cave. The project had taken only a month and a half because they'd used the free labor Abel gained from his followers.

Luckily, there hadn't been many obstructions to clear out in order to make the tunnel flat enough for the van to drive in and out of. The natural tunnel led away from the compound for more than a half-mile and came up about a football field from a dirt road that wasn't much wider than the track they had created.

Dobson drove with ease, taking it slowly, being careful, being cautious.

They left the radio off and the windows down. They listened to the sound of explosions from above. Abel closed his eyes and listened as if he were enjoying a live musical orchestra. The cacophony of explosions sounded loud and echoing, literally music to his ears.

The explosions did little damage to the cave, not until the final one that blew the main building to pieces. That one came at the end of a string of explosions.

At the sound of the first explosion, Abel spoke.

"Stop here," he ordered Dobson.

Dobson nodded and slowed the van to a complete stop. He kept his foot on the brake and waited.

Abel reached into his winter coat and pulled out a small burner cell phone. He dialed a number with the press of a single button. It was a pre-programmed number, set to fast dial.

He didn't put the phone up to his ear like he was making a call. He just waited and looked out the window over the trees.

There was only one simple ring, and then the burner phone went dead.

The other phone he was calling was installed as a trigger to several layers of C4 explosives plastered at structural points on the main building, the church, the barn, and the other buildings.

The second after the other line received the call, the C4 exploded.

Abel and his guys sat and listened to the discordant sounds of explosions and screams that followed. The explosions they heard with no effort. They heard the screams on the wind.

The final explosion came as the loudest. It echoed over the trees and across the sky. The last one rocked the cavern behind them. Rocks tore off the ceiling and fell to the ground as if a giant were stomping on the ground above.

With the touch of a button, Abel killed anyone who was left inside the main building, the church, the barn, all the remaining buildings.

Abel smiled a cold, ominous smile. The polished whites of his teeth matched his coat.

He smiled because he had convinced the Athenians to martyr themselves, but none of them knew about the C4 explosives. They didn't know of the forty-one pipe bombs or what they were for. They only knew the lies they were told, and they believed them as truth.

Abel figured the ones left behind were certainly dead now. It was doubtful anyone would survive the explosions, and if they did, so what? No one had all the pieces to what he was up to other than himself and his core guys.

He delighted in it all. He delighted in the deception, in his plans, and in the carnage he caused.

Abel tossed the burner phone out the window and over the van's hood. It landed on the cavern floor in front of the van.

"Run over it. Okay. Let's go."

Dobson nodded and took his foot off the brake and pressed down on the gas. The van rolled on and forward and over the burner phone, crushing it to pieces.

Abel stared out the window, listened to the cracking and shattering of the burner phone, and smiled.

11

TRICKING THE ATF INTO A TRAP, killing his followers, and covering his tracks was all part of the plan. However, one thing that Abel lived by was to expect the unexpected. Plans go to hell when the first action is taken, always. It is a good measure to forecast that things will go wrong, or at least different from expected.

About five miles down the winding backroad from the compound and the fires—backroads that were supposed to be clear—Abel and his men came to their first unexpected obstacle.

"General," Dobson said.

Abel looked forward and stared out the windshield ahead.

"I see him."

Up ahead of them about a hundred yards away from the van's grille, through overhung trees, at the intersection of the snowy, dirt road they were on and the one they needed to turn on, a lone highway patrolman was parked in the middle of the inter-section.

The light bar on his car flashed blue light through the gloom.

"What do we do?"

"Keep going."

"What if he wants me to stop?"

"He will want us to stop. So, stop."

Dobson nodded and drove slowly to the end of the dirt road.

The highway patrolman stood a few feet out in front of his cruiser's grille. The car's engine idled. The driver door hung open like he had just thrown the car into park and stepped out, which is what he did. He was cruising along, patrolling the sector that he was assigned to patrol, which was just a confusing section of backroads near the Athenian compound's property line. That's when he thought he heard explosions, forcing him to pull over and step out. That was only moments ago.

The highway patrolman wore a bulletproof vest outside his uniform, but under a heavy police coat. The vest was plain and obvious. It was a bulky thing that made him look like he wore a deflated tire around his torso.

The patrolman had one hand resting on the butt of a holstered Glock.

He watched, a little confused by the oncoming black van and the headlights coming toward him. Behind the van, far above the trees, he saw black smoke coming from the direction of what he thought had been a series of explosions. He couldn't confirm this because, so far, he couldn't get anyone on the radio to update him. He heard a bunch of inaudible chatter back and forth between cops and ATF agents. He heard nothing concrete, nothing definitive, not even anything that made coherent sense, not yet. There was too much excitement. He wanted to leave and drive over that way, find out what the hell was going on, but the incoming van might be worth stopping to check them out.

Still, he was a good cop. He didn't ask questions when the time wasn't right for questions. And by the sounds of the chatter, this wasn't the time to be asking questions. Dispatch had enough going on with the operation to the south.

He was sure that he had heard something that sounded like explosions. It all had to be connected. He figured the Athenians engaged in a firefight with the ATF. Maybe he heard grenades or explosives. A lot of times, these cult-militias are armed to the teeth with all kinds of military hardware. There was no telling what the Athenians had in their arsenal. He had never heard of a militia group using grenade or rocket launchers on law enforcement before, but it wouldn't shock him if that's what they were doing.

The patrolman watched as a black van pulled up out of the gloom from the direction of the compound grounds.

But there were no roads into the compound from there. Why were they there?

The van's tires rolled slowly through white mist and darkness. It pulled up slowly and stopped at a four-way stop sign, about ten yards from the toe of his boot.

The patrolman raised both hands and stepped out into the middle of the road. He signaled for the van to stop. As it slowed, he lowered his gun hand and dropped it back onto the butt of his Glock. He walked straight and then curved to approach the driver. As he gained ground, he noticed that there were multiple people inside the van. He wasn't sure how many because of how far away the van was, but he counted more than three. Through the windshield, he saw two figures seated in the front, one in the driver's seat and another in the passenger seat.

He approached all the way and stopped and tapped on the window with his other gloved hand. Dobson rolled the window down manually and leaned out with a big smile on his face.

"Hello, Officer. What's going on?"

The patrolman stayed back a couple of feet and peered into the van's cabin. First, he looked at Dobson. The guy had unremarkable features. Then he looked over at Abel, who wore all white. The guy smiled at him, almost sinisterly. Then he craned his head and tried to look in the back of the van, but could make out nothing but shadowy figures—several of them. It was pitch black in the van's rear.

He unclipped a flashlight off his belt and clicked it on. He pulled it up and shined it at Dobson, and then at Abel and then behind them. He saw a little more than nothing, but not much. The hole between the front seats and the rear of the van was narrow. He saw a black guy sitting behind Abel. The guy wore all black like he was in the military or something.

The patrolman asked, "Did you boys hear that explosion?"

Dobson looked at Abel as if he was looking at a commanding officer.

Abel said, "We heard something back that way. It sounded like a bunch of transformers exploded. That's happened out here before. There's a lot of forgotten power company equipment out here. It's all worn and old. They really need to fix that stuff. But you know how it goes. The power company doesn't give a crap about us country folk."

"Uh-huh."

Abel smiled.

The patrolman said, "At any rate, I don't think it was a transformer."

"Oh. What was it, then?" Dobson asked.

The patrolman shifted on his foot, tilted away from them like he was making himself a harder target to hit in case one of them drew a gun on him.

It didn't work.

Right then, about as fast as a gunslinger from the Old West, Abel whipped to the left, over the center console, and reached his hand across the steering wheel and out the window.

A Glock 17 was in his hand, tight in his grip.

He squeezed the trigger.

Once. Twice. Three times.

Three bullets scattered in short patterns across the patrolman's face and neck. Red mist exploded and puffed and lingered in the air after the patrolman's body plummeted backward.

His body hit the snow with a loud *thud!*

Dobson knew the attack was coming. He had no doubt. He wasn't misled or betrayed by Abel's attack. He expected it because they had already trained for it.

He reached to cover his ears the moment the highway patrolman denied the explosion had been a transformer, which was smart on his end because the shots would've rocked his eardrums. It probably would've busted them.

After the patrolman's body was on the ground, Abel retreated and holstered his weapon. Not as fast as he drew it, but with the same grace. The gun went right into his holster like it was well oiled, which it was.

Dobson asked, "What you want us to do with him?"

"Leave him."

"What about the lights? Someone will see them eventually."

"Let them. They'll know it was us whether they find him dead like this or hidden in his trunk a month from now. Makes no difference."

One of the other guys slid the van's side door open, and the rest of them piled out to look. Only one of them stepped away from the van and approached the patrolman. He stopped just over the body and stared down at the three holes in the guy's face and neck. They were the size of nickels and bleeding out like waterspouts.

He spun around.

"General, those're helluva shots."

Abel said nothing.

One of the others asked, "They close together?"

"Pretty close."

The guy on the dirt track turned back to the patrolman and then whipped back around again.

"Hey, guys."

They all looked out.

"This pig ain't dead."

"What?" Dobson asked.

One of the other guys stepped farther out from the van and joined the one standing over the patrolman. He looked down.

"He's twitching."

"Could be after-death. That happens."

"He's blinking, though."

Abel didn't get out of the van. He leaned over Dobson and barked an order out the window.

"Leave him. Come on. Let's get going."

Abel's men returned to the van, returned to the back, and returned to their original seats.

Dobson rolled up his window after the last of the others returned to the back, and the van door slid home. The sound was loud in the stillness.

Dobson took his foot off the brake and rolled forward, skewing the van's trajectory in order to drive around the patrolman and the abandoned police cruiser.

12

WATCHING the black panel van roll away in the cold, blue lights from his police cruiser, the patrolman barely turned his head to see it all.

He could hardly move. He could hardly think. His brain pounded in his skull. His ears rang louder than he had ever heard before. He felt nothing but cold and heat at the same time.

His body temperature heated intensely at first, but quickly it reduced its degrees to a cold, minimal level, swapping out its intensity for extreme cold. The cold came on fast, and before he knew it, he was freezing. He felt it on his face and cheeks. He could taste smoke and sulfur in his mouth, both at the same time. The smoke wasn't there, as if he was inhaling it. It was more like he was exhaling it like the smoke was produced from his own body. Instead of breathing in oxygen and exhaling carbon dioxide, he breathed oxygen and exhaled smoke.

It didn't take long before the cold consumed the rest of his extremities and then swallowed the rest of him. His core temperature dropped. Everything dropped. Everywhere.

The patrolman's right hand moved involuntarily. He saw it. He couldn't think clearly. His thoughts came out in broken phrases. He felt himself slipping away.

His hand continued to move. It crawled up over his body armor and his chest like the severed hand in that old TV show, The Addams Family, only his hand wasn't detached. It was still attached to his arm. It just moved on its own, without him trying to move it, like falling down and having a hand whip out in front of you to break the fall.

The hand clawed itself up his body armor and up his chest to a radio mounted on his top left shoulder. The hand pulled the radio down and rested it just under his chin.

The whole act took a long minute.

His thumb clicked the talk button like it was trying to call for help. He didn't speak. He couldn't. All that his mouth did was gurgle blood.

He released the button.

No one answered.

He clicked it again and tried to speak.

All that happened was more gurgling, with some added wheezing from the holes in his cheeks. There was no speech, no sound of any known letters or parts of speech, of any known language.

He released the button again.

He was getting colder and colder. The end was near. He knew it. His body knew it. But his hand wouldn't give up. His right hand automatically took action. It defaulted to its second nature.

He clicked the talk button on and off for another solid minute or two; he wasn't sure. He repeated this until a voice finally picked up.

"Who's clicking their talk button?"

He clicked it again and tried to speak. He tried to call for help, but nothing came out.

"Hello? Who is this?"

The patrolman clicked one last time.

That was the last thing he did before his right hand stopped moving. He stared up at the night sky and watched the stars for the last time, and took his final breath.

13

WIDOW HAD DRIVEN the Lexus through the day and into the night, stopping three times for gas, stopping once for lunch, and eating dinner in the car. He drove beyond nightfall into the early morning hours.

He passed through Illinois, Indiana, Kentucky, Tennessee, part of North Carolina, putting Chicago behind him, enjoying the journey. Widow stopped about twenty miles before the border of the two Carolinas because of a roadblock that could've been for him, for throwing a bad guy off a roof back in Chicago. Although he figured that was unlikely, it was better to err on the side of caution.

Widow wasn't much worried until that point, but he was technically in a stolen vehicle, stolen from three dead criminals that he killed, not in Chicago, but back in Deadwood, South Dakota.

Nothing much special to say about them, not over any of the other people he had killed in the past. They were bad guys, doing bad things to innocent people. In Widow's opinion, if you do bad things to good people and you cross his path, then justice has sentenced you already.

Widow wasn't a vigilante, not in the Charles Bronson-Batman kind of way. It was just that he was a guy who couldn't let injustice go unanswered. That and he had enough bad luck that it seemed injustice crossed his path a lot more than the average person. Or it could've been he just noticed more?

Widow preferred things to be done by the book, by law enforcement. Someone breaks the law, let the cops sort it out. That's what they are there for. Unfortunately, that wasn't always enough. Justice was about balance, about setting things right. Sometimes the law isn't enough. If Widow was around, then he would do what needed doing to reset the balance.

Like in South Dakota, innocent people got hurt. Cops weren't doing anything about it. So Widow did something about it. He was retribution walking. He was justice incarnate.

He killed the guys who needed killing and didn't give it a second thought. What would be the point? Only a Buddhist monk would go around thinking about a cockroach he stepped on. Widow was no Buddhist monk. He believed in karma. What goes around, comes around. He was karma. He was what came back around.

The three bad guys he stole the car from weren't model citizens either. They had just shot up a hospital, killed an FBI agent, his friend. He didn't figure the Feds would be in a prodigious hurry to track him down. He figured they probably wouldn't be looking for him at all. Not over three dead cockroaches, but he had thrown a Saudi prince off a building back in Chicago.

The prince was the top of the food chain for a certain nefarious criminal enterprise that crossed Widow's path, leading him to be the karma, coming back around, once again.

That was one that they might look for him over. Saudi princes were well connected. It was definitely the kind of murder that grabbed headlines.

So, maybe they were searching for him. If the FBI would ever hunt for him, it would be for something like that.

Not hunting him, per se, but the Lexus he was cruising around in. They had no clue who he was—no evidence of his identity.

Still, the roadblock he came to made him uneasy.

There were several things that could be what the roadblock was all about.

The Saudi prince's servant girl, who saw his face, might've ratted him out. Maybe they pulled the vehicle description from the camera back in the alley leading to the prince's building, or maybe they pulled it off a CCTV camera on the street, or a streetlight camera, one of those that takes photos of cars running red lights.

There were about a million ways that the police might've gotten a description of a black Lexus leaving the crime scene after a prominent, wealthy citizen took a nosedive off his own penthouse balcony.

Up ahead, Widow saw brake lights and cars bottlenecking up into a single lane to pass through a row of highway patrolmen.

Widow wasn't interested in the idea of spending a month in jail while the authorities tried to figure out if he was their guy or not. And what if they figured he was their guy? Potentially, he could face life in prison. Does Illinois have the death penalty? He didn't know and didn't want to find out.

The other side of the coin, the X-factor, was the Saudi royal family, which was a bigger problem for the FBI. The prince might've been exiled by the royal family, but that didn't mean they condoned his being tossed off a roof. Just like Hans Gruber at the end of Die Hard, Widow suddenly realized.

He smiled again and saw a turnoff that led to a gas station and a hotel.

Widow took it. His tank was running low again.

He pulled down the ramp, a bumpy, neglected patch of interstate. He pulled into the gas station.

A single highway patrolman's cruiser was parked at the station. After Widow pulled in, he realized his mistake. The car was parked there as a precaution in case someone tried to do what he had just done, avoiding the roadblock.

Widow pulled the Lexus in and slowed. He looked over the gas pumps and the station for security cameras. He counted two, one in front of the door to the station and one over the pumps. Plus, there were certainly going to be some in the store, at least one over the register.

Widow avoided the outside cameras and drove past the pumps, past the corner of the station, and past the highway patrolman's car, which was a souped-up Dodge Charger, painted gray, with a black stripe down the side. It had the police interceptor package: battering ram mounted on the grille and an extra layer of armor skin over the metal exterior.

Widow saw a highway patrolman step out of the store and into the cold as if he had been staying inside in the warmth, waiting for cars to pull in. He stared at Widow as he passed.

Widow gave a friendly nod to the guy. He doubted they had a physical description of him or a photograph of his face—if they were looking for him at all.

He leaned forward and smiled, and waved at the patrolman as the Lexus glided past. He went to the far reaches of the lot, as far as he could, out of the cameras' views, and stopped at a set of self-serve air and water pumps for tires and radiators.

He parked the car, killed the engine, and stepped out.

He glanced over the roof of the car at the patrolman who stood on the corner, staring at him.

Trying to look like he was there for the air pump, he looked at the nozzle, at the coin insert slot. To engage the operation, it cost one dollar, coins only, which meant quarters only.

Widow checked his pockets quickly with a self pat-down and found no coins. He turned back to the Lexus and ducked down into the car, and searched the cup holders for loose change.

He lucked out and found two dollars in quarters: three coins in a cup holder, a fourth stuffed down in the passenger seat and another dollar's worth in an unused ashtray that ejected from the bottom of the stereo when pressed with a finger. He took them all and backed out of the car. That's when he saw the patrolman coming straight toward him.

"Shit," he said under his breath.

The patrolman walked slowly like he would if he were approaching a suspect. He didn't go for his radio, which was a good sign. He wasn't reporting a suspicious suspect or requesting backup, but suspicion flashed across his face.

Widow knew this look well. He seemed always to be the prime suspect every time there was a crime in whatever town he was passing through. He had that look, he guessed, which was probably one of the reasons the NCIS recruited him to be an undercover agent in the first place, a lifetime ago.

In the civilian world, none of that mattered. Only the guys in the uniforms got the glory, the respect, and the public gratitude for their service.

Widow had been a double agent, working for the NCIS in an elite unit, but stationed with the SEALs as one of them.

He had worked black-on-black ops.

No one knew who he was. And no one cared.

In the civilian world, he was the ultimate book cover—judged and labeled and sorted away as the prime suspect.

He looked the part.

If the cops searched for a mad-dog killer based on looks alone, he fit the bill, and in more ways than one.

Usually, Widow wasn't the guy the cops were looking for, but this time it could be. If the roadblock up ahead was for the murder of a member of the Saudi royal family, then he was the guilty party.

Widow unscrewed the rubber cap on the air nozzle to the front driver-side tire. He returned to the machine and whipped the quarters in and fired it up. He turned to kneel to begin the fake air-pumping process and stopped. He stared at the patrolman and pretended that he was only seeing him for the first time.

He jumped back a little, pretending to be startled.

"Oh. Hello, Officer."

The patrolman picked up his pace and stepped into a cone of light that shone down from a light high on a pole above them both.

He stopped ten feet from the rear of the Lexus and paused, scanning his eyes over the vehicle. He was checking the interior as best he could, in case there were others inside.

The windows were tinted.

Without skipping a beat, the patrolman whipped up a Mag flashlight seemingly out of nowhere and clicked on the beam. He shone the light into the tint, saw no one was there.

He clicked off the light and stepped up to the rear of the car.

"This your car, sir?"

Widow thought about the plates. He didn't know where they were registered. He had taken the car from South Dakota, but he presumed it was a rental. It could've been from anywhere. Rental cars are moved cross-country all the time, every day.

So, he said, "It's a rental."

The patrolman nodded.

"Nice car."

"It is. But out of my price range. I'm just an employee. My company paid for it."

"You having tire trouble?"

"Yeah. The damn tire pressure light keeps coming on. It's annoying."

"Did you turn off when you saw the roadblock?"

Widow paused a beat.

"Yes. But not because of the roadblock. That warning light came on again, and I saw the gas station. Figured now was as good a time as any to fill up the tire. Don't want to be stuck in that line and have the tire go flat. You know how long those things can last?"

Widow chuckled.

The patrolman stayed behind the Lexus; his lower half was out of Widow's sight, which told Widow as much about where his hand was, as if it was right there in plain view.

The patrolman had one hand on his gun—no question.

"What's your name?"

"Jack Widow."

"Mr. Widow, you got identification?"

"Sure. What's this all about?"

Widow asked the question like an involuntary reaction, like exhaling. It surprised him, but what was more surprising was the look that the patrolman gave him. The patrolman's face shot a look of disbelief at Widow, as if he was shocked that Widow didn't know what the roadblock was about.

"Where're you driving in from?"

Widow didn't want to say Chicago in case they were searching for a guy from Chicago who fit his description. Plus, he figured the Lexus's plates were from South Dakota. He didn't know for sure, as he'd never checked the plates. Which was a rookie mistake, he realized. He should've taken a gander at them much earlier. The Lexus had originated with some bad guys before he stole it from them, which was in South Dakota. He figured the odds were good that they'd rented the car there. Of course, the odds decreased when he started thinking about how often rental cars are transported from one state to the next with no return to their home.

He took a chance and pulled the trigger on the lie. He answered.

"Rapid City."

"South Dakota?"

Widow nodded.

It must've been a good guess because the patrolman didn't take a second look at the plate. South Dakota, it was.

"ID, please?"

"I've got the pump running."

"Sir, ID, please?"

Widow nodded, furrowed his brow like he was annoyed, dug into his back pocket and took out his passport. He let the hose for the air pump fall to the concrete and walked back around the Lexus to meet the patrolman. The timer on the air pump ticked away, using up his quarters.

He handed over the passport, hoping the patrolman didn't ask about his driver's license because that was a problem. He didn't have a driver's license. He would have to think of a way to distract the man so that he wouldn't even think to ask for it. It would have to be something really distracting to work.

The patrolman took the passport and flicked it open.

"Jack Widow. As you told me."

The patrolman shook the passport one-handed. The pages flicked from page to page. He studied them all the way to the last page, fast.

"You got a lot of stamps here."

"I travel for work. Always on the road. You know how it goes."

The patrolman nodded.

"Where do you work?"

This posed a problem for Widow. He didn't want to give the guy the name of the company that the stolen car was probably rented under, the bad guy's company. The fewer lies he told, the better it was for him not to get caught in one. That was under-cover cop 101, but sometimes lies were necessary, for the greater good and all.

"I work for a major conglomerate."

"What's that mean?"

"I don't want to give my company a bad name. But we're into everything."

"Like what?"

The patrolman closed the passport and leaned into Widow as if he was about to learn a deep, dark secret, something juicy.

Widow thought of his distraction tactic. He thought of two.

"Ever heard of Starbucks?"

The first distraction.

The patrolman leaned back, nearly leaping back.

"You work for Starbucks?"

"I do."

"What do you do for them?"

"I work for corporate. I'm a corporate hitman."

The second distraction.

"A what?"

"A corporate hitman. Oh, don't worry. It's not like an actual hitman. And it's not my actual job title or nothing. Officially, they call me a corporate consultant."

Widow finger-quoted the word consultant like he was giving the cop a wink and a nudge.

"What do you do for them?"

"I take out the trash."

"What's that mean?"

"I handle their ugly business, like reconning the competition and noting their weaknesses. You know? I record their vulnerable spots. I form strategies to take over regions and markets. If mister and missus so-and-so own a small but lucrative regional coffee shop, I take them out. I analyze them, check for weaknesses. I access the best course of action to take them over. Sometimes, we buy them out. Sometimes, we strategize to run them out of business. It's all perfectly legal. Not ethical, maybe, but legal."

The patrolman paused. He looked both dumbfounded and suspicious and amazed all at the same time.

He asked a question that seemed like he didn't know what to ask.

"Reconning. You ex-military?"

Distraction worked.

"Former military. We don't say ex. Once military, always military. That's what G.I. means."

"What does G.I. mean?"

"It means Government Issue, which translates to government property. Once you sign on the dotted line, your ass belongs to them for life."

"Really?"

"When they get you, they get you for life."

"I thought you served and then got out."

"We do, but they can always recall us."

"Is that right?"

"Yep. You ever serve?"

"Nah, I didn't. My daddy was a cop, and then I was a cop. Cop family."

"Same here. Military family."

"So, even if you're an old man rotting in a nursery home, they can reinstate you?"

"Recall. They recall you. Technically, they got policies ending the use of recall at a certain age, or certain situations, but the government makes the policies. They can always break them. There are loopholes in everything in government."

The patrolman seemed to buy it. He nodded along. They were both quiet for a long moment.

The patrolman asked, "Starbucks, huh?"

"Yeah. Business is where war is fought nowadays."

Just then, the patrolman's radio burst to life with clicks and chatter and voices saying radio codes.

The patrolman tossed the passport back to Widow, who caught it, and the patrolman stepped back and away to get a better listen to the radio.

He stepped out of earshot. Widow tried to listen to hear the radio code being used, but couldn't. Instead, he watched the patrolman's lips.

He read partial words, which weren't enough to pinpoint the exact conversation, but the gist that he got from it was that there was an officer down. At least, that was his best guess.

After another few exchanges from the patrolman and then the voice on the other side of the radio, the patrolman clicked off the radio and gave an "over" prompt. Then he walked back to Widow.

"Sir, I'd advise you to get your tires aired up. Then get back in your car, turn on your radio, listen to the local news, and keep heading south to wherever you're headed. Don't stay here."

"What channel?"

"Any of them. I'm sure you'll hear what's going on. For now, good luck with the tire pressure light and Starbucks. Be safe out there."

The patrolman said nothing else. He just turned and jogged away, back through the dim parking lot, back to his cruiser.

Widow was left confused.

Apparently, the roadblock wasn't for him, but something was going on. Still, he thought it best not to be caught in a stolen vehicle that was linked to the events of South Dakota and Chicago in case the cops at the roadblock got more thorough in checking him out.

He had pressed his luck too far already.

It was time to ditch the car.

He returned to the Lexus, reached a hand into the trunk button, and popped it. He walked back to the trunk and looked inside for a rag or cloth so that he could wipe the car down and get rid of his fingerprints.

He thought about the chore ahead. Wiping the car down was going to be a nightmare. His prints were all over the place. Then he realized so were the prints of the dead guys back in Deadwood.

He found a pair of car rags on the floorboard. They were still punched together by the plastic tab they had when bought from a store.

Widow took both rags, tore the tab away, and dropped it into the trunk. He came out of the trunk, closed it. He paused and looked around when he noticed a sign that solved part of his problem.

It was for an automated carwash.

Widow returned to pumping air in the front tire with what time remained of his dollar in quarters. He wanted to maintain the lie in case the patrolman was watching him. He wasn't watching. That fact was confirmed when Widow saw the cruiser pull out of the gas station with the patrolman at the wheel. The sirens were off, but the light bar was on, flashing blue.

The cruiser pulled out into the direction of the traffic on the interstate.

Widow watched him drive off until he was gone from sight. He continued to fake-pump air into his tire until the machine stopped humming and stopped pumping. Once it was quiet, he put away the hose and returned to the Lexus's driver seat and drove the car to the carwash to take care of the car's exterior for him.

THE AUTOMATED carwash took care of any fingerprints or forensic evidence that Widow may have left on the exterior of the vehicle. He paid for the full service, including the tire wash.

He pulled out of the carwash and drove the car back around to the dark side of the gas station, avoiding getting his face on any of the security cameras. He parked the Lexus back near the air pump because he needed to use the vacuum hose, attached on the opposite side of the machine, so he could clean out the floorboards and seats in case whoever found the car was thorough enough to have a forensic team go through carpet fibers and upholstery. He doubted that would happen, but in the million-to-one chance the FBI was ever called to check out the vehicle, they might use a forensic team on it.

Don't run to your death was a Navy SEAL motto he lived by. Being a little overzealous wasn't always a bad thing.

Widow stepped out and started the vacuum machine. He vacuumed the seat he used, the floorboard beneath the pedals, the pedals themselves, and the dash. He vacuumed the cup holders and the middle console and the stereo. He did the knobs, the buttons, and the air vents. He vacuumed the other floorboards and the backseat and the rear footwells.

He stepped out and did the same thing to the trunk. Next, he wiped everything down with both rags twice.

After he was done, he locked the car, wiped down the keys, and threw them as hard as he could into the black woods and snow behind the station.

He tossed the rags into a trash bin and popped the collar on his coat, blew onto his hands to warm them up, and shoved them deep into his pockets. He headed out of the gas station with his head down and chin tucked in. He made no eye contact with anyone. He was just a drifter, a nobody.

Widow wanted to head southeast, the direction he was already going. He had no intention of turning back, but he thought it best to avoid walking straight through the roadblock. A man on foot was far more suspicious than one driving through.

He walked to the end of the gas station's service drive and took a right and walked along the interstate's shoulder. He walked over a hill and saw the roadblock up ahead. It was clear as day.

He didn't see the highway patrolman who had spoken to him back at the gas station, which was good. There was no chance of anyone else recognizing him unless they had a physical description of him, or worse yet, a photo.

He knew they had neither of those things. If they had either, he would already be in handcuffs. If the cops had a photo of him, so did the highway patrolman who interrogated him at the gas station.

Widow decided he had two options going forward.

One, he could try to hitch a ride with one of the vehicles that were already waiting in line to pass through the roadblock unimpeded, but this was not a viable option, as they would be wary of a roadblock. A total stranger asking for a lift right in front of it was going to get turned down ten times out of ten.

The second option was to divert from his path and head into the woods, maybe fifty or a hundred yards out, and walk around them. This was risky, but would probably work. He was dealing with highway patrolmen and not a foreign military force. It was unlikely they were watching the woods.

Widow looked to the sky. He saw no helicopters scanning with searchlights overhead. He saw no drones, either. Of course, why the hell would they have drones just for him? Not likely. It was hard to believe that they might've figured out the network of interstates that he had been driving on. All of this assumed they were even looking for him.

Widow looked at the cops, at the roadblock. Under the blue and red flashing lights, he counted them. He could see five. The cops were pretty distracted by the cars in line. No one paid attention to the shoulder. No one saw him. Not any of the cops, anyway. Some drivers sitting and waiting in the cars saw him, but they didn't know what was going on. None of them looked concerned about one guy walking on the shoulder.

He stood on the hilltop for another moment, double-checking everything one more time before making his move. After a second look, he descended and vanished over the other side of the hill toward the woods, back off the shoulder. His boots sank down into the snow up to the calf, burying it in some places.

Widow slogged through it down to the tree line. He stepped into the trees like a crocodile sinking back into the brackish water of a river. Within seconds, Widow was camouflaged in the darkness and lost to the sight of anyone who might watch him.

He walked on, traversing the trees and the snow in the dark with no problem. The snow slowed him down. He stepped cautiously. He didn't want to sink down into a hole.

The cold and wind created the biggest issue. The temperature wasn't that bad, and he had a good winter coat on, but the wind picked up and gusted cold air in his face. Several times it slapped his breath off his face.

A good five minutes passed before he stopped in a clearing. He took the time to confirm his bearings. He stared up at the sky and took notice of the moon. It was exactly where he thought it should be.

The sky was too gloomy and overcast to see the North Star, or any stars. But the moon was big and full and bright. It broke through the cloud cover. The moon told him he was starting to veer a little off, so he readjusted his path and headed east, parallel with the interstate.

Widow continued walking straight for a while. Then he began veering toward the road in a slightly diagonal direction, because eventually he wanted to get back on it. He walked until he figured he was a good hundred yards from the interstate, which was close enough for now. He changed his path again, heading back east, parallel with the interstate.

He walked for fifteen more minutes, mostly being over-cautious, until he finally figured it was safe to return to the road, but he didn't. He stayed in the concealment of the trees and the snow and maintained the same distance from the road for another fifteen minutes.

Don't run to your death; he reminded himself.

After thirty minutes of walking through the brush and the snow and the trees and the darkness, he figured he had gone far enough under cover of darkness and woods. Any longer would be overkill.

He turned and tracked back northeast. He walked until he saw the road, gave it another look-over. He stepped out of the woods and walked up a low hill and onto the pavement and the shoulder.

Widow turned right, walked on. He popped his collar up once more, only the wind knocked back down. He blew into his hands again and rubbed them together, trying to stay warm.

He walked along the side of the road and popped out his thumb.

15

THE EXPLOSIONS QUIETED down to silence, but the ringing in her ears continued. Adonis lay on the ground, in the snow, like when she was a little girl and her parents moved up to Albany, New York, where she would lie in the snow and make snow angels with her dad, one of her best memories with him in it.

She looked up, shook off thoughts of snow angels, and looked at the same sky that Widow was seeing. Only hers was covered in smoke. She couldn't see the moon.

The fingers on her right hand were the first parts of her body to move. They wiggled for a while. She was grateful they worked to begin with, and grateful that they were still attached. Without looking, she feared that many of her friends and colleagues weren't so lucky.

She felt multiple sharp pains in her chest, like little needles stabbing her all at the same time. It hurt badly. It felt like she had taken a shotgun slug to the vest, but she didn't remember anyone shooting at her, just the explosions and the carnage.

She lay there for a long minute, trying to let her body recover to a more normal state so she could do her job, so that she could act like a leader and a professional ATF agent. But there was also the possibility that she was stalling. Not that she was afraid of seeing the devastation. That didn't scare her. What frightened her was if she couldn't handle it. She feared seeing it and not being able to manage it as she was supposed to do. If Clip was dead, then Adonis was the only one left in charge. She didn't know what to do. She stayed there on the ground, paralyzed, until her heartbeat slowed to a normal rate, and she couldn't stay frozen any longer.

After finger wiggling, her strength returned, and her breathing returned to normal, and her heartbeat slowed to normal. The wind had been knocked out of her, unlike anything she had ever experienced before.

Adonis hauled herself up slowly, using her rifle like a crutch. She planted its butt in the snow and pulled herself up and plopped down on her butt.

She reached up with her free hand, shoved it into her line of sight, and stared at her other fingers. They were still there, too. All fingers and toes accounted for.

She pulled hard on the rifle and got up on one knee. She reached a hand over her Kevlar and felt what was causing her pain in her chest.

Her Kevlar was covered with shards of glass busted out of the SUV's windshield by the blasts. There was some metal shrapnel as well, but she felt nothing had penetrated through, which was good.

Several tiny metal fragments of undeterminable origin had also stuck in her vest. One piece stuck out to her. She grabbed at it and pulled a short, headless, broken nail out of her vest. That one could've gotten her if it had been an inch longer or had more force behind it or if it had hit her vest at a different angle. She was lucky.

She dropped the rifle onto the snow and slipped off her coat, slowly, as if she had just woken from a coma and had completely forgotten how to take off a coat. She dropped the coat to the ground. The cold hit her instantly like a bucket of ice. She shivered as her core temperature dropped. She became more alert as she realized she needed to get warm again quickly.

Adonis squirmed and wriggled to get the Kevlar vest off. She pulled it off and dropped it in the snow next to her rifle. She stopped and stared at the vest.

The damage it took for her was far more than she had thought. There were more nails than she had noticed before when it was on her.

Adonis gazed out over the area around her and the SUV. The SUV's windshields and windows were all busted out from the blast wave, but the police lights embedded in the grille were still intact and swirling. Blues and reds washed over the surrounding snow, reflecting off the shards of broken glass and shiny metal pieces.

Around her, she saw dozens of nails, screws, pieces of glass, and metal fragments—all homemade bomb shrapnel like the contents they'd found in the shipping boxes in the postal station in Augusta, the thing that had kicked this whole operation off and led her to now. It was that event that she would later regret, deeply, but now she had no time for regrets, no time for second guesses or hindsight. Those things lead to doubt, and doubt kills an investigator's ability to investigate.

She forced herself to shake it off and scan the rest of the surrounding grounds. She saw more bolts and screws and nails and broken glass littered across the yard, as if the bombs had been packed with them. But dynamite sticks are already packed tight. There's no room for shrapnel or anything else. It was the vests themselves that were packed to the gills with shrapnel.

Adonis left her Kevlar where it was. It was useless now, anyway. She lifted the coat, shook it off, and slipped it back on. She hauled her rifle up slowly, in case she needed it. She low-carried it and tried to walk straight, but she stumbled instead.

Her head ached. Her vision was foggy. She waited for it to clear up, and when it finally did, she stared out and scanned over the damage that had been done.

The main building burned in bright red flames. Thick black smoke rose profusely from it and covered the sky.

She watched the only section of the main building left standing as it burned and then collapsed in on itself while the fire raged on, consuming everything but a brick fireplace. Eventually, that would likely crumble and fall over too. But she wouldn't stay long enough to watch it.

Adonis slowly craned her head and let her eyes soak up the horror. She was glad that her vision was still foggy. She didn't want to see what she saw. It might've been worse not to see because her imagination filled in the gaps.

All around her, dead bodies lined the ground, slumped in the snow. They were everywhere. Some whole. Some not. Some burned without moving. Some still moved. One man was on fire, far in the distance. She watched him for a short moment as he ran around in panic until he stopped and fell flat on his face. He was so engulfed in flames that she couldn't identify him as an agent or Athenian, friend or foe.

Screams from the living filled the air, but she hardly noticed them. Her ears continued to ring, and her eardrums pounded.

Standing, Adonis could barely see the helicopter in the sky until it was coming down on her, partially because of her vision, but mostly because of the black smoke. She was amazed that Ramirez could pilot it.

The helicopter came down slowly through the smoke. She felt the rotor wash over her face. It whipped her hair back behind her head. She stepped away and watched it land right behind where she had been lying, about ten yards from her SUV.

She saw Ramirez in the pilot's seat. She automatically smiled at him because she was glad to see a face she knew, and he was alive. She watched him land the helicopter and waited until the skids touched the snow before approaching. The rotors kept turning, whirling a hole in the smoke above it. The rear door slid open and several agents she didn't recognize and whose names she didn't remember hopped off one by one.

Adonis stumbled toward them, desperate. She almost fell twice.

One of them ran over and caught her, helping her back to the helicopter.

"Don't worry, Adonis. Help is on the way," the ATF agent shouted over the noise. She instantly felt bad for not remembering his name. He grabbed her by both arms to keep her steady.

She shouted, "It was a trap!"

The agent nodded.

"I need to sit down."

He nodded again and helped her stumble back to the helicopter.

Ramirez stayed in the pilot's seat. The engine stayed running. The rotors slowed to a crawl, but continued to rotate.

ATF policy would dictate in a case like this that Ramirez remain in the pilot's seat in case he needed to perform a quick takeoff. But there was no case like this one. Still, that's where he stayed because he realized that one trap could lead to another.

Adonis climbed into the back of the chopper and dumped herself down on an empty seat.

The agent looked her over quickly. He checked for wounds, checked for bleeding. She was all there, all intact.

After he was certain that she had no external injuries, he shouted again so she would hear him.

"I'm going to run out and help the others. You stay put. Okay?"

She nodded.

Once he was out of the helicopter, she reached into her pocket and called her boss. She put the phone on speaker and cranked the volume up all the way. She could barely hear it ring, but she heard it over the ringing in her ears.

The phone rang and rang until she got a busy signal, and it cut off automatically. No voicemail. No error message. No nothing. It just died as if the phone call had never been made.

Adonis waited for a callback, but there wasn't one. She stayed staring at it, expecting the answer to what to do next would come from the phone. It didn't.

She didn't realize at first that Ramirez was saying something to her. Then she looked up and saw his lips moving. He was shouting, trying to speak to her over the rotors, but it was no use. They were too loud. She couldn't make him out.

She showed a hand to him, signaling him to hold on a second. He nodded and stopped shouting.

Adonis picked her phone back up, looked at the screen, and texted her boss.

Her message read: *I'm alive.*

16

AFTER THEY MURDERED a highway patrolman on a backroad not far from the Athenian compound, Abel and his guys headed east and slightly south through a network of backroads, slowly and steadily until they were twenty miles away from their crimes.

Abel knew it would take time before the cops and the ATF figured out what had happened. The highway patrolmen would be faster, since they were all stationed at an outer perimeter. Plus, the poor bastard Abel had shot was a highway patrolman, just in the wrong place at the wrong time—unlucky. Once his body was discovered, the highway patrol would be out on the hunt for Abel and his guys in full force.

Abel wasn't worried. He was still ahead of the cops.

He ordered Dobson to stay the course and take all the backroads they could, just as they had laid out in their contingency plan in case they had to run. Dobson knew the destination, but none of the exact routes to take. The backroad system in Spartan County was unmapped. Dobson had driven them in several test-runs so he could learn them. He had slacked on that detail. He hadn't memorized the exact routes, not down to the fine details, not like he should have. He did several trial runs. He thought that would be enough, but it wasn't.

He sweated but hoped that no one noticed. He wasn't sure if he was going the right way or not, but he knew the destination, the coordinates, and the direction he was expected to head. So far, no one seemed to notice that he wasn't exactly on track.

He was a little scared. He hid it as best as he could, trying to take advantage of every stop sign to look like he was pausing so he wouldn't raise suspicion, but really he was navigating his next turn, trying to remember his trial runs. He hoped something would click, but it hadn't yet.

So far, no one was on to him.

One thing benefiting him was how fast the ATF had raided them. They weren't expecting it, not until they caught that agent. The fast raid and need for them to vanish quickly sped up Abel's terror plot. The whole thing acted as a smokescreen for Dobson to hide his inadequacy.

The ATF raid was a stroke of bad luck for them, but things always went to hell when the first bullet was fired. That's just the way it goes in war, and they were at war.

When asked if he had done his part and memorized the correct escape routes, Dobson had lied to them. He wouldn't tell them he wasn't exactly sure which way to go. He wasn't stupid.

He had taken them in the right direction, he thought.

They headed southeast from Carbine toward the coastline, where they had a large boat anchored in Hague Marina, about thirty miles south of the coastal North Carolina border.

On the way, they had one stop to make, the most important stop. There was a guy whose name was unknown to Dobson. They were supposed to hand over all forty-one pipe bomb packages to him.

The unknown guy would disperse the packages for Abel, mailing them from twenty different locations around the Eastern Seaboard, only three at a time, in order to keep the number small and unnoticeable to postal workers.

The man was a no-questions kind of guy. He was reliable. They had worked with him before. He knew nothing about the packages, nothing about Abel's lieutenants personally, and they had the same lack of knowledge of him, keeping everyone in the dark and keeping the mission secure.

The unknown guy was good at that. For a large fee, he would deliver anything to anyone within the US, unnoticed, and without asking questions.

Abel would insist that one of his guys go along for insurance, but the guy didn't know that yet. Abel planned to alter the arrangement when they met with the guy in Florence, South Carolina.

First, they had to survive the dragnet unseen, but Abel had it all planned out. That's why they were taking the backroads. They would find a big hole in the net to slip through, and then the plan would proceed.

It was the ATF and the South Carolina Highway Patrol versus seven highly trained US Special Forces turned militant cultists, and the ATF was crippled. A bunch of backwoods, unorganized, late-night patrolmen were no match for Abel's crew. They had been running covert missions all over the world, beating out some of the world's best-trained soldiers. What was South Carolina Highway Patrol going to do?

Abel stared out the window at the darkness and the snow-covered landscape. First, he saw endless fields of trees. Then he saw farmlands—empty, large farms that looked abandoned, resembling something out of a post-apocalyptic world.

He checked his watch. They were on schedule with time to spare, a whole day if they needed it to lie low—perhaps two at the most.

It didn't look like they would need spare time. Barring another stroke of bad luck, they would be right on time to meet with the no-questions guy and mail the bombs. Then they would head to the boat, where he planned to spend the rest of his days sailing the coast of South America, reading news clippings of a US thrown into terror and searching for him.

The US authorities would be chasing their own tails. That was the goal, anyway.

Abel considered himself to be a patriot, not a terrorist.

He wanted his country to pay for two hundred forty-three years of tricking its citizenry that the government was in charge.

He was an anarchist. He didn't really care how the world was governed, or by what type of philosophy. They were all shit. None of them were acceptable. He wanted the world to have no government. That was the only way to be truly free. Even the anarchist ideology was too limited to describe him.

Deep down, Abel had no deep down. He was just a guy who liked to blow shit up and see people suffer.

Abel looked back out the window at the abandoned farms, which reminded him of a government that burned its own people in the 2008 bailout.

He had a plan, but plans always go to hell when the first bullet is fired. That was a Navy SEAL motto, one he didn't know. Too bad.

Just then, the headlights on the van flickered, and the dashboard flickered, and the engine died down as if they had been hit by an EMP attack. If it was jamming from an electromagnetic pulse attack, they could be dead in the water. It was just a quick succession of events, but they all noticed.

Dobson held his breath, hoping it was nothing.

Abel said nothing. He just stared forward, but Dobson could see his hand had formed a fist.

Dobson finally took a breath and then held it for a long moment.

The engine idled again and kicked and hummed and whirred.

The dashboard lights flickered again, rapidly, as if the engine was going to die. The tire pressure light flicked on, and the fuel light and then the engine light. The radio had been playing low music, but now it flickered on and off. The volume shot up to full blast, and then it died back down to nothing.

The van sputtered like the engine was fighting to stay alive.

"What's going on?" Abel asked.

"I don't know," Dobson said.

"You said the engine was good!"

"It is good."

Abel said nothing.

Dobson said, "I can't predict everything."

"Will we make it?"

But Dobson didn't have to answer because right then the van answered for him. It sputtered once and twice more, and then the engine light lit up brightly and flickered. The engine ran like it was back to normal for a few seconds, but then everything died. The engine, the interior lights, the heater, the radio, all of it cut off.

Dobson pumped the brakes and pressed them down slowly to avoid an abrupt stop, possibly followed by a skid. He kicked the emergency brake pedal seventy percent down to the floor, and the van slowed and stopped dead in the middle of the snowy backroad.

Dobson slammed the gear into park and switched the ignition to off, even though the entire van was dead.

"What now?" One of the guys from the back asked.

"Could be the battery. I suppose."

Abel said nothing, and undid his seatbelt. Dobson undid his. They both stepped out of the van into the cold, empty night. The side panel door followed suit, and all five of the other guys stepped out. The interior light flashed on, which shocked them.

"What the hell?" one of them asked.

"Guess it's not the battery," another said.

Four of the men from the back went around to the rear of the van and opened the rear doors. They started taking out their assault rifles and distributing them as if they were headed to combat a precaution.

The five from the back, including Flack, weapons handler, circled out and around the van, setting up a defensive perimeter, ready for any attack. The whole thing went down like an operation in Afghanistan or Iraq like they were on just another military convoy that broke down.

Dobson popped the hood and opened it, and set it down on the prop bar and studied the engine, trying to keep the look of surprise on his face.

Smoke billowed out from under the hood and from more than one exact location on the engine. Seeing that actually baffled Dobson, making his pretending less work.

Abel joined him at the nose of the van.

He asked, "Battery?"

"No."

"The smoke doesn't look good."

"That's nothing. It'll clear," Dobson said, hoping it was true.

Abel stood back. They both waited to see if the smoke would clear. Lucky for Dobson, it cleared.

Dobson stuck his head in under the hood and over the engine and studied everything thoroughly, as if his life depended on it, which it did.

After five minutes of touching things and shifting wires and inspecting hoses and critical engine parts, most of which was for pretend, he came out and gave his professional opinion.

"I think it needs a re-flash. Gotta be electrical."

"And what about all the smoke?"

"Just a side effect. The engine overheated. It was like a chain reaction from the onboard electronics bouncing around faulty signals from one system to another. It's gotta be. The interior lights are on now. So it's not a power issue."

"All that was caused by an electrical problem?"

Dobson nodded.

"So, you're telling me that the engine got confused and set off an electrical disturbance?"

"That's pretty accurate. Yes. I'd say the onboard computer got confused."

"So, it needs a re-flash?"

"Yes."

"You knew that just by looking over the engine out here? You don't need a diagnostic machine?"

"That's my guess. Just a guess, but it explains the power failure."

Abel said nothing.

Before Dobson spoke again, he gulped hard. Abel heard it.

"Any major mechanical interruption wouldn't have affected the power inside the van."

"I don't suppose you can do the re-flash here?"

"I'll need special software to do it. No one's gonna have that but an auto shop. I won't be able to do it out here unless we find an auto shop."

Abel palmed his face animatedly like he was on stage, playing a part. He rubbed his forehead in frustration, all part of the melodrama he loved.

Dobson had seen him behave this way before. They all had. It was the same expression he made before he flipped out and murdered Iraqi prisoners. He liked to toy with them and then fly off the handle.

He had never murdered one of his own guys before, which gave Dobson some reassurance. And Dobson lucked out because Abel didn't murder him.

Abel stayed standing there like that, making the same gestures of frustration and disappointment, for a long second, face buried in his palm.

One of his guards said, "You okay, General?"

"Give me time, boys."

Abel raised his head and then stepped away from the van. The headlamps were back on. He walked the cone of light out in front of the van and traced the snow until he was out of range. He stared around in the darkness and looked at the road ahead and the road behind and then the empty farms.

He returned to the van, to his men, and gave them new orders.

"Boys, regroup. We're setting up camp for the night."

Dobson asked, "Camp?"

"We can't get the parts we need tonight, and we can't just sit here in the middle of the road. The cops are steps behind us. And worse, once they find the dead patrolman, they'll be searching everywhere for us, like exterminators hunting rats. We need shelter till we can sort out transport."

Abel paused a beat and looked around and put his hands out like he was a wizard, showing off a spell.

"We need to commandeer a new vehicle. We're not gonna find one. Not out here, middle of the night. For now, let's requisition one of these farms. They look abandoned. We can scout for a vehicle at daylight."

Dobson nodded, as did Flack and the others.

"Brooks, you and Jargo go check out that one."

Abel pointed out the closest farm in view to Jargo, his sniper, and Brooks, who was just a great all-around soldier, a wingman. Brooks was Abel's right hand.

Brooks was a tall black man. His skin was darker than the shell of his rifle. He stood tall, just over six-foot-five, but not quite six-foot-six. He was taller than many professional basketball players.

Brooks had been with Abel for the longest time of them all. They went way back. Abel's guys were long out of the military, but there was an established, respected chain of command, and Brooks was second from the top. They all knew it, and none of them ever questioned it.

Brooks was tall but wiry, loose in the joints, with long arms. He was also the second oldest, next to Abel, but he remained in incredible shape for a man over fifty. He put in serious exercise time, but none of it was inside a gym. He liked to get his exercise by doing things outside. At the Athenian compound, during warmer weather, that's where he could be found every morning, outside lifting heavy tires and rocks and pulling things.

Out of all of Abel's guys, Brooks was the most terrifying. No one wanted to go up against a six-foot-five-plus guy with fists like sledgehammers and skin that camouflaged him into darkness.

Brooks had graying temples and a tight fade, but he was slightly balding on top, which he usually covered with a baseball cap. At the moment, he wore a black ball cap, unmarked so that no witnesses could identify him by saying they saw a giant black man wearing a baseball cap with a specific sports team logo on it.

Brooks was the largest, strongest, and second-highest-ranking in their crew. The sniper named Jargo was almost his opposite, as far as physical descriptions go, but he was just as deadly.

Jargo was a white man from Kentucky with family ties to white nationalists, a fact that he wasn't embarrassed about, but he didn't share in those philosophies. His allegiance was only to his unit and Abel's cause. Still, he kept close touch with his family. Some of the Athenians' best allies were cousins of Jargo, who were members of backwoods militias all over the state of Kentucky. None of these groups were as serious or dedicated to the cause as the Athenians.

Jargo never held that over them. They were strong allies to have, even if a joke.

Jargo stood two inches under six feet. He was stocky, built like the sidewall of a lighthouse. In regular sparring matches, Brooks feared losing to Jargo the most, even though Jargo was far shorter. Jargo was fearless and tough. They were all tough; even Dobson wasn't a guy to take for granted in a one-on-one street fight.

Brooks said, "What're the parameters?"

Jargo asked, "Shoot to kill?"

"No. No killing. You likely won't find anyone there. But if you do, take them alive. We might need a hostage or two."

"You got it, boss," Brooks said.

He took up his M4 assault rifle and led Jargo with his sniper rifle through the snow and darkness toward the farmhouse.

Abel looked back at the others and zeroed in one of them.

"Flack, get behind the wheel and slip the thing into neutral. The rest of you grab a corner. You're pushing the van down the driveway."

They all hugged a corner. With Dobson hustling to the passenger side door, which Abel corrected with a single order, as if he were singling out Dobson to take on the brunt of the work as punishment.

"Dobson, grab the rear."

Dobson stopped and nodded and didn't protest.

Dobson and the others grabbed positions on the van and pushed toward the farm's snowed-over driveway.

Abel stepped aside and reached into his inner coat pocket. He took out a pack of cigarettes, a guilty pleasure of his that he also used to kill his nerves whenever he got nervous.

Broken down in the middle of nowhere, about twenty miles from a massive explosion that he was responsible for, all while a hundred Feds and probably an equal number of South Carolina cops would be frantically searching for him was plenty of validation to be a little nervous.

He lit up a cigarette and took a drag, releasing slow exhales of smoke into the early morning darkness.

Sixty seconds later, he saw Brooks's flashlight beam light up and flash in their direction, signaling that the coast was clear.

"Okay, boys, get that van up to the house. See if you can hide it in a barn or something."

Dobson, Cucci, and Tanis, the rest of the crew, gave affirmatives, while Flack nodded from behind the steering wheel.

It took them twice as long as Abel would've required back in their Army days, but the snow-covered driveway made it difficult, especially pushing uphill for part of the track.

Once the van was up and near the house, Jargo and Brooks rested their weapons against the brick around the front door and joined in to help push the van the rest of the way.

They got the van inside an old, empty barn with untouched cobwebs in every corner. They closed the doors behind the van.

After it was all complete, Abel pulled Brooks aside and asked, "How's the inside of the farmhouse?"

"It's good. Must've been a foreclosure, and the bank took everything because the place is fully furnished."

"Any beds?"

"Yeah. Four."

"Good. I'm going to get some sleep. I'll be in the master. If this shithole has a master."

He paused a beat and turned and stared at the barn.

A shutter from an open window at the peak flapped in the wind, clacking against the barn.

"Tell Jargo to set up there. You stay with him. Keep an eye out. Take turns sleeping. Tell the others to do the same."

Brooks said, "Our old Army motto."

Abel asked, "What's that?"

"Sleep when you can. You forget?"

Abel didn't answer that. He turned and walked away, disappearing into the abandoned farmhouse.

17

SEVEN MILES southeast of the roadblock that Widow snuck through, and further away from the explosion in Carbine, and the Athenian compound, Widow sat comfortably in the passenger seat of a roomy Toyota Tundra that looked like the owner had put it to the test as far as being a workingman's truck.

It had a certain worn but well-maintained feel about it. The guy driving sat in the seat like a cowboy on his trusty horse.

The truck was Widow's first ride after the gas station and after the roadblock. He ended up walking past the roadblock for two miles before someone pulled over. It all happened right on cue too because it had snowed, not hard, but enough for the Tundra driver to take pity on Widow and pull over to the shoulder and offer him a ride.

The driver was a man of an age somewhere between his last birthday, being in his early thirties and being old enough to run for president. Widow wasn't exactly sure where the guy sat on his life's timeline because the guy was in good shape with a youthful demeanor like he was full of life, but he also drove the truck with a mature, confident way, like driving the truck was part of his business and business was doing well.

The Tundra driver was cheery and friendly. He had crinkles above his cheeks from smiling a lot. He had wrinkles across his forehead like he also worried a lot. Widow saw in his face, behind the smile, a guy with the weight of the world on his shoulders. He was a family man and a businessman, Widow guessed.

The Tundra driver had calloused knuckles, but not the same callouses that a boxer would have, or that Widow had. These were more of the workingman's telltale callouses.

Widow figured the guy was a business owner, but had probably worked his way up. Maybe his father had made him work from the bottom of a family-owned business until he proved himself ready to take over.

The Tundra driver was probably second or third or fourth gener-ation in the same business. Now, the brunt of the weight was his to bear. It was a handed-down family business, probably defining his future before he was even born, like a prince inheriting the throne and all the responsibilities that come with it.

Widow wasn't sure what the business was, exactly. He figured it was farming-related. But what? Maybe the Tundra driver was given a hauling business, delivering fertilizer or farming goods to all the nearby farms. Maybe the guy was a farmer himself. Maybe his daddy had handed him the reins recently, possibly when he turned thirty like his daddy's daddy had done before him.

A pair of rough utility gloves was stuffed into one of the cup holders. They were the kind that a lineman might wear, or those guys who tossed around large bundles of hay all day. They were hard and tan and worn. The material was part canvas, part suede. They looked durable.

A wedding band dangled from a chain around the Tundra driver's neck, which at first signaled that he might be a widower, but that didn't seem likely because the guy sat back with a sense of pride and was chipper like he was doing well with his business, with his family, and with his own life. Not the kind of bearing of a man who was unmarried.

Widow figured the ring on the chain was related directly to the gloves and the physical labor he did for a living. He probably didn't want to risk losing his ring, so he kept it close on a chain instead of on his finger where it might slip off or get him caught in some work-related machine.

The interior of the truck was clean, spotless, and worn with use. The seats were clean. The dashboard and upholstery were oiled and polished. Everything in the truck was used and worn, but maintained with the utmost care.

The Tundra driver was a ginger. He had a red beard, about three-quarters of an inch grown out. Widow figured the guy was completely bald on top. He wore a baseball cap, but the sides of his hair thinned just as it vanished under the rim of the hat. The cap's bill was flat, as if it had just been bought off the rack ten minutes ago.

Widow had seen this style around many, many times in the last couple of years. It was a trend. Lots of guys his age and younger stylized their hats this way. It didn't bother him, but every generation was different.

He remembered seeing photos of his dead grandfather, his mother's old man. He had been a Marine. In most of the old photos that Widow saw, his grandfather wore his hats on the top of his head. They were just set down on top like a soft lunar landing. The hat rested there and was never pushed down all the way. The brim barely set on his head, not pushed all the way down. It looked like a brisk wind would've knocked it off, but that never happened.

Widow remembered seeing the same style on the old guys in his grandfather's other photos. A group of aging vets hanging out, playing dominoes, and they all wore their military caps this way.

At least the driver wasn't wearing it with the sales sticker left on it. Widow had seen that, too. Millennials liked to do that. He found that one annoying.

The first five minutes of the ride was mostly awkward silence, with neither Widow nor the Tundra driver wanting to speak first. In the end, the Tundra driver spoke first.

"That roadblock was something, huh?"

Widow smiled and answered with what he thought was a lie.

"It had nothing to do with me."

"Oh, I know that."

Widow looked over at the driver, curious.

He asked, "How?"

"What?"

"How do you know it has nothing to do with me?"

"They did that because of that thing over in Carbine."

"Carbine?"

"It's a town. Close to where I picked you up. It's in this county. I passed through it. I go there sometimes for supplies because it's closer to my home than Charlotte."

"Carbine, is where you're coming from?"

"No. I'm driving back from Knoxville with a couple of stops along the way there and back. I brought samples to a wholesaler last night. A bit late, but he's in a pinch, and he was the last on my stop, anyway. Needs more trees. So, I made the trip because we need the business. He'll send them down his pipeline to new vendors throughout his region. Hopefully, one of them will buy from us."

Widow didn't ask what the samples were. He got the impression it was some kind of crop, or possibly nursery-related. He figured if the Tundra driver wanted him to know what they were specifically, he would tell him.

The Tundra driver talked and talked, answering questions that Widow didn't ask.

"But Carbine's where I go for quick stuff, sometimes. It's easier to get to and get out of than driving all the way to Charlotte. Well, normally, it is."

"Why? Is that far for you?"

"I live in Cherokee Hill."

"Where's that?"

"You never been out here before?"

"Nope."

"Well, let me introduce myself, proper," the guy said with a bigger smile.

He held onto the steering wheel with one hand and reached over with the other one and offered it for Widow to shake.

"My name's Walter White."

Widow took the guy's offered hand and shook it awkwardly because their positions were side by side and not dead-on straight like most handshaking scenarios.

White chuckled like he and Widow were in on an inside joke, except Widow wasn't in on it. He was clueless why White chuckled. He thought maybe the guy was famous or something, and he was used to people recognizing him.

"I know. Now, you're wondering if I cook meth."

Widow looked at him sideways.

"I don't judge," Widow said, which is half-true. "Live and let live is my motto. You wanna cook meth, that's on you. Knock your socks off. I couldn't care less."

"No. No. I mean, like the TV show."

"What?"

"It's a joke. You know?"

Widow stayed quiet.

"Walter White? My name is like the guy's on that TV show. You know?"

Widow looked at him, dumbfounded.

"You don't know the show, do you?"

"I don't watch TV. Don't own one. Never have."

"You don't own a TV?"

"Nope."

"And you never have?"

"Can't say I have. My mom had one in our home, but that was twenty years ago."

"What're you? A priest or something?"

"More like a monk."

"Say what?"

"I'm more like a monk. Priests own TVs; they vow a life of celibacy, not boredom."

White said nothing to that.

"Guess you can say I'm a nomad, which is kind of like a monk. Nothing says that a monk must live in a monastery."

"You're a drifter?"

Widow nodded.

He saw White's smile shrink slowly. He stared at Widow before turning his head straight. Widow could see that White was having second thoughts about picking him up.

One of the tools in Widow's tradecraft from his deep cover days was simply developing a camaraderie. So, he kept talking.

"I don't know about Walter White, but I remember old TV show about the monk who wandered the Old West, righting wrongs."

"You're talking about Kung Fu? That show starring Bruce Lee?"

Widow shook his head.

"No. Bruce didn't star in it. He created it. The story goes he wanted to star in it, but the studio wouldn't let him. They wanted a white actor."

"That true?"

"It is. According to his autobiography."

White nodded.

Silence filled the cabin once again, and they drove on. Widow listened to the heat blasting from the vents. He heard the hum of the engine and the tires on the road. He heard the wind gusting outside, beating on the truck's skin. And suddenly, he realized he hadn't introduced himself.

"My name's Jack Widow. Nice to meet you."

"Likewise."

"Thanks for picking me up."

"No problem."

"What's the roadblock about? You said you knew."

"It's been all over the radio."

"What has?"

"Back in Carbine, there was an explosion. But the media doesn't have all the facts about it."

"But you do?"

White reached down with his left hand and pointed underneath the Tundra's stereo at a black metal box drilled into the bottom of the dashboard, aftermarket. The box had buttons and knobs and a lit-up screen with digital channels displayed. The power was on, but the volume was all the way down.

Widow asked, "Police scanner?"

"Yep. I get bored doing long drives. I like to listen sometimes. Plus, it's helpful if there's lots of police activity on the road. I don't trust Apple Maps always to guide me through the quickest routes."

"So, what's going on?"

"There was a raid on the Athenian compound."

"Athenian? That a company or something?"

White leaned forward and stared out the windshield at the sky. The snow picked up speed and density. He flicked his left wrist and flipped on the wipers to the slowest mode and then inspected it and went up one more level to a slow, steady rhythm.

The snow fell slowly and haphazardly, almost as if it was dancing on the wind.

The wipers flicked the snowflakes off the windshield with ease.

A solitary early morning flicker of light appeared on the horizon as the sun started its climb to a new day. The sunlight looked like a spark on the horizon.

White said, "The Athenians are a cult."

"A cult?"

"Yeah, you know? Like Jamestown, or Waco, or that guy that convinced a bunch of women to be his wives. You know? The inbreeding thing?"

"Aren't they all like that?"

White chuckled and shrugged.

"I think this one is like a militia slash religious cult. You know? The most dangerous kind—a bunch of religious nuts with lots of guns."

"That is just like Waco."

"Well, just like Waco, this one ended badly. Only without the long standoff. Didn't that one have like a month-long standoff between the cops and the Waco people?"

Widow thought, More like two months.

He asked, "What happened?"

"FBI raided them this morning. They must've got wind of stockpiles of weapons or something. I guess."

"ATF, you mean?"

"Huh?"

"The ATF raided them, not the FBI. The ATF handles illegal weapon stockpiles and the like."

"ATF?"

"The Bureau of Alcohol, Tobacco, Firearms, and Explosives."

White mouthed the words and asked, "Wouldn't that be BATFE?"

"Too long. The Justice Department likes three-letter acronyms. FBI, DEA like that."

"CIA?"

"The CIA is part of the State Department, not Justice. It's not a criminal investigation agency. It's a spy agency."

"ATF handles alcohol and tobacco?"

"They were formed long ago."

"Oh, during Prohibition?"

"Before that. Eighteen-eighty-six."

"Was alcohol illegal back then?"

"It wasn't originally about alcohol. It was part of the Treasury Department. Then it became an IRS unit. Then a Justice Department unit. They regulate the sale and transport and stockpiling of…?"

Widow trailed off and stayed quiet, waiting for White to say it.

"Alcohol, tobacco, firearms, and explosives?"

"All the good stuff. They're federal like the FBI, and they come with all the red tape and bureaucracy."

"You sound like you're not fond of them?"

"I got nothing against them. They stay out of my way, and I stay out of theirs'."

"ATF. The radio made it sound bad."

Widow stayed quiet.

White said, "There was an explosion, actually a bunch of them. The cult blew themselves up. Killed a bunch of ATF guys."

Widow looked at White with surprise shadowed over his face.

"They blew themselves up?"

"Yeah."

"That's unusual."

"Not really. Isn't that what they all do?"

"They don't usually blow themselves up. Or take out law enforcement when they do. Cults usually poison themselves or some other insane thing, but not explosives. It's cheaper just to drink bleach than to rig elaborate explosives."

White shot Widow a sideways look.

Widow asked, "How many died?"

"A hundred, I think. Not sure how many Athenians versus ATF agents."

"A hundred?"

"That's the toll I heard. I shut it off soon after. The waves are too frantic to understand what's happening now. Too many cops were talking over each other."

I imagine so, Widow thought.

"So why the roadblocks?"

"What do you mean?"

"If the Athenians are dead, then why the roadblocks? They only put up roadblocks when they're hunting someone."

"I guess there're stragglers?"

"Maybe. But not just any. More than likely, they're hunting some really bad ones."

"The roadblocks are in all directions on all major roads leading in and out of Carbine."

"I didn't even notice passing through Carbine."

"Were you riding with someone else?"

Widow paused a beat. He couldn't tell him he was driving a stolen car. So, he lied.

"Yeah. I got dropped off before the roadblock. The guy I was with turned around, headed back the other direction. He didn't want to be caught up in whatever was going on."

"That's not surprising. People around here are very particular about their privacy and their constitutional rights. They don't like cops butting into their affairs. And they hate Feds coming around. Not because this county is full of criminals or anything. It's just an old political view that stuck around. I guess you could say people around here are libertarians. They love their guns, like conservatives, but they also love their civil liberties like liberals. It's a real 'mind your own business' attitude."

"I can understand that. I have a similar motto."

"What's that?"

"Live and let live," Widow said.

He thought, *But you shoot at me, I shoot at you.*

White said, "I'm down with that. That's a good way to go about your life."

"I think so. Life's short. I don't have time to be a downer on other people for the way they want to live. If you want to live on a compound and spend your days worshipping a man-child who convinced you he's a living messiah, that's your business, not mine. Doesn't affect me."

White cracked a half-smile and nodded. He agreed, but he changed the subject.

"So, Mr. Widow, where you headed, exactly?"

Widow stared out the window at the road ahead.

Good question, he thought.

"Guess I'm headed to the Atlantic."

"You guess? You don't know?"

"No. Just figure I'll go where it's warmer, and I like beaches."

"You really are a nomad."

Widow said nothing to that.

"You don't have any bags?"

"Nope."

"Where do you keep all your stuff?"

"I'm wearing it."

White looked him over from across the wheel.

"The only thing you own is the clothes on your back?"

"And the things in my pockets."

"A nomad and a minimalist. What you got in your pockets? Pocket-lint?" White said jokingly, but Widow had nothing to hide.

He clicked off his seatbelt, let it reel back home. He leaned back in the seat and shoved his hands into both front pockets of his jeans and turned them out. The right pocket turned out to reveal nothing but pocket lint, as predicted. The left pocket turned out to reveal no lint, but a cheap gas station-bought toothbrush. It wasn't the foldable type he preferred. Those were scarce these days.

The toothbrush was a ninety-nine-cent piece of plastic with bristles and not much else. That was all he carried in his front pockets.

Stuffed in his back pocket was his passport, crinkled and well-worn, but still valid and still valuable. Bookmarked inside was his debit card, also well-worn and still valuable, not much though; sometimes, it felt like it was barely useful. His checking account wasn't what it used to be. When you're not depositing money, but spending and spending, your account will shrink fast.

Widow wasn't a rich man, not in the monetary sense. He had zero net worth. He wasn't in the game of savings accounts and stocks and holdings and IRAs and 401k's. Widow's financial plan was no plan. He lived off what he had or what he earned, and when that ran out, he would earn more.

No one would call Widow rich, but he colored himself wealthy in the sense that he had everything he needed. What he needed was all right there—clothes on his back and enough money in his pocket, or in his bank account, to buy coffee and breakfast and motel rooms.

White stared forward through the windshield to the horizon and drove on.

Widow stared forward and stayed quiet for a beat.

The early morning glow slowly turned into bright, early morning sunbeams. The snow continued to dance across the sky, but the sun rising made it seem a little less gloomy, like hope was on the horizon.

They drove on for a while before White spoke again.

"Mr. Widow, you got any family?"

"Can't say I do."

"Is that a no?"

"I got a father left. Somewhere. But I never met him."

"So, what do you do for Christmas?"

"Nothing. I'm alone. But it's no big deal. I like it that way. It's all part of the price I pay for my freedom."

White was quiet again.

Traffic was light, heading southwest, but heavy going back the other way.

On their drive, they saw several police and military and medical emergency vehicles driving back the way they'd come. The police vehicles had sirens wailing and light bars flashing, almost violently, almost palpable, like gunfire.

White said, "You know Christmas isn't that far away?"

"It's pretty far away. More than three weeks."

"True. Still, it's a real shame to spend it alone."

Widow stayed quiet.

"You're not getting a big family dinner or anything?"

"There's no one—no distant cousins. No aunts. No uncles. No one."

White shifted in his seat like he was trying to stretch out his back from slouching during his long, overnight ride.

"You know what you should do?"

"What's that?"

"You should spend a day or two with us. You can have a real Christmas dinner."

Widow looked at him.

"Have what?"

"Christmas dinner."

"How? It's a long way off."

"Not Christmas dinner on Christmas, but a big family dinner like most people have on Christmas. A lot of families split up the exact days they have dinners and go to different places. We can do that tonight. Hell, all our dinners are like Christmas dinners. That's when we're all together, which we are right now."

"I don't know."

"Come on. You should experience it, at least. Do it with us."

"You serious?"

"We got plenty of food. Plenty of room for you to crash a night. We have big family dinners all the time. You're not putting us out or anything. It'll feel like a Christmas dinner, minus the decorations. We've not done that part yet. Lord knows we got plenty of Christmas spirit lying around."

Widow wasn't sure what he meant by that almost as much as he had no idea what to say. He had never been invited to spend a big family dinner with a stranger's family before, not since he'd left the NCIS.

He repeated himself.

"You serious?"

White paused a beat like he was rethinking the offer, but it was too late now. The offer was made. The negotiations were in session.

"Yeah. That's it. You can spend the day and night with us. Me and my family. You'll love it."

The day and night?

Widow thought about this for a moment. His first instinct was to run. He didn't enjoy staying in one place, standing still, but when was the last time he'd experienced a slice of American family life?

A Christmas dinner, even if it was three weeks early, with strangers, was better than no Christmas dinner experience, he figured.

"You sure it's not an inconvenience?"

White paused and stared in the rearview mirror at his own reflection as if he was having a meeting with himself, discussing it with himself.

"Sure. You ain't got no real plans. And my family'll love having you around. The Atlantic's not going anywhere. It'll be there day after tomorrow."

"I'll only stay for the day. Then I'll take off. Ok?"

"And night. I insist. We got plenty of empty beds. You can stay the night with us, and in the morning, I'll drive you in the direction you want to go, at least to Lancaster. You can catch the bus from there."

Widow glanced out the windshield once again, quickly, and then over at White.

"Sounds good to me. I appreciate it."

"Great. You'll love my family."

18

A RADIO DISPATCHER, who had worked for the South Carolina Highway Patrol for two decades, thought that she had seen it all. During her tenure, she thought she had heard it all. She knew all there was to know within the department: all the radio codes, all the officers on the ground, and all the terminology. She believed that there was nothing left to surprise her—she was wrong.

Tonight had been quiet until the ATF thing in Carbine went sideways. One moment, her radio was quiet as a church mouse, and the next, it erupted into a cacophony of radio chatter. Parts of it were pleas for help, but most of it was inaudible. When the radio chatter after the explosion slowed to where officers could understand each other across the network, she stayed quiet, trying not to interrupt, staying out of the way.

She stayed quiet for ten long minutes and slowly counting, listening to the chatter. She heard familiar patrolmen voices and unfamiliar ATF voices over the airwaves, using words like explosion and bodies and body parts. She heard things that made her cringe, that made the hair on her neck stand straight up. It sounded like a war zone. No! Not a war zone. It sounded like the aftermath of a bombing. Warzone implied a war, a battle being waged, but her side, the good guys, weren't fighting back. It sounded like they had been attacked and were down for the count.

She stayed quiet, stayed listening. Her mind went to thoughts of her dead husband, who had been a retired patrolman. He didn't die in the line of duty. He died from colon cancer—five years ago. He had retired, and a year later, he was diagnosed and died. He was buried two miles from her home, in a nice little cemetery that she visited every Sunday morning, after Mass. The church was right down the street from the cemetery, which made it almost an obligation for her to visit.

She had stayed with the department. She was still a year away from retirement age.

Suddenly, her thoughts were interrupted by the radio, but not by loud chatter or another explosion. It was interrupted by silence because just a second ago, she'd heard nothing but chaotic chatter. Now, she heard dead silence, not static—silence.

She pulled her chair up closer to the edge of her cubicle desk and listened.

The silence turned to repeated clicks, but no voices, like someone was pressing the talk button down, but saying nothing. She listened closely, expecting someone to say something. But they didn't. No one said a word. Instead, she heard continuous clicking as if one of her patrolmen was clicking the talk button, trying to say something, but not talking at all.

This went on for five long minutes. Her first thought was someone's radio was malfunctioning, but it needed to stop. It was important to keep the channel clear.

She listened and still heard nothing but clicking and dead air.

She grabbed the receiver on her headset and adjusted it, and spoke.

"Who's clicking the button?"

She listened, heard nothing. No response.

"Hello? Who's this?"

She listened again and heard nothing again. But then she heard the click one more time—one last time.

After, she heard a sound that wasn't clicking or a radio code or anything that she had heard before over the radio. It was a sound that she rarely heard over the police channel. But she had heard it before. She knew it well. She'd heard the sound many, many times over the emergency nine-one-one phone lines, whenever she worked the emergency dispatch station and not the police radio station.

The sound was heavy, irregular breathing, like someone who had holes in his throat. It sounded like someone blowing through a straw that had multiple punctures in it. It sounded like a deranged, broken flute that didn't play music, but played terror. It sounded like drowning.

The sound she heard was someone's last breath, their last sounds. The last sounds of breathing turned to someone's death rattle.

19

WIDOW LEANED TO THE RIGHT, his shoulder squeezed against the Tundra's front passenger door. He blinked. His eyelids flapped slowly and heavily until they fully closed. On the last blink, his eyes closed and stayed closed, and his head rolled to the side and down against the Tundra's window, involuntarily. Sleep overcame him so fast that it seemed almost like being under the power of a heavy sedative. It happened as fast as if someone had shot him with a tranquilizer dart.

No one had shot him. Widow was tired, and that was all. He had just finished a long drive alone. It was early in the morning. He dozed off. His brain powered down like he was lying in a comfy king-sized bed and not sitting upright in a truck.

Spending sixteen years in the Navy SEALs, traveling all over the world at all hours of the night, Widow had learned to sleep wherever he could and at whatever time he had available. He could bounce around the back of a cargo truck, barreling down a rocky mountain road in Afghanistan, or along a dusty dirt road on the plains of Africa, and he would stay asleep. A car could backfire, and he would stay asleep. He could be on a battle carrier in the Gulf, rocking and swaying, and a major storm could disrupt the ship, and he would stay asleep.

Only three things could wake Widow up—gunfire, the brush of his skin from a beautiful woman, or freshly brewed coffee. He couldn't explain it, other than to say that it was all part of the SEAL programming.

White noticed the silence and turned his head, glancing over. He saw Widow was asleep. He stayed quiet and turned back to the road. He drove on, taking it as easy as he could, keeping the bumps and dips to a bare minimum because he was unaware of the power of Widow's sleep patterns.

He knew he didn't want to wake a sleeping giant.

Widow slept for what felt like an hour-long nap. Actually, he had only been out for about fifteen minutes. However, his brain had transported him right into the REM cycle. At first, he woke up a little groggy, but then he felt refreshed, alert like he was heading into combat. He had to force his energy power back down to medium readiness.

A cramp in his left leg caused him to shift in his seat. Widow was cramped even in a roomy Tundra's footwell. He turned his foot left and then right, making the best of it. White noticed and saw he was awake.

"We'll be there soon, Mr. Widow."

"No rush."

"You can push the seat back more if you need to."

"Thanks."

Widow reached down under the seat and snapped the adjustment bar up and held it there until the seat slid all the way back on its tracks. Then he released it. It made little difference, but it was enough for him to feel more comfortable. He stretched his legs out to the maximum capacity of what the truck's footwell would allow.

He opened his eyes wide and held them like that, feeling the heat from the vents on the dash blowing on his face.

"Where're we now?" Widow asked, staring forward, looking out over a scene of huge, swaying trees and white snowy everything and a wintry sky that was half gloom, half sunlight.

"Welcome to Cherokee Hill."

Widow looked out the windshield ahead and then panned his view over to the right. He saw faint streams of early morning light and darkness, and more trees caked in snow.

"I don't see any hills."

"It's Cherokee Hill, singular. There's only one hill. Well, there are lots of little hills, but one big one. You're on it. The whole place is named after it."

Widow nodded.

"Why Cherokee?"

"Indians lived here once. I think."

Widow nodded.

"Possible. The Cherokee lived throughout both the Virginias and the Carolinas."

"See, there ya go. That's probably why. I don't remember ever hearing a story why. It's always just been called Cherokee Hill. That's the name I've always known."

Widow looked forward and saw the faint early morning sun rays again—hope on a gloomy day.

"Your family up this early?"

White chuckled once, unexpectedly and involuntarily, like gagging on a doctor's tongue depressor, like a gasp of laughter.

"Oh yeah, they'll be up. The whole family will. At least my parents will be. We're farmers."

"Right."

Widow shifted again, back toward the door. He twirled his left foot around and around, fighting a cramp in his shin.

White didn't notice this time.

Widow looked back at the trees and the snow to the right, and then forward to the road they were on. It was a single-track, snow-covered road. There were no streetlights on the shoulders. In fact, there were no shoulders or ditches on either side, just more huge trees.

"Are we on a dirt road?"

"Yes. We're taking the backroads. It's faster than going all the way around down the highway."

Widow stayed quiet.

White said, "It's not a route you'll find on Google Maps on your phone. That's for sure. That app used to send me all over the place back here. I got lost once coming back because I tried to use it."

Widow didn't own a phone, but no reason to mention that, so he didn't. He just nodded along.

Out the window. After they'd gone about a hundred yards, Widow saw farmhouses and long rolling plots of land with over-grown grass blades sticking out of the snow. The plots of land were huge, surrounded by long, snow-covered wooden rail fences, some broken in places, some rotten from years of neglect.

There were long winding driveways and far-off structures that looked like well-built homes, only like the fences. They were forgotten and unlived-in and unmaintained. Beyond the houses were barns and long, snaking fields, all covered in snow.

After they drove past the first and second farmhouses and plots and then the third and fourth, Widow noticed an obvious pattern.

"What's going on with these farms? They all look empty."

White answered big and loud as if he was talking over the roar of a tank engine.

"I'd say fifty percent of the farms around here are still empty."

"That many?"

"Oh yeah, my family's farm is one of the few ones left. Tons of our neighbors had to leave back when the banks were foreclosing on everyone. It was a massacre. They pulled the notes on hundreds of farms in the area."

"You mean back in 2008? The financial crisis?"

"Yeah, but it wasn't just a fast thing. There was an initial wave of foreclosures, but then it slowed to a lingering thing for many. Most of us held out. But the ones who didn't make it ended up going out the second and third and fourth years. The rest all went over the next ten. Sad thing."

"Strange."

"Why do you say that?"

"People gotta eat. I didn't think the food industry slowed just because the banking and housing ones did."

"We all got hit. Just like everyone else."

Widow looked around, and on both sides, he saw nothing but emptiness, like a post-apocalyptic world. It made him think of what rural civilization would look like after nuclear fallout. It was a nuclear winter, a humanless earth, a world gone to shit. Despite the grim thought, it was strangely peaceful, the way the earth used to be, perhaps.

"Looks like your family really got lucky."

"We did. But not just luck. Our primary business isn't food or agriculture like the rest of these farms. We grow something different. Something that's stayed lucrative for us."

"What's that?"

White thought for a moment. The answer seemed visible on his face. He almost blurted it out, but stopped himself.

"Nah. You know what? I think it's better for you to see for your-self. It'll be a nice surprise."

Widow's first thought was that White was a pot farmer, which added up when he thought about the reference to drug-dealing earlier. Was marijuana legal in South Carolina? He didn't think so, but he wasn't sure. It was becoming legal in a lot of states, so eventually, it might be here. However, he figured that would be far in the future. The South was always the last holdout on every national issue.

He didn't ask.

They drove on down long, winding backroads, turning left once and right twice and snaking around countless loops and near corners until the road straightened out to a long, endless track ahead.

Finally, White slowed the truck like he was preparing to turn onto one of the empty farms, but he didn't turn. Instead, he looked over to the left side of the road down a long, snowy-white and tree-covered plot of land to a farm in the distance.

There was an old, forgotten For Sale sign out front, posted to a dilapidated wooden fence.

"Huh, that's weird."

"What's that?"

"The lights are on at Pine Farms."

"It's weird?"

"The Pines left years ago like everyone else. They were one of the first to go. It was the first sign of trouble for the rest of us, like the first lifeboat to go into the water."

Widow stared at the lights on at the Pines' farmhouse.

"Looks like candlelight, not electricity."

White squinted his eyes like focusing the scope on a rifle.

He said, "Yeah. You're right."

"We should check it out. Might be squatters."

"Does it matter?"

"They're squatting on private property."

"The bank's property."

"Does that make it better?"

"Hell-yeah, it does. The banks screwed us all over."

Widow shrugged and said, "That's a fair point."

"Plus, it's been a cold night, and it's Christmas season. Whoever's squatting probably just wanted out of the elements. They needed a place to sleep for the night. We should be kind."

"Yeah."

"They're already here, anyway. Cops won't come out right now. Let them stick it out. I'll call the sheriff in the morning."

Widow nodded and stared out the window at the candlelight. He let his gaze follow it as they drove past. He had a strange feeling that they were being watched.

20

THROUGH HIS SNIPER rifle's scope, while lying in a prone position, Jargo watched as two guys in a white Toyota Tundra drove up and then stopped on the road that he and the others had come up.

The vehicle drove at around thirty-five miles an hour at first, right over the rise of a hill just before the Pine Farms property line and fences, but then it slowed just at the foot of the driveway and stopped like they were lost or couldn't decide on which way to go. There was a driveway across the street that led to a farm that wasn't abandoned. They could've continued straight, but they could've done that without stopping. So why did they stop?

Jargo watched, with a bullet standing by in the rifle's cold chamber. His finger was in the rifle's trigger housing. His index fingerprint brushed the rifle's trigger. They were old friends, and both his trigger finger and the rifle's trigger were eager to go.

Jargo breathed in, slowly, and he breathed out slowly. His heartbeat slowed in seconds the way he had practiced and practiced controlling it for years. It was from years of Army sniper service. Just as much as practicing breathing, heart rate control, and shooting, Jargo also practiced restraint.

Restraint was probably the hardest skill in his sniper arsenal for him to learn. It was in his nature to shoot now and be restrained later. He wanted to fire. He wanted to see the red mist that smoked out of a human head when shot from his weapon. He wanted to squeeze the trigger, and it wanted to be squeezed. He felt it. But he didn't fire. He just watched—for now.

There was enough early morning sunlight to make out the driver, face, and all. But not the passenger. He was obscured in shadow and darkness.

First, Jargo targeted the scope reticule on the driver. The man was ginger and in his early thirties, probably. He had a jolly look to him like he was full of Christmas spirit or something.

The rugged work truck, the area, Jargo figured the guy for a farmer.

Jargo watched him for a second more, left both eyes open, but envisioned the guy's head exploding like a pumpkin from an accurate bullet. One shot, cold too, but he could blow the guy's brains out the back of his head—easy.

Jargo made a silent bang sound with his lips, an intimate whisper, just as he'd done many times back in Iraq, before he joined up with Abel's team, because, before Abel, he operated within the confines of the Army's Rules of Engagement, which dictated that he was almost never lawful in shooting a bad guy whenever he felt like it. He was glad those days were long behind him. Still, he couldn't just shoot the Tundra driver for no reason. Not without Abel's orders. Doing so would be far worse than violating the Army's bureaucratic bullshit.

Disobeying Army law came with courts martial and hearings and investigations. Being found guilty came with jail time, which came with three squares a day, daily recess time, and a warm cot. Crossing Abel came with none of that. It came with a bullet to the head and nothing else.

Even though he couldn't shoot, it didn't mean that he couldn't imagine the squeeze of the trigger, the rocketing bullet, and the explosion of the red mist surrounding the Tundra driver's head.

Jargo smiled at the thought; then he slowly panned his aim up and to the left. He stared through the windshield and waited. He couldn't see the face of the second man, but he could still kill him. There was no clean headshot, but the guy was tall, which meant that from Jargo's angle, he could see the man's gut from the scope. A perfect gut shot would kill the passenger without fast medical help—no question. But it would be a slow and painful death.

He stared through the scope into the darkness of the cabin and aimed at the passenger's gut.

He whispered to himself once again, and, once again, it was intimate.

"Bang!"

Jargo waited a long moment to see what the riders in the truck were going to do. They were stopped dead-on the middle of the snowy road. The driver was staring at the farmhouse behind Jargo, inspecting it.

The candlelight. They must see the candlelight, he thought.

It was good that the candlelight made them pause. It was good because it meant that they were locals, probably neighbors, because only neighbors would stop in the middle of the road to suspect lights on a property that had been empty for years. A passerby wouldn't have noticed because they wouldn't have known.

The guys in the Tundra were doing the concerned neighborly thing—good Samaritans watching out for their neighborhood. Maybe they were even charged by the house's owners to watch over the property from time to time.

Short of them being police, Jargo wasn't sure what to do about them. If they were cops, he'd shoot them on sight—no questions asked—but with nosey neighbors, he simply marked them, logged them into his memory, and watched to see what they did next.

He needed further instructions. So, without moving away from the gun or the scope, without compromising his shot, he called out.

"Brooks?"

No answer.

"Brooks?"

Nothing.

He took a mental snapshot of the neighbor's exact location in his mind, as if his mind was an accurate tracking system. Then he broke off his gaze and took a quick look back over his shoulder for Brooks.

Brooks was curled up twenty feet back, up against the barn's cold wall in the loft space, near the ladder going back down.

He was sound asleep and snoring.

"Brooks?"

No answer.

Jargo pedaled his right leg up and back down to a pebble on the floor behind him. He scooted the rock along the floorboards and up to his stock hand. Quickly, he scooped it up and tossed the stone at Brooks, and returned to his rifle.

The stone zipped through the air and nailed Brooks right on the chin.

Brooks's eyes shot open fast, like a pair of airplane doors being blown out at twenty thousand feet. He was wide awake in a split second, a soldier's natural reaction to being woken up abruptly.

"What?" he asked.

"Get over here. Intruders."

Brooks hopped to his feet in one fast effort. It seemed almost like fancy martial arts move. He was limber for a huge guy in his fifties. His M4 rifle rested against the wall, butt on the floor.

He left it where it was, walked over, and joined Jargo down in the prone position. He picked up a pair of small field binoculars that cost as much as a used car and spoke.

"Where?"

"Dead ahead. The road. Front of the driveway."

Brooks looked through binoculars, while Jargo returned to peering through the scope.

They both watched at the same time at the Tundra stopped in the front track across the street, brake lights lit up.

"They been there long?"

"Maybe a minute. No longer."

Suddenly, the brake lights dimmed as the driver took his foot off the pedal, and the truck rolled away slowly.

"Who are they?"

"Neighbors. That's my guess."

Brooks paused a beat.

"Saw the driver for a second."

Jargo said, "Yeah. He looks like a farmer."

"Did you see the guy in the passenger seat?"

"I couldn't make him out. Too dark. And too tall. His face was covered by the roof. What about you?"

"All I can see is his gut."

"Same here."

"That means his head's close to the roof, then. He's tall like me. I got the same problem. When I drive, I gotta sink down in the seat in order to see up high enough for traffic lights."

Jargo made a barely audible, affirmative grunt.

"Get the plates and watch to see where they go. If they're nearby, then they just solved our problem."

"What problem?"

"Transportation. That's a big truck."

Jargo cracked a smile.

"True. Good thinking."

Brooks got up abruptly like he was leaving a conversation. He returned to his wall, slammed his back against it, slid down to his butt, closed his eyes, and gave one last order before going back to sleep.

"Wake me if there's anything else."

"Affirmative," Jargo replied. He memorized the license plate, as ordered, and logged it into his memory. Then, he watched the truck pick up speed and drive along the bumpy track and uphill for about another football field length, past a large mailbox. He had thought they were farmers who lived in the neighborhood, maybe even on the same road, but he was shocked that they lived that close.

The Tundra drove some ways past the abandoned farm they were holed up in, but then it stopped at the end of a narrow, private drive. The truck turned onto the snowy drive and drove past a big metal mailbox stuck up on a red wooden post with writing along the side.

He watched the rear lights as the truck vanished down the drive and into the trees.

He smiled.

They were neighbors after all, which meant that maybe he was going to get to see the red mist sooner than he imagined.

21

SPARTAN COUNTY ENCOMPASSED a large area of land smack on the border of South Carolina and North Carolina.

Flying over Spartan County by air would reveal long stretches of abandoned farmlands and sprawling forest trees and networks of backroad country. There seemed no clear design when they were plowed, and the ditches were dug like a bunch of guys with heavy equipment had gotten together, drunk lots of beer, and just started plowing roads.

The roads spider-webbed into hundreds of uncharted branches and dirt tracks, all going nowhere in particular.

Spartan County was one of the smallest counties in the state and the least populated per square mile. The locals often joked that a man could walk for a whole day along the backroads and never come across a single vehicle.

That was what Joseph Abel was counting on.

Ninety percent of the county was farmland, forests, and backroads, while the remaining ten percent included a handful of small towns where the tallest building among them was three stories. Not a sprawling metropolis by any means, just the way locals liked it.

Spartan County was home to quintessential small-town America that politicians always boasted about supporting, but hardly ever visited except for photo ops.

The local towns had everything the locals needed and nothing they didn't. For some, it was a laid-back fairy-tale kind of life. For others, it was drive-through country.

The towns' main streets were lined with shopping centers and churches and local branches of government and public schools and community centers. There were hospitals, naturally, but none of them was equipped to handle big patient loads from a catastrophic event like a commercial plane crash, a convoy of overturned school buses, a major terrorist attack, or a hundred cultists blowing themselves up along with dozens of ATF agents and local cops.

The local hospitals weren't the ATF's first phone call.

First, they contacted the nearest major hospitals immediately after the explosions were reported. One was located across the border in North Carolina, and the other was to the southeast. They both had emergency helicopters—one each. Both were in the air, bound for the Athenian compound in Carbine to airlift injured agents and police and Athenians. They picked up only the most critical cases. The second criterion for who went in the helicopter was selecting patients who were most likely to survive a helicopter ride. There was no sense in evacuating people who were going to die in minutes.

An unwritten, unofficial request that Adonis's boss had made clear to the general managers of each hospital was that injured children came first, before everyone else, because children being children meant they were innocent. The second priority was the injured ATF agents and police. The rest of the adult Athenians were not to be given any special treatment. They brought this disaster on themselves.

The hospital's general managers didn't argue.

The closest hospital to the Athenian compound and the explosions and the dead and injured was the hospital in Carbine, which had only six ambulances.

It was overrun with injured and wounded within minutes of the explosion.

There weren't enough ambulances and hospitals on the ground to handle a level of injuries from a major explosion like the injuries at the Athenian compound.

The grand total number of ambulance fleets for the entire county was eight, and the number of working ambulances including Carbine's was twenty-three. They were all less than state-of-the-art, but all seventeen others were headed to the scene. Even with lights flashing and sirens blasting and early morning traffic being slight, some of them would take forty-five minutes to an hour to reach Carbine.

Lucky for Adonis, she was already seated on the back of one of the ambulances from Carbine. She sat on the back, inside two swung-open doors, her legs dangled over the rear bumper. Her feet were just above the ground.

She was fifty yards from the compound's front doors.

The main building was still on fire. So were the church and the outbuildings. Everything was on fire.

Fire trucks were parked between the ambulances and the main building and behind the police cars that the ATF had arrived in. Most of them were damaged. Two were on fire; several had blown out windows and front fender damage. One had its two front tires blazing fast and furious in a raging fire.

Three firemen stood in front of that truck blasting the flames with fire extinguishers before the flames reached the engine or the gas tank or spread anywhere else. The last thing they needed was another explosion.

The rest of the firemen were spraying the main building with water from fire hoses attached to two fire trucks or dragging survivors out of and away from the building and the blazing fire.

They started with the ATF agents and police. They worked fast to lift, carry, or drag the ones who were breathing as far back from the burning building as possible in case of more bombs or explosions.

All six ambulances, and the pairs of paramedics that came with each of them, tended to the wounded ATF agents and police first.

Adonis had a head injury, a superficial gash across her left temple that curved around to the front of her forehead just above her brow. It looked worse than it was. It bled profusely. The EMT told her to keep the bandages tight and clean.

She also had several other cuts from broken glass, not from any of the bombs, but from the passenger window of the SUV she had arrived in. Like all the other vehicles they stormed the property in, all the vehicle windows shattered from the explosions and the shock waves.

The paramedic finished a quick field dressing for her head. He told her she was lucky it didn't look like she would need stitches, but that she should go get it checked out at the hospital anyway, but what he was really saying was that she should wait and check it out tomorrow at a clinic. He knew good and well that she wasn't getting any face time with a local doctor. Not with even more urgent injuries out there.

She thanked him and insisted that he move on to the more important victims, which he did. He left her there alone.

Adonis ignored the physical pain and took her phone out and looked at the screen. She had several missed calls, all from her boss, as well as several text messages. They all asked versions of the same question: *Where are you?*

Adonis was the Resident Agent-in-Charge of the local region of South Carolina. She answered to the Deputy Director, a man named Mike Gibbs.

Her first instincts told her she had hearing damage because she hadn't heard her phone ring, not once, not at all. But she realized she could hear everything around her just fine.

She heard the paramedic when he was asking her questions. She heard the ambulance sirens when they were blaring past the destroyed gate and entrance to the compound. She heard the fires crackling and sparking all around her as they burned on. She heard the screams and cries for help from injured agents and

Athenians left lying on the ground among the soot and ashes and the dead.

Her hearing was optimal, no problem there.

She checked her phone. The ringer was switched on. She played with it, pushing the outer switch up and down, testing it out. The screen notified her each time that the phone ringer was on and then off.

She pulled up the settings and tried to hear the ringer. It didn't ring; then, she realized that both the ringer and the vibration function were both busted. Maybe when she landed on her butt from being thrown back by the explosion, she had crushed some vital internal piece of the ringer's configuration.

She swiped and pressed on the missed calls and tried to call him back.

The phone rang.

He picked up on the first ring.

"Adonis!"

"Yeah. I'm here."

She pressed the phone close to her ear and jabbed a finger in the other one to plug it up. The surrounding commotion was too loud to hear what he was telling her otherwise.

Adonis had trained hard, back in the day at the ATF National Academy in Glynco, Georgia. She wasn't the only female in her class, but she was the only one to make top marks in combat courses, something that she was proud of. She was proud of showing the boys that a woman could do it, too. This sense of pride was short-lived ever since because she was one of a handful of female agents on the ground in command positions. The men in the same positions outnumbered the women by a lot, by leaps and bounds. She liked to think she was fighting the good fight.

Adonis was a rebel at heart, but very much a part of the system now. She was institutionalized. She was the lead agent-in-charge, which meant no more sticking it to the patriarchy. She was the patriarchy now. She had responsibilities and duties. She owed everything to the agency.

The National Academy instructors beat the rebel side of her into submission, as best they could, and now she was part of the cog of upper management. A tough spot for a girl who was a rebel at heart. She liked to look at it this way: she was still fighting the good fight, only she was also upholding justice for all—very egalitarian.

Part of being institutionalized made her wonder if she should do a situation report for her boss. She didn't know how much he knew already. So, she gave it to him.

"There's been an explosion. Several, actually. There are dead on the ground: Athenians and ours. I don't know where Clip is. I don't see him anywhere."

Her boss interrupted her.

"Adonis. Adonis. I know what's going on."

"You do?"

"Yes."

"It's all over the media. Everyone knows. It's Waco all over again!"

She paused a beat, and then she said, "I'm sorry, sir."

Her boss was quiet for a second. He spoke in a tone that sounded like the ones she had used in the past when she delivered to the nearest relative the sad news of an agent dying in the line of duty.

"Clip is dead."

"Oh, no!" she said faintly, almost in a whisper.

"The director has ordered Agent Marson's team to get down there and take over. From this point forward, you're relieved of command."

"What? Why?"

"I just explained it to you! Are you listening! We've screwed up! We got agents down! We got citizens dead! Adonis, they're airing reels of Athenian children storming out of the compound, and then they're cutting to the video of explosions. It's playing on CNN! Over and over! You're done!"

"I did everything by the book!"

Mike Gibbs, her boss, paused a beat and breathed in.

Adonis felt like she had been punched in the gut, like they just clipped her wings. She said nothing, just waited, and listened.

Gibbs said, "Sometimes, that's not good enough. Sometimes, our best is good enough. Sometimes, the bad guys win. This time, Abel won."

She held back tears.

"Am I fired?"

"I don't know. I'll be fired, I'm sure."

"Why? It's my Op."

"I gave it to you. And that doesn't matter, anyway. Like I said, we're all over the morning news. It didn't make the morning papers, but we're all over the online pages. Damage is done. It doesn't really matter if we did our jobs or not. The agency will hang this disaster around our necks and feed us to the lions. The higher-ups have to protect the agency and sidestep the blame."

"I'm sorry, Mike."

"Forget it now. Listen up. Marson's guys will be there in two hours, probably."

"Two hours? Why not now?"

Adonis looked at her watch. It wasn't there. She stared at an empty wrist. Her watch was gone. She lost it somewhere. It must've blown off in the explosion.

She frowned. She liked that watch. It had sentimental value.

She took the phone away from her ear and checked the time. It was nearing eight in the morning, later than she thought. She synchronized the time in her head to a two-hour countdown.

"Let me run cleanup till then. I need to. Let me make it up as best I can. They're dead because of me."

Dorsch is dead 'cause of me, she thought.

"Adonis."

She stopped and listened.

Gibbs sighed. She heard it over the phone.

"I'm not saying it's your fault. If you think that's what I said, then I misspoke. I apologize. This is the fault of Joseph Abel and his followers. No one else. Don't you take a single iota of blame. You got nothing to feel guilty about. Put those thoughts straight to bed. That's a direct order."

No response.

He asked, "Got it?"

"I got it."

"Good. Now, are you okay?"

"Yes."

"Any injuries?"

"No," she lied.

"Good. Now, listen carefully."

She listened.

"I'm instructed to tell you; you're off this case. As of now, you're suspended. We're all off the case. The FBI will take over whenever the hell that is. Me too. I'm done. We're all done."

Gibbs paused a beat, swallowed.

"Now, that's out of the way. We got one chance here, and it's not to catch this bastard. Don't bring him in alive. Do you understand what I'm saying here, Adonis?"

Her boss couldn't see her face, but if he had, he would've seen utter confusion on it.

She said, "But, Abel is here. He's dead. We probably won't find his body for days. He's under a ton of brick and ash and not much else."

"Toni, you're not listening. Please."

She swallowed hard and tuned in her ears.

"Okay?"

"No one knows this except some of the South Carolina State Police. So, keep it quiet. I mean it. No one knows. Not the FBI. Not yet. No one above me. I've not reported it yet."

"Okay. What is it?"

"I've been looking over maps of the area and analyzing data for the last two hours with my team, in secret. We're supposed to be shut down here, too. I didn't hear from you, so I just kept looking, myself."

"Okay?"

"Spartan County has miles and miles of backroads."

"I'm aware. During your raid, the highway patrolmen ran a perimeter, checking out all the backroad-country they could. And...Adonis."

"Yes."

"This morning, right after the explosion, a radio dispatcher with the South Carolina Highway Patrol got a radio call on the police frequency. No one spoke on the call. It was just breathing and silence. It lasted for only a couple of minutes. It disconcerted her, but meant nothing. Everyone was up in arms, running around like chickens with their heads cut off. Which is understandable, right?"

"Yes."

"An hour passed, and about six a.m., someone over there noticed a patrolman wasn't answering his radio. Their cars have GPS trackers in them. Naturally."

"Of course."

"So, they sent someone to the patrolman's car. When they got there, they found him dead, Toni. He was shot on a country road."

Adonis said nothing but listened as if her life depended on the information being transmitted.

"It happened five miles northeast of the compound on a back-road off Six-Oh-One."

Adonis's ears and face perked up. Before she knew it, she was on her feet.

"The patrolman's dead. His CO is there now. I've asked them not to touch the scene."

Adonis moved away from the back of the ambulance involuntarily. She didn't realize her feet were moving. For a split second, she thought she was floating away.

Where was she going? She didn't know.

"Adonis."

"Yeah?"

"South Carolina Highway Patrol cruisers have dashcams, like everybody else."

She listened closely.

"The head of the state police out there called me. He told me they've got the video. He emailed it to me. I watched it."

"And?"

"It shows a black panel van. I saw the patrolman get shot through the driver's side window. I watched the driver, and a passenger get out, and then I counted five others."

"Five?"

"And…Adonis."

"Yes?"

"I saw Abel. He was the passenger. He was the shooter. He stood there over the dying patrolman and stared at him like he was getting his jollies watching the poor guy dying."

"Abel? You sure?"

"Yes. I'm sure. He was dressed in a white getup like one of those phony TV evangelists. Like he was a high priest or something. In my twenty-three years of law enforcement, I've seen nothing like it."

Abel was alive.

Adonis felt the hairs on her neck stand up. She felt shivers all over her body. She felt the rage coming on like a bad cold.

"Abel got away. He planned this whole thing."

"He caught Dorsch. Probably killed him in some horrible way. He must've set this whole thing up, killed so many of his own people just to cover his escape."

"How? He had a two-day notice we were coming. Tops. Are you saying he had all these explosives lying around already?"

"Yes. He's been planning it for years."

"How did he know we were coming?"

"He didn't know that we were coming. Not us specifically. But he's always known that someone would come. Someday. We knew they ran shooting drills. We came here based on the luck of finding materials being shipped to them for packing bombs. There's no telling how many shipments came before. Could be hundreds. Abel's wanted this day to come."

"If he planned for this, then he must have a phase two. He must have something coming next. Doesn't seem likely he would plan such a terrifying escape and nothing else."

"I agree. We gotta find him. Where's the dead patrolman exactly?"

"I've ordered Ramirez to fly you there. Find him. He should look out for you. Go with him. Check it out. There are two patrolmen on the scene, waiting. I've been reassured that they'll be cooperative, but Toni…"

"Yeah."

"He killed one of their own. Hopefully, they'll play nice. I told them we would do the same, but tell them nothing. See what you can get and report back."

"Okay. Got it."

She clicked off, but he said one more thing.

"Before you take off, I counted seven of them—Abel and six others. They will be tough. Probably his guys from the Army. So, grab as many other uninjured agents who'll fit on the helicopter. Take them with you. Tell them to do as you say. If they give you shit, call me. Now, go get this bastard before the Feds take over."

She looked around, instinctively, and surveyed the agents who looked like they would be useful going further.

"Toni, we're on the clock, but off the books here. You get the shot; you take the shot. I've gotta go. Be careful."

"Always."

She pressed the phone end button, and slipped the phone back into her pocket.

She left the ambulances and the EMTs behind her and reentered the scene. She walked past police, past police cars, past wrecked police cars, and searched for able-bodied ATF agents.

Without thinking, she walked to the front of the mess. She tried not to look below the level of the horizon. She didn't want to see how bad it was. She didn't want to see the severed limbs and the dead bodies of her friends.

A moment later, she heard the *whop, whop* of helicopter rotor blades. She thought it was Ramirez circling overhead, probably looking for her, but then she heard another set of rotor blades and then another.

She looked up and saw two helicopters flying in from the north.

They were both stamped along the sides with emergency services markings from different hospitals, but flying in from nearly the same direction.

They were big helicopters—bigger than the ATF's own helicopter.

She watched them swoop in and circle around, looking for landing spots. They both found spots not far apart within the Athenian walls. She watched them land.

Suddenly, the paramedics on the ground seemed to breathe a sense of relief at the sight of several more paramedics coming out of the helicopters to help.

Adonis turned back to looking for agents.

She walked toward the main building, which was nothing but one big blazing fire and surviving brick sections.

On the ground, she found a long set of tracks in the snow leading up to the back of a small convoy of fire trucks. She looked at the fire trucks. She never even heard them come in, or at least she hadn't noticed.

The fire trucks' emergency lights swirled on top of the roofs, mixing in with the red lights from the ambulances. The snow in the cones of the lights appeared red, like seeing it through a red filter.

Some of the fire trucks were being used to spray water over the blaze, but a few were unused. They seemed forlorn and forgotten in the red snow.

The main building blazed, and the flames roared on, no matter how much water was sprayed on them.

There were firemen fighting the fires. There were firemen swarming and scattering all over the grisly scene of carnage. They were picking up scared children and injured elderly, moving them out further from the buildings and the flames. They carried many of them out to the cluster of ambulances back where Adonis had come from. They dropped them off there as fast as they could. Then they scrambled back to the carnage to repeat the pick-up-and-carry process.

Right then, the firemen weren't firemen. They were paramedics. Their number one goal was to save lives, not fight the flames.

Adonis finally spotted Ramirez. He had circled his helicopter around to the back of the compound. It was parked on landing skids in an open snowy area, waiting for her like a personal chauffeur.

She scrambled to meet him, but halfway she stopped and remembered that she was supposed to grab backup. She had forgotten for a second.

Along the way, she grabbed the attention of two other ATF agents who looked strong. Their names were Swan and James. They were helping the firemen move people away from the flames.

Both Swan and James were officially part of the SRT. They were Clip's guys. They weren't investigative, which was fine by her. She didn't want anyone else butting in and tracking down Abel without her.

She wanted to find him. She knew Dorsch was dead. Why wouldn't he be? Why would Abel leave him alive?

Adonis wanted to find him first because now she was out for blood—Abel's blood.

22

THE TUNDRA'S tires scaled slowly over bumps on the track as they climbed uphill. The driveway was long and winding. Thick trees covered the first part. The trees were big and leafless, twisted, brooding guardians that stood eternal watch.

Over the crest of the hill, White slowed the truck, turned the wheel and lowered the volume on the radio with a button on his steering wheel. He glanced at Widow with a half-smile on his face, as if he was waiting for something.

He watched Widow's expression.

Widow looked across at him and then back out the windshield. He stared at something he was not expecting to see. Suddenly, White's cheery personality and obsession with Christmas made complete sense.

Out across the Whites' farm at Cherokee Hill, as far as the eye could see, Widow saw fields and fields of undecorated, untrimmed, and pristine Evergreens, Christmas trees. They were of all sizes and varying ages. They grew everywhere but were laid out in a kind of organized insanity.

He saw acres of them, spanning and sprawling in three compass directions like something out of one of L. Frank Baum's Oz children's books because of the greenness. He closed his eyes and pictured that field before Dorothy, the Scarecrow, the Tinman, and the Cowardly Lion reached the Emerald City. They crossed a big, green meadow filled with red poppies that made them drift off to sleep.

Not in Kansas anymore, he thought.

Some trees were half-buried in snow. Some had everything from roots to tops exposed. Some had only the tops exposed. Others were half and half. Most had lush green needles, white-capped by snow.

The closest collection of trees stood big and tall in perfect rows inside different big, square sections, which he could see were done on purpose to separate the trees. Each section must've been a different batch. They appeared to be divided by age. The oldest section probably being the ones to be harvested first and sold.

The early light filled the fields. White blankets of snow, topped off by the green of Christmas trees, presented quite the sight to see. It flooded Widow with nostalgia of the only Christmas mornings he ever really knew. It was as if the memories were buried in ancient tombs deep within him.

They were images of his mom, alive and young and single, and of himself as a little boy. No father. It was just the two of them— mother and son against the world.

The trees stood majestic in the early morning sunlight. The whole farm looked pristine in a gloomy, wintry sort of way, like a storybook. He supposed that was the beauty of Christmas trees; anywhere they are, they add something festive to everything around it.

Widow asked, "What's this?"

"It's a Christmas tree farm. We grow the trees here. They're our one and only export. Welcome to Cherokee Hill Farm, or as I like to call it, A White Christmas Farm."

"That's funny."

"Right? It's our real last name, I promise."

"Why not actually call it that?"

"Tradition. The farm wasn't always Christmas trees. Before my time, other crops grew here."

"Okay."

"We discussed changing. I wanted to change it back to other farm crops, but I was outvoted. We vote on major things like that as a family. Guess now I'm glad I lost that one. We might not have made it through the recession if we'd been in the middle of converting everything."

"I've seen nothing like this before."

"You've never been to a Christmas tree farm?"

"No. Is that unusual?"

White shrugged.

"It is if you grew up here. I guess. Don't really know. Lived nowhere else."

"I've seen Christmas tree lots before. The kind set up in parking lots. You know? But nothing like this."

"It's pretty cool, right?"

"It's outstanding. You guys should do Christmas shows here or something like a Christmas tree tour. I bet parents would bring their kids out from miles around."

"We used to do that."

"What happened?"

White shrugged.

"Times are hard for everybody. Cuts had to be made. A big spectacle like that costs money to maintain. We used to decorate them with lights, and we hired local teenagers to drive people around on tractors."

"Shame you don't do that anymore."

Then White said something that Widow had heard before but hated because it was a throwaway excuse that meant nothing.

White said, "It is what it is."

It is what it is. Cars, trucks, trains, trees, dogs—they are all what they are. Widow hated that phrase, but he didn't say so.

Instead, he repeated himself.

"It's still awesome."

"Isn't it? Can you imagine what it was like growing up here?"

"Bet that was something special?"

"It was. My brother and I used to play hide-and-seek in trees. Still do it with my son, sometimes."

"That's a pretty great childhood."

"It really was."

"Does it always snow like this?"

"No. Maybe like every ten years. But not usually like this. This is new. It's been a cold winter."

Widow didn't respond.

They drove on another minute in silence.

White took the curves slowly so that Widow could see it all as if he was on one of those tractor tours. Widow took advantage of the slow drive. He looked left and traced the horizon all the way right. His eyes stopped on some heavy farm equipment that he couldn't identify, so he mentally tossed it into the big tractor category.

Behind the heavy tractor-like equipment, he saw a section where trees were missing. They were cut down. Nothing was left other than the stumps sticking out of the snow.

He asked, "What's with the different sections? I mean, how do you choose which trees are ready for sale and which aren't?"

"It takes trees ten years to grow to the size where they reach their market potential. Not too big, but big enough."

White lifted a hand off the wheel and pointed.

"Each section's a different year. That empty section over there is exactly ten years old. Those are the ones we've cut and sold for this year."

"Looks like you still got plenty left?"

"Yeah. The Christmas tree business has slowed in the last decade. Several other farms across the country have gone out of business."

"Why is that? People don't celebrate anymore?"

"That's a part of it, but mostly it's because people get those fake trees. Lots more Americans are conscious of the environment now. Those trees are more economical and, even though they're plastic, they have repeat value. Better for the evergreen. That's probably how the consumer thinks of it. I suppose."

Widow nodded.

White said, "It's okay. We've picked up some of their territories, which helps."

Widow looked back out and saw White's farmhouse appear from behind the trees. It was a two-story red brick house with a huge wraparound porch with a barn off to one side. The whole estate looked like something from a Norman Rockwell painting.

Widow was shocked; there were no Christmas lights or decorations. He figured they just hadn't been put up yet. Or maybe they were waiting for later in December.

As the Tundra closed in on the farmhouse, a big, white front door swung open, and an old man stepped out with a big smile on his face. He was followed by a woman, younger than him, but over sixty-five. She stepped out behind him in the sort of intimate way that told Widow they must've been married to each other, and for a long time.

They must've been Walter's parents. He looked just like them.

The pair stepped out onto the porch. The older man stopped at the top of the stairs and waved at the Tundra.

White waved back.

Widow knew the old man couldn't see the wave because of the sun reflecting off the windshield.

They drove up to the house and swung around a circular drive that wrapped around a big tree.

Off to the left, between the barn and the farmhouse, there were two other vehicles. One was another Toyota Tundra. It was an older model, maybe twenty-plus years old. It looked like it had been worn out and abused down to its bare bones, but was still in working condition.

The other vehicle was covered by a tarp, but its shape was weird. Widow couldn't identify it, not exactly. It might have been a van or maybe an SUV, but the nose was weird.

He figured maybe it was an old classic car like one of those nine-teen-forties cop cars, the kind Dick Tracy would drive. Maybe Walter and his father were fixing it up in their spare time, which was something fathers and sons did together, something he would never experience.

The top of the driveway, around the tree, was completely shov-eled. Widow saw some concrete underneath the dust of snow left behind. Another set of tracks went off to the barn.

White parked the truck right in front of the porch and killed the engine. He swung open the door and stepped out. Widow followed.

The old man came down and hugged his son tightly as if he hadn't seen him in months, which wasn't the case, according to White's story.

Close family, Widow thought.

"Dad, that's enough," Walter White said.

The older man stepped away from his son, but then the mother moved in, and it was the same story, repeated, and far worse. She threw in kisses all over his cheeks and face, which required him to bend down to her level so she could reach him. He bent down as required, as he must've done a million times before. He did it, recognizing the highest point of the family's established chain of command—the mother.

Walter White greeted her in a boyish, after-school kind of tone that he might have used when he was six years old and stepping off the school bus coming home from his first day of school.

"Hi, Mom."

"We missed you, son," the mother said.

"I've only been gone one day."

"Doesn't matter," the old man interjected.

The mom let Walter go and stared at Widow. Her eyes started at the most comfortable position for a person to look naturally—eye level, which, for her, was only five inches north of Widow's navel because she stood around four-foot-five inches tall and Widow was six-foot-four.

She looked up at him like she was looking up at a high, unclimbable rock face.

"Oh, my, you're a big guy."

Not knowing what to say, Widow said, "Thank you."

"Son, who's your friend?"

"Sorry, Dad, this is Jack Widow."

Widow stepped away from the truck and closed the door behind him. He walked up to them and reached his hand out for the old man to shake first. He smiled as best he could.

"It's a pleasure to meet you, sir."

The old man was bald, with red hair around the sides and red stubble on his face. He had a squint in one eye, like the old Popeye cartoon, only not as dramatic or exaggerated.

Widow had seen that squint before in older Navy guys. Usually, it resulted from a stroke where the left side of the face went numb and never quite oriented back to normal.

The old man gave Widow a huge smile and took his hand and shook it. He gave it a hearty squeeze like he was trying to impress Widow.

"It's a pleasure to meet you, son."

They shook for ten seconds and then stopped.

Widow smiled at the old woman and offered his hand to her next. She took it and gave him an equally hearty smile and strong squeeze, even harder than her husband's.

White said, "Widow, this is my mother and father."

"It's nice to meet you both, Mr. and Ms. White."

The old woman said, "You can call me Abby. And this is Abe."

"Abe and Abby?"

Abe White said, "Yeah. We know. It's a coincidence. It's how we met—blind date. Our friends put us together because of our names. I think it was a joke. But the joke's on them 'cause I fell in love with her and then I did what you-kids say. I put a ring on it."

The Whites chuckled, all of them. Abby and Abe carried it on a little longer than Walter. He acted more like it was a required laugh; he'd probably heard that joke many times before, but he was required to laugh out of some sort of White family SOP.

"I didn't marry her for her name. Trust me!" Abe added.

"And I didn't marry him for his name, either. I married him for his money," Abby said. She looked around, eyes locked with each of the men for a split second, and then she added a big, maternal smile.

Abe said, "You could always call up Patrick Mickey Mouse and see if he's available."

Widow continued to smile, continued to stay quiet, but this time, his face showed confusion, involuntarily.

Abby said, "It's Mickey. His name was Patrick Mickey, not Patrick Mickey Mouse. You made that up. And I haven't seen him in more than fifty years. The poor guy's probably dead now. Why do you keep harping on him?"

After she mentioned the guy might be dead, her fingers added the sign of the cross over her face and chest as if she wished the dead to rest in peace, or she had just said some blasphemy, and she had to repent for it immediately.

Widow didn't belong to any religion, but in his life, he had the most proximity to Catholicism. During his early years, most of the town he grew up in was Catholic. In the Navy, he had encountered chaplains before. His religion was the world.

Widow stared at Walter, who offered an explanation.

"He's some guy that Mom dated for about a week back when they were teenagers."

Widow nodded.

Abby stared at him.

Walter White asked, "Where's everyone? Sleeping?"

"Maggie's awake."

Walter nodded, turned to Widow.

"That's my wife."

Abe also turned to Widow and spoke.

"What brings you here, Mr. Widow? Looking for work? I'm afraid we're already staffed up. Walter here already hired four new guys for the season. Too many, if you ask me."

"It's not too many. We could use more, Dad."

"No way. If we hire more, you'll just get lazy. You're able-bodied. You can help them."

"I already do help them. And I shouldn't be doing that. I'm the boss."

"Plus, your kid can help too."

Walter ignored that.

He said, "Widow's not looking for work, Dad. I just picked him up."

"He's a hitchhiker?"

Widow said, "That's right."

White's parents both looked at him.

"I'm not looking for work. I'm just passing through. Your son was kind enough to give me a ride."

Abby said, "That's how we raised him. Always be kind to others."

Abe said, "Yeah, but why is he here?"

White interrupted.

"He's got nowhere to spend Christmas."

Abe said, "You told him he could stay till Christmas? That's almost a month away!"

"I'm not staying till then, sir."

Walter said, "I didn't invite him to stay till Christmas. I just asked him to stay the night and have at least one big meal with us. It'll be the closest thing he'll ever get to a family Christmas dinner."

Abby asked, "Oh, why's that, Mr. Widow?"

Abe said, "You running from the law?"

"No, sir," Widow half-lied.

"He's not a criminal," Walter said.

Abby looked at Widow.

"Are you?"

"Technically, we're all criminals."

They all stared at him.

Widow said, "We've all jaywalked or gotten a speeding ticket or parking ticket or run a red light or whatever. At some point. Right?"

As if it was spliced into their DNA, the Whites all shrugged nearly in unison.

Abe said, "I like you, Mr. Widow. No matter what you did or didn't do, it doesn't matter. We're not turning you in. We're not a family of snitches here."

"Don't worry, sir. I'm not wanted for anything, and I'm not running from anything. I'm just a nobody going nowhere in particular. That's all."

Abby intervened.

"You're welcome to stay with us today and tonight. No problem."

Abe said, "But tomorrow morning, you got to get going. No offense, son, but we're not running a bed-and-breakfast here."

"Understood. Don't worry. I'm not staying. I've got miles of road to cover."

"Good. Now, come with me."

"Where are you taking him, Dad?"

Abe looked at Walter.

"You been up driving all night, son."

"Yeah."

Abby reached out her hands and touched her son's collar and spoke to him.

"Go inside. Get cleaned up. Take a nap. We'll wake you up."

"I gotta unload the truck."

Abe said, "Nonsense."

"But, Dad?"

"You heard your mother. I got the truck."

"You can't lift anything, Dad."

"I don't need to. Jack will help."

They looked at Widow, who looked at them—confused for a moment because he had forgotten who "Jack" was. No one had called him Jack.

Widow said, "I'll be glad to help. Of course. No problem."

"See. There you go. Now, go enjoy a couple of hours rest next to your beautiful wife," Abe said.

He leaned into his son like he was passing along a dark secret.

"Trust me. They get old fast."

Abby shoved her husband from the back, a quick hard shove, but not strong enough to budge him much.

"You're no spring chicken yourself, sir!"

"I wasn't talking about you, babe."

"Yeah right."

Abby said nothing else, but she stepped over to her son and took his arm like the father of the bride escorting his daughter down the aisle. Then they walked off back up the steps to the porch and into the house.

White turned back once before entering.

"Dad?"

Abe looked at his son.

White reached into his pocket and pulled out the keys to the Tundra and tossed them to his father.

Abe caught them.

They said nothing about it.

White turned to Widow.

"My dad will take care of you. See you at breakfast."

Widow said, "No problem. Thanks for the hospitality."

White nodded, and he and Abby vanished completely into the large farmhouse.

Widow heard birds and let his eyes gaze up over the porch, where he watched a lone blackbird fly and land on the corner of the roof.

He saw smoke puff out of the chimney about ten yards to the right of the bird.

"Okay, Jack. Let's get to work."

Abe looked at his watch.

He said, "We're late already."

"Are we going somewhere else?"

"Farm work starts early."

Widow nodded.

They both climbed into the Tundra. Widow looked in the back as he went around to the passenger side. He hadn't peeked in so far to see what was in the back.

He had expected farm equipment, or machines, or bales of hay for horses or whatever a Christmas tree farm would haul in a work truck.

But there was none of that.

The back of the truck had stacks of lumber packed in tight, with a thick stack of roof shingles wrapped in white plastic that was torn and falling off. They were held down by cables and bungies, which might've been overkill because they were heavy enough to stay in place unless Walter's truck got rear-ended.

Widow hopped in next to Abe and shut the door.

Abe fired the engine back up and jerked the gear into reverse like he was angry at the truck. He backed up and switched the gear to drive and drove around the circle driveway and over to the barn.

They passed the vehicle with the tarp over it and the older Tundra.

Abe stopped in front of the barn's huge double doors.

"Jack, hop out and open those doors for me?"

"No problem."

Widow did as he was asked. He stepped out and closed the passenger door behind him. He traced around to the nose of the Tundra and pulled the doors open, one by one.

The inside of the barn was dark, but not pitch black. A large cone of light was coming from way in the back.

A cold draft swept over Widow like he was standing in a wind tunnel. He heard the wind blowing from inside.

It whistled.

Widow had expected to see horses, maybe chickens, and maybe goats lodged inside the barn. This was a farm, but there were no animals.

In the darkness, he could make out stalls where horses would go, but they were empty.

In the corners of the barn, he saw various farming tools. The thing that stuck out to him was a pitchfork that looked old, almost medieval, like something from the devil's weapon rack. It had wicked prongs on the end. They looked strangely sharp. He wondered if they were supposed to be that sharp.

Abe opened the Tundra's driver's door a crack.

"You gotta step aside so I can pull in."

Widow turned and nodded. He stepped out of the way.

Abe flipped the Tundra's headlamps on.

The inside of the barn lit up, and Widow saw exactly why there were no animals inside. He saw why he had felt the wind. He saw why he had heard it.

The barn was long and narrow, but with plenty of room inside.

In the far back corner, there was a huge hole in the wall and the roof. The wall wasn't missing from never having been put up. There was a hole that looked like a giant had come along and ripped it out of the barn, like a small bomb had gone off, blowing out that section of wall and roof.

Abe pulled the Tundra into the barn slowly.

He slipped the truck into park and left it running and hopped out.

Widow pointed at the hole.

"Is that why the lumber?"

"Yeah. Damn barn is old as dirt. We had a twister blow through here last summer. We just got the insurance check for it two months ago. Bastards took their sweet time. But it was fine. We had other priorities anyway. So, we never got around to fixing it. You know how it goes. We used the money for other things.

"We ain't got no animals. Fixing the barn wasn't a priority. Things pile up ten times faster on a farm when you don't stay on top of them. Anyway, Walter had the time and opportunity to pick up some lumber last night since he was down in Atlanta."

Widow nodded.

Abe said, "Don't worry. I won't make you repair it or anything. We got guys for that."

Widow smiled.

Abe closed his door and joined Widow at the rear of the truck.

Widow let the tailgate down.

Abe asked, "You don't mind doing this?"

Widow shrugged.

"You guys invited me to stay for dinner. It's the least I can do."

"It'll be slow going. I'm old. Can't lift a lot at a time."

Widow took another look over the lumber and the shingles.

"I can do it all myself."

"No. I can't allow that. If you can do it, then I can do it too. I'm old, not dead."

Widow shrugged and said, "The boards are easy. We can take them one at a time. The shingles are too heavy in this bundle. Got a knife? We can cut them loose."

Abe smiled and reached into his inside coat pocket.

Most men carried wallets in their inside pockets, but not Abe. He pulled out a large folding knife.

"That's a big blade."

"Biggest in the county on a folding knife."

"That so?"

"Oh, I don't know. I just like staking that claim."

Abe smiled.

It wasn't the biggest blade that Widow had ever seen, not even close, but it looked five inches, which was probably illegal to conceal and carry in the state of South Carolina. He wasn't sure. He knew that lots of states made it illegal to conceal and carry a blade longer than three inches.

Abe opened the blade and reversed it and offered it to Widow.

"You can do the honors."

Widow nodded and took the blade by the handle and climbed up onto the tailgate.

"Don't cut the cables and bungies. You can just remove those. They clip to the bed," Abe told Widow.

Widow unclipped them and tossed them aside to the side of the truck bed. After that, he saw the next layer of security from the lumberyard that loaded the truck. The lumber and the shingles were all secured with plastic ties. He cut them all free; then he double-checked to make sure he got them all.

He closed the knife and returned it to Abe.

"Where do you want them?"

Abe said, "We'll pile everything over by the hole."

Widow nodded and began taking as much as he could carry. He started with the shingles.

He picked up a huge stack and lifted it, and got down off the tailgate. He walked them over to the back corner near the hole and began a neat pile.

When he turned back, he saw Abe, still near the truck, desperately trying to pick up a stack of shingles the same size as Widow's stack.

"Let me get that," Widow said, and he scooped up the stack with ease, piled it up on top of the stack he'd already started.

Abe said, "You're a strong guy."

Widow stayed quiet.

Abe asked, "You a bodybuilder or something?"

"No. I could never do that stuff. I just move a lot. It keeps me in shape. I'm always walking."

"You like that kind of life?"

"I do."

"Must be lonely, not having a place to go on Christmas?"

Widow shrugged.

"It's not so bad. It's only one day a year. Not a big deal."

"I couldn't do it. I love Christmas-time."

"Did you start this farm yourself?"

"No. My daddy bought it after the war."

Widow didn't ask which war because of how Abe had said it. He said the war, which Widow took to mean World War II.

Widow continued to unload the back of the truck until the work was finished.

23

THE ATF HELICOPTER buzzed over the Athenian compound, over the trees, over several wide-open fields, missing Agent Dorsch's dead body, which lay partially buried in snow, over a pool of cold blood.

The helicopter flew onward without a second look back.

They lost enough agents for one night. Seeing Dorsch, they would've stopped and landed and recovered the body, but it wouldn't have changed anything. He was dead. Their colleagues were dead.

Abel was out there.

The two new de facto agents inside the helicopter stared at Adonis. Ramirez flew the helicopter, staying steady on course toward the dead patrolman.

They all wore headsets to hear and communicate.

Adonis explained a brief rundown of what they were doing and who they were after. She explained the explosion, which they already knew about, then she explained about Abel, whom they had a briefing on before the raid. The new part was that he had escaped with six of his operatives. The other new part that she added were the words: *clear and present danger*, and then *shoot to kill*.

The agents and Ramirez all nodded in agreement.

Now, they felt re-energized because their guy wasn't dead in the explosion. It had been a fake-out that cost them more than was acceptable. It was personal.

Abel was still out there—free. And that couldn't stand. They owed it to the agency, to the dead, and to the injured. Adonis owed it to Dorsch.

During her briefing—perhaps unnecessarily—perhaps she was overcompensating; she made the point to them that no one had seen Abel during the raid. And terrorists wanted the credit for their suicide bombings. Abel should've been the first one to step out of the compound. He should have made it a point to step forward so everyone could see him and then watch him blow himself up. He would want to be on TV, blowing himself to bits. That was the typical terrorist martyr standard operating procedure, not to blow up women and children while staying behind in a burning building.

After she brought them up to speed, she said one more thing.

"This guy is a psychopath, and so are the guys with him. You can bet that they're still alive. You can bet that this whole thing was a diversion. He wanted to escape. Rigging the compound to explode like that means he put in months of planning for this scenario. We can bet that he knew we were coming. Maybe not us specifically, but he had planned on someone coming for him. Convincing those people to blow themselves up takes months and maybe years of brainwashing.

"And you can bet that if he planned that part, then he planned the rest of his escape. Probably. So, be ready for anything."

The two agents nodded. They took up their weapons and locked and loaded right there in front of her, both primary assault rifles and their sidearms. They made the gesture big and huge like they were telling her: hey lady, we got this. She outranked them, a woman. They were making a statement saying nothing. And she knew it, but it didn't matter. She was beyond proving herself. Now, she wanted them to be deadly.

She saw the hunger in their eyes. She saw the desire to kill in their faces. And she was okay with it.

Adonis got up off her bench, shaken a little from the helicopter ride. She squatted and steadied herself and then scrambled past them on her way up to the cockpit. She climbed up a narrow space and around the center console and dumped herself down in the copilot's seat.

"Everything good?" Ramirez called out to her.

She reached up and grabbed a headset that was locked above her. She slipped it over her head. A coiled, curly wire connected the headset to the console above her.

Once she got it situated right on her head, she spoke into it.

"Everything's good. You know where we're going exactly?"

"Not the exact road, but we can't miss it."

Adonis looked out the windshield and saw nothing but confusing backroads that stretched on for miles in every direction, criss-crossing multiple times.

She saw trees and snow and shadows. The morning light didn't help illuminate the shadows much.

"Why can't we miss it?" she asked.

Before he answered back, she saw why.

Up ahead, about two klicks, she saw blue lights washing over the trees, bouncing and strobing and climbing out of a gap between trees.

Ramirez pointed.

"There."

"I see it.

The helicopter yawed and circled out over the treetops like a heavy car trying to make a sharp turn. Then it came back and swooped down at an angle.

Ramirez called back over the headsets to the guys in the cabin.

"We're going to land."

They each gave a thumbs-up. They were ready.

The helicopter zoomed like it was going to pick up speed, then Ramirez pulled back on the stick and pressed his foot on the rudder pedal.

The machine jerked back.

"Sorry," he called back to the guys in the cabin.

The hole between the trees wasn't wide enough to make a comfortable, slow landing. The helicopter hovered downward, slowly, and appeared above blue lights.

Below, Adonis saw four state patrol cruisers.

Three of them had blue light bars rotating out of sync. The lights combined and lit up the trees and the surrounding forest. They made everything look blue.

Ramirez said, "They knew we were coming, but they didn't even clear us an LZ."

He said it as a statement, which Adonis picked up on. She didn't respond.

They came in as slowly as Ramirez could and hovered over the patrolmen and their cars, which was on purpose. He buzzed them, like flashing a frown at a driver who cut him off in traffic.

Two of them wore uniform hats, which they clamped their hands down on to keep them from blowing off.

Adonis saw them fighting to hold them down.

"That's enough," she said. "You're messing with the crime scene."

Ramirez nodded and swooped the helicopter up and over the cruisers. They ended up landing about twenty-five yards south of the cluster of cars.

Ramirez left the engine running, and the rotor blades slowed to a light rotation.

"Stay here," Adonis told him.

She took off the headset and hopped out of the flight deck.

Swan and James followed behind, weapons ready, which wasn't necessary, but they liked to put the patrolmen on notice that the ATF were the big guns.

Adonis stopped halfway to the patrolmen.

"You guys stay back. Let me do the talking here."

Swan looked at James, and they nodded.

"Okay."

"You're the man here," James said.

Adonis said nothing to that. She turned and approached the patrolmen.

One of them said, "Your boys tryin' to ruin our crime scene?"

Adonis said, "You didn't clear us a landing space."

"Not my job, lady."

"It's your job to assist us in our investigation."

The other patrolman said, "Your investigation? That's rich."

The first one said, "Wasn't it you guys that botched the Athenian Raid in the first place?"

He walked up into what she considered her personal space.

Adonis stared him down with a hard, terrifying look that she had practiced in the mirror forever. It was her cop look.

He backed off a few feet.

Another man, without a hat on, stepped forward from behind the trunk of one of the cruisers. He had a half-smoked cigarette in his hand. He took a last drag off it and tossed it. It went spiraling into the snowy shoulder of the road.

The hatless patrolman was probably over fifty, but in great shape, like a guy who gets up at four a.m. every day to run ten miles while most of the world sleeps.

He stepped up to her. He was dead-on six feet tall, towering over Adonis's five-foot frame. Plus, the patrolman was two hundred fifteen pounds, not built like a rugby player, but he could pass for a baseball player. Either way, he had a hundred fifteen pounds on her easily. Adonis was a hundred pounds soaking wet.

The other thing she noticed immediately about the guy was his cop stare. He wore it right then, the same as her. But it was much better than hers. It demanded obedience. He commanded respect with it. She already respected him and didn't have a single reason to, other than professional courtesy.

It was his stare, his presence. He walked and carried himself like a commander.

He looked down at her. His stare lightened up a bit, and he stuck his hand out for her to shake.

"You Adonis?"

"Agent Adonis."

She took his hand and squeezed hard, and shook it.

The hard squeeze was something she'd learned long ago. Ninety-nine percent of the men in her field had a thing about hand-shakes. The stronger the handshake, the more dominant the man, they believed, which was a dumb fraternity thing to her, schoolboy even, but whatever. She played the game as well as any man. Therefore, she gave him a hard, strong handshake, as she did every man she met.

To the fraternity of professional men, a soft, gentle handshake showed a soft gentleman, which equaled weakness, helplessness almost.

The whole handshake thing was just another tool in Adonis's arsenal. Only part of her job was shaking down bad guys, but a bigger part was navigating the world of modern-day, corporate and bureaucratic law enforcement.

If Adonis were ever interviewed on a "Life in the ATF for a Woman" documentary, she would say that navigating the bureaucracy scene was "one big pissing contest."

Adonis thought about writing a book about her experience as a high-ranking female in the agency. Nobody writes tell-all books about the ATF, and especially not women. She figured it might be an interesting book and unique. She'd never heard of a female agent of the ATF revealing all her experiences in the male-dominated world of policing alcohol, tobacco, firearms, and explosives.

On today's bookstands and headlines, it's the FBI who gets all the glory and respect, as well as the CIA. The CIA has its own mystique to help them out. It's glamorous to read about spies. No one wants to read about the ATF, unless maybe a story from a woman's perspective, something that comes with a sexy, political topic, perhaps a black woman's rise to leadership in the ATF. Of course, now she probably could focus the whole book on the Athenian nightmare that she found herself in.

Luckily, if she got fired today, at least a book on this whole debacle could bring in future paychecks.

She snapped out of thinking about it and shook the hatless patrolman's hand, hard and strong. He returned the same hard, strong handshake.

"I'm Patrolman Shepard Pittman, but everyone calls me Shep. You can too. I prefer it."

He spoke, and she noticed the way he spoke. He moved his lips as if his mouth was full, but she saw nothing in his mouth. It reminded her of a horse chewing grass.

And then she realized; he was a dip chewer, which made her wonder if he had been a baseball player once upon a time, like Dorsch. The thought made her lips curl downward into a sad frown. It was involuntary. She quickly fixed it.

"Okay, Shep. I don't have time to kill. Show me what I'm here to see, please."

"Okay. Right, this way."

He turned and passed through the other patrolmen. They parted like the Red Sea, like he was royalty and they were peasants. They jumped to as if they would do anything that Shep bade them to do.

"We touched nothing. Except to make sure that he's dead."

Shep dropped his voice a little at the end. She heard it like a lump in his throat.

She followed him past the patrolmen and around the cars. The blue lights flashed and washed over her face.

The dead patrolman's car was the last in the cluster, a good twenty feet from the nose of the closest car. It was parked on a three-way intersection of old, faded roads.

They walked across the snow, through cones of spiraling blue lights, to the dead patrolman's car.

Adonis said, "Tell me about the backroads."

Shep said, "There's nothing to tell. These are paved. Most aren't. They're backroads. They go nowhere. This whole part of the county is a smorgasbord of them. There's no rhyme or reason. They were here when I was a boy, and they'll be here long after I'm dead."

Shep continued walking, but Adonis stopped him with a hand on his shoulder.

He spun around to face her.

"You saw the video feed?"

"I saw it."

"What did you see?"

"Didn't you see it?"

"It was described to me. But I want to know what you saw. Did you get a look at the shooter?"

"Sure. I saw both the driver and the guy who shot Daniel. Pretty good look too. I saw the other guys, but their faces were harder to make out. Couldn't offer any kind of positive ID. The shooter, though, he wore all white like he was giving a sermon just before a human sacrifice or something. He was weird."

She reckoned Daniel was the first name of the dead patrolman.

"The driver wasn't the shooter?"

"Don't you already know?"

"Just humor me. Tell me what you saw."

"No. The shooter was the front passenger. He leaned over the driver and fired from inside the vehicle. No hesitation. He just shot my guy like he was nothing. Like a piece of trash."

Adonis nodded. She saw what she was hoping to see in Shep. He wanted retribution for his dead friend just as she did for a hundred of her dead friends.

She looked ahead at the dead patrolman. His body was sprawled out in front of his car at the center of the intersection.

Shot dead on backroads going nowhere, she thought.

Dorsch's face flashed over her mind's eye like a taunt, like a curse. She thought of a specific photograph of him. He was smiling, big, and happy. It was on her phone.

"Did you know him well?" she asked.

Shep nodded. His eyes glazed a bit, like a raindrop on glass, but there were no tears.

"What was his name?"

Shep cleared his throat.

"Patrolman Daniel Brant. He is a good man. Was a good man. He's got a wife. Just married. Like a month ago. I went to it."

Adonis reached out her hand and brushed his forearm, an automatic thing she'd learned at the academy from a course on dealing with the public.

"Let me look alone. Keep your guys back. Okay?"

"Okay."

Shep stepped back and away.

Adonis stepped over to the intersection and circled the dead patrolman.

She whispered to him like she was talking to his ghost.

"What you got to tell me?"

Standing over him, and staying a few feet back, she saw everything she needed to know pretty quickly. Brant's crime scene held no secrets back from her.

The shooters hadn't even tried to hide or cover up anything.

She saw the van's tire tracks in the snow. She saw they came from the direction of the Athenian compound. She turned and looked in that direction. She looked up over the trees.

She could see the smoke from the burning buildings filling the sky. It was five or six miles away, but plain as day.

The tracks veered off to the right, to the east.

They'll be easy to track, she thought.

They would need someone on the ground, though, and she didn't want to use the patrolmen. At least, she wanted to keep them out of it as much as possible. Abel was hers to catch or kill. That's the way it was going to be.

She walked around Brant's body.

His eyes were wide open and dead. He stared up at space. She craned her head all the way back, slowly, and followed his gaze.

She saw the morning sun and the sky above.

She figured he must've looked up at the stars right before he died.

She didn't want to waste any more time. She turned back to Shep.

"You described the asshole that shot him to me."

"Yes?"

"You remembered what he was wearing, but would you recognize his face?"

"I'll remember it till the day I die."

Adonis went into her jacket pocket and pulled out her phone. She scrolled through it, through the photos, until she found one she wanted. She selected it and turned the phone to Shep to look at.

"Did you see this man?"

Shep reached for the phone with one hand, instinctively, but Adonis held on to it.

He stepped closer and looked down at the screen. He stared at the image and the face in the image. He pinched his fingers and zoomed the image up to a bigger size. He stared at it.

He closed his eyes tightly, recalling the video from Brant's dash-cam. He opened them again and looked at Adonis.

"That's him. That's the shooter."

Adonis took the phone back and nodded.

"His name is General Joseph Abel."

"General?"

"He was US Army."

"Great. I bet they'll love that headline."

"He's a former general turned cult leader. I'm sure they'll spin his crazy behavior and so on. But that's not my concern. What-ever the Army does is their problem, not ours. My concern is that he's graduated from cult leader to weapons smuggler to terrorist."

"And cop killer?"

She nodded.

"I've seen the Army file on him. We know he's got the knowledge to wage war on our government, but now we know he's got the balls, too."

"So, what are you thinking?"

"I was thinking shoot-to-kill."

"But now?"

"We gotta take him alive," she lied. If she had the chance to put him in her crosshairs, then she would squeeze the trigger. There was no doubt in her mind. She would kill Abel for Dorsch, for Clip, for all the other lives destroyed in one night by that maniac.

But in her mind, she knew that if she could make a clean arrest, then she had to. There was no telling what valuable secrets Abel's twisted mind held.

She said, "There's no telling how many explosives are out there. If he's connected to other networks, we need to know what he knows."

She stepped back and pulled the phone away from him and returned it to her jacket pocket.

"Thanks, Shep. That's what I needed to know. We'll take it from here."

Shep said, "Like hell! You're not shutting us out! No way!"

"Look, I know this is hard. You've lost a guy. I get that. I've lost dozens, maybe as many as a hundred ATF agents. This is my investigation. My crime scene."

"I'm going after this guy. With or without your help. We'll follow you if we have to."

Adonis looked back at Swan and James. They returned her stare. She saw their fingers tapping the trigger housings of their rifles like they were telling her just to give the order. Which frightened her a little because she wasn't sure they would say no to shooting at cops. Then she saw the anger in their faces. They had lost brothers tonight, too. They wanted blood as much as she did, probably.

Adonis looked over past them at the helicopter. She saw Ramirez waiting. He had the same look of anger on his face. It was the same that was on the faces of the patrolmen. It was the same that was in Shep's eyes.

They needed boots on the ground if they were going to track the van. She worked it out in her head. She could use the extra manpower, the extra guns too.

Adonis turned away from Swan and James and Ramirez and the helicopter and looked down at her wrist at the exact place where her Timex used to be. It wasn't there. She had forgotten that it was gone now.

She shook herself out of thinking about that. She didn't need to know the exact time. She knew it was after eight in the morning, and she was running out of time.

They were all losing time. Abel had a head start.

She suddenly wished it was still nighttime because the daylight made it worse. With the night, they could've searched for tail-lights from the air, but now they couldn't. The morning meant the locals would get up and out—more cars on the roads meant more people to weed through.

Shep interrupted her thoughts. He saw she was working things out in her head. He also didn't want to lose any more time.

He said, "We can help you. We don't have to step on each other's toes. We all want this guy. We can get him a lot faster together."

He was right. With most of her agents down or headed to the hospital, the local resources of the South Carolina Highway Patrol were better than no resources at all.

Shep looked over at the helicopter, and he picked up on her problem right off.

"You need a man on the ground, anyway. You may never track them from the air. You can't see the tire tracks from up in a bird. You need us on the ground. Plus, the treetops are dense. I know that. I've been up there in helicopters plenty of times. You need our cars to follow the tracks on the ground."

She nodded slowly.

"Okay. But one car. You and I will go by road. My guys will follow overhead. Deal?"

"No one else? Just us?"

He seemed like he wasn't crazy about that.

"Send your guys to join roadblocks. They can coordinate with us to cast a dragnet. It'll be better this way."

Shep didn't respond. He just stared back at his guys in silence.

Adonis asked, "That gonna be a problem?"

"Your guy killed one of us."

"He killed more of mine."

"I know. I know. I'm just saying my guys won't be happy about that."

"We're not here for their happiness. This is the way it's gotta be. I don't want their trigger fingers to get in the way."

"Like your guys' trigger fingers won't?"

"It's not a pissing contest. You agree or not?"

Shep sighed and nodded.

"Okay. I agree."

"Good."

"Come on. We'll take my car."

He walked off away from the dead patrolman and toward his car. He went over to his guys without Adonis and barked orders at them. There was a brief argument, and then he barked louder. The two other patrolmen seemed upset but didn't dare question Shep's orders.

Shep came back to his cruiser and opened his door.

"Come on. Get in."

Adonis looked at her guys and signaled for them to rejoin the helicopter. She did a couple of hand signals for Ramirez to understand the plan. He nodded and fired the helicopter back up. Swan and James strapped into the rear again and shut the door. The bird was up in the air seconds later, hovering above Adonis and Shep and his police cruiser.

Adonis got in the passenger side, and Shep fired up the car. They took off slowly and steadily.

Adonis rolled her window down and stuck her head out occasionally to double-check that they were following the right tire tracks and to look up at the ATF bird.

The helicopter followed overhead.

24

By SEVEN O'CLOCK in the morning, Abe had Widow doing all kinds of lifting and pushing and moving things around in the barn and around the outside of the house and then around the farm, like they were working in planned concentric circles. All of this at the price of coffee—naturally. But the extra coffee was promised to him at breakfast time.

By eight in the morning, Widow had arranged the heavy items in the barn, moved firewood from a stack of chopped wood up to the house, and learned the general layout of the terrain as if he had worked there for a week already.

Now he and Abe were talking about going out into the field.

Abby stepped outside in different clothes than she had worn earlier. She appeared to have taken a shower and applied makeup and dressed for the day. She wore the same winter coat as earlier, but now she had blue jeans and a white sweater on underneath. She'd changed her earrings as well.

After Widow's last chore, he and Abe sat on a pair of patio armchairs on the front porch. They were taking a break, or Widow was. Abe was fully energized and ready to oversee Widow on the next project. Abby overheard Widow and Abe talking about going out into the fields on a pair of ATVs that Abe had stashed in the back of the barn. Widow was trying to make the short break last long enough for him to be rescued. Abby picked up on it right away. So she swooped in for the rescue.

Widow was trying to make the short break last long enough for him to be rescued. Abby picked up on it right away. So she swooped in for the rescue.

On the porch, she looked at the men and then at a pair of empty coffee mugs on a small glass-top table between the two men and the two patio armchairs.

She waddled over to them in a way that made Widow think of a momma duck, but she hovered over them like a momma bear and stared at the mugs.

She moved her eyes up and inspected Widow's face the same way she would her own son.

"Mr. Widow, have you been up all night?"

Widow and Abe looked at her. Widow looked tired. She saw black circles around his eyes and the look of defeat on his face, a look she had seen before on Walter's face when Abe was in an overzealous, pushy mode.

Abe looked at her like she was interrupting the boys during poker night, which he never played anymore. He had been grounded from poker nights because he kept losing their money.

Nowadays, the only poker he played was against his grandson, even when he lost all their quarters and dimes and nickels, which were Abby's coins. She was the one who collected them in an old cookie jar.

Widow cracked a smile at her. He was glad to see her.

"I have, ma'am."

"Are you tired, son?"

"Yes, ma'am. I'm exhausted."

"Abe, what the hell are you trying to do?"

"What?"

"You've been makin' this poor boy work all morning. Look at him. He's tired."

"What? He's fine. Look at him. He can take it."

"Abraham!"

"What? He seems okay to me."

Widow yawned right there as if on cue, a desperate attempt to reiterate her point. Which it was. The only thing more obvious would've been if he said: *Hint, Hint*, with air quotes around it.

He said, "I'm okay."

Abby asked, "How many coffees have you had?"

Widow stuck up one hand and counted on his fingers. He held up four.

"Four?"

"If you are asking how many I've had since last night, that's the number. If you're asking how many this morning, the answer is one here at the house."

"That's a lot of coffee. You don't know what you want."

"I'm okay," he repeated.

"I've made up a spare room for you. I think you should go up there and lie down. Get some rest."

Abe said, "But we need to get out to The Sevens."

The Sevens, as Widow understood from Abe's explanation, were not yet at the height and weight where they could be harvested and sold. The process took about ten years to mature enough for the market. Out in the fields, there were dozens of large plots, sectioned off by growth years, so they could track each batch, as Widow had seen on the drive in.

The Sevens were the seven-year-old trees. They renamed them according to year. Each section moved up a number grade, once the Tens were cut down and sold. That's how they designated, which were ready.

Widow vaguely understood that there was work that needed to be done out at The Sevens, involving the sprinkler systems and a backhoe and his hard work. Hearing Abe explain it, the only thing that Widow got out of it was the realization it would be his back put to work and not Abe's.

"You boys come inside. We're having breakfast soon."

"But morning time is work time," Abe protested.

"I said work time's over. Widow doesn't work here. He's our guest. Now, he's already paid us back for the ride from Walter. In fact, I'd say we owe him now."

"Owe him?"

"Yes. How much do we pay new hires?"

"I don't know. Twenty dollars an hour?"

"He's earned forty dollars then. Probably more. I'd say ten for the ride is fair. Now, we owe him breakfast."

Abe stared at his wife. He couldn't argue with that. His lips didn't move, and no sound came out of his mouth. But Widow could see that they were still communicating, a side effect of decades of marriage.

Widow made it easy for them.

"Thirty dollars is an expensive breakfast. What are we having for breakfast, ma'am?"

Abby turned and stepped away from them so they could get up and follow her. She spun back on one foot near the top of the porch steps and smiled at Widow.

"We're having scrambled eggs, bacon," she paused. She put one finger on her chin, and her eyes rolled up a bit to the sky like she was recalling something to add.

Widow started to speak, but Abby wasn't finished.

She said, "Pancakes with Vermont maple syrup, which I get delivered here special. You'll love it."

Abe said, "You're serving the Vermont maple?"

He scratched his bald head and smirked with a genuine disappointment at offering such a fine condiment to an outsider.

"Widow, we're done here. Thanks for all your work. We appreciate it."

Widow smiled and stood up from the chair, followed by Abe.

Abby said, "Good. Take off your boots when you come in. Abe, show him the bathroom so he can wash his hands. And hurry; we're waiting."

"Yes, ma'am," Abe said.

Abby spun around like a ballerina and walked back into the house.

"Sorry I put you to work. Guess I got carried away."

Widow said, "Don't worry about it. I enjoy doing things. And I appreciate your letting me stay, also for the family home cooking. I never get that anymore. The negative part of being out on my own."

Abe smiled and went into the house behind Abby. Widow followed.

The front door opened to a grand country estate on a small scale. The place was exceptional. It could've been featured in a magazine. It looked like a new build on the inside. It was probably a recent renovation. Either that or Abby slaved away all day, making it look so new. It even smelled new, but only in the front foyer.

The foyer had country wood everywhere; some painted white, some were unpainted. He smelled freshly polished wood, which could've been the large oak table near the entrance with a potted plant on it. It could've been the walls or the baseboards or the floor tiles, or it could've been all of it.

Beyond the foyer was a big, open floor plan with a construct of wooden stairs zigzagging right at the front. One landing was presented to visitors like a stage. Widow imagined having a lone guy with a guitar and a stool up there, playing for parties.

The stairs disappeared into a floor above, which had to be the bedrooms because the first floor was so open that Widow could decipher what every room was right from the front door. Every square foot was easily reconned.

In his head, he calculated the size and layout of the space.

Off to the left, the first room's door was wide open. Inside, Widow saw a mudroom.

Abe stomped his feet on a large welcome mat inside the front door and then went straight through the foyer, careful not to track any dirt or snow through. He went to the mudroom like his life depended on getting the house procedures right.

Widow followed suit, stomped the snow off his feet onto the mat, and headed to the mudroom behind Abe.

The mudroom had two sets of cubby stations—one to the left, one to the right. In the center, on a back wall, was a cushioned bench with welcoming pillows on the back.

The bench, the pillows, and the cushions were all white and clean. There was no sign posted warning off people from using the bench, but Abe stood over it for a second, seeming to calculate whether it was worth his life even to risk dirtying it up.

In the end, Abe decided he had no choice and plopped down on the bench, leaving room for Widow to his right, but Widow waited for him to be done first.

Abe slipped off his boots and stuffed them in a cubby to the left. Then he leaned to the other side and pulled out a pair of comfortable, well-worn slippers from the right cubby. This assembly line process was refined by strict instructions from Abby, no doubt.

Widow stayed in the doorway to the mudroom with his boots on because he had no slippers to complete the process, and he didn't think Abe wanted him to walk around in only his smelly socks.

Abe realized the dilemma.

"You can borrow Junior's slippers."

Widow thought he was referring to Walter.

Abe got up off the bench, standing in his slippers, relishing the comfort of it for a split second. Then he stepped over to the right cubby and reached to the top shelf and pulled out a pair of men's slip-on shoes.

He held them to his face, looked down at Widow's boots, and stopped.

Widow turned fast and glanced back at the left cubby. He looked at the cubby from that side and saw a pair of recently shined black combat boots. Like the slip-on shoes, they belonged to a big man, this Junior, he figured.

He remembered on the drive up the track to the house, Walter mentioned playing in Christmas tree fields with his brother. That must have been Junior. These must've been Junior's combat boots and his slip-ons.

Abe asked, "What size do you wear?"

"Fourteen."

Abe stared at the shoes but didn't check the label. He looked at them and knew the size almost as well as anyone knows their own size.

"Oh. Well. That won't work then. Junior was a twelve."

With little brainpower behind it, Widow let out a question before he put two and two together. Instantly, he felt stupid.

"Was?"

"What's that?"

"Junior was a size twelve?'"

Widow stared past the slip-ons in Abe's hand and looked at the cubby. He confirmed what he had already seen and felt even dumber because he knew the answer before he uttered the first dumb question.

Both cubbies were divided into sections for each family member. It appeared to be divided by height, so if a teenager grew taller, then everyone else in the family was downgraded to a lower cubby. The next section of shoes to the right was smaller than size twelve. Maybe they were tens or elevens. They were probably Walter's shoes, Walter's cubby. Next down were women's shoes, and then another set of women's shoes, and then Abe's, and then what looked like shoes for a teenage girl, and next Abby's—he figured by the style—and finally, there were shoes that had to belong to a boy. Judging by the style and size, the boy was somewhere in middle school, a growing boy. He would be the x-factor, the decider in who would move down the ranks in the White family shoe cubby hierarchy.

The thing that made Widow feel like an idiot was that now he realized the first section of shoes belonged to a dead son.

Abe stayed quiet.

No tears came from his eyes, but they glazed over so fast it was like his brain flipped a switch to make them do that.

Widow asked, "What branch was your son?"

Abe smiled and reached up, unzipped his coat all the way down. He unbuttoned the top button on a collared shirt and reached into the top. He grabbed onto a metal-beaded chain around his neck and reeled it out. He let it dangle out in front of his chin.

It was a set of dog tags.

Abe said, "His name was Second Lieutenant Abraham Michael White, Jr. of the 2nd Battalion, 1st Marine Regiment, 1st Marine Division."

Widow stared at the dog tags, read them, and confirmed the name and rank. He stayed quiet.

Abe added, "Marine Expeditionary Force."

"The Professionals. Their nickname. Marines love nicknames."

Abe nodded.

"You know them?"

"I served. Navy. Sixteen years. But can't say I ever met a Marine from The Professionals."

He didn't say his rank or that he was a SEAL, or NCIS. No need to tell a grieving father his rank if it was higher than his dead son's. It wasn't a pissing contest. Widow felt that just saying Navy was good enough to illustrate that he understood.

"Did you go to Iraq?"

"More times than I can count."

"Did you see combat?"

"More times than I can count."

Abe nodded.

"My son was a good Marine. He died in what the official US Marine Corps after-action report described as 'enemy action' in a place I never heard of before called Al Anbar Province. It's in Iraq."

"I've been there. Tough place. All of Iraq is tough. He must've been a great Marine to get that assignment."

Widow put one hand on Abe's left shoulder.

Abe smiled at him.

"Thank you for your service."

"Thank you for your sacrifice. It's not in vain. Don't you ever think that it was."

Abe nodded. He returned the dog tags to their place under his shirt.

He stepped back. Widow removed his hand and let it fall back down to his side.

Abe stepped away over to the only other wall in the room, which had a plethora of different sizes and styles of winter coats, all hanging on hooks along the wall. The largest percentage of coats looked like they belonged to a single owner, a teenage girl. It was probably thirty percent of them.

Widow recognized styles and colors as something he had seen traveling across America. He had seen more teenage girls traveling alone on buses than he would've expected before he started his nomadic lifestyle. And the thing these teenage girls had in common was that they were stylish and trendy. So were the coats. The process seemed to go like this: The coats were selected according to the latest trends and then neglected a week later. It reminded him of the stock market. Investors bought something they thought was hot or trendy, then they dumped it a week later.

Trends in fashion and stocks were like the moods of a schizophrenic, depressed mental patient with multiple personality disorder; everything changed fast.

Widow thought they should change the saying from death and taxes to fashion and psychosis.

Widow had never been fashionable. Not ever. He was lucky to fit in with the cool kids at all.

Widow shook off his overthinking and snapped back to reality, where Abe was waiting so they could join the others at the breakfast table.

Widow slipped off his coat and hung it on a hook. That part was easy, but then he looked at Abe. Now they had to face a serious problem together. No way was Abby going to let him inside with his boots on. But there was no size slip-on for him to borrow.

"You gotta leave your boots here. Sorry, I don't have shoes for you."

"It's no big deal. I can keep my socks on. Is that okay?"

"It'll have to be."

Widow didn't sit on the bench. He put one hand on a cubby and leaned and kicked one boot off, trying not to shake any snow and dirt off onto the tile. Then he repeated the process with the next boot.

Afterward, he picked them both up by the neck with one hand and set them down on the top back corner of one of the cubby structures.

Widow cracked his knuckles before they went to join the others. He didn't want to do it at the table.

After that, he said, "Ready."

Abe turned and led the way back through the door. Widow followed in his socks.

25

ADONIS AND SHEP turned the wrong way down a one-way street, but they never knew it because there was no visible sign posted. The sign wasn't visible because it wasn't there. A year earlier a thunderstorm had stomped right through Spartan County on its way north. The thunderstorm took down the sign, along with other things. The next day, a pair of local farm boys stole it. They set it up in the back of one of their dad's properties and used it for target practice.

By now, it was no good as a street sign—too many bullet holes.

Adonis and Shep continued the wrong way down the street because they were following a pair of tracks they thought belonged to Abel, and that's where the tracks led so far.

They followed the tracks on the ground until the snow thinned out over the road. The helicopter flew over the backroad system for a bird' s-eye view, hoping to spot the van, but so far, Ramirez had seen no sign of it. The treetops were too dense, and the roads wound around so much it was hard to maintain a steady look without yawing or turning the helicopter's flight pattern.

Ramirez was sure that from the ground, they must've looked like they were flying mock dogfights.

Shep didn't notice the tracks thinning. He concentrated on driving. Adonis focused on the tracks.

As soon as she noticed the tracks were missing, she stuck her head out the window and stared down at the road and then up ahead to see if they came back into view, but they didn't.

"Stop!" she said.

Shep slowed and stopped.

"What's up?"

He looked over at her.

She hung out the window and stared at the road ahead.

He asked, "You see them?"

"No. I see nothing. The tracks vanished."

"They're gone?"

He looked out ahead, scanned the road, saw the thinning snow, and nothing else—same as her.

Adonis said, "The snow's too thin here. I can't make out their tracks anymore."

"Maybe it's because we're on a hill? The snow might get better up ahead."

Adonis looked ahead, saw the slope of the hill heading back down.

"Maybe."

"We should be able to pick them up again if we keep going."

"Let me get out and look first."

"Okay."

Adonis hopped out of the cruiser and stood still. She checked out the road ahead to confirm no sign of tracks. And then she flipped around and looked back the way they'd come. She saw where the tracks vanished.

She took her phone out of her pocket and pulled up the screen, and went to her maps app. She opened it and investigated her surroundings. The thing that didn't change was that she was still in the middle of a fifteen-mile network of backroad country. No amount of staring at her maps app was going to change that.

She stared at the perimeter of the map. She made mental pinpoints where she thought the roadblocks should've already been set up. Between her and the roadblocks was nothing on the map, just nameless roads.

She looked straight, looked left, looked right, and turned back to the car. She walked back and stuck her head near Shep's window so they could talk.

"Call the roadblocks. Check with them."

Shep stayed where he was. He had one hand on the wheel, and one draped out across the door's windowsill. He felt the cold on his knuckles.

"They've got nothing so far."

"How do you know?"

"They would've called."

"Check anyway. They should've tried to pass through by now."

Shep got on the radio and called one of his guys.

"Watts, come in."

"Go for Watts."

"Anything at the roadblocks yet?"

Watts came on over the radio.

"Nothing. No vans anyway. Bunch of trucks coming and going, and that's it."

"Copy. What about these trucks? Anyone fit our guys' description?"

"Nope. Only two trucks had more than two passengers so far. They were both old guys. Looked too old to be the guys you're looking for. They checked out, anyway."

Shep clicked the talk button.

"Okay. Keep a lookout for them. Be careful; we're dealing with low-down salty dogs, here. Over."

"You got it. Over," Watts said and clicked off.

Shep shrugged at Adonis.

Adonis got on her phone and called Ramirez. She looked up at the helicopter circling overhead. She saw it fly in and out of view above.

The call wasn't a direct call. Ramirez couldn't hear his cell phone up there, not over the rotor blades. She had to call her switchboard and have the call wired to the helicopter's radio.

It was fast, faster than usual. Within seconds, Ramirez answered from his headset.

"Adonis?"

"Yeah."

She stepped back from the police cruiser and jammed a finger in her free ear. There was a lot of background noise coming from his end, a combination of the rotors and wind and engine noise.

"What's up? Why we stopped?"

"I lost the tracks down here. You see anything from up there?"

She stared up at Ramirez, who had the helicopter hovering two hundred feet above. All she saw was the helicopter's outline. It was too high and too dark to see Ramirez's face.

From the helicopter, Ramirez looked out his windshield at the terrain. He looked clockwise in three compass directions, and then he completed the rotation to see behind him.

He took his time, double-checked, and answered her after thirty seconds.

"All I see is miles of nothing and snow and trees and more nothing."

"Nothing?"

"I see the fire to the west."

"Nothing else?"

"Lots of empty roads."

"Nothing else?"

"Looks like a bunch of farmland."

"Where?"

"North. South. East and West. Everywhere."

"Any of them look alive?"

"Not that I can tell from up here. I've got nothing. No sign of them. I see no disturbances anywhere."

"So, you see nothing?"

"Nope."

"Where are the closest farms?"

"Oh. Hold on."

Ramirez looked out the windshield again.

He said, "Keep going straight. The road veers to the north. Those are the closest farms I can see. We'll meet you there."

Adonis hung up the phone, pocketed it, and got back in the cruiser. She looked at Shep.

"Know anything about the farms up ahead?"

"Nope. Just that it's all we'll find out here. Bunch of empty farmland."

"Empty?"

"Lots of the farms here got hit back in the recession. They were hit about as hard as anyone else. Spartan County used to be a thriving agricultural region."

"What's the population look like now?"

Shep shrugged.

"Less than it was."

Adonis said, "They're here. I can feel it. Abel's smart—crazy, but smart. After he shot Brant, he would've known we'd find out, and throw up roadblocks. He's probably holed up here. Somewhere. An impromptu act, but he's military. He knows how to change course on the fly. I bet he thinks he can outlast us. Outsmart us, too. Thinks we'll have to give up, eventually."

"You talk about him like he's some kind of military genius."

"He's smart and tactical. Look what he did to us. It's a mistake to overlook that."

"He shot my guy. Think that was smart?"

"I think that was bad luck. He probably didn't expect to run into any cops. These roads are too vast to cover with a posted cop at each one. The odds of running into your friend like that were small. Plus, he's crazy too. Don't forget that."

Shep stared at her.

"He's sadistic."

"I don't deny that. Which is why we gotta find him. Put him down," Adonis said, figuring she didn't need to hide it anymore.

Shep asked, "Do you think Brant was bad luck?"

She shrugged.

"Don't be sensitive on me now. Look at it like a cop and not a pissed-off friend. At least until we catch him."

Shep tapped his fingers on the steering wheel, looked out ahead like Brant's ghost stood there, staring at him.

"Why do you think he would take refuge here? Wouldn't they be better off plowing ahead?"

"The roadblocks. Maybe they thought about it after they shot Brant. But then he thought we'd find Brant's body. They knew it would ratchet up the heat. Abel must've figured the roadblocks. Maybe he thought we'd set them up across several states."

"They are set up across states. At least, North Carolina has them set up on their side. Fifty miles into the state, I think."

Adonis pushed back from the edge of the car. She stood straight and nodded.

"See, killing a cop in South Carolina isn't just going to piss off South Carolina cops. Killing a cop pisses off all cops universally."

"Okay. But, we didn't know Brant was dead for thirty minutes. It took you close to two hours to get here."

"Yeah, but you guys ordered the roadblocks the second you found Brant, right?"

"Yeah."

"Abel doesn't know it took that long. He's smart, but crazy. Remember? He probably shot Brant. They drove on for a mile, and then he thought about the dashcam. Or one of his guys brought it up. Or maybe he got scared after seeing Brant. Maybe he figured his escape route was compromised. Maybe he didn't realize it was just bad luck. I don't know."

"Maybe. Or maybe they memorized the escape route and plowed through at high speeds until they broke through the perimeter before we put up the roadblocks."

"I don't think so. We can't think that way. He's still here, I'm telling you. I think they're holed up somewhere."

They were both quiet for a long beat until a thought occurred to Shep.

He said, "Or they swapped vehicles."

"I don't think so. Why would they have an extra one stashed this close to Carbine?"

"Stashed vehicles are commonplace for Special Forces operators like a bug-out bag to a spy. Or maybe they didn't use a stashed vehicle. Maybe they hijacked one."

Adonis hadn't thought of that. He saw it on her face. She raised an eyebrow, looked at him, and said, "Let's hope that hasn't happened yet. We need to find them before they have the opportunity. I know they're here. I know they're here."

She hoped he was wrong. She hoped Abel hadn't had a chance to do that. Too many people died today because of her mistakes. She couldn't stop now. She had to find Abel. It was more than her feelings for Dorsch. She had to avenge him. She had to avenge all of them.

Adonis looked at her wrist, where her Timex used to be. It was still gone, which she knew, but she looked anyway. She frowned at the empty spot on her wrist.

She said, "Abel's a terrorist, a lunatic. He's a career army general, Special Forces—yes. But, he's not some kind of messiah. He's just a man. He's a well-prepared man, but a man. Nothing more."

"Okay, Adonis. Get in. Let's hunt down this asshole until they shut us down."

She smiled and waved up at Ramirez.

"Where do we go then?"

"Keep going straight."

26

Less than ten miles to the north, the whole White family was present, together, sharing in family conversations, like a Hallmark greeting card. They were a tightknit clan, no doubt about it.

Before they sat down to eat, the whole family stood up around the table like the knights of Camelot. Joining hands, they said a long prayer, which included a short bit about Widow. They prayed he would get safe to where he was going and that he found happiness. They sat down after the prayer to eat.

No memories of long-lost family nostalgia struck Widow like they would a normal person because he had never known a family meal like this before. Sure, he had been to other people's family gatherings in the past. But never his own. He had only known a mother and no other type of family except for the deputies under her command. They had been the closest thing to uncles he had known. Kind of like Dorothy in Kansas with the farmhands, Widow had grown up with a family of unrelated men he thought of as uncles.

A big serving plate of crisp, delicious bacon occupied the table space closest to Widow. Beyond that was another big serving plate that started out filled with scrambled eggs, but only a third of the eggs remained. One large serving plate was once loaded with sausages, and, now, it was also half empty, a big part

Widow's fault. Next to that was another bowl, overloaded with breakfast rolls. Beyond that was a plate with sliced oranges, as well as a pitcher of fresh-squeezed orange juice and a pitcher of water.

It was a full-court press. Many of Widow's favorite breakfast foods were there in attendance.

The only thing missing from the table was a pot of coffee. The coffee was in the kitchen. Widow's eyeballs kept roaming toward the open kitchen door instinctively, like a heroin addict staring at the place where he hides his stash.

Every few minutes, his nose sniffed the air because of the coffee aroma. It drew him to it like a siren at sea.

The youngest member of the family was a boy, eight years old. He raced his sister to be the first seated and was closest to the serving plate with eggs.

The sister was sixteen and showed no interest in her brother's racing endeavor.

She was more interested in Widow, at first, as a teenager might be when a strange man sits at her family's table. Her interest was a combination of curiosity and trying to look cool all at once. That all faded away within minutes as she stared at her cell phone, which was strategically placed next to her place setting. Every ten seconds it seemed, she would tap the screen, light up the phone, and check her notifications like she was expecting a life-or-death text message from someone.

This must've gone on at the table pretty often because no one else seemed to pay attention to it.

Widow was surprised that Abby would allow for it, but that's the world today. The younger generations use smartphones like accessories they're born with, and the older generations tried their best to avoid them, but now, they are everywhere.

Besides the children and Widow, five other people sat around the table, making eight total. All eating, talking and enjoying their breakfasts. Seven of the eight were members of the White family. Widow was the odd man out; only he didn't feel that way. They made him feel welcomed and comfortable and included, which he appreciated.

The oldest branches of the White family tree, Abe and Abby, had two children, a brother and sister—Walter and Foster White. Foster was a doctor, as mentioned by Abby several times. She tried to pawn Foster off on Widow as a potential wife for him. Both Foster and Widow noticed. And neither mentioned the obvious tactic.

Foster was Walter's younger sister. She was an attractive woman, Widow thought, but he wasn't in the market for a wife, obviously. Where would he fit a wife into his life? But there was no reason to tell Abby that.

Foster was the last one to come out to the family room while Widow was in there with the rest of the Whites, minus Abby, who was still prepping the table.

Foster must've just stepped out of a morning shower. She came down the stairs with her hair damp, looking just-washed. She wore blue jeans and a white button-down shirt, tucked in. She was clean and smelled of lavender and rosemary that must've been from a fifty-dollar bottle of shampoo that promised its wearer that it would make an impression. It was truth in advertising because Widow noticed.

He shook her hand politely, gently. He respectfully called her Doctor.

She corrected him instantly with, "Call me Foster."

Abby stepped out of the dining room and into the family room and announced breakfast, acting like a member of the queen's staff.

They all gathered around the table. Widow waited to sit last so he could find the seat meant for guests. People are sometimes finicky about where they sit at their own tables. Humans fall into routines and patterns by nature, which was one of the reasons he loved the open road. Nothing was ever the same—no chance of falling into a stagnant life.

Walter sat next to his wife, Maggie. Their two children, Dylan and Lauren, the eight- and sixteen-year-olds, sat on the other side of them.

On the opposite side, and to Widow's right, were Abby and Abe. Widow sat at the head of the table on the south end of the dining room. No one matched him at the foot of the table, near the kitchen.

This posed a problem for him in a way because he was the farthest from the kitchen and, therefore, farthest from the coffeepot. The only plus of sitting there was that his back was to the wall, an old habit involving the advantage of keeping his eyes on all possible breaching points in the house in case a band of terrorists invaded, an unlikely event, but better safe than sorry.

He didn't tell them about the seating angle or his paranoia about bad guys storming their home. He felt stupid for having that fear, but it was based on sixteen years in the Navy and NCIS. Being an undercover cop gave him plenty of paranoia. At this point in his life, it had become normal, like breathing. A healthy amount of paranoia was a good thing. He preferred to think of it as being cautious and staying alive.

Ten minutes into breakfast, Abby saw Widow stirring in his seat, staring into an empty coffee mug. She saw the look of defeat on his face, which reminded her of a documentary she once seen about apes. She recalled seeing a smart gorilla being tested by stacking children's blocks, all different shapes. The ape painstakingly tried to piece them together into a table with different holes, each corresponding to the shape of the blocks—circle, square, and triangle.

Widow had the same look on his face, sitting at their table, as the gorilla had after spending twenty minutes getting the blocks wrong.

Abby said, "Mr. Widow, do you want more coffee?"

Widow's turned his face toward her. The smile that stretched across his face was like Dylan's on Christmas morning, when he could finally begin the most important part of Christmas: opening presents.

"I'd love more, ma'am. Thank you."

"You like coffee, huh?"

"It's the oil of the human body," he said. Then he thought that blood was more like oil in a car engine than coffee. But why correct his statement?

Widow sat at the White's dinner table with a full belly. He had eaten two plates of scrambled eggs, bacon and sausage, and one breakfast roll and drunk coffee and left a glass of orange juice full and untouched.

Abby had served up a big breakfast for them and not the Christmas dinner Widow was promised, but the breakfast was such a grand affair that he could picture a stranger walking in from off the street and thinking that the whole scene was an official family Christmas breakfast.

Widow scooted his seat out and stood.

Abby smiled, waved a hand for Widow to stay where he was, and got up out of her seat and turned to the kitchen.

Widow said, "I can get it, ma'am."

"No. That's okay, Mr. Widow. You stay seated."

"I feel bad making you get up for it."

"That's perfectly okay. You've done enough already."

Widow stayed seated. He wasn't about to ignore a direct order from her. Abby went into the kitchen. She came back out with the whole coffee pot and walked around the table, circling past her grandkids, and refilled Widow's cup like a waitress in a diner. He thanked her.

She stepped to one side and leaned on the back of his chair with her free hand so that she could reach around his shoulders, which was hard enough. Instead of refilling his mug and returning the coffeepot to the kitchen, she set the pot down on the table next to the bacon. A tactical decision.

"There, you can help yourself now."

"Thank you."

Abe asked, "Won't that get cold sitting out?"

Widow said, "Don't worry. I'll drink it before that happens."

"You're gonna drink that whole pot?" Dylan asked.

A grin cracked across Widow's lips. And everyone knew he was serious.

Dylan stared the hardest. With a stranger at his family home, Walter had ordered him to be on his best behavior ahead of time, before they sat at the table. Which he was. But now he saw an opportunity to mess with the stranger, to put some entertainment into his morning.

Dylan continued to stare at Widow, and said, "Mr. Widow?"

The family continued speaking to each other.

"Yeah?" Widow asked.

"You know what a dead fish is?"

"Like a fish that's dead?"

"No. It's a handshake."

"A handshake?"

"Yeah. Anyone ever give you a dead fish?"

Maggie started listening in.

"Mr. Widow doesn't want to hear about dead fish, son."

"Awe, mom. He might."

"It's okay, ma'am," Widow said.

Dylan smiled, and Maggie went back to eating.

Dylan slid off his chair and walked around to Widow. He held his hand out.

"Here. I'll show ya," he said.

"Okay," Widow said, and he put his hand in Dylan's for a handshake.

Dylan squeezed so Widow could feel the handshake, and then he let his hand go completely limp.

Widow shook it and smiled.

"That's a dead fish," Dylan said, taking his hand away.

Walking back to his seat, he continued explaining it.

"I do it to new kids I meet all the time. It freaks them out. It's funny sometimes."

Widow nodded and said, "Dead fish, huh?"

"Yeah. You should try it next time you meet someone new."

Widow said nothing to that. Instead, he followed his instincts, which were to stare at the coffeepot. It wasn't filled to the brim. He had already drunk one cup. Abe drank another. And Walter also drank two himself, but his seemed to be half-creamer, making his share only equal to one Widow-sized cup of coffee.

The pot in front of him was big, unlike any he was used to seeing. He always thought they came in a standard size, but this one was a little bigger, a little more bulbous, like an old southern tea pitcher, like a decanter, only it was made from glass instead of ceramics. Judging by the depth and size and the amount of hot coffee left, he figured it had enough for him to get three or four more mugs from it.

"Mr. Widow, you okay?" Foster asked.

Widow realized he was staring at the pot of coffee like a brain-dead, catatonic patient stares at a light bulb.

"Sorry. Yeah. I'm okay. Just enjoying the aroma of coffee."

He looked up at the table. The whole family stared at him, wide-eyed, as if he showed to breakfast with no clothes on.

"Sorry," he said again.

"Okay. Leave him alone. The man loves coffee. So, what?" Abby said.

Widow nodded at her.

"It's a legal drug more powerful than cocaine, they say."

Foster said, "Just worried for a second."

"Foster's a doctor, you know?" Abby asked, putting exorbitant effort into hooking her daughter up with a hitchhiking stranger, which Widow thought was weird.

After watching them interact, after a while, he figured it out. Abby was more trying to nudge Foster into finding her own mate than she was serious about Widow as a potential suitor. She was teasing her daughter, dropping hints as if asking, "Hey, when are you going to settle down, Foster?"

Foster's eyebrows furrowed, a combination of embarrassment and annoyance. She must've heard all the jokes and teasing before.

"He knows that, Mom," she said.

"I just thought I'd mention it."

There was silence for a moment, except for Dylan, who moved on with his plans to eat another handful of bacon, and Lauren, his sister, who was making slight noises of angst with her breathing, like quiet sighs. She stared at her phone screen and reacted to whatever was happening on her screen. Seemingly, it was some kind of big drama.

"Lauren, put the phone down," Maggie White demanded.

"Mom! It's important!"

"I said, put it away."

Walter said, "Not at breakfast, Lulu."

Lauren dropped the phone on the table linen with a *thud!* The act itself was an alternate method to backtalk without actually talking back.

She continued to stare down at it even though she was no longer holding it—a loophole in her mom's choice of words. Put the phone down. Technically, she had put it down. But her mom, knowing exactly what her daughter was doing, wasn't having it.

"Get the phone off the table this instant, young lady!"

Lauren made an inaudible gasp that translated to: *How dare you speak to me that way!*

Widow wondered if she would've just said it if he hadn't been there. Something told him the answer was yes.

Abe said, "We have a guest, Lulu."

Walter said, "You can check your phone after breakfast."

Abe said, "You've got the rest of the day to play around on it."

Abby added, "After she helps me clean up the kitchen."

"Of course, Mother. She'll help you first; then she can use her phone," Abe said.

Widow stared on with a bit of envy, a bit of admiration, and a bit of humility at the family interaction that he'd only read about in books. The White family breakfast. They truly represented an iconic image of the American family life he'd never had.

Widow sipped his coffee slowly, trying not to draw attention to himself, but fast enough on a race to the finish before the hotness and freshness of the batch of coffee died away. In the real world, there are thousands of types of coffees and beans and aromas and flavors and ways to brew and ways to enjoy. To Widow, there were only two types of coffee—hot and cold. He preferred the former. Although, he had seen people at Starbucks ordering iced coffee. The first time he saw it, he thought to himself, The world is ending. Who the hell drinks coffee with ice?

Apparently, many people did, too many people, in his opinion.

Widow looked at Walter.

"Did you call the sheriff?"

Walter smacked his head with a free hand.

"No. I forgot. I'll do it after breakfast," he said.

Abby asked, "Why call the sheriff?"

Walter had just shoveled bacon in his mouth. He put up a finger to tell his mom: one second. The table fell quiet, waiting for him to finish. Finally, Abby and Abe both looked at each other and then at Widow, looking for the answer.

He said, "We saw some lights on last night at that place across from you guys."

Abby asked, "Pine Farms?"

Abe said, "They've been gone for years now. No one lives there."

"Did we get new neighbors?"

Walter finished chewing and swallowed.

"No. We saw lights on. Like candlelight."

Abby said, "Well, who's there?"

"I thought squatters."

"Should we call Henry?"

Walter looked at Widow.

"Henry's the sheriff. Henry Rourke."

Abe said, "Everyone just calls him Henry. No one calls him by his last name."

Dylan wanted to add to the conversation.

He said, "He's been over for breakfast before too. I call him Mr. Henry."

Abe took a sip of coffee from his mug and set the mug down. Then he slid his chair back and folded his napkin over to the side of his plate. He got up and walked back to the kitchen, out of sight. He returned with a cordless house phone. It was white and slim and sleek. He wasn't dialing a number. He had done that out of sight. He already had his ear to the phone and was waiting.

Abe looked at Walter.

"I'll call him now."

Someone must've picked up the line because he spoke.

"Maddie, we got a problem. Maybe. Is Henry in?"

The sheriff must've answered the phone because Abe explained the situation. He said his son had seen lights on at the abandoned farm, and there shouldn't be anyone there and that it was probably squatters. There were pauses, listening on Abe's part, and nods and then further explanation of what they saw. He left no stone unturned.

Within a short minute, he was off the phone after a flurry of thank-yous and back at the table, back with the napkin in its original position and the coffee in his hand. Abby gently slapped his arm.

"What did he say?" she asked.

"They've got a lot going on today with the explosion and all."

Dylan looked at them; his eyes opened wide with interest. He perked up and sat up in his chair.

"What explosion?"

Maggie said, "Don't you worry about that. Eat your breakfast."

Walter put a hand on his son's shoulder and patted him with a father-son gesture of affection that Widow saw and knew he would never know. Walter turned back to his own father.

"What did he say, Dad?"

"Like I was saying. There's lots going on, but they're looking for some guys who might be involved with the Athenians. Apparently, the explosion sent the ATF and the cops into a frenzy. Everyone's a little out of whack right now, but they're following up on every lead, no matter how small."

"They're sending someone out?"

"Henry's coming himself."

"Really?"

"Yeah, he mentioned his boys are all out there helping and running roadblocks."

Abby asked, "Henry wasn't with them?"

Abe shrugged.

"Someone's gotta run the shop, I guess. Or maybe I just caught him at the right moment."

"He must be busy."

"He sounded tired."

Maggie said, "He's probably been working since early this morning."

"Probably. The explosions were around four-thirty."

Walter asked, "When's he coming out?"

"I guess soon. He'll probably stop by after. You know how he likes your mom."

They all looked at Abby.

"He doesn't."

Abe looked at Widow, who was confused.

"Henry dated my wife way back before you were born, when the dinosaurs roamed the earth."

Like Patrick Mickey? Widow wandered.

Abby said, "We didn't date. It was high school. We were friends, that's it.

Widow smiled. The family continued to chat and laugh and eat.

Several minutes passed with more conversation. Abby circled back around to Widow being up all night.

She said, "After breakfast, you can take a nap in the guest bedroom, Mr. Widow."

Abby had only just eaten her breakfast. She forked a pile of eggs into her mouth and then put the fork down and dabbed her lips with a napkin. A second later, she repeated the whole process. She ate like someone who was hungry, but on guard because of an old tradition of politeness and table manners.

Abe stared at his empty plate, contemplating a second helping.

He said, "Will you be able to nap with all that coffee in your system?"

"Never had a problem before."

"Really?"

Widow shrugged.

"Coffee doesn't keep you awake when you're trying to sleep?"

"Coffee keeps me awake until bedtime."

"Even in the daytime?"

Foster looked out from across the table through a grand bay window at the morning sunlight and the gray that covered most of it.

She said, "Who can tell the difference with this weather?"

Maggie said, "No one. This polar vortex is real, I guess."

"Real?"

"Yeah. I guess it's a real thing."

Walter turned his head and looked at his sister.

"Don't get started, sis."

"Don't get started?"

"Yeah. On your global warming kick."

"I told you a million times. It's called climate change, and it's real."

"I think the jury is still out on that," Maggie blurted out.

Foster rolled her eyes.

"No. Science agrees."

Abe got a second helping, only a smaller portion than he'd started with.

For a moment, Widow thought he was going to interject, but he stayed quiet.

Walter said, "Sis, don't start. It's morning, and Mr. Widow's here."

At that point, Widow was refilling his coffee mug again. Dylan stared at him like he was watching a natural wonder. Lauren was blatantly staring at her cell phone again, but not touching it.

Abby was eating and dabbing with her napkin.

Widow stopped and stared over the lip of his mug.

This was the American family at breakfast, at Thanksgiving, or Christmas, or just a large family gathering.

This was how it went, he thought.

These were people who loved each other, linked by blood, bonded by family love, arguing over something that causes great rifts in communities, but doing it with respect, with debate, with dignity.

He cracked a sad smile because he saw the beauty in what they had together, but also he felt a sharp sting, way down deep, that told him it was something he had never had and probably never would. Not the way he lived his life.

Suddenly, he noticed that the debate over climate change going on between sister- and sister-in-law had turned to him.

Foster stared at him.

Walter stared at him.

Maggie stared at him.

Foster said, "What do you think, Mr. Widow?"

"About what?"

"Climate change?"

He looked at their faces and thought he should stay out of it, but he was at their table, eating their bacon, enjoying their coffee, and they were asking him a question.

He shrugged.

"I think carbon gases are warming the planet. I've been to Antarctica and the Arctic in submarines. I've seen polar ice caps melting away."

Maggie threw her hands up in frustration.

"Of course he's going to take your side."

Foster said, "What's that supposed to mean?"

Abe finished a bite of bacon and decided it was time for him to step in.

"Ladies, who cares about this topic? We're at breakfast. And Mr. Widow's gotta be tired. Let's not drag him into family squabbles."

Widow didn't argue with that. He didn't want to be involved.

Maggie said, "You're right."

Foster nodded in agreement.

Silence fell over the table for a minute.

Abby spoke first.

"Did you know Foster is a doctor?"

Foster said, "He knows, Mom. I told him. We told him."

"Oh. Did you know she was single?"

They all turned their heads and stared at Abby; even Lauren stopped playing on her phone to look at her grandmother.

"Maw-maw, you've told him that like a million times."

"Oh, my. Well, excuse me."

The Whites all laughed.

Ten minutes later, they finished breakfast, or rather, Abby notified them it was over because she started clearing dishes. The Whites put down their utensils, with Dylan scarfing two last strips of bacon, and they began moving to the family room, leaving behind their dishes. Except for the children. They stayed behind to help clean up.

It all went down like clockwork, like a predetermined chain of command and duties. Abby was the commander, and Dylan and Lauren were the grunts.

Widow was the last man left. He had been given no assignment, no duties. He was tired and had already helped Abe outside. So, he figured no one would be upset if he joined the family in the main room, leaving the dishes behind. Widow was many things. He had been many things. But the original thing he had been was a southerner. Leaving behind dishes as a guest in someone's house wasn't in his DNA.

"Let me help you guys."

He carried his empty plate and stacked several others on top in order of emptiest to fullest, a plate half covered in uneaten food.

Widow followed Dylan into the kitchen, over to a counter, and stacked the dirty dishes next to a large farm sink. The sink was large enough to bathe a lamb in.

Abby walked over, waving her hands.

"Oh, no, dear. You go on out there with everybody. I can handle this."

Dylan took that as a dismissal of all of them because he headed out of the kitchen ahead of Widow.

"Not you!" Abby barked. "You're on dishwasher duty!"

"But Maw-maw, I emptied the dishwasher yesterday. Make Lauren do it."

"Lauren's wiping things down. You, empty and fill it."

Lauren was in the kitchen already with a damp towel in hand, wiping countertops.

"But Maw-maw."

"Dylan Abraham White, you do as your maw-maw says."

Dylan was young, but not stupid. He knew enough about life to know not to argue with his grandmother. So he didn't.

Dylan let his arms drop like an ape. He dragged them and his feet over to the sink and began cleaning dishes and stacking them. There were already dishes in the sink for him to clean and stack.

Widow looked around the kitchen.

Abby saw him and walked over to him. She gazed up at him like he was a tree standing in the middle of her kitchen.

"There's no machine dishwasher. If that's what you're looking for. Dylan is the dishwasher."

Widow smiled and nodded.

"Okay. Thanks for breakfast. And coffee."

"No worries, dear. You want more coffee?"

Widow thought for a moment and was tempted for that moment, but then he thought of the offer to take a nap in the guest room.

"No. I'd better pass. But I'll grab the pot from the table for you."

"Don't worry. Stop working, dear. Go out there with the others."

Widow laid his hands down by his sides and smiled.

"Yes, ma'am."

Abby smiled back. She moved over to Dylan.

Widow stayed a moment longer and watched her take her grandson's place behind the farmer's sink.

He looked excited.

"I can go to?"

"I done told you no. You're going into the dining room to fetch the rest of the dirty plates. Hurry now 'cause then you're taking my place back at the sink."

Dylan looked at Widow with a plea for help on his face.

Widow said, "Don't look at me. You heard the general."

Abby smiled at Widow again, a bigger smile than before, and he turned and left the kitchen to join the others in the family room.

As soon as Widow stepped through the kitchen door, he felt a warm heat brush over his face. A fire crackled and spat in a fireplace on the far wall in the family room. Everyone was stationed at spots in the room like a military unit huddled around a camp-fire out in the desert.

Abe stood at a back door on the far wall of the room. He had the back door kicked open. A heavy log from the fireplace propped it in place. A screen door separated the inside of the house from the cold outside.

Abe smoked a cigar near the open door. He puffed and exhaled the smoke out into the outside grayness.

The fire hissed a loud sizzle as if it had hit an extraordinarily flammable log. Then it died down to a normal, soft crackle.

Maggie sat with a hand on Walter's knee. They looked snug and comfortable on the sofa. Dr. Foster White sat on a loveseat across from her brother, with a big space next to her.

There were two empty armchairs across from each other, one in front of the fireplace, angled to see both the room and the fire.

Widow had three choices of where to sit. He got the feeling that the family had set up an ambush for him as if they would know if he was attracted to Foster or not by what seat he chose. Sit by her, and it was a red alert that he was interested. Sit at one of the armchairs, and he wasn't.

Foster was an attractive woman, around his age, and a doctor, which showed she had brains. All things he liked very much, but he yawned as he stood there and felt the urge to take the Whites' offer to nap in the guest room. *Sleep when you can*, was a universal military motto.

Instead of falling into their ambush, Widow joined Abe at the door.

"Did you enjoy your breakfast, Mr. Widow?"

"I did. Thank you for the invite, sir."

"Thank Walter; he's the one that offered."

Widow nodded.

"So, what would you like to do next? Want to join us out in the field for some work today?"

Widow looked out into the yard at the snow and the gray.

"You guys going out to do more work in this weather?"

Abe puffed the cigar and craned his head, looked up at the sky.

"Yeah, it doesn't look like friendly weather. That polar vortex is hitting us hard. So, no. I guess we're not. My wife would kill me if I sent you back out there, anyhow."

Then he went quiet, looked around the room like he was making sure no one was eavesdropping, which they weren't. He leaned in close to Widow and spoke in a near whisper.

"Guess you noticed my wife dropping hints about my daughter being single?"

He moved back to his leaning position. Widow smiled.

"Was pretty obvious."

Abe said nothing to that. He just chuckled to himself and puffed the cigar.

Widow said, "I am interested in your offer to crash in one of the rooms."

Abe nodded and said, "The sandman gets us all. No matter how much coffee you drink. You need to rest. It's the human condition. Our biggest weakness, we all gotta sleep."

Widow nodded and followed it up with a yawn that wasn't fake.

Abe took a last puff of the cigar. He pushed through the screen door, stayed half inside the house, and put out the lit end of the cigar on a brick wall on the exterior of the back porch. Then he returned to the house, shut the door, and set the cigar on a windowsill.

"Come with me. I'll show you to an empty room."

Abe walked past him and up a flight of stairs. Widow followed. The rest of the family followed them with their eyes.

Walter was the only one to ask.

"Going to take a nap, Widow?"

"Mr. Widow's tired. Let's try to keep it down so he can get a couple of hours' sleep," Abe said.

"We'll see you later Mr. Widow," Maggie called up.

Foster said, "Nice to meet you."

Widow waved back down to her and the rest of them. He followed behind Abe up the stairs.

The landing was visible from the family room. After that, the stairs vanished into the ceiling.

They walked up to the second floor and turned a corner in a short hallway that led to another hallway.

"This is a big house. It's kind of grand."

"Thanks. We love it. We like to think of it as our own Buckingham Palace."

The house was no Buckingham Palace. Widow knew that because he had been to Buckingham Palace. But it was a nice big family farmhouse.

At the end of the hall, Abe opened a door that led to a good-size corner bedroom.

"This is the guest room. There's a private bath with a shower in it over there. Help yourself."

"Think I will take a shower. I need one. Thank you, sir."

Abe paused at the door. He looked Widow up and down.

"What size clothes you wear?"

"Thirty-four tall in pants and extra-large in shirts are in my comfort zone."

Abe nodded, turned, shut the door, and left. And finally, Widow was all alone with a shower and a bed. He couldn't help but smile.

The guestroom had a king-sized bed against the back wall and two large windows and one armchair against the corner. Greens and blues and grays made up the colors. There were two rattan-framed mirrors and a long, waist-high dresser on the next wall, and two doorways on the last one.

Widow opened one of the doors and found a closet with shoe-boxes stacked on the floor and no shoes in sight. The rack for hanging shirts was empty except for wire hangers dangling from the bar. Clean bed linens were folded on a shelf above.

Widow closed the closet door and tried the next one. He found the shower and toilet and sink. Everything was simple and white except for the shower curtain and towels, which matched the green and blue from the room.

He stepped back to the room and yanked his socks off his feet. Then he undressed and left his clothes in a pile in one corner. He stepped back into the bathroom, naked, and hopped into the shower. He set the water to warm, and showered.

Widow killed the water when he was done and stepped out of the shower. He toweled off, slicked his damp hair back, and wrapped the towel around his waist. He stepped to the mirror and wiped the steam off it. He stared at his face. He could use a fresh shave. He wondered if it would be impolite to ask Abe to borrow a razor and a can of shaving cream.

Next to a stand-up squeeze bottle of toothpaste, there was a cup with several disposable toothbrushes wrapped in plastic like Widow had seen in some motels.

He needed to brush his teeth, but he didn't need to waste one of the Whites' disposable brushes. He went to his old jeans and fished out the cheap gas station-bought toothbrush out of one pocket and rinsed it good and used it, with the Whites' toothpaste, to brush his teeth.

Widow had all his own teeth, amazingly, given how many times he'd been punched in the jaw. He was proud to have them. In his life, he had never had a single cavity or major dental-related operation, except when he was seventeen, when he had all his wisdom teeth yanked out.

After he was done in the bathroom, Widow returned to the guest room just in time to hear the last of a series of knocks at the door.

He heard footsteps walking away, as if someone had knocked and hurried off.

"Just a second," he called out.

He double-checked the towel's staying power around his waist. When that was safely confirmed, he opened the door.

No one was there. The hallway was empty, but on a short table across from his door was a stack of neatly folded clothes.

He went over, careful not to drip water onto the hardwood, and scooped up the clothes. He returned to the room and shut the door behind him.

The clothes had belonged to Abe's dead son, he figured, like the house shoes and the combat boots from the downstairs mudroom cubby and the dog tags.

Widow thanked Abe to himself as if the gratitude could be transmitted psychically. Then he realized he was talking to himself. Widow noticed he did that more and more, a habit common to drifters, probably. He was spending too much time on his own on the road and not enough around people. That was probably not healthy.

Widow set the clothes on the bed and took off the towel. He toweled his hair some more till it was part dry, part damp. He hung the towel on a rack in the bathroom.

The dead son's clothes comprised a pair of dark blue jeans and a belt and a thick, long-sleeved black shirt. He checked the sizes. The jeans were thirty-six waist and tall. He guessed that's why Abe had brought him a belt to go with them. There was also a pair of clean black socks. No underwear, probably because that would be weird for Abe.

Widow put on the new clothes with his own underwear and checked himself out in the bathroom mirror. Everything fit pretty well, even the jeans. They were a little loose, but the belt kept them nice and snug at the waist.

After he checked the fit, he took all the new clothes off again because he didn't want to wrinkle them. He opened the closet and folded the jeans over a hanger, and hung them up. He repeated the process with the shirt. He left the socks on his feet and kept the underwear on.

He went back over to the bed and tossed the top layers of covered pillows onto the floor. He turned down the covers and blankets and sheets. He found several layers, more than he'd expected.

Before he knew it, he'd slipped his body under the covers, and his head was on the pillow. He turned to one side and stared out the window for a long minute, letting his mind run until it was empty of thought.

Clouds overcast the sky outside. Everything was gray or white. He closed his eyes and fell fast asleep.

27

Dobson crouched over the motor to the van with a look of confusion on his face, which he was faking to keep Abel thinking that he was also blindsided by the van's sudden breakdown.

A single hood lift held the van's hood open. He tinkered around with a screwdriver, tapping it on different parts of the engine.

While some of the other guys napped, Dobson went straight to work in the van. He knew he had better look like he was busy trying to fix the problem, even though he already knew what the issue was, and he knew he couldn't fix it.

He stood inside the barn to the abandoned farm. Overhead in the loft, under the roof's peak, and the high beams, Brooks and Jargo were chatting, occasionally checking out the road with the sniper rifle's scope.

Radio chatter flickered and buzzed throughout the barn.

Brooks was getting radio communication from Abel. Probably a status report or an update request. Abel wanted both often.

After a moment, the chatter died away, and Brooks went back to talking to Jargo.

Dobson could hear the reverberations of their voices, but not what they were saying. He heard them shuffle around, probably trading positions at the rifle.

Empty stalls surrounded the van. Stacks of old hay lined the walls.

Morning sunbeams crept out from behind clouds here and there. Most of the sky was overcast with gray and white, which made Dobson think it would start snowing at any moment.

Flack stood at the rear of the van with the doors swung open. First, he rechecked the pipe bomb packages, then checked the labels and the stamps. Everything was as Abel had instructed it to be. The labels were correct. The names and addresses Abel gave them were listed correctly. The correct name coincided with the correct street address. Each pipe bomb would be delivered correctly to the right person's home. As long as no mailman got curious and tried to open any of the packages, then they would hit the correct target's addresses.

They may not all be opened by the intended recipient, but that's war. Collateral damage was to be expected. Plus, Abel didn't much care if he missed his targets, but killed a wife or husband or even a kid instead. That was just as good a target.

The stamps were metered correctly for weight.

Next, Flack checked all the belts and buckles and locks and bars to make sure they were closed tight to keep the pipe bombs and their packages locked in place.

Flack closed the doors and came around to speak.

"How's it looking?"

"Not good."

"What's going on?"

"Like I said earlier. It's electrical. I can't do anything about it without a diagnostic machine and the correct software."

Flack reached a gloved hand up to his face and wiped his mouth.

He whispered, "Like in the cave?"

Dobson glanced back to make sure no one was listening.

"Yeah. Like in the cave."

Just then, as if on cue, one of the barn's huge double doors pulled open with an eerie creak, and Abel stepped inside. He stretched his arms out and up like he was just waking up. His white gear and coat blended into the gray and white behind him.

"How's it looking, boys?"

Dobson assumed he was talking to him.

"Same as before."

"Can't fix it?"

Dobson shook his head.

Abel walked into the barn, stopped about five feet from Dobson, reached out a long arm, and patted Dobson's shoulder.

"Well, we'll need new wheels."

"Yes, sir."

"Come out here."

Abel turned and walked out into the open air.

Dobson followed him out.

Abel walked him to the snowy driveway and stopped over the van's tracks left in the snow.

Abel stopped, turned, and faced Dobson. He held out an open hand.

"Are you armed?"

Dobson looked around. The others were gathering around him, except Jargo and Brooks, who were still up in the barn's loft behind him.

Dobson said, "Yes."

"Hand it over."

Dobson tried to look confused, but it wasn't confusion on his face. It was fear.

"Go on," Abel said.

Dobson reached a shaky hand into his coat and reached down to his side. He unsnapped a safety catch on a hip holster, brandished a Glock. He took it out and paused a beat, and then reversed it and handed it to Abel.

Abel turned to one of the others and tossed the pistol to him.

"How long have you been with us?"

Dobson still held the screwdriver in his hand. He stood there and said nothing.

"I'm talking to you," Abel said, pointing a shaky, pruned finger at Dobson.

An icy breeze blew across the farm and slapped Dobson in the face. He shivered. Some of it came from the breeze, and some of it came out of fear.

"I guess ten years."

"Ten years?"

"Maybe longer."

Abel nodded and said, "In all that time, how many times have you failed me?"

Dobson stopped, looked down at the ground for the answer, and thought for a moment. He looked up and saw the look on Abel's face. Fear overwhelmed him. He stopped, looking for the answer.

Abel grinned back at him ominously.

Dobson prayed Abel couldn't see his fear.

He said, "Never."

"Never."

Silence.

Dobson stayed put. He fought to keep still. He fought to stop his muscles from moving, but it didn't last. He shivered visibly.

"Are you going to kill me?" he asked.

Abel grinned wider and craned his head slowly, and looked up behind Dobson. His eyes moved up the barn to the opening under the peak.

Dobson turned and stared up.

He traced the barn's exterior until his eyes came to rest on the loft window at the top of the barn at Jargo's sniper nest. The loft shutters were wide open, but neither Jargo nor his sniper rifle was there.

Instead, Brooks knelt in the open window armed with his M4. He knelt in a firing position. The rifle butt was lodged against his right shoulder, his eyes lined over the sights, and his finger was on the trigger. A sound suppressor stuck out of the business end of the weapon. And it was pointed straight down at Dobson.

Dobson locked eyes with Brooks and froze. His jaw dropped, and his hands shot up instinctively to block the bullet from tearing through his face.

He screamed.

"NO! NO! NO! PLEA...."

Suddenly, Dobson felt a sharp, tight pain around his neck and in his throat and deep down where the voice formulates letters. But it wasn't pain from a bullet to the head. No bullet was fired. It was something else. He couldn't breathe. Something was strangling him.

Dobson's hands moved down to his throat in violent desperation. His fingers brushed across his skin and neck until he found the cause of strangulation. His fingers clawed and clung at a sharp wire around his neck. He scraped and pried and wriggled, trying to slip a finger under it, trying to get some slack, trying to get a fraction of a centimeter, anything. But it wouldn't give.

Suddenly, Dobson felt his feet come up off the ground. His leverage was wiped away in an instant. He still couldn't breathe. He couldn't pull the wire off his neck. There was no slack to give. He couldn't do anything but choke. He was completely helpless, completely powerless.

Moments earlier, and seconds before he walked into the barn, Abel had radioed up to Brooks and told him what was about to happen and what he should do.

Brooks distracted Dobson with the M4 while Abel crept behind him, slowly. Then Abel exploded to action and yanked out a long, homemade garrote and slipped it around Dobson's neck. The garrote was crafted from items he'd found in the abandoned farmhouse. The string was a high-grade fishing wire. He used a pair of wooden muddlers from the kitchen as the handles, stringing the line between them in grooves already left there around the bulbous bottoms of the muddlers. Finding the fishing wire and the muddlers left behind wasn't a surprise to Abel. Why would anyone bother to pack them? They were replaceable and not worth packing up. When the bank's coming to foreclose on your farm, the last thing you might think to pack would be trivial items like fishing wire and muddlers.

In a sick way, Abel chalked the stroke of luck up to God's will. Abel had been twisting and exploiting religion for so long that he actually believed some lies he spewed.

Abel walked up behind Dobson, slipped the wire over his head and jerked, and wrenched backward. Once he knew he had Dobson by the throat, he jerked and twisted and spun around in a one-eighty degree turn. He heaved and hauled Dobson up over his back and yanked forward, using Dobson's own weight, and gravity, to strangle the man.

Dobson kicked outward and wriggled in the air. His face turned blue. He tried to scream in pain, in desperation, but all that came out were gasps of the last slivers of air his lungs could exhale.

Dobson tried to call out for help. He stared up at Brooks, who watched him die with no emotion on his face, no signs of friend-ship or unit loyalty. Brooks showed no signs of anything until the last seconds when a smile grew across his face until it was big and wide.

Dobson kicked harder and harder into the air until his legs slowed, and he felt his energy levels dropping, dropping until nothing was left.

Abel pulled the garrote harder and harder until Dobson stopped kicking, stopped clawing, stopped moving altogether.

Abel strangled Dobson until the man died, until his corpse turned pale.

Finally, when Dobson felt like nothing more than a rag doll over his back, Abel released the garrote. Dobson's corpse collapsed into the snow like a sack of potatoes. It didn't bounce or move on impact. It just plopped down and stayed literally dead weight.

The wire was still tight around the corpse's neck. Blood seeped out slowly from around the wire. Abel had strangled him so hard the wire had cut through his skin. Blood seeped out of the cut.

Dobson's emotionless face stared up at the sky. His eyes were dead. His skin was almost translucent, as if the color had gone out like a light. His eyes bulged nearly out of their sockets. He was as dead as anything that had ever died.

Abel breathed in heavy wheezes, trying to catch his breath. Strangling someone like that was physically exhausting, especially for an older man who was past his prime.

Abel panted and gasped until he caught his breath. His guys stood around, waiting. After Abel's breath returned and his panting slowed, Flack stepped out from inside the barn. Brooks stayed where he was, but Jargo appeared from the loft and stuck his head out to look at the dead body.

A silent moment passed between them all until Tanis asked the first question that he and Cucci were both wondering. Not that they didn't suspect the answer. They just wanted confirmation from Abel.

"What'd he do wrong?"

Abel stood up tall. He twisted and turned to check his pants and his winter coat for blood droplets from Dobson's neck. He found nothing.

Abel looked up at Brooks, and then over to Tanis and Cucci.

He raised his arms in the air and addressed them like he was standing on a platform in the ancient Roman Colosseum, addressing a bloodthirsty crowd of spectators.

He spoke loud and articulated every word and every syllable.

"I only ask for the best. If you boys can't deliver, then you will suffer. Dobson lied to us. He failed. He knew something was wrong with the van. And he lied about it. Now, he's paid the price. Now, we're even."

Tanis nodded along, and the others listened.

Abel asked, "What do we call a man like that?"

Tanis said nothing. Cucci stepped back to the house and leaned on the railing for the steps. Abel's eyes looked from face to face. He turned and looked straight at Flack, who said nothing. Abel looked up at Jargo and then over to Brooks.

Brooks rested the sniper rifle down out of sight and spoke.

"Dobson was a saboteur."

Abel pointed up to him. He became very animated as his blood returned to a normal circulation in his veins.

"That's it. That's right. That's what we call them. Dobson was a saboteur, a traitor to our cause. He was a problem. Now, he is not."

He looked back down at Flack and then over to Cucci and Tanis.

"What's the punishment for treason?"

All at once, a little out of sync, a little out of unison, the men answered him.

"Death."

"Death. That's right."

Abel turned to the guys near the porch.

"Clean this up."

Tanis asked, "What do you want us to do with him?"

"Just dump him in the back of the barn somewhere, like garbage."

Tanis and Cucci both left their guns on the porch and scrambled over to the body.

Abel looked up at Brooks again.

"Back to it then, Major."

Brooks snapped to and barked out the order to the others like they were deployed.

"Get to steppin', boys!"

With that, Cucci and Tanis heaved up the dead body and hauled it away inside the barn. Flack held the door open for them. They dumped Dobson into an old, snowy horse trough, tucked away at the last stall.

Jargo returned to his sniping post. Brooks looked down at Abel again and waved at him. Abel looked up.

Brooks said, "I know where we can get some new wheels."

Abel called back up to him.

"Where?"

Brooks raised a gloved hand slowly and pointed east.

"There's a farm there. People living in it. They got a truck."

"Big enough for us?"

"It might be now we're down one. Some of us can sit in the back. Or maybe they got an extra vehicle. We can take two."

Abel grinned up at him.

"Want me to go check it out?"

"Not yet. Soon. Clean up this mess first."

28

ADONIS RODE in Shep's cruiser for almost an hour along more backroads than she thought would be in such a small radius. They went slowly, circling back, turning left, turning right, going up and down one road that connected to the next. They scanned the empty roads methodically until they were no longer empty. By this time, there were trucks driving the roads here and there and an occasional car. They saw several SUVs. There were local people going to work, going for supplies, or just passing through. It was getting too hard to track them all.

Adonis had to pray that Abel would get caught at one of the roadblocks because she was losing hope that he was still within the dragnet at all. But it was Shep who voiced it first.

"We've missed them."

"No, we haven't. They're here somewhere."

Shep reached up and tapped on the clock on the dashboard. The time was nine twenty-five in the morning.

"It might be too late. We should get the FBI on this."

"They already know what's going on."

"Why aren't they here yet?"

"I don't know," she said, but she turned her ringer off in her pocket. She knew the FBI was already in Carbine. Her CO had texted her. Technically, she was off the case. They were officially off the books now. There was no point in telling Shep or her guys that. If they got caught, they could have plausible deniability and just blame her for it.

Adonis wasn't planning on taking Abel in. She was planning to take him out.

"Don't worry about the Feds. We're on our own, for now."

Shep said nothing to that.

Adonis shifted in her seat. She leaned to the left and stared out at more abandoned farms and trees and snow and half-empty roads.

She said, "Let's just keep going. Okay?"

"Okay."

Shep continued driving. Ramirez continued scouring the skyline. And Adonis looked back out the window. She kept it together, but she knew that hopelessness was barking around the corner.

* * *

THE LOFT's shutters stayed open, but Jargo and Brooks crouched back inside in the darkness. The barn doors were closed, hiding their broken-down panel van. Cucci and Tanis and Flack were in the barn near what used to be horse stables, and Dobson's corpse, which was discarded in a back corner per Abel's instructions.

Abel was in the farmhouse. The candles were long extinguished, not that it would've made a difference at nine o'clock in the morning. It was no longer dark enough outside to allow the light to be seen.

Jargo kept his sniper rifle back away from the loft's hole to keep it from being spotted. But he kept it ready to pull up and take aim and fire if he needed to. The others were holding their weapons, ready to defend the pipe bombs, the packages, and Abel at all costs.

After Cucci and Tanis and Flack dragged the corpse into the barn, they heard a buzzing sound from above. A second later, Jargo spotted a helicopter in the sky, buzzing the trees and the road.

He called out to the others. Cucci and Tanis dragged Dobson's body all the way in past the van and dumped him. Flack pulled up the rear and shut the barn doors.

Abel came on over the radio. "What's it doing now?"

Jargo slipped his sniper rifle down and leaned into the inside corner of the windowsill so he could get a better angle on the helicopter without being detected.

He stayed where he was. He didn't take his eyes off the bird. But he raised his hands and gave Brooks a few hand signals. Brooks watched them and then talked on the radio.

"The bird is searching for something."

"Who is it? Police?"

"Hard to say. We count three onboard."

"Three? That's it?"

"Yeah. Three."

Abel asked, "Maybe FBI?"

"Wait."

Silence. Jargo held up a stop hand signal for Brooks to see. Everyone waited. Jargo lifted the sniper rifle and gazed through the scope. But he wasn't looking up at the helicopter. He was staring down at the road.

He scanned the road and turned like he was following something.

He lowered the rifle and then stepped back to Brooks. He took the radio and spoke.

"Sir, there's one police car on the road. It's a state patrolman. I count two inside."

"Patrolmen? You sure?"

"Yeah. Between the helicopter and car, there are five bodies in total."

"Patrolmen? I never heard of them using helicopters before."

"It might not be state patrol alone. The passenger in the car is a woman. She's not dressed as any state patrolman I've ever seen before."

"What's she wearing?"

"She looks like FBI to me."

"Then, she might be."

Brooks took the radio from Jargo and pressed the talk button, held it up to his mouth.

"The FBI would send a lot more than five people."

Abel said, "Flack, come in."

Flack's radio crackled low on his belt. He picked it up and spoke.

"Yes, sir."

"You get anything on the police radio earlier?"

"I've heard nothing about a helicopter. But I haven't listened to the radio for a while."

Abel asked, "Is it possible the neighbors called the cops?"

Brooks came on over his radio.

"That's probably it, sir."

Abel stepped up closer to the kitchen window and pulled the blinds down. He stared up in the sky. He could hear the rotor blades echoing over the treetops. Then he saw it. Everyone stayed quiet. He watched the helicopter fly over and out of his line of sight. Both the helicopter and the police cruiser were gone.

After another minute passed, Jargo came on over the radio.

"I got a better look at the riders in the car. They stopped at the mailbox for the neighbors down the road. They looked like they were contemplating driving down it, but they didn't. They drove off.

"And there's something else. The woman in the passenger seat looked to me like she was calling the shots. She kept pointing and talking over the driver."

"Interesting."

"And she had bandages on her forehead."

"Bandages?"

"Yes, sir."

"Boys, we still got an ATF agent alive and well. It seems she's after us. And I would guess she's on her own."

Brooks came on over the radio this time.

"She's got four guys and a helicopter."

"The ATF, FBI, and all the rest of the Washington pawns are just like the Army. For operations, they might skimp on the body armor and bullets, but not the manpower and machines. We blew up a hundred of their agents; they are gonna send a helluva a lot more than just a girl and a helicopter after us. Trust me."

"What's that mean?"

"It means for her; this is a personal endeavor. She'll try to take us on her own."

Abel was quiet until another thought popped into his head.

"Brooks, perhaps you should find out about that truck across the street. After they pass, why don't you pop over there?"

29

BROOKS APPROACHED the mailbox at the end of the long drive and studied it. It said Cherokee Hill Farm on it. No family name given.

He made a note to himself and turned and stared back at the abandoned barn in the distance. He couldn't see Jargo, but he knew he was there, watching him through the sniper rifle's scope. He waved and held up his radio.

His radio crackled and hissed.

Jargo spoke through an earpiece with a coiled wire going down from his head to Abel's radio that he'd lent to him.

"I see ya."

Brooks held the radio to his mouth.

"I'm entering."

"Okay. I'm gonna lose you as soon as you get ten feet farther up the track."

"Acknowledged. Going silent then."

Brooks waited for Jargo to give him an affirmative, which he did. Then he killed the radio and slid it into his coat pocket. It fit snugly enough to keep from creating a visible puff in his coat.

He looked left and looked right, then brandished a Glock from a hip holster at the small of his back. He checked it, made sure a round was chambered, and then re-holstered it.

Brooks walked the drive, making mental notes of everything he saw. He walked past huge trees near the front and then up the hill and over the crest. He stopped. He noted the Christmas trees and the snow. He noted that there was heavy farming equipment out in the fields, far off in the distance to the east. They sat unused, like long-forgotten machines. He noted the same to the west. He also noted no signs of farmhands, no signs of animals.

He walked the long track farther until he passed through some trees on a corner, and then he saw the farmhouse. He stopped at the base of the circular driveway and studied the house. He studied the red brick, the white door, the barn off to the side, and the vehicles.

Smoke plumed out from a chimney on one side.

He noted the two trucks and one vehicle under a tarp.

The one Tundra was perfect for them, but now they could commandeer two, which was even better.

Brooks walked off to the east, away from the front door, and watched the windows. He wanted to see how alert the people inside were, if they noticed that a hulking black man, a stranger, walked their property this close. He looked at every window. Not one blind flapped. Not one curtain ruffled. Not one eyeball peeked out.

He was also looking for family pets, like a big dog or a pair of big dogs. He hated dogs. They made for the most dangerous kind of alarm system a homeowner could own. Alarm systems can be disabled silently. Dogs make all kinds of racket. Alarm systems aren't dangerous. They don't attack intruders. They can't break human bones. They don't have teeth.

Many guard dogs can break bones. He knew a dog handler in the Army who told him that one of their German Shepherds could break the bones in a man's arm in seconds.

The Cherokee Hill Farm had no dogs. He was sure of it because he saw no paw prints in the snow. He saw no dog toys left in the yard, no dog houses, and the house had no doggie doors that he could see.

Brooks wanted to be as sure as he could, so he started whistling quietly. He kept his gun hand behind him, ready to go for the Glock in case a couple of dogs came running out of nowhere to see what the whistling was about, but nothing happened. No dogs. No movement at the windows. No one came out of the house.

He returned his hand to his side and scoped out the corners and tops of the house. He saw no security cameras, but he wasn't expecting any. He also saw no signs of an alarm system, which didn't surprise him. Way out here, what good would an alarm system do other than make a lot of noise? They were too far for an alarm company to send someone out.

The area was rural, which meant that most likely it was policed by sheriff's deputies from the county, a large territory for them to cover. It wasn't likely that he had to worry about that.

The one thing he was positive he would find was that a few of the males who lived here would be more than proficient with rifles and shotguns and maybe even AR-15s, but he wasn't worried about that.

Brooks took off his ball cap and stuffed it bill first into his back pocket to make himself look more trustworthy.

He cracked his fingers, frontward, and then backward. The knuckles cracked. He walked past the trucks and stepped up onto the front porch.

He could smell coffee and something else, something mouthwatering. He took a deeper whiff. His brain told him it was bacon.

He walked up to the big, white front door and listened. He heard no one shuffling to the door, but he heard muffled voices deep in the house.

He stepped to the side and peered into the closest window. He saw nothing through the blinds and the curtains but obscured shapes and shadows.

After closer inspection, he was certain they had no alarm system. No wires lined the interior of the window. He saw no sensors.

The door had a doorbell, but he didn't ring it.

He stepped back to the front door and knocked, light, at first, to test the sound. No one came. He knocked a little louder. No one came. He knocked one more time, louder. Then he heard sounds like voices that had been talking lively and now stopped for the interruption.

He stepped back and paused.

A moment later, he heard footsteps getting closer. There was more than one set of feet. The footsteps stopped.

He was sure that someone was on the other side of the door, looking through the peephole. Then he heard voices speaking and arguing like one person was asking someone else, Hey, you know this guy?

He reached up and knocked again.

He heard a female voice speak.

"Open it. Don't let the poor man stand there."

The doorknob creaked, and the door opened slowly.

It wasn't even locked, he thought.

The door swung all the way open, and he was greeted by three members of the White family. He stared and smiled at them.

Abe stood front and center. He had opened the door. Behind him was Abby, and behind her, about five feet back, was Walter.

Abe asked, "Yes, sir? Can I help you?"

Brooks smiled, looked down the hallway into a large, open living space. He saw a kid come around the corner and stare back at him. He saw no one else from that spot, but he heard another female voice speaking in the living room.

"I'm sorry to bother you, kind folks. My partner and I are lost back there on the road."

"You're lost?"

"Yes, sir. There aren't a lot of street signs out here."

"Where's your car?"

"Oh, sorry. I should've said, we're lost, and our car broke down."

Abby stepped from around her husband and spoke.

"Oh, dear. What a terrible place to be stranded in."

Abe said, "You should call somebody."

Walter said, "Where's your phone?"

"I don't have a phone. My partner does, but we got no signal."

"Oh, dear," Abby said again.

"Where's your partner?" Walter asked.

Brooks saw skepticism on his face and on the older man's face. He figured they were father and son because of how much they looked alike.

"He's waiting with the car back on the road. He's a little paranoid about leaving it alone. We're not from around here."

"Do you need to use our phone?"

"Oh, that would be so nice of you."

Abby turned and went back into the house and disappeared. Abe and Walter stepped out onto the porch with Brooks.

"My name's Abe. This is Walter, my son."

"Jim Nelson."

Brooks stuck out a huge gloved hand for the two men to shake. Abe shook it first, and then Walter.

"So sorry you got stuck out here," Abe said.

"Not as sorry as I am."

"Where you guys headed?"

"We're driving up to DC. My partner just went through a divorce. He's relocating up there."

"You're helping him move or something?"

"Nah, I'm tagging along. My sister lives there. It's kind of road trip for me."

Walter asked, "Where you guys from?"

"Atlanta."

"Oh, boy," Abe said, "You didn't get far."

"Nope. We didn't."

"What you guys do?"

"For a living?"

Abe nodded.

"Real estate. We're investment partners."

They were quiet for a moment.

Maggie stepped out from the living room and wrangled her son from staring at the stranger.

Brooks watched them vanish farther into the house. Then Abby came walking out from the kitchen. She had a cell phone in her hand. She walked down the hall and out onto the porch through the opened door.

She handed an old but well-maintained flip phone to Brooks.

"Here you go."

"Thanks, ma'am."

"Of course, dear."

He took the phone and studied it.

"Something wrong?" Abe asked.

"I was just thinking; I haven't seen a flip phone in years."

"It works. That's all I need," Abby said.

"Yes, ma'am."

"You're not calling long distance? They charge for that."

Walter said, "Mom, nobody charges long-distance anymore."

Abe said, "Not unless he calls out of the country."

"I'm not. Don't worry. I'll give this right back."

Brooks stepped back off the porch and out onto the drive. He flipped the phone open and dialed a number from memory, and put the phone to his ear. He listened to an automated voice from a bank, repeating the time and date to him. It was a generic number, no association to him.

"I got a problem. Yeah. We're broke down."

He paused like he was listening. He looked back at the Whites. They were quiet, listening to him and watching.

"Uh-huh. Right. Yeah."

He went silent for a second like he was getting instructions.

Brooks said, "Jim Nelson. We're out near Cherokee Hill Farm. Oh, you do? Okay. Great. See you then."

Brooks mimicked like he was clicking off the call and flipped the phone closed. He returned to the porch, returned to the Whites, and handed the flip phone back to Abby.

"Hope you got someone to come out and give you a hand?"

"Oh, yes, ma'am."

Walter said, "That was pretty easy."

His father said, "A lot easier than I would've guessed.

"We have a good Triple-A."

Abby turned and went back into the house.

Abe offered to shake. "That's lucky.

"Yeah. Thanks for the phone. I hope I didn't intrude?"

"No intrusion."

Abe smiled at Brooks.

Walter said, "Let me get my keys, and I'll give you a ride back to your vehicle."

"That's not necessary."

"Sure, it is. It's no problem."

"I'm not going that far. We're right down the drive."

Abe intervened.

"I insist. Let my son take you back."

"You know. I'm not bad with engines. I can even look for you when we get there."

Brooks shrugged.

"Okay. I won't turn down a free ride."

"Okay. Let me grab the keys."

Walter turned and went back into the house.

"Get your warm coat, too."

Abe turned back to Brooks.

"So, what brings you guys off the beaten path?"

"What's that?"

"You said you were heading to Washington from Atlanta. Why come out here? Why Spartan County? Seems out of the way to get to DC."

"We had to make a stop in Carbine."

Abe paused a moment.

"How did that go?"

"Fine."

"Really? What about the explosion?"

Brooks planted his hands on his hips like it was a normal habit of his, and got his gun hand in better position. The Glock was a second from being brandished in his hand and ready to fire.

"Oh, I heard about that on the radio. Yeah, it sounds bad. Actually, that's how we got out here. The cops directed us off the interstate. They had things buttoned up. We scraped around and thought we were taking a shortcut through all the mess. You know? Like we were trying to circle around. It seemed like a good idea."

Abe's lip tilted and twisted like he was struck with a math problem he was trying to solve. It was a facial expression that Abby had seen many times before. So had Walter and his dead older brother. They had seen it when they were children.

Abe did it involuntarily whenever he caught one of the boys in a lie.

"That's funny. My son got through the roadblocks just fine."

"There are lots of roadblocks. Maybe he went through a different one."

"That's true."

Abe's lips retracted and defaulted back to a smile.

"Of course. Of course. Makes sense."

No more words were said between them. They stood in silence until both Walter and Abby walked back out to the porch.

Brooks glanced casually in and down the hall whenever he got the chance. So far, he counted both Abe and Abby and then Walter and his wife. He also saw their son and a young girl, probably a teenager, and he guessed there was a seventh person in the living room because Walter's wife was conversing with someone, and it sounded like an adult.

Brooks guessed it was a woman. In his experience, whenever a strange man comes to the family door, most men come to the door to scope out danger, which was a good instinct, but it would make no difference. If he wanted in, then he was getting in.

Abby stepped out first. She carried two metal coffee thermoses. Steam emerged from the lip of both.

"Here, Mr. Nelson."

Abby reached out her hands, offering both thermoses to Brooks.

He ignored her at first because she had called him by his alias. It slipped his mind.

Abe noticed.

"Jim?"

Brooks course-corrected and took both thermoses against his instincts because now both his hands were occupied, which would've been smart by the Whites—if they had intended to do it. They didn't. He knew that.

"Oh, sorry, ma'am. What's this?"

"I brought you a hot coffee to keep you warm out here in this nastiness. Plus, a second one to bring to your friend."

"Thank you, ma'am. That's very kind of you."

"Not a problem."

Walter showed his truck keys to all of them.

"Let's get going. You don't want to miss Triple-A."

"Okay. I'm right behind you," Brooks said and turned and smiled at Abe and Abby.

"Thanks for being so kind. I'll send the thermoses back with your son."

Abe nodded.

"You get yourself back to your vehicle and keep warm."

Abby said, "Don't worry about the thermoses if you don't finish the coffee. Those are our beaters. They're not important. We got plenty. We drink a lot of coffee out here."

"Thanks again."

Walter stepped past his mother and father and off the porch. He walked out to the newer Tundra and got in the driver's side. Brooks followed and didn't look back. He opened the passenger's side. The first thing he did was stick the thermoses into the truck's cup holders to free his hands. Then he got in, making sure that his Glock didn't come out from under his coat. He was forced to sit on it haphazardly. He couldn't adjust it. That might give it away to Walter. He left his seatbelt off.

Walter fired up the ignition. The Tundra started right up, with no delays because of cold weather. It sounded vibrant and alive and built to last, perfect for Brooks's needs. He took note.

Walter slipped his seatbelt on. He pulled the gear into drive, and they slid off.

A minute later, the truck climbed uphill from the farmhouse side. The men were not speaking, but the seatbelt sensor kicked on with an annoying chime, and a dash light flashed on. The noise filled the silence.

Brooks did nothing.

He didn't put his belt on.

Walter cleared his throat.

Nothing.

Walter cleared his throat again.

Nothing. No movement.

Brooks didn't put his belt on.

The truck drove out of sight of the farmhouse.

"You mind putting your seatbelt on?"

Nothing.

Walter continued to drive forward. He eased up on the gas a bit, hoping that the reduction in speed would cut off the seatbelt sensor, but it didn't. Once the sensor was triggered, only buckling the other seatbelt would cut it off. Like a barking dog, it wouldn't stop.

"Buckle up, please."

No response.

"That sound is so annoying. So, buckle up."

Nothing.

Walter stayed quiet as the Tundra climbed to the top of the hill and then over it and picked up speed on the way down. The seatbelt sensor squawked gallingly.

As they went downhill, he couldn't take it anymore.

"Sir, please fasten the seatbelt. That sensor is never gonna stop till you do."

Brooks looked over at him cryptically.

"Oh. Sure. No problem."

Brooks reached his right hand back behind him like he was going to grab the belt. He didn't grab it.

Instead, he came out with his Glock and shoved it hard into Walter's ear. The whole thing was so fast Walter didn't know it was a gun until he felt the cold nylon-based polymer end of the muzzle.

"What is this?"

"Shut up!"

Walter took his foot off the gas.

"Keep going!"

Walter did as instructed. The truck continued to descend the hill and the drive. It bounced and sprang.

"Slow it down a bit."

"You said, keep going."

Brooks stared at him.

"It's just as easy for me to pull this trigger, splatter your brains all over that window, and kick you out and drive myself as it is to let you live."

Walter froze. His hands gripped the steering wheel at the ten and two o'clock positions. He stared straight ahead as if he kept Brooks out of his peripheral vision. The man and the gun would disappear like a nightmare he wanted to wake up from.

Brooks pushed the gun harder.

"Are you paying attention?"

"Yes!"

"Good. Drive straight."

"Okay. Yes."

Walter drove the rest of the way down to the backroad. The truck came to a stop at the mailbox.

"Which way, Jim?"

"Brooks."

"What?"

"That's my name. Not Jim."

"Okay, Brooks. Which way?"

"Go straight."

"Straight?"

Brooks pointed with his free hand at the abandoned farm driveway down the road.

"There."

"Pine Farms?"

"The what?"

"The Pines. They used to live there."

"Whatever. Go that way. Take it slow."

Walter took his foot off the brake and then gassed slowly like he was told. He drove over bumps and crossed the backroad, and drove to the end of the Pines' drive.

Brooks fished his free hand into his pocket and jerked out his radio. He thumbed the knob to switch the radio on. Static crackled.

He clicked the talk button.

"Jargo. It's me. I'm coming home."

A second passed, and a voice came over the air.

"Who you got with ya?"

"One of them."

"Affirmative."

Brooks slipped the radio back into his pocket, and he retracted his gun hand. He rested it on his lap.

"Keep going. Don't think that you are out of danger. There's a sniper rifle trained on you right now."

Walter didn't question. Instead, he leaned forward and looked up at the barn in the distance.

It was automatic. He never served in the military as his brother had, but he was country-boy enough to know about rifles. The barn's loft was the best setup for a sniper's nest.

Brooks noticed.

"It's a Barrett fifty cal. You know what that is?"

Brooks lied. Jargo's rifle didn't fire fifty-caliber bullets, but no reason to tell Walter that.

Walter leaned back. His shaking increased.

"I don't. Not exactly. I've never seen one."

Brooks chuckled.

"Of course you've never seen one. They're expensive. Therefore, not practical for a guy like you. Know how much?"

Walter didn't answer.

Brooks reached the Glock up fast and poked him in the arm with the muzzle.

Walter answered.

"How much?"

"Close to ten grand. Not quite ten grand, but close to ten grand."

"That's expensive."

"Sure is."

They continued until the Tundra got close to the farmhouse and the barn.

Walter saw the sniper in the loft. It was the guy from the radio, Jargo.

Suddenly, the barn doors sprang open, and the abandoned farmhouse's front door opened wide.

Five men appeared from different directions, all but one were armed. Walter saw assault rifles and two shotguns.

The only one not armed was an older man decked out all in white as if he just stepped out of a store's showroom with brand-new winter clothes.

Walter asked, "What's this?"

Brooks didn't answer him.

Instead, he said, "Park, right there."

Walter pulled the Tundra up and over towards the barn doors, stopped twenty feet back, and parked where Brooks had pointed out.

"Kill the engine."

Walter cut off the engine and pulled out the keys.

Brooks showed him his free hand, opened it up. It was big and massive, like a baseball glove.

"Keys."

Walter shivered and held the keys up and dropped them into Brooks's hand. The moment they hit his skin, Walter felt that his life was over, as if giving up those keys destroyed the last ounce of hope he had to escape.

"Get out."

Walter got out, and Brooks followed. They closed their doors one after the other and met in front of the truck's grille.

Walter held his hands up in the air like he was surrendering to police at gunpoint.

The old man in white walked out slowly, his hands up at eye level and visible as if he was giving a peace offering.

"Hello, neighbor."

Walter said nothing. He just stood in front of the truck's grille, hands up, shaking.

Abel walked over and stopped eight feet away from Walter. Brooks kept his Glock out and down by his side, his finger on the trigger.

"What's your name, neighbor?"

Walter said nothing.

Abel looked at Brooks.

"He mute or something?"

"No. He can speak."

Abel stared at Walter.

"Walter White."

Flack stood with a shotgun in the barn's doorway. He chuckled out loud.

Abel turned to look at him.

"Something funny, soldier?"

"Walter White."

Abel shrugged. Flack looked at Cucci and Tanis, and then Brooks.

"No one?"

"What?" Abel asked.

"Walter White? It's from that show. About the drug-dealing school teacher?"

No one spoke.

"Never mind. Sorry for interrupting, General."

Abel turned back to Walter.

He offered his arms like he wanted a hug.

Walter stayed where he was.

Abel said, "Come on. We're neighbors and neighbors hug."

"We are? They do?"

"Mr. White, are you a man of scripture?"

Walter nodded.

"Well, so are we. The Bible says: *Love your neighbor as yourself. There is no commandment greater than these.*"

Walter looked around slowly. He saw the faces of each man, except Jargo. They stared back at him intensely. He saw nothing but insanity. They saw nothing but sheer terror.

He stepped forward, slowly, and stopped in front of Abel.

Abel reached out fast, grabbed him, pulled him in, and embraced him.

"Good. Good. We were neighbors, and now we're friends."

Walter shook. Abel let him go and stepped back.

"Now, from one neighbor to another, we need your help."

"You do?"

"Yes. See, we have a problem. Several, in fact. But the most pressing one is we need wheels."

Walter stayed standing, but he felt his knees shake. His body felt heavy.

"Take my truck."

"Oh, thank you. That's kind."

Abel stared at him, hard like he had another request, but didn't speak it.

Walter asked, "What?"

"I'm afraid we may need more than that.

"What else do you need?"

"We may need hostages. A little insurance. And this is a maybe. I haven't decided yet."

"No. No. Take me. Leave my family out of this."

Just then, Jargo called down from his sniper's nest.

"Cops! Cops!"

Abel pulled out his radio, spoke, and waited for Jargo to respond.

"Where?"

"At the end of the drive."

"Boys. We got company. Grab cover."

Abel got off the radio, and his men hopped to action. Jargo slipped back into a prone position, making sure his rifle was out of sight. Cucci and Tanis took positions on the outside of the house. Flack slipped back into the barn, closed the doors behind him.

Brooks stayed where he was.

He asked, "What about his truck?"

Abel stared at the truck.

"No time to hide it now."

"What do you want to do?"

Abel pointed a long, bony finger at Walter.

"Get rid of them."

"What?"

"Get rid of the cops, or we will pay your family a visit."

They all heard tires on snow and gravel climbing the bottom of the drive.

"They're headed this way."

"Do it! Get rid of the cops, or you're dead. Your family's dead."

Walter stood frozen.

Brooks walked closer to him and grabbed his forearm. He squeezed it hard. Walter felt instant pain. Brooks pulled it up into the air and then clamped his fingers down on pressure points in Walter's wrist.

Walter belted out in pain.

Brooks reached his other hand out and held Walter's truck keys out, and dangled them in front of his face.

"I've got your keys. You say something. You tip the cops off. I see you wink or smile or twitch—anything. I'll take the keys and slip into your house. I'll kill the old man first. Then I'll have my way with the women. All the women. Including that peachy teenager. Got it?"

Walter swallowed hard.

"I got it! I got it!"

"Good. Get rid of them."

Brooks released him and pocketed the keys. He went off to the side of the driveway to a cluster of trees and a rotten fence. Walter followed him with his eyes until Brooks was gone from sight. He blended into the trees and brush like a chameleon, like something out of a nightmare.

Abel headed into the house and stopped in the foyer. He left the door ajar.

Walter saw his face. Abel winked at him and put one finger on his lips and mouthed a single, taunting word.

"Sh."

30

Adonis rubbed her forehead, brushed over the bandage on her brow, and closed her eyes tight like her brain would explode from frustration. She thought of that thing people always said about someone who rides horseback for the first time. Something about not the first day or the day after, but the third day was when you felt it.

The gash on her head didn't hurt; none of her cuts hurt, not compared to what hurt her on the inside. The thought of all the dead agents, the injured, the Athenian children, and Dorsch cut her deep. And they would haunt her for days, weeks, months—hell, probably for the rest of her life. But she couldn't think about that right now. She couldn't worry about the dead. She had to focus. She was running out of time. Soon the ATF would replace her; the FBI would get involved, and her chance to make it all right on her own terms would vanish.

Even if she was off-script here, eventually, the FBI would catch up to her. If they found out what she was doing, they'd put her in cuffs. Her window was closing.

She, Shep, and the others were posted up at one of the road-blocks intersecting the borders of Spartan County and Interstate Seventy-Seven, with North Carolina within seeing distance.

Both Adonis and Shep stood outside of his cruiser, parked on the shoulder ahead of long stretches of backed-up cars, crossing over into North Carolina. Swan, James, and Ramirez stood around outside the helicopter that was parked off in an abandoned parking lot for a derelict shopping mall. The stores were all gone. Most of the windows were boarded up and covered in graffiti.

Adonis had told everyone to stop for ten minutes. It wasn't to take a break, but for her to regroup and think of the next step before she had no steps left.

Ramirez spoke on his phone. Swan and James paced back and forth with their weapons ready. They were more eager than she to get the job done.

Shep sat on the hood of his cruiser, smoking a cigarette, which might've been against department regulation for the South Carolina Highway Patrol. They probably had a subsection of a paragraph about dealing with the public that prohibited smoking in public areas like the side of the road. Adonis didn't know and didn't care.

North Carolina State Troopers and Highway Patrol cars lined up on the other side as a precaution. South Carolina police handled the stops and checked IDs and inquired of vehicle occupants' identities and destinations. They took special care of vans and SUVs and any vehicles with multiple male passengers.

The light bar on Shep's cruiser flashed, bathing Adonis's dark skin in blue light. She looked around, frozen in her own thoughts. The way she saw it, the only thing she could do until her phone rang again was to get back out there.

They came to the end of their hastened search when they hit the roadblock. They reached the end of the dragnet's radius and still no sign of Abel, not even a clue. She was sure that Abel had come the way they came. The path they took was the only one that made sense. It was the straightest line to the North Carolina border.

Adonis joined Shep at the hood of the cruiser and sat down next to him.

Shep said, "Think we're done?"

"I don't know."

"What time are they supposed to be shutting you down?"

Adonis flicked her wrist like she was going to check the time on her watch again, but she didn't look. She knew it was gone. She reached into her jacket and took out her phone, and stared at the clock.

It was after ten in the morning.

"Now. I think."

"Why haven't they called you yet?"

"Who knows?" she said, but they had been calling. She just ignored the calls. She felt bad for lying to Shep about it.

Shep wasn't stupid. He took a drag from his cigarette and offered it to Adonis, like passing a peace pipe around a Native campfire.

She nodded and took it, and took a long drag from it.

He asked, "They gonna fire you?"

"Oh yeah. Probably."

"Even if we catch this bastard?"

"I don't know. Probably. If I catch him, maybe they'll give me a glowing recommendation to be a crossing guard or something."

"Hey, I was a crossing guard once."

"You were?"

"Yeah. Way back in the day. I did it for a week."

"Why? Was it court-ordered or something? What, did you sleep with the boss's wife?"

Shep chuckled and shook his head.

"It was a volunteer thing. I did it at my son's school."

She nodded, but didn't quite understand why he volunteered to work as a crossing guard.

Shep took out his cell phone and clicked through apps and pulled up a photo. He raised it to show Adonis. She took the phone from him and stared at a photo of a young boy.

"He looks happy."

Shep took the phone back, stared one last time, and pocketed it.

"He is. He's full of life. You got kids?"

"No kids. I'm not very good with them, to be honest."

"Oh. That's probably not true. You just don't have any of your own. Once you have kids, your instincts will take over, and you'll discover a whole side of yourself you didn't know existed."

She nodded along because she had nothing to say to that. They were smoking the rest of the cigarette when Ramirez came striding over from the empty parking lot and the helicopter. He wasn't running, but he was moving fast like it was urgent.

Adonis hopped up off the hood of the car and handed the cigarette back to Shep.

She stepped forward about six paces from the car.

Ramirez stopped dead in front of her. He panted a couple of breaths, and then he spoke.

"Adonis. I called the Spartan County Sheriff's Office like you told me."

"And?"

"They got a report of some squatters at one of the farms."

"Squatters?"

"Someone saw lights on at a farm that's been abandoned for years."

"They check it out?"

Ramirez shook his head.

"I doubt it. They're spread pretty thin. They said they would get to it when they got to it."

Adonis's face lit up with a glimmer of hope for the first time since her nightmare had begun.

"You got the address?"

"I do."

Shep stood up off the hood and joined them.

He asked, "Out there, the address is pretty meaningless. How are we going to find it?"

Ramirez said, "I know exactly where it is. They said it's across from a Christmas tree farm. I saw it when we were in the air. It's not far. You can follow us from the ground."

Adonis said, "Let's get rolling!"

Adonis and Shep jumped into Shep's cruiser. He fired it up, and they both buckled their seatbelts. Ramirez ran back to the helicopter and started it up. Swan and James loaded back into the rear. The helicopter was in the air, rotating until it faced the correct direction. It flew off, and Shep and Adonis followed, hitting the gas, maxing out their speed when they could. Shep hit the switch for the light bars. They left the sirens quiet and sped down winding dirt roads, taking curves as fast as they could.

31

THE LAW ENFORCEMENT vehicle stopped at the end of the drive to the Pine Farms, as if the officer behind the wheel wasn't sure he had the right address. But in the end, he turned the wheel, and the vehicle's tires climbed over a bump of snow and dirt and onto the track.

The vehicle wasn't a South Carolina Highway Patrol car. It wasn't Shep behind the wheel, either. The vehicle was a truck, and the driver was an older man with white stubble on his face and bags under his eyes. He had gone to work the day before clean-shaven and ready for another slow, uneventful South Carolina day at the beginning of winter, before the ATF bungled a simple late-night raid on some crazy cult's compound up in Carbine. Now, he's been up all night trying to run his department.

The driver was Sheriff Henry Rourke. He drove a Chevy Silverado marked with both a Chevy emblem on the grille in front of the engine and Spartan County Sheriff decals on both outer door panels.

Sheriff Henry Rourke liked to tell people he was close to retirement age. He was a little past it, which was a drum that his opponents constantly banged on. Rourke was well known. In Spartan County, clout counted for more than technicalities of a man's age. Besides the clout, he had no intention of retiring. He would ride his clout-wave until it killed him.

Normally, Rourke wore a ball cap on his head, but not while driving or when indoors. He was from a generation that still sported Southern manners, which dictated that a man always took his hat off indoors, even inside a truck.

He wore the same uniform design he always wore, which was brown on brown, with a heavy blue winter coat that had a warm wool lining. He unbuckled his seatbelt at the mouth of the drive to let his belly have a little breathing room—not too much was required, but enough for his wife to make comments about him quitting doughnuts. At least, that's what she used to comment on when she was alive. But she had been gone for about three years now.

Rourke drove up the track. So far, all was quiet. He saw no sign of disturbance at the farm, but he wasn't far enough along yet. Since Pine Farms had been abandoned near ten years ago, no one kept it up. Therefore, the trees over the drive were overgrown, and the grass was so high that even under cover of snow, long blades stuck out like frozen hands sticking out of the ice of a frozen lake.

But, what was strange was that there were fresh tracks in the snow, driving up the long drive to the farm.

Rourke wound along the drive, following the tracks in the snow, cut through the overhanging trees, and arrived at the mouth of the driveway, which opened to a large flat area with the Pines' long-abandoned farmhouse and their old barn. Right in front of the barn was a white Toyota Tundra. The engine was off. At first, he saw no one around, but then he saw Walter White standing off to one side of the truck, awkwardly, cumbersomely. Rourke thought this because White wasn't on the driver's side or leaning against the hood as a normal person would be. His placement on the track was of a man waiting for someone to drive up, but his posture—his demeanor—was like someone who had gotten caught doing something he wasn't supposed to be doing, in a place he wasn't supposed to be.

Rourke had known the Whites for years, as he did many of his constituents. He had known Walter since he was a boy. Being from a good family doesn't mean a man is immune to doing bad things. And White looked like he was up to no good.

Rourke pulled the truck up to the rear of the Tundra and slipped the gear into neutral and kicked the emergency brake all the way down. He leaned forward to the right and reached over to the dashboard. He grabbed his lucky ball cap and slipped it on over his silver hair, and returned to an upright position. He left the engine running and got out of the truck.

His gun was holstered on his right hip. Rourke was old, but not slow, not with his weapon. He unbuttoned the safety catch on the holster in case he needed to quick-draw.

Rourke made a mental note that it was now loose in the holster like he might forget it. Since getting a little older and a little more forgetful, he started making a habit of ticking off things from a mental checklist. Now it was second nature to him to tick off his mental checklist. He especially did this in potentially dangerous situations. Although this didn't appear to be dangerous, it still made the cut—better safe than sorry. You didn't make it as sheriff, lasting as long as Rourke had, unless you were vigilant. It didn't matter that Walter White was there or not. If his own mother had been there, Rourke still would've done it.

His ball cap was also on his mental checklist. The hat was a Yankees ball cap he had owned since the nineteen-eighties. It served no law enforcement function, like the bulletproof vest he wore under his uniform shirt or the holstered Glock 22 on his hip or his badge. In fact, the Yankees ball cap was frowned upon by the people in the county because the Atlanta Braves were the region's baseball team of choice. But Rourke wasn't one to conform for the sake of conforming. He was from North Carolina, which had more Yankees fans than Braves fans.

His Yankees cap was his good luck charm. Every time he didn't wear it, bad luck followed him. He saw it as just as much a part of his uniform as his Glock 22. If forced to choose between them, he might take the hat over the gun.

Rourke closed the driver's side door and put the ball cap on, and slipped his hands into his coat pockets.

He walked halfway around the nose of his Silverado toward Walter and met him in front of the Chevy emblem on the grille.

"Mr. White, what you doing here?"

White was quiet. He looked like he was at a loss for words. His mouth opened to speak, but all that fell out was a bunch of vowels at first.

Rourke asked, "Walt, you all right?"

"Oh yeah. So sorry. I guess this looks odd. Me being here."

"Depends on what you're talking about. What're we talking about here?"

"I came over here to run off the squatters. I called you earlier to let you know I saw lights."

Rourke nodded along.

"That's why I'm here now. I'm checking it out."

"Where're your deputies?"

"They're around."

Walter looked right toward a cluster of trees and to where he saw Brooks vanish. It was a glance. He didn't turn his head, not completely, but the gesture was noticed. Then he looked back at Rourke.

White said, "I feel like such a fool."

"Why? What's going on?"

"I saw nothing here. I searched the whole property."

"Why did you do that?"

"My dad. He got all upset. He kept complaining about it taking you too long to come out here. You know how surly he is."

Rourke nodded, but he didn't know that. He also didn't know it to be true. He couldn't remember the last time he had talked to Abe White and not had the man behave pleasantly.

White said, "You know what happened was I was driving in late last night. Probably tired. I should've stopped off the road some-where and got a motel room. Anyway, I heard the whole thing on the radio. You know the explosions and standoff in Carbine? Think it made me paranoid—a little. When I was passing here, I thought I saw something, but it was just a reflection. There's no one here."

"A reflection?"

"Yeah. From off the glass. One of the windows reflected my high beams—is all. It was nothing. Sorry to waste your time with this."

"What're you doing here now?"

"I told you. I thought I'd come over and scare off the squatters, but there's no one here."

White held his arms up like he was presenting the farmhouse to the sheriff.

He said, "See. No one's here."

"You just got here? Just now?"

White nodded.

Rourke looked past him at the farmhouse and the windows. His eyes scanned over it. He saw no one. He saw no evidence of anything other than what White was claiming.

"You came over here to chase off squatters?"

"That's what I said."

"Unarmed?"

White glanced back at the tree cluster.

He said, "Yeah. Dumb me. I forgot to bring a rifle."

Rourke nodded along. But in his mental checklist of things to suspect, he checked a box right there.

"You already checked the place out, huh?"

"Yeah. Oh. See that glass over there?"

"The windows?"

"Yeah. The windows. My headlights reflected off them this morning. That's what I saw. No reason for you to even be here. Sorry, I wasted your time."

Rourke looked at him.

"Yeah. You said all that already."

White was quiet.

Rourke asked, "You been drinking, Walt?"

"Oh, no, sir. Not me."

"So, nobody's here? You already checked the whole place?"

White repeated, "Sorry to waste your time."

Rourke looked past White at the farmhouse windows, at the front door, and then at the barn.

"Nobody in the barn?"

"Nope. There's no one here."

"Okay. No reason to waste time here then."

"No. I guess not. Sorry again."

"Okay. We'd better get going then."

Rourke said it, and Walter nodded along like he agreed, but he faced a big problem. Rourke acted as though it was time to leave, but Walter couldn't leave. He didn't have his keys.

Rourke motioned to the Tundra.

"You coming?"

"You want me to ride with you?"

"No. Take your truck and go home."

Again, White looked fast to his right at the trees and brush where Brooks was supposed to be hiding. Nothing happened.

White said, "So, here's the thing."

Rourke listened.

White opened his mouth like he was going to speak. But nothing came out. He couldn't think of a way out of this. He couldn't leave with Rourke. No way would they let him. And he couldn't get in his truck and start it up. Brooks had the keys.

Before he could say a word, before he could come up with a ruse to get Rourke out of there, Brooks shot his weapon.

There was no gunshot sound, no boom. There was only a single, quiet purr that echoed across the trees like someone hitting a two-by-four against the tree's trunk.

There was only one muted gunshot. The bullet hit Rourke right in the center mass. He was flung against the grille of his truck. His Glock 22 came out in his right hand, but it faced upward.

White responded without thinking, a reaction. He grabbed the Glock with both hands and squeezed it. He didn't want Rourke to shoot it. Somewhere in the back of his mind, he knew that if that gunshot went off, his family would hear it. They might react. Abe might come to investigate. He didn't want Brooks and the others going to his house, either. He thought that if he could step in and show that he was cooperating, then maybe they would let his family stay out of it. He was wrong.

"What're you doing?" Rourke yelled. There was blood in his mouth, in his teeth. His voice was plagued with pain and agony.

His ball cap was off his head. It was back near the tire. His Glock was gone. White had swiped it from out of his hand before he could fire. He was helpless.

White stood over him with the Glock, a look of utter confusion on his face.

A tall black man came walking out of the trees to the far left. He had fired the shot that hit Rourke in the chest. The black man was holding the smoking gun.

The black man yelled out.

"Put the gun down!"

He was pointing the gun that had shot Rourke at White now.

Suddenly, four other guys appeared from out of nowhere. Rourke counted them. One wore all white as if he was some kind of high priest or something.

The man in white winter gear spoke to Walter.

"Son, drop the gun."

White didn't move. He stood there with the Glock in his hands. He was holding it the wrong way like he had never held a gun before. The business end was pointed back at himself.

White paused. He was thinking about what to do next. Brooks, Abel, Rourke, and all of them could see it on his face.

Brooks shouted.

"If you don't drop that gun, we're going to shoot you where you stand."

White looked up at the loft shutters to the barn. Rourke looked there as well. A sixth man appeared up there, holding a serious-looking sniper rifle. It looked military, like a ten-thousand-dollar piece of hardware.

Rourke kept his eyes on the sniper, who aimed down his barrel right at White's chest.

Rourke spoke in a whispered voice.

"Walter?"

White twisted fast, which scared Rourke at first. He thought for sure they would shoot him dead right then, but no one fired.

White looked down at Rourke. Tears streamed in White's eyes.

"I'm sorry," he said to Rourke.

"Walter, drop the gun. They'll kill you if you don't."

"I'm sorry. I was scared for my family."

"Just put the gun down."

"They'll kill you if I do."

"You don't know that. Put it down."

Abel said, "Mr. White, what's with the deliberations? Put the gun down."

White begged to Abel, "Don't kill him. Please?"

Abel walked slowly from out of the farmhouse and over to the parked trucks and the bleeding sheriff. Cucci and Tanis were close behind him. Abel was the only one not pointing his gun at Walter.

Abel looked at the sheriff and then at White. He raised his hand and opened his palm.

"Hand over the weapon. And I'll let him live. You have my word."

White looked into Rourke's eyes, apologetic beyond anything he could say.

Rourke nodded.

Abel inched closer.

White dropped one hand off the gun and handed it over.

Abel took it and put a bony-fingered hand on White's shoulder.

"Good choice, my boy."

Brooks approached and came up to Rourke. He stopped his boots inches from Rourke's head. He pointed his silenced gun at Rourke.

"Kill him?"

White shouted, "No! You promised!"

Abel looked at Rourke. He stuffed the Glock 22 into one of the pockets of his winter coat and fluttered the tailback off his butt. He squatted down, balancing on the soles of his boots.

He looked Rourke up and down.

Rourke was pressing at his chest hard with both hands. He was in pain from the bullet impact.

Abel reached his bony hand down and opened the sheriff's coat. He grabbed both Rourke's hands and forced them to separate from his chest. Rourke didn't fight back.

Abel looked at Rourke's brown shirt, which was pooling with blood. He reached out a long finger and tapped on the chest, getting blood on his finger.

"Bulletproof vest, huh?"

Rourke nodded.

Abel said, "An old, shit one too. You're lucky it worked at all."

Abel cocked his head like a doctor examining a wound. He grabbed both Rourke's hands once again and returned them to the wound.

"Looks like the vest saved your life," Abel said and glanced at a name patch sewed into the breast pocket of Rourke's shirt and said, "Sheriff Rourke. But your vest is old and shitty. Looks like the bullet penetrated and got you, but it's mostly superficial. The round is jammed into the vest."

Rourke said nothing.

Abel repeated, "You're lucky."

Brooks kept his weapon ready to kill the sheriff right there on the ground.

Abel stood back up and backed away. He stepped over to White and wiped the blood off his fingers onto White's coat shoulder.

"You want him to live?"

"Yes."

"You do what we say, and no one will die. Got it?"

"Yes."

"You disobey me, or one of my guys, just once, and he dies."

White swallowed hard out of relief because he thought by the way Abel talked he had abandoned the idea of taking his family hostage. That was shattered when Abel said one more thing.

Abel looked at Cucci.

"Pick him up. Take him into the barn and find out if the police know anything."

Abel saw the look of betrayal on White's face, and he added one more thing.

"Check his wounds and fix him up first. Then talk to him. That's all."

Cucci asked, "Want me to hurt him?"

"Give him some time. If he's not cooperative, then we can use other methods."

White interrupted.

"You said you would let him live."

"I didn't tell him to kill him. He's just going to have a conversation. And I wouldn't worry about what happens to him, Mr. White."

Just then, Jargo came over the radio.

"Boss?"

Abel snapped a nod at Brooks, jerked a radio out of somewhere in his white robes that White hadn't noticed, and tossed it to Brooks.

"See what he wants."

Brooks caught the radio and clicked the button. He looked up at Jargo in the barn and pulled the receiver end of the radio in front of his lips.

"What's up?"

"Helicopter! Same one from before, I think."

Abel, White, Brooks, and Tanis were all in earshot and heard it. Flack heard it off his own radio. Cucci heard it but didn't react. He had been given a direct order, and he was carrying it out. He lifted Rourke like Frankenstein's monster, carrying a victim away into the night.

Rourke didn't resist. Cucci scooped him up and carried him off into the barn.

The rest of them first looked up at Jargo, who pointed out to the northeast. Abel and White both had to spin on one foot to face that direction. Brooks and Tanis stayed where they were and looked up over the trees. Flack stepped farther out to the drive, away from the barn door and past Cucci on his way. He stopped behind Abel and looked up.

Several of the men raised their hands over their eyes. The sunlight that was there shining through the clouds beamed into their lines of sight like lasers.

They waited and searched the sky. Abel glanced at Brooks. Brooks got on the radio.

"Jargo, how far?"

"It's three klicks away, but coming on fast like they know where they're going."

Brooks looked at Abel.

"We should take it out."

A look of horror came over White's face.

Take it out, he thought.

Abel thought for a second. They didn't have the luxury of firepower heavy enough to take out a flying helicopter, not from the ground. The only possibility would be if Jargo took out the pilot. Could he do it? Sure, but not from three klicks away. But once it was a closer range, he could.

Abel made a decision.

"No. We could use the helicopter."

"How? We can't get the pipe bombs out of here by helicopter. Someone will notice a helicopter flying around."

Abel glanced at White, whose facial expression changed to an emotion that was a combination of confusion and utter terror. He heard the words. He heard the right sequence—pipe bombs.

The confusion was the same, normal, expected expression that anyone would have. The terror part came on because White realized they didn't intend to leave him alive. Before he heard those words, he thought he stood a chance of surviving. Not now.

Now, he was a dead man walking. Knowing there were pipe bombs meant he had heard too much. It may have been a slip by the one called Brooks. Whatever. It happened. He couldn't unhear it.

Abel smiled a sinister grin at him that was supposed to be reassuring, but White doubted Abel knew how to be reassuring or comforting.

Abel turned back to Brooks.

"We can find many uses for it. It'll get them off our back. For another, we can use it to get as far as possible. Just do it. Okay?"

"Sure."

Jargo came over the radio.

"Boss, what do we do?"

Brooks answered.

"Nothing. Observe only."

Brooks got off the radio and said, "We should take cover again. If they're coming for us, they'll do a sweep first."

Abel said, "Of course."

"What about the vehicles?"

"Leave them. They'll see them and stop to look."

32

SHEP PARKED the patrol cruiser past the circle drive in the spot where Walter's Tundra had been parked only twenty minutes earlier before Brooks tricked him into driving out to the road.

Shep unbuckled his seatbelt but left the car running. He looked at Adonis in the passenger seat. She undid her seatbelt and slipped her fingers into the handle to pop the door open and get out. She stopped there because Shep was looking at her, his left hand on the steering wheel. He didn't get out.

Shep was about to brief her. She knew it. Over her career, many guys like Shep, lifetime cops, had looked at her the same way before giving instructions or a warning or briefing.

He pointed the index finger on his right hand across his chest at the farmhouse in front of them.

"Listen, this is my state. These are my people. I can tell you about the people who live here. They're not gonna cooperate. Not likely. People out here don't volunteer cooperation with cops. It's just a way of life for them. If they have trouble, they take care of it themselves."

Adonis waved her free hand up in the air like she was waving off tiny, invisible rockets. Like an old west quick-draw, Adonis ripped her sidearm out of a shoulder holster padded down on her left ribcage under her breast. She pulled it faster than Shep had ever seen someone do in real life, outside of shooting competitions.

The weapon was a standard ATF Glock 22 with fourteen rounds in the magazine, and one chambered. She ejected the magazine and showed Shep the bullets.

The Glock 22 has a 7.32-inch slide length, eight inches overall from the corner of the butt to the tip of the barrel, and it looked huge in her small hands. But she held it like she had fired it a thousand times a month at the shooting range, which was true except during months when she had too much caseload to make it into the shooting range.

"You were being a really good guy before. Don't give me this you're a little lady bullshit! I'm a Resident Agent-in-Charge in the ATF and I've seen shit too. I'm not some fragile little woman who got this badge and this gun from affirmative action. I earned it. I earned this badge, and I earned every bullet in this gun. Got it?"

Shep raised both hands in the international sign of giving up like she was pointing a gun at him.

Adonis reinserted the magazine into the Glock and smacked it home. A little melodramatic, but she had learned long ago that men responded to visual aids and drama.

"Okay. Okay. I get it. I just wanted to warn you they may not cooperate with us."

Adonis re-holstered her weapon—fast, almost as fast as she had drawn it.

"Let's go."

She pulled the door handle, opened it, and got out. She closed the door behind her. Shep followed suit, and they both approached the front door. They stepped up onto the porch. Adonis took the front and center position. She rang the doorbell. They both heard the standard doorbell chime through the house. They heard scurrying footsteps, like a child's, and slow, regular footsteps, like an adult.

The door opened after the doorbell chimed and echoed through the structure and died to silence.

Standing in the doorway was a man wearing a worn, gray knit skullcap. Adonis would've guessed that underneath, he was bald, judging by the way his red hair seemed to end above the temples, where most people's continued.

Standing directly behind him was a woman who was shorter than him, shorter than Widow by nearly two feet. She had curly hair and big eyes. She glowed angelically. Standing behind both of them was an entire clan, squeezed into a foyer that opened up to a huge floor plan.

Adonis quickly counted six people in all. Everyone looked related, like members of a family tree hanging out for a family day. One woman looked different. Adonis figured she was married into the family. But everyone else looked like the same genetics, even the two children. One was a boy who pushed his way to the front to see what was happening. Adonis could see his eyes weren't on her, but were locked onto Shep's holstered sidearm. The other child was a teenage girl. She came with the rest of them to see who was at the door, but once she saw Adonis, she lost interest and turned and walked back to whatever piece of furniture she had probably been glued to before Adonis rang the doorbell.

The old man was the first to speak.

"Hello. Can I help you?"

Adonis pulled out a black leather wallet with her badge pinned into one side. The wallet was shaped the same as the badge. It was only a badge holder. There was one empty pouch on the rear for her to stuff money in. It was empty. She showed the badge to the whole family. The boy's eyes flicked from inspecting Shep's holstered gun to Adonis's badge.

"My name is Toni Adonis. I'm with the ATF."

She left off the Agent part because she wanted to seem friendly and accessible, at Shep's implied suggestion that country folk around Spartan County didn't take kindly to law enforcement.

Abe White leaned into the badge. He squinted his eyes and stared at the gold badge's blue center. He mouthed the words he read on it.

"Department of Justice. A-T-F. Special Agent."

Then he retreated to his stance and asked, "How do I know that's real?"

Adonis dropped her hand and pocketed the badge into her coat pocket.

She nodded and said, "It's real."

"Okay. What can I do you for?"

"This is Officer Pittman with the Highway Patrol."

Abe put his three fingers on his chest and introduced himself like he was teaching someone how to pronounce his name. Adonis didn't know if he was mocking, or it had been a stupid impulse. Either way, he did it.

"Abe White. And this is my family behind me. Now, why are you here?"

"Sir, how many people do you have in the house right now?"

Adonis's eyes wandered behind him; only it wasn't to recount the family. Her eyes darted behind Abe to see if there was any evidence of anyone else in the house.

Abe said, "Why do you want to know? You got a warrant?"

"Sir, we're looking for very dangerous men. We're not here because of you or your family."

The wife grabbed at Abe's arm and jerked him back.

She said, "Dangerous men? What men?"

Shep interrupted.

"Ma'am, it's urgent that we find these men."

Adonis stepped back in and raised a hand for Shep to stay quiet.

She asked, "Mrs…?"

"My name's Abby White."

"Mrs. White, we're searching for any sign of a group of very dangerous men. Did you all hear about the explosion at the Athenian Compound?"

The whole family nodded, like real-life bobbleheads.

Abe said, "We heard about it."

"Several of the men responsible for it have escaped. We believe they're in this area."

Terror overtook Abby's face. Everyone else looked at each other like they were all keeping a secret.

Adonis looked at Shep and nodded. He took out his cell phone and swiped and clicked like he was searching for something. He stopped at his Notes app and read off it.

"Do you guys have a son named Walter?"

Abby nodded so hard it looked like her bobblehead might fall off. She dug her fingers into Abe's forearm.

Abe said, "Yes. He's not here right now, though. Why?"

Shep continued to half-glance at his phone.

"Did he call Sheriff Rourke about something to do with squatters at one of the farms nearby?"

"Yes. He saw some lights on or something when he drove in late last night."

Adonis said, "Maybe the squatters are the men we're looking for."

Shep said, "They might've found one of the farms and are hiding out there."

Abby said, "Oh, my."

Adonis repeated, "How many people are on the premises? Here I mean?"

Abby said, "Six. Plus, our son. But he's out."

"Where's he?"

Abe said, "He drove off to help a gentleman who came to the door. He said he broke down, up the road."

"A man? What, man?"

Abe said, "Oh, an African fellow? He was tall. Maybe late forties."

Adonis asked, "African?"

Foster stepped forward and gently shoved her mother aside.

"He means a black guy. He wasn't from Africa. Least, he sounded American. There was no African accent or anything."

Adonis nodded and asked, "Who are you, ma'am?"

"I'm Doctor White. Just call me Foster. The one who left with the black guy is my brother, Walter."

"Okay. Where did they go?"

Abe said, "Walt took him back to his car. He said it was broken down out there on the road somewhere."

Maggie, who had been holding her son by the forearm to keep him close to her and to keep him quiet, moved Dylan back behind her, and she stepped forward. Now, four members of the White family were huddled close to the front door. Abby stepped a little to the right and hugged the wall, but the chain of White family members stepping forward forced Abe to take a step out onto the front porch. He was still in his house slippers. He felt the cold between his toes.

Maggie spoke.

"You mentioned something about dangerous men?"

Adonis said, "Yes, ma'am. Very dangerous."

"Could one of them be the tall black man?"

Adonis stayed quiet for a moment, but Maggie and the rest of the White family could see her brain searching through the dossier of bad men that she was looking for.

It only took a second for Adonis's face to register that she located one name who fit the description from her memories of Abel's files. There was a guy in his circle named Brooks. She couldn't remember his exact designation or rank or military function. There were seven primary names in his circle.

Still, recognizing the description was enough for her face to send the wrong output to the White family. Maggie reacted first. She grasped a hand to her chest, and worry overtook her face. Abby followed next. They both started speaking over each other in near hysterics.

Shep said, "Now, we said nothing, ladies. Walt is probably fine."

Abe looked at Adonis.

"We have to go get him."

Adonis reached out and grabbed both of Abe's shoulders.

"We will, sir. I promise."

Shep interrupted.

"We need to ask you a few questions first. Just quick questions."

"But my son. I told you he's out on the road with that guy."

Adonis said, "Step out here with me, sir."

Abe shivered in the cold but didn't go back to the mudroom for a coat. He folded his arms into his chest and stepped out onto the porch, and followed Adonis down to the bottom step. She led him just out of earshot of his wife and family.

"Mr. White."

"Abe. Please."

"Okay, Abe. We just came in from the road. We've already been up this way once, and we saw no broken-down car or any sign of anyone being out there on the road."

It took Abe a second to figure out what she was saying. And when he did, his face went blank, like his mind checked out right there.

"Abe, earlier, there was a call from this house to the sheriff's office."

Abe snapped out of it and looked at her.

"Yeah. My son called. He thought there might be squatters at the place down the road. As you've already mentioned."

"Right now, the sheriff isn't answering his phone. We think that may be where they are now."

"Pine Farms. That's where he called about the squatters. But all he saw were some lights on at night."

"Where's Pine Farms?"

"It's right across the main road, sort of diagonal. It's our closest neighbor. Pine Farms' driveway is probably fifty, maybe a hundred yards, mostly south of our mailbox. You can't see it from here. But it's that way."

He pointed in Pine Farms' direction.

Abe said, "It's the closest driveway over there."

"Okay."

Adonis took her phone out of her coat pocket and looked up in the sky. She said, "See that helo up there?"

Abe had back problems, so he had to wrench his entire torso back to look all the way up.

"I see it."

"He's with us. I'm gonna call him now and tell him to fly over. Okay?"

"Yes. We should call Henry too."

Adonis didn't actually call Ramirez. She texted him and talked at the same time.

"Henry?"

"He's the sheriff."

"I told you. His switchboard operator is saying he's not answering. Not his phone. Not his radio. She said that means nothing. They're slammed busy, just like the rest of us."

Adonis glanced back past Abe and saw that Shep was talking to Abby White and the sister, Foster. He wasn't paying attention to Maggie White, who just took out her own cell phone.

Adonis watched her swipe and dial a number. There were tears in her eyes.

Abe was still talking. She didn't hear what he was saying. He was mumbling.

Adonis put a hand up for Abe to wait a moment. She pushed past him and stopped a few feet short of the porch steps.

"Shep?" she called out.

Shep stopped talking to the ladies and looked back at her. Adonis pointed at Maggie.

"Cell phone!"

Shep turned and saw Maggie trying to call her husband. He stepped over and snatched up the phone.

"Hey!" Maggie called out.

"Sorry. But you can't be calling your husband right now."

"Why the hell not?"

Adonis stepped away from Abe and walked up the steps.

She said, "Mrs. White, if you call him, you might warn them. If the guy your husband left with is one of our guys, trying to make an escape or something, our best chance is to make him think that his cover isn't blown."

"Cover?" Maggie asked.

Shep said, "It's to protect your husband. You could give him away to the bad guys if you call him. That goes for your kids too. They got phones?"

Maggie spun around to look at her daughter, but Lauren wasn't there.

"Lauren!"

No answer.

Maggie stormed back into the house. She kept one hand on Dylan's arm, dragging him along with her automatically like she would never let him out of her sight. His feet touched the floor only every few steps. Shep stayed where he was. Technically, they hadn't been invited inside, but Adonis took it upon herself to follow into the house to get a better look. The wool had been pulled over her eyes too many times since last night. She wasn't just going to blindly believe a family she didn't know. So she stepped in behind Maggie, who stormed back into a huge living room and ripped her daughter's phone out of her hand.

While Maggie was busy doing that, Adonis stopped at the mudroom and took a peek inside. She pushed the door open and popped her head in. In a flash, she checked the ground for mud-covered boots. She saw the cubbies, the organization, and the names neatly printed in longhand on placement tags posted above each cubby.

She counted six muddy boots placed where she considered them to be the corresponding names of their owner. She saw Walter White's cubby. She saw that posted in front of his was a space with snow and dirt on the tile in front of it like there had been boots there before, only now they were on Walter's feet.

There was a seventh cubby with clean, freshly polished combat boots set inside the cubby. Adonis inspected the ridge between the bottom of the boots and carpeted bottom of the cubby. She could see dust edging out from underneath the boots like they hadn't been moved in ages.

Above the combat boots was a Marine uniform and the name of another son, she guessed. She realized right then that cubby wasn't a cubby at all, but a shrine to the fallen. The other son must've died in combat.

Adonis moved on from the fallen Marine's shrine and saw one last pair of muddy boots. They looked like cheap, but durable, secondhand workman's boots. They were huge. She couldn't see the label to read the exact size, but she wouldn't have been surprised if they were size fifteen. They belonged to a big man, and so far, she had seen no one in the house who fit them. She wondered if the missing son was a big guy. Maybe he had worn those boots when he came in from his ride the night before and left with a clean pair on. It was possible. However, it wasn't likely because inside of the cubby labeled Walter, there was a pair of house shoes, and they were no bigger than a size ten.

So, who owned the muddy boots?

"Agent Adonis?" Abby said.

Adonis turned and saw the mother standing behind her.

"Oh, I'm sorry. I got curious."

Abby nodded.

Abe stepped in and asked about the helicopter. Adonis nodded and returned to the foyer. She didn't ask permission to stay inside. She took out her phone and completed the text message to Ramirez.

She looked at Abe and asked, "Pine Farms is the one in that direction?"

She pointed southwest to confirm the right direction. Trust, but verify was imprinted in her ATF DNA.

Abe nodded.

"That way. That's what I said."

"Okay. I'm sending my guy to do a flyover," she repeated.

Both Abby and Abe thanked her.

"No need. If Walter's there with the guys we're looking for, my guy will tell us in a minute. Everything's going to be fine. We're going to get him back. That's our top priority here," Adonis lied.

Adonis walked out of the foyer, back onto the porch. She nodded at Shep and told him about the flyover. Then she turned back to Abe and asked him a question.

"Mr. White, you told me that your family members were the only people in the house?"

"That's right."

Adonis asked, "Who's the big guy?"

33

WIDOW WOKE FROM A DEEP SLEEP, albeit not that long, but his previous double life as a cop for NCIS forced him to master the power nap, a vital tool. He woke to feel boosted energy levels as much as someone who had slept a full eight hours.

Although there was a table alarm clock on the nightstand next to the bed, it only provided the time, which was ten forty-five. He guessed it was in the morning since it was gray out and not a black night. The problem with abruptly waking up from a deep sleep was that he couldn't tell what day it was right off. The brain needs time to orient itself.

Part of him assumed it was the next day, after his huge breakfast with the Whites. But that couldn't be right because he still felt satiated, full, and he didn't remember going to the toilet. If he had slept since the morning before, then surely he would've gotten up for the bathroom at least once. He was a healthy specimen of a man, but he was older. And no one over the age of thirty-five has a bladder that good. No one's bladder is immune to aging.

Therefore, he realized it was the same morning.

Widow slid his legs and feet around. His bare feet landed on the floor. The carpet felt nice between his toes, warm and comfortable. He ran his toes over it like a dog scratching an itch. He wasn't ashamed. He was as primitive a man as they come. It was the simple pleasures in life that Widow appreciated.

He blinked, adjusting his vision, shaking himself awake. He ran both his hands over his face and then up through his hair. He tousled it to make what the kids called the bedhead look.

He looked around the room and saw the dead Marine's clothes where he left them. He decided maybe he should get up, even though he hadn't slept long. But if he went back to sleep, then he would end up being a nocturnal creature for the next several days until he could readjust his body back to sleeping at night.

Widow's favorite time of day was early morning. It coincided with coffee time, even though all times were coffee times.

He stood up, in his underwear and socks, and stretched himself all the way out. From his fingertips down to his toes, he felt the stretch. He let out a yawn and approached the closet and the borrowed clothes.

He stopped before he got there because he heard a sound. It was faint at first, but grew louder. It sounded like distant humming, like a giant industrial fan had just been switched on.

The sound grew louder. He recognized it. It was the whopping of helicopter blades. It was over the Whites' farm. He was certain.

Widow stayed in his underwear and socks and walked away from the closet to one of the windows. He stepped to one side near the curtain and pulled it aside. He tugged between two blinds and looked up and out.

His eyes scanned the sky. He saw nothing but light snowfall and white and gray overcast. He waited, listening to the rotor blades. They grew closer. He saw the helicopter. It was circling the farm, maybe sixty-five meters overhead.

He only glimpsed it because of the grayness, but it was there, big and black, like a giant house fly, buzzing overhead.

He saw no tail number, not a visible one, anyway. He guessed the helicopter was a Bell 205, or as he knew it, a UH-1, which was the military designation for the same large transport helicopter. It was often used by military forces for transporting attack teams.

The helicopter's presence over the farm meant there were probably armed law enforcement agents on board. How many was anyone's guess. But it was safe to assume there was more than one guy. But from what agency? There was no official designation on the bird. FBI maybe? Which meant that if the Bell 205 was like the UH-1, it sat two crew members and thirteen passengers, making a potential of fifteen armed Feds coming for someone.

That can't be for me, Widow thought.

Without realizing it, he crossed his fingers and hoped it wasn't for him.

He watched out the window for a long moment as the Bell 205 made a third and then a fourth circle around the farm. Then he heard another sound. It was the front doorbell.

Widow arched an eyebrow involuntarily. He craned his head toward where he thought the front door was located from his position and looked out the window. He pushed his head against the blinds to see better, but it was no good. He wasn't at the front side of the house. In fact, he wasn't on the side of the house that he had thought because he saw nothing out the window but rolling hills with long sections of growing Christmas trees and snow. He was at the back corner of the house.

Widow stepped back from the window and retreated to the bed. He thought about what he should do. He decided it would be best to go downstairs. His best guess was that the helicopter had something to do with the Athenian thing. It made little sense to send in a black helicopter and armed Feds for him, just because he threw a bad guy off a roof. Then again, depending on the federal agency that was using the Bell 205, it was plausible. If it was the FBI, they liked to use their toys as much as the Navy. They might come all the way out here and search for him door-to-door.

Whatever the reason the cops were out and about wasn't the fault of the Whites.

Widow put on the borrowed clothes and his own underwear. He slipped on a fresh pair of socks and headed out the door.

At the bottom of the staircase, he was surprised that no one noticed him, except for Lauren, who sat on one of the sofas near the center of the living room. She folded her arms the moment she saw him step off the bottom step. She didn't make eye contact. She stared at a calming fire that burned in the fireplace.

Widow slipped past her and walked down the hall toward the voices. Everyone was out front. Just then, he stopped and listened beyond the voices, past the sounds of the crackling fire, and away from the creaking sounds of the old, wintry farmhouse. He heard nothing else but rustling wind, and he realized that the helicopter's rotor sounds were gone as if it had flown away.

He continued down the hall and stepped out onto the edge of the foyer. He stopped in his socks in the doorway and realized that he had forgotten the house shoes upstairs.

On the front porch, Widow counted seven people, none of them Walter White. He was missing. There were two new faces—a man and a woman, both law enforcement, obviously. The man looked like the avatar for everyone's first thought of what a patrolman would look like. He was fit, approaching middle age, and seasoned. The woman was a different matter altogether. Widow knew she was no street cop. She carried herself with both a professional and a bureaucratic way about her. Immediately, that told Widow she had been through the Quantico wringer, as he had, once upon a time. He didn't know her credentials exactly, but he would bet all the coffee in the world that her career had started in a classroom in Quantico, or somewhere comparable.

The woman was a Fed, no doubt about it. But from which American alphabet agency, he would only be guessing. The first guess would be FBI. But if she was here about the Athenian thing and not for him, then she was ATF.

Everyone stared at Widow, including the Quantico woman.

She quick-turned and faced Widow directly.

"Who's this?" she asked, with alarm in her voice. He saw her right hand grab the middle of an open coat and rest there. It was an odd placement, but he knew exactly why she put it there. Under her coat, a gun waited inside a holster on a shoulder rig.

"I thought you said there was no one else in the house?" she said.

Abby turned to Abe and stared at him. Abe blinked twice like he had forgotten who Widow was, and then he spoke.

"Oh, sorry. This is Jack. Ah…"

Abe trailed off, and Foster saw her father drawing a blank. She stepped in to help him out.

"Cousin Jack. He drove in with Walter late last night. Father didn't know he was here. I saw him come in. He went right to sleep. Long drive. Isn't that right?"

"That's right. What's going on?"

Widow put a hand out, instinctively thinking Adonis was going to shake it. He glanced up to the sky and saw the tail end of the helicopter he'd heard flying off in a southwest direction.

Where's it going? he thought.

Adonis stuck out her left hand, opposite of Widow's, and offered it up for a handshake, like a counteroffer. She wouldn't remove her right hand from where it was. That was her gun hand. Widow smiled and reframed his handshake with his left.

His hand consumed hers like a python, coiling and constricting around unsuspecting prey. She squeezed hard. As soon as she saw her hand vanish in his, she doubled her effort and squeezed as hard as she could. She stared up into his eyes and realized that he didn't even notice, which pissed her off in a way. She said nothing about it.

"Cousin Jack, my name's Agent Adonis. I'm with the ATF."

Adonis didn't introduce Shep, and she didn't go into the whole story again.

"Widow. Jack Widow."

"Right."

"Most people just call me, Widow. Except the family here. A pleasure to meet you. So, what the hell's going on?"

Adonis pulled her hand away, which was much easier than she had thought it would be. Her first impression of Widow was that he was one of those guys who held onto a handshake long enough to be considered harassment. She had faced those kinds of hand-shakers before. Widow wasn't one of them. His hand-shake was firm but gentle. It seemed almost like he had practiced it to get it that way.

Maggie spoke first, still holding onto Dylan's wrist.

"It's Walter. They think he's with some men from last night."

Foster said, "The Athenian explosion thing. You know?"

"What about it?"

Abe answered first. He held Abby in one arm, comforting her. Widow could see that all this talk about it was making her uneasy.

"According to Adonis, several of the leaders went missing."

"They escaped after the explosion?"

Adonis said, "They may have escaped before. The explosion might've been a diversion."

Abe said, "There was a guy who came by. You were napping. He said he and his business partner broke down on the road…"

Suddenly, Widow knew the rest of the story before they explained it. To save time, and perhaps because he may have been lacking in some manners, he interrupted.

"Walter took him back to his car?"

"Yes."

Adonis asked Widow a question.

"You rode in with him last night?"

"Yes."

"Before the explosion?"

"After. It was on the radio."

"Did you see these squatters Walter called the sheriff about?"

"No. Neither of us saw anyone. Just lights on in what's supposed to be an abandoned farm."

Adonis nodded right as her phone was buzzing. There was an incoming text message. She looked at her phone. She saw the message, read it, and turned back to Shep.

"Come on. Let's go."

Shep nodded and started back to the police cruiser they came in. He stopped halfway and called back to Adonis. She looked, and he showed her he was still holding Maggie's phone. He tossed it to her. She caught it and walked to Abe and handed it to him with one final order.

"Keep your family off the phone. Stay here. We'll be back."

"Is it them? Did your guy see Walter?" Abe asked, desperate for information.

Adonis was already running back to the car. She shouted back to him over her shoulder.

"Just stay here. Stay off the phone. Lock your doors. We'll be back. Everything'll be fine."

Adonis hopped into the cruiser, and Shep kicked it into drive, and they were off a lot faster than they had arrived. Snow kicked up behind the tires, gusting into the air, and the cruiser vanished back down the drive.

Widow stepped farther down the porch, away from the family. He reached out two hands and leaned on the hand railing. He looked up at the sky for the helicopter. It wasn't there. All he saw were blackbirds and gray clouds.

Behind him, he heard Maggie trying to keep it together. He heard the concern in Abby's voice that was quickly receding into motherly worry. Foster comforted her mother and then Maggie, staying strong. Abe stared at his family and stayed quiet. But it was Dylan who spoke.

"Don't worry, Mom. They'll bring Dad back. They got a helicopter."

Abe looked back at Widow, who stayed leaning against the porch handrails with no coat on. He looked deep in thought.

"Fossie, take Mom and everyone back into the house like Adonis told us."

Foster said, "Dad, what about you?"

"I'll be right in."

Everyone had disappeared back into the family home except for Abe and Widow. Abe walked over and leaned next to Widow, but then he returned to a full stance because he felt Widow towering over him.

Abe said, "What do you think, Widow?"

Widow breathed in.

"I wish I would've heard this other guy ring the doorbell. I could've gone in Walter's place."

"He didn't ring the doorbell. He knocked."

"Why?"

Abe shrugged.

"Some people aren't doorbell ringers. Some people are just knockers. I guess."

Widow said, "Maybe. Tell me about him."

"He was a tall black guy. He was big. Not as big as you, but big, like he had a lot of brawn."

"He look dangerous?"

"He was very pleasant, but sure. He looked like he could handle himself."

Widow stayed quiet.

Abe asked, "What're you thinking?"

Widow returned to a full stance and pointed down at the phone in Abe's hand.

"You got internet on that phone?"

"Of course. They all come with it."

"Does it got a passcode?"

Abe looked at the screen and touched it.

"I don't think so."

"May I use it?"

"Sure."

Abe handed him the phone. Widow took it and looked at Abe.

Abe asked, "What?"

"There any coffee left?"

"I can make some."

"Okay. Let's go inside."

34

THE TEXT MESSAGE on Adonis's phone read out the vehicle descriptions that Ramirez saw from the sky, parked in the Pine Farms' driveway. It was followed by the suggestion that they should call it in.

Adonis replied only to the second message with a firm NO!

"What now?" a second message on her phone read.

She replied, "See anyone at all?"

Ramirez replied, "No. But lots of hiding places."

"What about a place to land?"

"On the farm? I can land about fifty yards away from the driveway."

"No. For a raid?"

There was a pause. Shep drove out down the Cherokee Hills Farm driveway and stopped at the end by the mailbox. He paused there for her to give him instructions on what was next.

Adonis said nothing to him. She just waited and stared at her phone. Then Ramirez texted back.

"There's an open field near some broken fence. By the road. To the south. Not far."

She replied, "Good. Meet us there."

She slipped the phone in her pocket before he replied. It vibrated once, but she ignored it.

"Turn left. Drive slow."

Shep nodded and turned the wheel. The road was still empty, which was normal because not much traffic went through it to begin with—not anymore.

Shep parked the cruiser on the shoulder just shy of a snow-filled ditch, and they killed the engine. They stayed put in the car's cabin. They both looked up at the Bell 205. They watched it descend and then hover in a circle until Ramirez saw the right spot. Then the Bell started coming down in the field near the broken section of the fence, just as Ramirez had texted. The rotor wash swept up snow and revealed long blades of centipede grass that had survived the polar vortex so far.

The Bell 205's landing skid tapped down on the field once and then twice, softly, before settling down. Shep and Adonis stayed in the car until the Bell's rotors slowed.

Adonis was the first out. She slammed her door behind her. Shep followed suit; only he popped the trunk open before exiting the vehicle. He went around to the rear of the car and opened the trunk. Adonis stopped near the ditch and waited for him.

Shep disappeared behind the lid for several seconds. Then he came back out and shut the lid. He took off his coat and shivered in the wind. He set the coat over the trunk. He took a bulky police radio off his belt and the receiver and wire that coiled up around his back and over his shoulder and clipped to the front of his shirt for fast, easy access. He set all of it down on the trunk lid. He picked up a department-issued brown bulletproof vest with: *Department of Highway Patrol* etched across the chest. He slipped it on and then pulled his coat back on over it. He scooped up the radio and was going to clip it back on, but it was so bulky against the vest, he left it in the cruiser. Besides, Adonis implied they were off the grid here. The radio was a temptation to call it in.

He hesitated before leaving it in the car, but he did.

He leaned back out and closed the car door.

Shep returned to the trunk lid and picked up a Mossberg 590 shotgun and a box of shells he had set down as well. He walked over to Adonis, digging his fingers into the box, which seemed not to be full. He loaded six shells into the riot gun. Once it was full, he shoved four more into his coat pocket. He pumped the gun and carried it by his side.

Adonis arched an eyebrow.

"Got another one of those?"

"Sorry. Just the one. Your boys got an extra rifle in that bird?"

"Guess we're going to find out."

They turned and headed to meet the Bell 205.

Ramirez left the Bell's engine on and waited for the rotors to slow to a soft spin. Then he took off his radio headset and helmet and hopped out. James and Swan got out the back. The three men walked toward Adonis and Shep. They all converged fifty feet from the helicopter and met in the field closer to the broken fence than the Bell.

Adonis asked, but she already knew the answer because Ramirez hadn't bothered to get a rifle out of the back for himself.

"Any firepower stacked in the rear?"

Swan answered.

"No. Sorry."

James said, "Nothing back there but us. Is this where they're located?"

He turned and raised a hand and pointed at the top of the barn, which was the only visible part of Pine Farms over the trees from their position.

Adonis said, "We think so. Did you see anything else up there?"

"Just two vehicles."

Shep thought back to the video he'd watched from Trooper Brant's dashcam. He remembered the brutal murder of his friend. He remembered the vehicle he saw them driving in.

He asked, "Is one of them a black panel van?"

Swan said, "No van."

Ramirez said, "Not that we saw. But there's a Toyota Tundra—white, and a truck. And it's got badge decals on the door and a light bar on the roof."

Adonis said, "That's the sheriff's truck. He came by here to check out the supposed squatters that White had called in."

Swan and James looked at each other and then at Adonis dumbfounded. They had been left out of the loop.

Adonis ignored the questions in their eyes, and they didn't ask them. They didn't care about answers. They only wanted to shoot the Athenians.

She said, "Okay. Let's assume that they're there. This is what we know. There could be seven hostiles. They're heavily armed. Probably have body armor. They're highly skilled. And they murdered or injured dozens of our brothers."

She looked at their faces. James and Swan were brute force types. Not much thought behind their eyes, but they were well-trained and deadly. She had no doubt about that. Ramirez was more of a thinker, but he could shoot straight and was probably reliable in a firefight. Otherwise, he would never have been given an ATF badge. Shep was the wildcard here, but she figured he might've been the best of all of them. She was glad he was there. He had the right motivation and probably knew exactly how to use that shotgun.

Shep said, "So, we're probably outnumbered?"

Adonis said, "Possibly outgunned."

The others stayed quiet.

Adonis added, "Joseph Abel is a crackpot who killed innocent cops today. We could call the FBI right now. But I want this bastard myself. Any of you got a problem with that?"

She looked over their faces. Swan and James answered immediately with no words, but actions. They both raised their assault rifles up to their chest like they were soldiers ordered to fall in.

Ramirez hesitated, but said nothing. No objection. He reached down and pulled a Glock 22 out of a hip holster. It looked identical to Adonis's. They were standard issue by the ATF. He held it down by his side.

She looked at it and nodded.

"Okay, then."

She didn't need to ask Shep. She knew his answer. He was in.

She said, "You guys know what this is? I'm not here to take prisoners."

Shep said, "Shoot to kill."

"Okay. Let's go."

James asked, "What's the plan?"

Swan asked, "Where do you want us?"

"They probably know we're here. So, stealth is out the window. I say let's just go in hot right here."

She pointed up the line, through the trees to the tail of the sheriff's pickup truck.

Shep said, "Guns blazing. That's the right way to go."

Adonis said, "If you see Abel, try not to shoot him unless you have to. He's mine."

Ramirez said, "We got two hostages in there. Let's not forget."

Shep said, "One's a South Carolina sheriff."

Adonis said, "I know. If they're still alive, the hostages are our top priority. But that's a smidge above killing these Athenian bastards. Got it?"

James asked, "How'll we know the hostages?"

Adonis said, "They'll be the ones unarmed."

Shep said, "The sheriff here is an old coot. You can't miss him. Plus, he'll be in uniform."

Swan asked, "What about the civilian?"

Adonis said, "I imagine he'll stick out like a sore thumb."

James and Swan nodded almost in unison.

Adonis said, "Let's go. No warning. Guns blazing."

35

WIDOW AND ABE sat at the kitchen table. A half-empty coffee mug rested next to Widow's hand on the table, and a steaming coffeepot was in front of Abe. He sat next to Widow while they both stared at Maggie's phone screen.

Widow googled the Athenians. There were lots of news articles and videos about the explosions, the dead and injured, and official statements from the governor's office and the White House and the FBI. There was nothing official from the ATF, just a lot of speculation by news outlets.

There was also a lot of coverage of a man named Joseph Abel.

Abe said, "Who the hell is Joseph Abel?"

Widow didn't answer that.

Both Abe and Widow stared at the man's face. There was no video of him, just a recent photo of the guy wearing all white. It looked like it was taken without his knowledge from a cell phone camera. The image was a little tilted and out of focus, but his face was visible enough.

Abe said, "He's all skin and bones."

Widow scrolled down the page they were on and read some of the article. His eyes skimmed to key points, and he was done.

"It says he's the leader and founder of a militant religious group called the Athenians."

"But who is he? Where did he come from?"

"Where do these wackos always come from?"

Abe shrugged.

Widow said, "Out of nowhere. It seems. Only normally, they've always been the way they are. Hiding in plain sight."

"Google him."

Widow clicked on the screen, and a keyboard came up. He typed, but Abe reached over him.

"Hold up," he said, and he clicked a little microphone button on the screen, and the keyboard vanished. It was quickly replaced by a blank screen with some sort of audio monitoring app and a bell sound that indicated the phone was recording or listening.

Widow didn't know what to call it.

Abe spoke.

"Show me: *Joseph Abel.*"

The phone screen changed again to the internet and started showing results from the search.

Widow said, "That's neat."

Abe looked at him.

"You really live off the grid, don't you?"

Widow shrugged.

Abe said, "I'm an old fart, and I know how to operate a cell phone."

"I know how to operate a phone. I just haven't owned one."

"You've not owned one in years or something?"

"Nope. I haven't owned one ever."

"Ever?"

"Not really."

Abe smirked, and they both looked at the results on the screen.

Abe said, "Scroll down."

Widow did until Abe spoke again.

"There. Click on that link."

The link he was talking about came with a photograph of Abel. Widow clicked it, and they both looked it over. It was some sort of profile on the guy.

Widow skimmed it like he had the previous articles.

"This one's some sort of fluff piece on him like he wrote it himself."

Abe was squinting, trying to see it.

He said, "I don't have my glasses. What does it say?"

"Not much. Just about how great he is and how the Athenians offer a different way of life. It's like a human-interest piece full of propaganda and spin. But..."

Widow trailed off.

"What?"

Widow leaned back in the chair.

"It says he was a one-star."

"A one-star what?"

"A one-star general."

"In the Army?"

"That's the only place that has generals."

"What does that mean?"

Widow stayed quiet and clicked out of the page they were on. He returned to Google and typed General Joseph Abel.

Abe asked, "Now, what are you doing?"

"Reconning."

Google came up with several articles related to the term: *General Joseph Abel*. He clicked on one and read. He read about Abel's time at Fort Polk in Louisiana and as much as he could about the guy's mentions in Iraq.

After several minutes of silence and the rest of the cup of coffee had vanished, Widow put the phone down.

Abe asked, "Anything helpful?"

"Yes. This dude isn't good news. He's some kind of war god."

"War god?"

"It's like a war hero, only without the hero part. From the impressions I can get off the info scattered across the internet, I'd say he's got plenty of battle experience, and it seems he's highly regarded by his guys."

"That makes him sound like a good guy."

"Not necessarily. I can tell there's plenty here that's redacted."

"Redacted?"

"Omitted by the Army from public knowledge. Plus, there's one more thing."

"What?"

"He was sent to Polk straight from Baghdad."

"So? What's that mean?"

"Fort Polk is called Fort Puke."

"What? Why?"

"It's an awful assignment for a general who loves combat. And this guy loves combat. I can tell. This is like a punishment. The Army promoted him to general and gave him the worst assignment they could."

"I don't know. Sounds good to me. Promotions are a good thing. Plus, he's out of the fray. He wouldn't have to worry about IEDs."

Widow stopped and looked over at Abe. He stared into his eyes. He swallowed a lump in his throat and asked a question, softly, compassionately.

"Is that what happened to Abraham?"

Abe looked down at his right hand. He stared at a piece of jewelry that Widow hadn't noticed him wearing before. It was a ring that was far too large for Abe's fingers. He wore it on his middle finger. He looped it around and around, slowly, staring at it like he was lost in memories.

Widow looked at the ring. It was a class ring. It wasn't a normal class ring. It was military.

Widow asked, "That his Annapolis ring?"

Abe nodded.

"He graduated back in 2003. I was so proud of him when he got in to Naval Academy. He was so excited to go to Iraq. He wanted to help so much. You know? He wasn't in it for the glory, or to hurt people. He wanted to save lives. He believed in what we were doing over there. He truly did."

Widow clicked the cell phone off and set it down on the table between the two men. He reached out his hand and placed it on Abe's shoulder.

A single tear, nothing dramatic, just a single drop streamed out of the old man's eye.

He said, "He was blown up by an IED. Outside of Al Anbar."

Widow stayed quiet.

Abe reached up and wiped the tear away.

"I lost one son. I can't lose the other, Widow. I can't. Abby can't. We can't take it. Not again."

Widow said, "You won't. You have my word."

Abe looked at him.

"He might already be dead. If he's really been taken by this Abel guy."

"He's not."

"How do you know?"

"They came over here for him. A living hostage works better than a dead one."

"Why didn't they just come for all of us?"

"I imagine it's not your family that Abel's interested in. They probably needed Walter's truck. They might be stuck because of roadblocks or the FBI dragnet."

"Or they really broke down. Maybe they told the truth about that part."

"Maybe. They might've sent one guy here to see how many of us there are. I don't know exactly. We're just spitballing here. But all are equally plausible reasons."

"What now? We just pray that Adonis brings him back alive?"

"We could do that. She probably will. They're the ATF. They've got a helicopter. Plus, the federal government is behind them."

Abe said, "That doesn't sound very promising."

"The federal government isn't completely useless."

Abe paused and looked at Widow's face.

"I'm the proud father of a veteran son. Don't bullshit me. I can see past the facade on your face. You're worried."

"Okay. I'm a little worried."

"Why?"

"Because of Adonis."

"Why? She seemed competent. She seemed eager to catch this whack job."

"I agree. She's a special agent-in-charge or whatever the ATF calls them. She definitely looks like a leader to me. She's tough. And pissed off."

"But?"

"Look back at her face. What do you remember seeing?"

Abe hesitated a moment.

"She's a woman?"

"No."

"She was tiny?"

"No. Forget about her physicality. It's a mistake to underestimate her as a cop because she's a small woman. They're tougher than most men. Trust me on this. I speak from experience. They've got to deal with all the shit we give them. Plus, they get shot at like everybody else. No, it's something else."

Abe thought back for a moment.

He said, "She had bandages on her head. Like a wound. She was injured."

"She was injured hours ago."

"She was there. At the explosion."

"She was not only there. She was probably in charge of the whole operation. I think it's personal for her. They're searching for the men responsible for blowing up all the agents that she's known and worked with and probably commanded. This is her Op. And it went very bad."

"What're you saying, Widow? You don't think she can be trusted to follow through with her job? She's compromised?"

"I'm saying that if this were the Navy, she'd been taken off post the moment everything went sideways. Not fired or stripped of her command, but she would've been benched. She's not thinking clearly like an agent is supposed to. I wouldn't be. Would you?"

Abe said nothing.

Widow said, "She probably saw people she knew die today. What? Six or seven hours ago? She shouldn't be out here. She shouldn't even still have a sidearm."

Abe nodded.

"So, what now? What can we do? Should we call somebody?"

"She said the local sheriff couldn't be reached. I guess we can call his office and tell them. We could call the FBI. That's probably who should be here."

Abe said, "Okay. I'll call the sheriff's office."

Widow nodded.

Abe left Maggie's phone on the table and fished his own out of his pocket. It was a smartphone, only old like a first-generation. He looked at Widow like he was going to ask the phone number and then decided just to dial nine one one.

He put the phone to his ear. It rang and rang; then, he heard a busy tone.

"It's busy," he said.

"Is the sheriff the only law enforcement out here?"

Abe nodded.

Widow said, "Must be inundated with calls from people, probably claiming all kinds of things. Terrorist attacks flood local cops with bullshit calls. Try their landline."

Abe nodded and went into his phone's internet browser to locate the number. Once he had it, he dialed.

He stared at Widow while it rang.

After five long minutes, he clicked off the phone.

Widow asked, "Busy too?"

"No. It just keeps ringing and ringing."

Widow nodded and thought for a moment.

Abe asked, "What's it mean?"

Widow said, "Either they're all too busy right now, which is plausible. This is a small county, and their sheriff is missing. They probably are scrambling to keep up with calls from worried locals. The TV is probably playing loops of the whole situation being a terrorist attack. Which would stir everyone up, causing them to flood the sheriff's office with calls."

Abe nodded.

Widow said, "Or, Adonis told them not to respond. Or she shut them down."

"Can she do that?"

Widow shrugged and said, "She can, I guess. Maybe she told them since their sheriff is missing that the ATF was commandeering their post. She might've told them to work the roads and leave the phones off."

"Which means we should worry. She's gone rogue. Like you said, it's personal for her."

"And the other guys with her. We can assume the ones in the helicopter are under her command, and the patrolman she's driving around with might have some stake in this as well."

Abe said, "So what do we do?"

Widow tilted the coffee mug and stared into it. He had consumed all the coffee in it. It was bone dry.

He asked one question, and it wasn't about coffee.

"Got any guns here?"

36

ADONIS TOOK THE LEAD. It was her show. She held her Glock 22 out and ready to go, pointed outward, following her eyes—none of that muzzle pointed at the sky bullshit like in the movies. If someone stepped into her line of sight, chances were that she wanted to shoot him. As far as they knew, there were two potential hostages. If she was honest with herself, she wasn't there for a rescue. It wasn't her primary aim. It was secondary. Certainly, she wanted to rescue the sheriff and Walter too, but that's not what weighed on her mind. She thought about nothing but leveling a bullet between Abel's eyes.

Swan and James spread out to the left, and Ramirez and Shep to her right. Adonis walked front and center. They stepped slowly, keeping their limbs loose, staying on course. Adonis walked up through the brush and over the snow. Shep was the closest man to her. The distance between them and the barn was about the same as from where they were to the farmhouse porch.

Shep kept his finger out of the trigger housing to the Mossberg shotgun. He noticed Adonis did not. He said nothing about it.

Shep whispered, "It's quiet."

They heard natural South Carolina sounds and nothing else. The wind gusted and whistled. Tree branches rustled and swooshed. Light snow fell, mushing on top of the roofs. A dog barked in the distance.

They heard nothing else. The farm looked like a ghost town. Shep thought of one of the many bombed-out, abandoned villages he had seen in Iraq, back when he was a know-it-all jarhead. Now he was older and a little wiser. His wisdom was telling him this didn't feel right.

Adonis kept walking; so did the others.

Shep said, "It's too quiet."

Adonis said, "Just keep your eyes peeled."

Suddenly a memory flashed through Shep's mind.

"Keep your head on a swivel," a commanding officer from his past had said. He couldn't remember which, but one of them. Ninety-nine percent of the time, patrolling the deserts of the Middle East was like any other desert—boring and filled with long stretches of nothingness combined with distant echoes of wind and more nothingness. Only one time, it had not been nothingness. One time his patrol unit stepped into an abandoned town that appeared to have nothing more than empty-looking rock buildings and abandoned huts and a single sand-covered road, but it turned out the village wasn't abandoned. His unit was vastly aware of insurgents setting up ambushes for patrols. So, they hadn't walked into a trap blindly. They surveyed the area first with field glasses and sniper scopes. They actually had set up camp the night before outside the village. They took shifts staying awake, keeping eyes on the abandoned structures through the night. The next morning was when they walked through it.

It turned out it wasn't a trap, but it also wasn't abandoned.

They found twenty-one dead bodies left inside the huts and the rock buildings and the shanty structures. The villagers hadn't abandoned the town. Neither had the insurgents left an ambush for the Marine patrol. It turned out that the early fighters for ISIS had butchered the villagers and left them behind. It wasn't a message. It wasn't a sign. It didn't have some morbid meaning. It was just sheer brutality, a bit of reality of an unstable Iraq. Some infighting was already there.

Even though that didn't turn out to be an ambush, the memory still clung to Shep's memories like a stowaway he couldn't shake.

Adonis said, "Don't worry. We know they know we're here."

"Then it's probably an ambush."

"You're free to go back to the car and call it in. Wait for backup. We're going in."

He looked in her eyes. There was something different there. Before, she looked like a pissed off ATF agent. Now she looked like a woman out for revenge.

Shep said, "I want them dead too, but I don't want to walk into a trap blindly."

"We're already in a trap."

"We should get back to the car. Let me call for backup. Seriously."

Adonis said nothing. James and Swan stopped walking. Ramirez stopped just after that. They stayed in their positions, scanning the buildings for movement.

"Toni," Shep said.

She twisted at the waist and looked up at him.

He said, "I want them dead too. They killed one of my guys. But I don't want to die. They got the best of you already once today. Let's not make the same mistake twice."

"We're already here."

Just then, James leaned over and whispered something to Swan. Adonis saw it and put a hand up to Shep to wait.

James turned and looked at them. He stepped back and walked over to them.

"Adonis."

"What is it?"

"Over my shoulder. Top of the barn. Don't stare."

Both she and Shep glanced up at the barn quickly, acting as blasé and uncoordinated as they could. Both of them saw what James was pointing out.

Adonis asked, "Is that what it looks like?"

James said, "It's a sniper. A rifle is looking out toward us."

"Is he aiming at us?"

"Can't tell."

Shep asked, "Why aren't they shooting?"

Adonis said, "Are they waiting for us to get in closer?"

Shep turned and looked back toward the road. He couldn't see it through the trees, but he knew the distance. He looked at the treetops.

"No way. They could've shot at us back on the road. He's got a clear enough view through the trees."

"So why aren't they shooting?"

Shep said, "Maybe it's a diversion?"

"What do we do?"

Adonis said, "It's gotta be a trick. We'd be dead already."

Shep said, "I agree."

Adonis said, "Just in case, James, you and Swan take the barn. Ramirez, come with us. We'll get the house. Yell out when it's cleared. Tell the others we bum-rush on my mark."

James nodded and walked back to Swan. He passed Ramirez on the way and relayed the orders. Ramirez glanced at Shep and Adonis and nodded. He crossed over to them.

They all walked a step forward. Then Adonis yelled out like the commander of a unit from the Union Army, charging a hill in the Civil War.

"Now!" she shouted.

All five of them took off running. James and Swan made it to the barn and hugged both sides of the barn doors. Shep was the first to the farmhouse. He leaped over the broken porch railing and slammed his back to the wall next to the front door.

Adonis followed Ramirez, who came up the steps and went down in a crouch. He covered the front door with his weapon, keeping his eye over the sights.

Adonis climbed the porch steps and stopped in front of a door. She paused a beat and listened. She heard no sound coming from the house other than the same gusts of wind tunneling through the old wood and brick.

She stayed where she was and reached out a cold hand and checked the doorknob. It was locked. She gazed around the doorframe. It was old and cracked and loose in a bunch of places. Luckily, she could see that the deadbolt wasn't engaged through a long half-inch slit in the jamb. It was just the lock on the knob.

She brought her hand back to her gun and waited.

Shep and Ramirez held their positions. Then she heard what she was waiting for. Diagonally behind her, and across the driveway, she heard James and Swan rip the barn doors open hard. The two men stormed into the structure.

Adonis stood strong on her left foot and stepped back fast with the right. She came back up with momentum that surprised Shep. She slammed her right boot into the door just under the knob and the lock. The door crashed open, and the wood splintered around the knob and the lock. The door swung back until it stopped on the opposite side of the wall.

Adonis breached first, and Shep followed. Ramirez took up the rear. They stormed into the house like a SWAT unit that had trained together for years.

Shep took the right, through an open doorway that led into a downstairs family room, followed by a dining room and a kitchen. The family room was mostly empty, with some old furniture remaining. Settled dust was everywhere. He saw no personal items left behind. There were no photographs or paintings on the wall or books on a shelf.

He saw empty flowerpots near a window. Cobwebs stretched from wall to floor in some places. Dust kicked up as he walked. A fireplace mantel was covered in both webs and dust.

He skirted to the right and scanned an open doorway to a kitchen beyond. He stepped through the doorway. Floorboards creaked underneath him. The kitchen was the last of this side of the house. Like the other parts, it was empty and derelict, except for a remaining farm sink. But everything else was pulled out and gone already. All the normal appliances were gone. Even the faucets were missing.

Ramirez followed behind Adonis for a beat until they came to a closed door to the left of the hall. She waved him to check it out.

He opened it slowly and peered in. It was a second hallway. He followed it, finding nothing but an empty study, bathroom, and a guest bedroom that had a mattress on the floor. It looked recently slept on.

Adonis followed the hallway to the end, stepping on creaking floorboards and over a rug that was left behind. She found a single door next to a staircase leading up. She looked up the stairs and listened. She heard nothing. She went for the door first. She opened it and shoved the Glock forward, ready to shoot. She found she was staring into utter darkness.

She strode to the right and used her left hand to feel along the wall for a light switch. She found it with the tips of her fingers. She flicked it, and nothing happened. Then she realized how stupid that was. There was no power for the lights.

She stepped back into the hall and felt around her pockets for a flashlight, but she had none. She pulled out her phone and clicked the button to convert the flash to a flashlight. A bright but short beam flashed out. She used it to check out the room. It was a basement. She saw the top of the steps and part of a wall along the bottom of the basement's ceiling, but nothing else, just darkness.

"Anything?" a voice asked from behind her. It startled her, and she jumped. The phone sprung out of her hand like it was covered in cooking oil.

"Shit!" she said.

Her phone clattered and bounced and clanged down the stairs all the way to a cement floor in the darkness below her. The light bounced and shone all over the basement, revealing it to appear completely empty. The final bounce on the cement floor was the end of the phone. She knew it because it made a loud crashing sound that sounded bad. And then the light from the flash shone up and back at her and then died away. It flashed once and twice and didn't come back on.

She glanced back over her shoulder and found Shep standing there with the shotgun pointed up the staircase. A second later, she saw Ramirez coming back from the other hallway.

Shep said, "Oh. Sorry."

Adonis said, "Nothing so far. What about you?"

"Nothing for me."

Ramirez said, "Same here. Just an empty house. I found a mattress. It looks slept on, but that's it."

"Let's go upstairs."

"Want me to grab your phone?" Shep asked.

Adonis looked back down at it.

"Nah. I'll get it."

Shep pulled a flashlight out of his belt and clicked it on.

"I'll light the way for you."

"Thank you."

Adonis started descending the staircase. She stepped lightly, not knowing how old the wooden steps were. They creaked under her weight. She made it to the bottom and quickly swept over the basement with her Glock as best she could. There was too much darkness to see everything. At the bottom, she scooped her phone up with one free hand and shook it.

"It still work?" Shep asked.

"Nope."

She brushed her fingers over the phone and screen, feeling for damage. She found a long crack along the screen that spider-webbed as she moved it. The phone was black. No power.

Shep asked, "Anything down there?"

"No. Nothing."

"Let's get upstairs."

She slipped the shattered phone into her pocket and scrambled back up the stairs and to the hallway.

Shep closed the cellar door behind her, and they prepared to ascend into the second level. But before they could, they heard something—voices calling out to them from the front of the house.

"Agent Adonis," the voice called out.

"Who's that?" Shep asked.

Ramirez said, "Sounds like James."

Adonis nodded, and they followed her back down the hall to the front door.

Shep asked, "Want me to check the upstairs?"

"No. But keep an eye on it in case someone comes down."

Shep nodded and pulled up the rear. He followed them, walking backward, keeping the Mossberg trained on the bottom of the stairs.

Adonis and Ramirez walked back out to the front door, through it, and onto the porch.

This time, she kept her Glock pointed at the ground for safety. She didn't want to shoot James by accident. But the moment she stepped out onto the front porch, she regretted it. She wished she would've had it pointed straight out.

She and Ramirez stepped onto the porch and saw the guys they were hunting—all of them, minus two. Dobson was technically there. His body rotted in the barn in a dirty old horse trough. And Jargo was posted up in a sniper's nest in the barn's loft.

Most of their targets stood in the center of the large space between the barn and the farmhouse, just in front of Walter White's truck.

Five feet in front of the Athenian men stood James. His hat was gone. His assault rifle was gone. His sidearm was gone. His hands were zip-tied behind his back. Blood streamed down his face from a fresh rifle butt to the nose, which was cracked and broken.

Swan was next to him; only he was on his knees. All his weapons were also gone. His nose hadn't been broken, like James's, but the zip ties were there, wound around his wrists, which were also pulled back behind him.

Both men looked defeated, scared, and ashamed.

"Get down on your knees," said a man standing behind James. He kicked James in the back of the knees, knocking James down onto his knees and into the dirt and snow.

Adonis looked out over the Athenian men in front of her. They were armed. Sound suppressors were screwed into the ends of their weapons. She glanced up behind them at the barn where she had seen the flapping shutter in the loft with the sniper rifle set out with no one at the helm—only now, there was someone there.

The sniper was in a shooter's seated position, one elbow up on one knee and butt on the ground like he was curled into a half-ball.

He was staring right back at Adonis. One eye trained through the rifle scope. The other was wide open next to it. She stared back at him. They shared a brief staring contest. But then the sniper did something different, not weird, but menacing. He moved his head and took his eye off the scope and looked at her with both eyes. She saw his face.

He smiled and winked at her.

It reminded her of seeing a bad guy that she caught and arrested at his sentencing in court. He was sentenced to life in prison. That look he gave her, she would never forget. It was the most menacing expression she had ever seen. That was, until today.

Today, the sniper took that trophy.

Five other guys from her list were there. They were all on the ground, fanned out in front of the parked trucks.

The man behind James, the man who kicked him in the legs, was a tall black man. It was Brooks, the same guy who went to the Whites' farm.

Adonis recognized him, too.

Beyond the group of men, the barn's doors were wide open, propped open by two homemade wooden wedges, jammed underneath each door.

She saw in the very back of the barn, the two missing guys— Walter White and Sheriff Rourke. They were zip-tied to the grille of a black panel van. Dirty rags were stuffed into their mouths.

Adonis's eyes refocused back onto the black man and then over the others until she found the one she was looking for.

Right at the head and center was Joseph Abel—big and obvious. She was surprised that she hadn't looked directly at him first.

He stood there tall but scrawny, more so than she pictured. He was outfitted all in white.

He spoke, and the others stayed quiet, pointing their rifles straight up at Adonis and Ramirez, who stood frozen like deer in headlights. Adonis could literally feel Ramirez quivering in his boots.

Both of them raised their Glocks, pointing them at the enemy. Adonis swept across the Athenian men for a second and then focused her sights on Abel only.

Abel was the only one of the Athenians not pointing a weapon back at them. In fact, Adonis saw he wasn't even holding a firearm.

In a slow, I-am-your-Messiah type way, Abel stepped forward. He stretched his arms up and out like he was going to give them a bear hug. His reach was long. From fingertip to fingertip, Adonis thought of it as the full wingspan of a California condor.

Abel's presence loomed, like doom itself.

He spoke in a charismatic and enigmatic voice.

"Agent Adonis, I presume."

Adonis stared at him in utter disbelief.

She asked, "You know my name?"

She asked, even though he probably knew it because James had just called out to her.

That notion went out the window when he explained how he knew her name.

Abel said, "I know you. Tommy told us all about you."

Ramirez glanced over his shoulder at her.

Adonis paused a beat and asked, "Where is he?"

Abel didn't play with her. No teasing or beating around the bush. He just told her flat out.

"He's dead. I killed him."

Adonis felt her heart plummet in her chest. She felt, for the first time, the wound on her head pound. She wondered if it had been pounding the whole morning only she hadn't noticed.

"He's dead?" she asked out of instinct, out of blindness, out of having no words to express the gut-punch of knowing.

"He is. Dead as a doornail, as they say."

Adonis's head pounded harder. Her heart hurt. Her throat swelled. Knowing that Dorsch was dead was the straw on the camel's back. Abel saw it on her face.

"Oh, dear. I know you loved him."

Adonis stayed frozen.

Ramirez lowered his aim and his gun a degree and glanced back over at her.

"What's he talking about? You loved him?" he asked.

Adonis whispered, "It's a secret."

"You were having an affair with him?"

"Yes," she said, with shame in her voice.

Abel said, "Now, Toni, be a good ATF agent and drop that gun. Both of you."

Adonis held back tears and a feeling of shame coursed through her veins, as if showing tears during a standoff with the man who had killed the guy she loved was shameful.

"Adonis," Abel said, "I'm not going to ask twice."

Ramirez said, "Adonis?"

"Lower your weapon," she whispered.

"Toni?"

"Lower it."

"No. We can't."

Abel arched an eyebrow at her. She locked her eyes on his.

"Adonis?" Abel asked.

She stayed still with her eyes locked on his.

Adonis said, "Do it, Ramirez."

Ramirez waited like he was waiting for Adonis to act first.

She lowered her Glock slowly like the hour hand on a clock face. She lowered it all the way to her side. Reluctantly, Ramirez did the same, changing his firing stance as if a regular at ease command had been given.

"Toss the pistols," Abel said in a calm voice.

Adonis tossed her Glock ten feet to the right. It sank into the snow near Walter's truck's front tire. Ramirez paused a long beat.

"Both of them," Abel said in the same calm voice.

"Ramirez, get rid of it," Adonis said.

Ramirez threw the Glock off to the left but kept it in sight in a last shred of hope that he could make a run for it if he needed to. That was completely shattered a moment later.

Abel said, "Tanis, pick up the guns, please."

One of his guys, the one called Tanis, Adonis figured, stood farthest from her left. He nodded at the command and kept his combat shotgun aimed at Adonis as he walked past the sheriff's parked truck. He walked around the tail end and over to Ramirez's Glock in the snow, bent over, and scooped it up. He stepped out in front of the two agents, keeping his eyes on them, and walked over to Adonis's thrown gun. He scooped it up. Then he took a position to the far right of her. He stopped, reversed the combat shotgun, and wedged it under his arm. He ejected the magazines from both Glocks, one at a time. Next, he racked the slides on both weapons, expelling the round in each chamber out into the snow. Last he tossed both weapons into the back of Walter's truck along with their magazines.

Tanis returned to aiming his combat shotgun at the agents.

"Now, that wasn't so hard, was it? And no one had to die," Abel spouted like he was pleased with himself.

His eyes stayed glued to Adonis. She stared back, with daggers in her eyes.

"There, no more standoff. Now, we can all be friends," Abel said.

Adonis stayed quiet. She couldn't take her eyes off his grin. Brooks burst the bubble between them.

"General, there's another one. In the house."

"What?" Abel asked, and realized one was missing.

No one spoke.

He turned on one foot and faced the farmhouse and called out.

"You in there. Come on out, or we'll shoot one of your pals."

Brooks stepped back from James and stood behind both men. He lowered his rifle behind them, swaying back and forth between them like he was going to pick one to shoot in the back at random. A sadistic game of Eeny Meeny Miny Moe.

Abel looked at Adonis.

"Tell him to come out."

Adonis paused a moment, contemplating what to do until she realized she had no choice.

"Shep, come out here."

Nothing happened. He didn't come out.

"Shep! Get out here!"

Nothing.

She stared at Abel. He arched the other eyebrow this time.

She called out, "Shep, if you don't come out, they'll shoot one of us! Please get out here!"

Abel said, "You really have little command over your guys, do you?"

"He's not one of mine."

"What is he then?"

Ramirez answered for her.

"He's just a highway patrolman."

Abel turned his head and looked at Brooks.

He said, "Highway patrolman?"

Brooks said, "Like the guy you killed this morning."

Abel nodded and called out.

"Shep, is it? Guess you're being stubborn because I killed one of your guys."

Shep didn't come out. He was in the farmhouse, back to the wall, next to a front room window. He held his shotgun up, pulled into his chest. Sweat ran down his cheeks. In one hand, he had his phone out. He was trying to get a signal, but there was none. Like in a cheesy horror movie, his phone coincidentally, tragically, was useless.

"Damn it," he muttered to himself. He tried calling his department. Nothing. He got a signal for a moment and dialed nine one one.

"Thank you!" he muttered. He put the phone to his ear and got an automated message.

"Because of high call volumes, the number you're calling can't be completed," the voice said.

"Shit!" he cursed. He redialed his department—hoping, praying he could get through this time.

The phone rang, but he got the same automated message with the same robotic tone.

"SHIT!" he shouted. It was so loud he knew they heard him outside. He cursed himself for listening to Adonis, for making a deal with her. Giving up his body radio was a huge mistake. He never should've done it. He should never have left it behind. He never should've left his guys out.

"Shep," Abel called to him.

"What?" he called back.

"You've got three seconds."

Abel started a loud count, while Brooks continued the twisted game of Eeny Meeny Miny Moe, swaying the barrel of his M4 from man to man behind their heads. The weapon's silencer was only inches from each ATF agent.

Adonis could see both James and Swan's faces. James bled out from his nose, but she could still see the panic in his eyes. Swan squeezed his eyes shut tight. His lips pursed and then moved. He whispered to himself. She read his lips. He was praying.

Ramirez whispered, "We should've never given up our guns."

Adonis said nothing, but felt more shame come over her. He was right. It was better to die fighting than like this, executed in the middle of nowhere, South Carolina, like dogs.

"ONE," Abel shouted.

"TWO."

"Wait! Wait! I'm coming out," Shep said.

He frowned and cursed at himself. He slid his phone into an empty pocket and stepped away from the window. He stepped in huge strides to the front door and stopped. He grabbed the front door, which wasn't shut all the way, and jerked it open. He stepped out onto the porch with the Mossberg raised. He pointed it at the group of Athenian men, flicking it from target to target until he recognized Abel, the man he watched on Brant's police cruiser's dashboard camera murder his friend in cold blood. He stopped, leaving the gun pointed at Abel.

Shep said, "You. You're the one who shot my friend."

Abel's grin remained.

"I did. You must've watched it on the dashcam?"

Shep said nothing to that.

"Shep, is it? Do us a favor and toss the shotgun."

Shep didn't respond.

"Do it, Shep," Adonis ordered, hoping not to lose more agents. But it was no good. He didn't respond.

Everyone stood their ground. Shep was the first to move. Foolishly—he knew—but he needed to close the gap, so he walked forward and stepped down off the porch. He was giving up any hope of cover he had, but he needed to get closer. He aimed to get as close to being behind the sheriff's truck as he could. The Mossberg's range was far enough to hit Abel or some of his guys, but it might hit Ramirez or Adonis first.

He needed to shorten the distance between them. Maybe he could get close enough to dive behind the sheriff's front wheel well. That would make for good cover.

And even if he got shot, it was okay by him as long as he took out Abel. Maybe give Adonis and Ramirez a running chance.

But he had to think of a tactic first, something to keep them busy. Talking seemed to be the best option. From what little he knew of Abel, he knew the man loved to talk.

Shep asked, "Why? Why did you do it?"

He continued to step forward, closing the gap more and more.

Abel said, "Why did I kill your friend? That's simple. He got in our way."

Shep stayed quiet. He took a step, stopped, paused, and took another step. He repeated this as much as he could without drawing suspicion.

Abel said, "Like you are. Right now."

Shep got as close as he could to a distance that would let him leap behind the truck's wheel wells and stopped.

Abel said, "Really, Officer Shep or Patrolman Shep or whatever your name is, this little charade you're doing, trying to get me to talk long enough for you to get into close range with the shotgun, is pointless."

As much as seemed that Abel couldn't widen his grin anymore, he did. But he also did something else. He nodded his head up and to the right twice like he was signaling for Shep to look over Abel's shoulder.

Shep glanced up over Abel's shoulder and saw nothing there to see, just the front of the barn, and the open doors. He saw the black panel van inside it and White and Rourke zip-tied to the grille and old hay and animal stalls and nothing else.

Abel saw him look.

He said, "No, Shep. Not there. Look higher."

Shep feared it was a trick, but what kind of trick?

He couldn't help but look. He glanced up again, but this time, he let his eyes linger on the barn's front side.

Abel said, "Up. Higher. Look higher."

Shep looked past him and up over his shoulder and up the barn's front side. He looked up to the open shutters, exposing the loft. Then he saw the sniper rifle they had seen earlier, only this time it wasn't down on the floor of the loft, as if it had been placed there as a trap. This time it was higher, in someone's grip, and it was pointed straight down at him.

He saw a sniper behind it, smiling back at him. The sniper's eye was behind the scope.

Shep knew this was the end. He didn't hesitate any longer—no more running up the clock. Time seemed to slow down. The muscles in his neck and jaw fired on all cylinders to traverse his head back down to look at Abel. The muscles from his arms down to his waist fired up and torqued, all of it working in unison so that he could raise the shotgun up and lower his vision to aim. The butt of the shotgun slammed into his shoulder, and his eye lined up as fast as he could down the sights. He nearly had Abel in his line of fire when his upper chest and collarbone exploded—partially under the bulletproof vest and partially above the plate. The pain was immediate, but the muzzle flash seemed like it came after he had already been nailed by a bullet.

The force of the impact jerked him off his feet, but he got in one pull of the trigger. The shotgun fired up as he went back off his feet.

Abel ducked, as did the rest of his guys, minus Brooks, who stayed behind James and Swan like human shields. Jargo didn't have to duck. He was out of range.

Shep landed on his back and dropped the shotgun. He felt the pain from the bullet amplified through his chest and bones, as if the bullet were still moving.

Adonis stayed standing, hands up. She was completely frozen. Ramirez went for his gun, but Cucci fired a warning shot into the ground in front of him, and he froze.

The others returned to standing and just stared at Adonis and Ramirez.

Adonis turned and looked down at Shep. She moved to run to him, but Flack fired a warning shot at her. The gun was silenced, but the bullet shot up snow and dirt right at her feet. She froze in place. She didn't look away from Shep.

He stared back up at her. Blood spurted out of his mouth from pooling in his lungs and throat. He tried to speak, tried to say something, but nothing came out but the blood. He tried to mouth something, but she couldn't make it out before he was dead.

37

WIDOW FOLLOWED ABE INTO THE WHITES' house, closing the front door behind them and dead-bolting it. They walked back through the family room past his daughter, his daughter-in-law, his grandchildren, and his wife.

He made eye contact with Abby. She knew not to ask where they were going. She knew where they were headed.

They threaded through the furniture, over to the fireplace and to the sliding doors at the back of the house. Abe slid one side open, and they stepped out onto the back porch.

Abe waited for Widow to walk through. Then he leaned in, looked at his wife, and said, "Lock this, hon."

Abby did as he asked and walked over and locked the slider behind them.

Abe turned and walked around the outside of the fireplace to a door that Widow hadn't known was there. It was a part of the house's structure but wasn't built in brick. It was all wood, painted white, including the door. The door had a padlock on the outside.

Widow figured it was a shed. He was mostly right.

Abe took a set of keys out of his pocket, not from his truck key chain. This was just a simple keyring with five keys on it. The others must've been related to the barn and wherever they stored Christmas tree farming equipment. He sifted through the keys until he found the right one. He unlocked the padlock, replacing the lock on the metal hasp.

He opened the door and stepped into the darkness, and Widow followed.

Abe pulled on a string, and a low-hanging light switched on. It was dull and yellow but lit the room enough to see everything but dark patches on the ceiling above it. The bulb dangled from a cord and swayed back and forth from the wind whooshing through the open door.

The exterior room with the lock on it was mostly a shed. All kinds of different regular, everyday tools littered built-in wooden shelves along three of the walls. There was a long wooden table in the center of the room. It looked heavy and hulking, as if there was no way the builders squeezed it in through the door. Widow thought the shed must've been built around the thing. That was not true, but that was his first thought.

The table had a bottom shelf underneath it with boxes and boxes of hand tools crammed into them. The boxes were labeled in black marker, but that made little difference regarding organization. The whole shed was disorganized, but in an organized, chaotic way, like only Abe knew where everything was located. It made sense to him.

The one exception to this was the twenty percent that wasn't related to a typical tool shed. That was the far wall.

On it, there were five layers of mounted hooks from top to bottom with a built-in mantel underneath, placed just below Abe's waist level and far below Widow's waist level.

On the hooks were three classic rifles, placed with care, and below that were two scoped hunting rifles. Below that, on the mantel, were boxes of ammunition.

Abe stepped past the light and rounded the table, and stopped dead in front of the rifles. He paused, looking over them like they were his pride and joy. Then he sidestepped to the right and turned back to Widow. He put his hand out like a stage presenter, revealing a new car for a game show contestant to win.

Abe said, "I've got these guns."

Widow walked full into the shed and rounded the same table on the opposite side, and stopped in front of the weapons. He looked them over and reached his hands up to the top one. Then he stopped.

"May I?"

"Be my guest."

Widow smiled and lifted the top rifle, one of the classic ones. He pulled it off the hooks and twisted it and studied it from top to bottom.

"A Winchester. 1894."

"You know guns? Well, I guess, of course, you do."

"It's the most popular lever-action rifle ever made."

"Some would argue that. Me included."

"This is a classic. You've kept the original steel butt."

Widow dropped the lever. The weapon was obviously unloaded, but he liked to be sure—an old habit.

Abe said, "Yeah. I found that one antiquing through west Texas."

"You've got three of them?"

"Yeah, the other two came from the internet. And the others are for hunting. Although we used to use the 1894s."

Widow repeated the lever-action fast, and dry-fired the rifle, testing the firing speed just for the kick of it. He repeated the process several times, rapid-firing it. A big smile flickered across his face.

He said, "Works great."

"They all do. My sons take good care of their rifles. I taught them that."

A cloud seemed to shade across Abe's face when he realized one of his sons was dead. Widow saw on the stock of the rifle he held, a set of carved letters—A.M.W. for Abe's dead son: *Abraham Michael White, Jr.*

Abe said nothing about it, and Widow didn't offer to return the weapon to its rightful place. Instead, he tried to reroute Abe's attention to the situation at hand.

He said, "What kind of load-out you got?"

Abe brushed a single hand over the boxes of ammunition stacked neatly on the mantel—the only thing in the shed that looked organized. He stopped over a stack of three boxes and pulled one off the top, handed it to Widow.

"That depends. If you want that gun, it's chambered to thirty-thirties. So are the other two, but the hunting rifles are long range."

"Thirty-thirty is fine."

Widow took the box of thirty-thirty bullets from Abe's hand. Then he took the box and the Winchester rifle and rotated all the way around on one foot, a hundred eighty degrees. He stopped in front of the huge worktable and placed the rifle down. He popped open the box. It was full. He took out nine bullets and lined them up under the gun, one in front of the other, on their sides, nose to tail. He left no space between them. He compared them to the length of the gun barrel. Exactly nine bullets appeared to fit perfectly.

Abe paused a beat and asked, "Sure you don't want one of the hunting rifles? The repeater's a good gun. Don't get me wrong. And I ain't got no problem with you using my son's rifle. But the range on those old guns is two hundred yards. Sure, you won't want something with a longer range?"

"No. This is perfect. If there's trouble here, you'll need the scoped guns."

"Trouble here? You're not sticking around?"

Fast—faster than Abe had ever seen anyone in his life—Widow's fingers moved like a magician's sleight of hand in performing card tricks. Within seconds, he had slid each bullet into the side-loading gate, using the right amount of pressure not to jam the bullet or force each one in.

Once the rifle was loaded, he scooped it up and racked the lever, loading the first bullet into the chamber from the magazine. The rifle was ready to fire. Widow moved his hand up over the trigger and lever and held it down safely from firing.

Abe stared at him. The look on his face was like he was staring at both a skilled rifleman and a circus performer at the same time.

He asked, "You ever been in the Marines?"

"I told you. I was in the Navy."

"Yeah. You did, but that was like watching the boys in the Marine Honor Guard. I mean, you're fast with that."

Widow shrugged.

Abe said, "What part of the Navy?"

"I polished hulls."

"What?"

"Boats. I was the underwater hull-polisher. You know? A diver."

Widow smiled.

Abe asked, "A diver?"

Widow nodded.

"I know what that means. You were a SEAL?"

Widow stayed quiet, continued to smile. And Abe took that to be an unofficial confirmation to the question.

Question asked. Question answered.

Widow said, "We better scoop up the rest of these rifles. Take them inside. If something goes down and Adonis's plan spills over to this house, then we'll need all the firepower inside. They'll be useless to you out here."

Abe nodded and walked over to the rifles. He started picking them off the hooks one by one and placing them on the worktable.

Widow asked, "Got a sidearm?"

Abe stopped on the first hunting rifle and said, "Walter used to carry one in his truck, but he got rid of it. He's not a gun person. Not since he's had kids. I'm not a crazy gun nut. I don't collect them or anything—just these rifles. But when Dylan came along, Walt insisted on getting rid of our handguns. He wouldn't even let me keep them in here. I think it was Maggie and not him. But they're parents, and that's the way it goes."

"That sucks. We could use a few handguns."

"You're planning to get close to these guys?"

"It may come to that. Better prepared than dead."

"Okay. I have one handgun. I couldn't let him sell it. It's upstairs."

Widow took bullets out of the box of thirty-thirties. He shoved as many of them into his pockets as he could carry without being bulky and uncomfortable. If he needed to sneak around outside, he didn't want bullets slapping together in his pockets, making all kinds of racket.

Next, Widow grabbed the remaining rifles off the hooks for Abe and carried three out the door, his initialed A.M.W. rifle included, along with as many boxes of bullets for the three rifles that he could palm in his hands or wedge between the rifles and his ribcage. Abe followed suit as best he could. Together, they left the shed, leaving it unlocked in case Abe had to run back in for more bullets.

They came to the back porch sliders. Abby stood on the other side, waiting as if she hadn't moved. As hard as it might've been for some people to believe, Widow had a mother once. He knew motherly expressions. They were universal among the world's mothers. And one such expression was worry.

Worry was stretched across Abby's face like a face mask. It couldn't possibly get worse or more obvious. At least, that's what Widow thought.

Abby saw them coming and waited till Abe was at the door. She unlocked the latch and slid the door open. She stepped out to help take some of the ammunition and one rifle from her husband. Foster came out from behind her and took as many of the spare boxes of ammo that she could from Widow.

Right then was when they heard a sound that solidified their growing anxiety.

In the distance, off toward the direction of the Pines Farm, they heard a loud gunshot. It echoed over the trees and across the sky.

They all froze and stared at each other.

Widow said, "Shotgun."

38

ABEL WATCHED Shep die right there. His guys stood around him in a semicircle like some sort of ritual—all of them except the one in the sniper's nest. He remained on guard and vigilant. Adonis was on her knees, zip-tied, next to Ramirez, who was the same, next to Swan and James. All their hands were restrained behind them. Their hats were gone, thrown off in the distance. James and Swan showed no emotion. They had stayed tough to this point. James's nose continued to bleed, not a steady flow as before. Now it was a slow trickle—a faucet that needed tightening.

Adonis felt Ramirez shivering. His teeth chattered. His eyes darted from side to side, watching the skyline like a pilot waiting for rescue, knowing that backup was coming.

His knees shook in the snow. His body shivered and bumped into hers.

She whispered, "Keep it together."

Ramirez shook. He said, "We're gonna die."

"We're not going to die. Keep calm."

"You got us into this. We're going to die. It's your fault."

"Shut up!" Adonis ordered.

Ramirez didn't listen, not really. He lowered his volume and muttered under his breath incoherently like he was praying to himself.

He was afraid. She couldn't blame him. For her, it was slowly coming on. She felt her heart pounding, her knees slowly chattering like his. She might've been distracted by her need for revenge more than him, more than the others. That was what kept her from feeling afraid. But that wouldn't last.

After Shep was dead, Abel knelt beside him and hovered one bony hand over the body. He spoke over the corpse like a priest giving a benediction.

"The Bible says, 'Do not take revenge, my dear friends, but leave room for God's wrath, for it is written.'"

Abel reached out and swiped his long fingers over Shep's eyes and closed them.

He said, "God's wraith. That's what I am. That's what we are."

The others stirred like true believers. They whooped and hollered and stabbed their rifles into the air. They chanted. It was a mishmash of Army, Marine, and Navy cheers.

"HOORAH! OORAH! HOORA! HOOYAH!"

Abel said, "Vengeance belongs to God!"

The men said, "HOORAH! OORAH! HOORA! HOOYAH!"

Abel said, "Revenge belongs to God!"

"HOORAH! OORAH! HOORA! HOOYAH!"

Abel said, "Justice belongs to God!"

"HOORAH! OORAH! HOORA! HOOYAH!"

Abel said, "But I am God's wraith!"

"HOORAH! OORAH! HOORA! HOOYAH!"

"I am God's revenge!"

"HOORAH! OORAH! HOORA! HOOYAH!"

"I am God's justice!"

"HOORAH! OORAH! HOORA! HOOYAH!"

Right then, the four men on the ground raised their rifles as Abel rose slowly. He lifted his hands and looked up to the sky.

He said, "Revenge is mine. Soon, those who deserve it will feel it."

"HOORAH! OORAH! HOORA! HOOYAH!"

The men lowered their rifles. Abel lowered his hands and adjusted his head to look forward. The four men saluted him.

That was when it hit Adonis. That was when she felt fear. That's when the truth hit home, and she uttered it to herself.

"You're insane."

Brooks was the first of the men to speak after their strange behavior.

"What do we do with them?"

Abel walked over to his prisoners, away from Shep's corpse. He stopped at arm's length away, hovering over them like a vulture.

His four guys stood around behind them, weapons lowered by their sides.

Abel paced out in front of them from left to right, slowly, and then back again. He stopped in the middle between Ramirez and James.

"Which one of you is the pilot for the bird?"

No one answered.

Abel wasn't the ask-for-something-twice kind of leader. So, he reached into his white garb, under his coat, and pulled out his Glock, big and obvious. He wanted them to notice it.

Ramirez whispered to himself faster and faster. He squeezed his eyes shut and swayed back and forth like he was about to go into a spasm.

No one spoke. No one answered Abel's question.

Abel sidestepped and pointed the Glock at Adonis. She stared up and back at him over the barrel.

He looked in her eyes.

"You. You're their leader. Who is the pilot?"

She said, "You're a fake!"

"What's that?"

"You're a fake! All this religious bullshit! You don't believe in God! Or anything else! You're a fraud!"

One of Abel's eyebrows arched.

"How so?"

"You know who the pilot is. Your guy in the barn watched us. He saw who got out of the helicopter. You all probably did. You're just toying with us."

Abel cracked a grin and shifted his aim to Ramirez.

"You the pilot? 'Cause we could use that bird."

Ramirez stopped moving. He raised his head. Hope filled his eyes, thinking they needed him to fly the helicopter. He was of value, and Abel wouldn't kill someone he needed.

"Yes. I'm the pilot."

Flack stood behind Ramirez. But just then, he took a big step back and sidestepped to the left.

Abel said, "Too bad. We don't need a pilot."

He shot Ramirez in the head. The head and body jolted back from the bullet. It was through and through. The bullet slammed down into the snow and dirt where Flack had been standing. The bullet buried itself somewhere underneath the snow, into the earth below. Snow kicked up high, and a snow cloud filled the air around Ramirez.

James and Swan both squeezed their eyes shut, but Adonis kept hers open. She watched as the snow cloud slowly wafted off in the breeze. She was the first to see the look on Ramirez's face as his body slowly slumped forward, and he landed face-first. A big chunk of the back of his head was gone.

Adonis's fear of death was gone, replaced by guilt. She knew it because it had been the second thing she felt all morning long, right after revenge. That feeling was gone.

Abel waited for the snow cloud to clear, and then he stared at her.

She screamed, "You're insane! You're just tormenting us!"

Abel shrugged.

Adonis said, "Just kill us already! If you're gonna kill us in cold blood, get it over with."

He stared at her. He stared deeply into her eyes, deeper than any man had ever stared into them before. She was terrified of him, but she struggled to keep that from being read on her face or in her eyes.

Finally, he lowered his Glock, re-holstered it somewhere inside his garb. He stepped back away from her.

He said, "You're not scared. You're different, Agent Adonis. Different from these other clowns. But not that different. You're not the first to defy me."

Abel stepped away and turned and looked up to the sky. Then he returned and looked up at Jargo in the sniper's nest.

"Brooks, give me the radio."

Brooks tossed his radio to him. Abel caught it and clicked the button.

"Jargo?"

"Yes, sir."

"Any movement?"

"No. Nothing on the road. Nothing in the sky."

"Good. Keep a lookout. They must've heard that shotgun blast over at Walter's place."

"Got it, boss."

Abel pocketed the radio this time. He went back over to the group.

"Boys, I think we have almost everything we need."

He looked at Tanis.

"Get over to the bird and make sure you can operate it."

Tanis nodded and took off, running toward the direction of the helicopter.

Abel said, "Cucci, grab the keys off that body and move that police car off the road. Bring it into the driveway. Don't block the trucks. Leave it running for now."

He pointed into a field off the drive.

"Flack, get the keys from the good sheriff, and move this truck off somewhere, too. Just get it out of the way of the driveway."

Adonis was staring at Brooks when he looked up, as if a light bulb had gone off in his head. He had an idea, and she didn't like the way it made him smile.

Brooks interrupted Abel.

"Sir, wait."

"What?"

Brooks went over to Abel, leaned in, and explained his idea to him. Adonis watched the whole time. She cringed when Abel's smile matched Brooks's. It was a sinister grin, from ear to ear.

Abel stepped back and looked at Adonis.

"That's why you're my number one, Brooks. Whatever I don't think of, you think of. Okay. Get over to Walter's place on the double. Just sit on them till we get there."

"Don't want me to take them now? They might call the cops."

"Take out their phone lines. And wait for us."

Abel took out the radio and called Jargo.

"Yes, boss," Jargo answered.

"Look around for cell towers."

Silence came over the radio for a moment.

Jargo came back on.

"There's one due south. Maybe six to eight klicks."

"Thanks. Keep an eye on that driveway across the street."

"Ten-four."

Abel spoke to Brooks again.

"I'm not worried about it. I'd bet we got the county's only cop right here. Just sit on them. We'll be over momentarily."

Brooks nodded and started off, jogging to the Whites' house.

Abel stopped him one last time.

"Brooks."

"Yeah?"

Abel showed him the radio.

"Take it with you."

Abel tossed it. Brooks caught it and tucked it into his coat. He turned back and ran off down the driveway to the Whites' house.

Adonis watched him go.

She asked, "You going to kill us now?"

"I've got use for you yet," Abel said. He retreated to the barn and signaled for Flack to come over. Flack was already in the sheriff's truck, the ignition on and running. He had to slip the truck back into park before he could get out.

Adonis watched as Abel explained the new plan to him. They looked like two men conspiring.

James spoke.

"Are they going to kill us?"

Adonis said, "I don't know."

But she did know.

39

"WE HEARD A GUNSHOT!" Dylan shouted. Excitement filled his voice.

He and Lauren stood at the top of the stairs, phoneless. Maggie was behind them, at the railing, looking down at the main room. Foster paced the hallway. Abe and Widow stepped back into the house. Abby shut the slider behind them.

Just then, like out of the sound effects of an old radio show, they heard a new sound. Thunder cracked and rolled deep in the sky.

Maggie called down.

"Was it thunder?"

Abby said, "It might've been."

Abe tugged on Widow's arm, readjusting to keep the rifles in his arm.

"That's what we heard."

He looked at Widow and whispered.

"No reason to tell the kids yet."

Widow disagreed but kept it to himself. The kids should know, in his opinion, because being prepared for battle was part of being victorious in battle. But they weren't his kids, and this wasn't his house. Besides, Dylan was the youngest at eight years old. He was going to figure it out in seconds because they were transporting a small armory into the house.

They moved into the dining room with the rifles and the boxes of ammunition. They laid them out on the dinner table with care, all unloaded, minus Widow's Winchester.

Abby followed them in and helped to take things from Widow's arms. After they laid them all out, she began doing grandmotherly things like shuffling boxes of ammo around and placing them in rows of caliber and ordering them alphabetically according to the name of the manufacturer—A's first, B's second, and so on.

It was a pointless endeavor, Abe thought, but he knew better than to question his wife's way of helping.

Widow helped her.

After they were through, she asked, "Want me to make some fresh coffee?"

Abe didn't think they could drink any more coffee, but Widow smiled and figured it was best to keep Abby busy doing what she felt like she could do to help.

He said, "Coffee is always brewed and available in the mess on a Navy ship or in the officer's hall. Twenty-four, seven."

"Okay, Widow."

She shuffled off to the kitchen and poured out the old pot and made a new one. It took only seconds before the aroma carried over into the dining room, and Widow's nose caught it. To him, the effect was working already.

Abe interrupted him.

"Now what?"

Widow said, "We've got to prepare for a siege."

"You really think that something bad has happened?"

"You heard the same gunshot I heard. Besides, they'd be back by now. We'd have heard from them."

Foster came into the dining room.

"What's going on?"

Abe said, "Nothing. Just some thunder."

"Dad, I know a gunshot when I hear one."

Abe said nothing to that.

Foster asked, "If nothing's going on, then why the hell did you bring in all the guns?"

Widow spoke to Abe.

"Look, we have little time. We need all hands on deck. No reason to hide anything from the adults."

"Okay. Okay. We're preparing in case something bad is going down."

Foster asked, "How can I help?"

Widow said, "You know how to shoot one of these?"

Foster grabbed one of the hunting rifles and the correct box of ammunition for it. She loaded it and showed him.

"I'm a woman, but I'm a countrywoman."

"Good. Can you shoot that one?"

Abe said, "She can."

"Then that one's yours. Who else is best with the scope? Can Maggie shoot?"

Abe and Foster looked at each other.

"Maggie?" Abe asked.

Foster said, "No way!"

"I can," Abby said, and she stepped out of the kitchen with a single hot cup of coffee.

Abe said, "She can shoot straight enough."

"I can shoot," Abby repeated.

Widow said, "Then take the other scoped rifle and a box of ammo for it."

Abby asked, "What about you?"

"I'm going to have to go out there. If they come over here, they won't expect me to be out there. They probably don't even know that I'm here."

Foster said, "Unless Walt told them."

Abe shook his head at her immediately. At first, she couldn't figure out why until it hit her. If he told them anything, it would have been under duress.

Foster said, "Oh."

Widow said, "Let's not think about that. Right now, we need to secure the house as best we can. Afterward, we can talk about getting Walter back."

Widow looked over at Abby. She still held the coffee for him. He walked around the table and took it, set it down.

"Thank you, ma'am."

Widow put the coffee down on the tabletop and looked at Abby.

"Can you tell Maggie to keep trying her phone? Someone needs to keep trying the cops. Tell her to call the nearest county over and try their sheriff. She can try the ATF's line. Or the local FBI's field office. Whatever. Just keep trying. Tell her to take both kids up to an upstairs bedroom and stay there."

Abby nodded and left them.

Abe said, "What now?"

"We need cover on as much of the house as we can. Foster, take your rifle and get to a corner window, close to the south side as possible. Make sure you have the driveway in view. Abe, where's the best window to cover the back from?"

"The master."

"Okay. Take the other hunting rifle and ammo there. Set it up for Abby and make sure she knows where it is. Then I want you back down here. Stand guard on the first floor. Quarterback the whole thing."

"What about the other Winchester?"

There was one left unassigned.

Widow said, "Give it to Maggie. Show her how to use it."

"That's a bad idea. I'm telling you. She's more likely to shoot one of us."

"Then set Foster up with it."

"Okay."

"Also, you mentioned a handgun?"

"Yeah. Follow me."

Abe picked up both the last hunting rifle and Winchester, but Widow took the extra Winchester from him and scooped up the extra boxes of ammo. They both went up the stairs and past Abby, helping Maggie wrangle Dylan into one of the bedrooms and out of the way. They turned a corner, opposite where Widow had slept and came to a room with the door shut.

Abe pushed it open. It was a huge bedroom with a bathroom and three big windows—the master.

Abe picked a window with a big sill and a small nook of built-ins with a cushion on top for sitting by the window. He set the hunting rifle and his ammo boxes down.

"Put the extra rifle there. I'll give it to Foster later."

Widow nodded and set down the other Winchester and all his extra ammo. He followed Abe back out into the hallway. They walked down the hall and came to a closed door. Abe pushed it open. It was another bedroom.

The bed, the dresser tops, the nightstands, the closet, and the floors were all cleaned and neatly organized.

Widow asked, "The corporal's room?"

He already knew it was because it looked like a Marine lived in it, which was to say it looked like no one lived in it. It was kept and maintained so well it could've been the model room for a house they were trying to sell.

"Yeah. We haven't changed a thing. I'm very insistent on that. I know he's dead, but I like to keep it just as he left it. Like he might still come home someday."

Widow stayed quiet.

Abe walked to the closet, paused, and brushed a hand over the hanging shirts. They fluttered like a glissando, like fingers over piano keys, as he brushed over them.

He tried to reach up to the shelf above the clothes, but couldn't quite reach the back. He stepped back.

"It's up there. In the far back."

Widow stepped up and reached all the way to back of the shelf and found a gun case. He slid it out and followed Abe over to the bed. He set the case down. There was a small lock on it.

"Got the key?" Widow asked.

Abe fished into his pocket, came out empty-handed, and then fished into his other one. This time he brought out the right key. It was a small set of two keys. One was the backup. They were gold and on a small ring.

He unlocked the gun case for Widow.

Inside, there were two magazines, fully loaded, and a Beretta M9, polished and oiled as if Abe's son were still alive, still keeping his gun to Marine standards.

"It's pristine. You've kept it clean?"

Abe said, "I use the chair from the desk to get it down."

He blurted it out like he was stuck thinking that Widow thought he was short.

Widow said nothing to that, either.

"You take it. You'll make better use of it."

Widow thanked him and took out the weapon. He racked the slide, checked that it was indeed empty. After he confirmed there were no bullets in it, he dry-fired it, as he always did, to make sure it worked properly. To him, the sound of an empty Beretta M9 dry-firing was like hearing the voice of an old friend.

Widow took out a full magazine, loaded the gun with it, and pocketed the other one. He chambered a round and slid the Beretta into the waistband of his jeans, tightening the belt afterward to make sure it stayed put.

Another roll of thunder sounded loud and looming over the farm, followed closely by a second one.

Abe said, "Now what?"

"Now, I go out there and see what the hell is going on."

40

CELL PHONES WORK in a hexagonal tower system called a network. There is no standard range for a cell phone tower. One tower doesn't measure the same range as another. They don't all equal X. Some are the same, some are similar, and many are different. A tower's range depends on several factors, including the direction of the antenna array, positioning, terrain, height and width of the antennas, signal frequency, and transmission power.

Civilian communities use simple tower systems with little security. Phone calls and text messages and signals bounce from one local tower to another tower and so on. If you take out one tower on a network, local communication involving mobile devices will go dark. Cell phones and mobile devices become handheld screens good for playing video games and keeping track of time and not much else.

Police don't depend on this technology. Neither do military bases. They utilize more secure network systems. But Abel's guys weren't interested in police communications, and they were not going head-to-head with a military force. They were interested in silencing the Whites, the only witnesses for miles around. From what Brooks told them, there was only one male to worry about, and that was Walter. He wasn't much of a threat. They had him zip-tied and at gunpoint, no problem there. But the shotgun blast from Shep was a concern. The sound of the blast, coupled with

Walter being gone, would raise eyebrows at the farm down the road.

The Bell 205 circled the closest cell phone tower, about ten miles from Cherokee Hill, with Tanis controlling the bird and Cucci seated in the rear. The tower looked to be the only one within a three-hundred-sixty-degree view from the Bell 205. The next closest one wasn't in view from Cherokee Hill, so they didn't worry about it. All they needed was to take out this one and create a black spot for them to operate in.

The helicopter yawed, and the rotor blades rotated. Tanis kept the Bell hovering against the winds at about fifty feet above the tower's base.

Tanis called back to Cucci, who sat on the rear bench, packed in as close to the rear door as possible without falling out of it. The door was slid all the way open. Cucci was armed with one of the M4s, with a suppressor attached to the end, along with an ACOG scope.

"Is this close enough?"

"Yeah. Hold it here."

Cucci aimed through the scope at the base. He clicked the firing switch to full auto and squeezed the trigger. The weapon fired several rounds out of the magazine. He didn't count them, but figured from this distance he might not need all thirty rounds from the magazine.

The suppressor kept the gun quiet over the rotor noise. The weapon kicked and purred in rapid succession. Bullets ripped into the base of the tower. Sparks ignited. He fired until he was satisfied the base was inoperable. Then he stopped and called back to Tanis.

"Take us up to the top."

Tanis nodded and pulled the flight stick back slowly. The helicopter's nose lifted, and the machine ascended two hundred feet to the tip of the antenna. He evened out the helicopter and circled around the top antenna.

Cucci aimed the M4 and squeezed the trigger. The gun fired, and bullets slammed into the antenna parts all along the top. Every bullet hit home.

The antenna sparked and exploded. Blue flames flashed and danced off the top. The heat was more than they expected.

Tanis reacted and pulled on the flight stick, hauling the Bell up and away fifteen feet. But Cucci stayed on target and fired until the M4 ran empty.

He called out to Tanis.

"That should do it."

Cucci ejected the magazine and loaded a fresh one from out of his coat pocket. He tossed the old one out the window. There was no reason to keep it. He doubted he would ever reload it.

Cucci said, "Okay. That should do."

They both looked out at the tower one last time. Both the base and the top antenna burned with several small fires.

Tanis said, "Taking us back."

The Bell 205 flew up and forward, the nose dipped, and then it circled back around the fiery antenna and flew back to Cherokee Hill.

* * *

Close to the same time, in front of Pine Farms, Brooks made his way up the drive to the road. Jargo watched him through the scope.

Brooks got on his radio.

"Jargo?"

"I'm here."

"Is the coast clear?"

Jargo paused a beat, leaving Brooks to listen to dead air for twenty seconds, until finally, Jargo came back on the radio.

"I don't see anyone for miles on the road. No traffic. No people."

"Okay. I see a bunch of power lines. It looks like the one straight ahead will do the trick. I should be able to take it out and kill their power and landlines. Can you confirm?"

"I see it. I'd put three rounds in the transformer just to be sure."

"Copy that."

Brooks aimed his gun at a transformer on his way out of the drive and onto the main road. He aimed through ACOG scope on his rifle, but he set the fire selector to single-shot. He paused a moment and squeezed the trigger—once, twice, three shots.

The transformer and all the conduits and cables lit up in a blue flash of sparks and flames, similar to the tower. The result was another long flash of blue flames and sparks, then the top of the pole lit on fire.

Both the landlines and cell phone communications were now down for miles. Plus, one more thing happened. The power at the Whites' went out.

Brooks smiled and carried on, staying parallel to the Whites' long uphill driveway.

41

THUNDER BOOMED over Spartan County and Cherokee Hill. Widow heard it. They all heard it. It might help Widow out. Potentially, it could provide some sound cover. He was only one man and on foot. If the elements favored him, so be it. He would take all the help he could get.

Widow carried the borrowed Beretta in his borrowed jeans. He held the Winchester rifle by the wood grain stock just ahead of the trigger and lever. He carried it with a loaded chamber. Ready to fire. Ready to kill.

After Widow helped Abe to evaluate key defense points to set his family in, he went out the slider in the back of the house. He wasn't sure, but he suspected that they might have eyes on the front. He wasn't sure what these guys were up to, what they were after, or why they were who they were. What he presumed, using the intel that he had, was that they were trying to escape capture, plain and simple.

Widow could understand that. Anyone could. He had no stakes if they escaped, or not. But they made a mistake when they involved Walter White, a man Widow had known for only seven hours—max, but a good man with a good family. Widow had no stake in what happened at the Athenian compound. He saw in Adonis's eyes that she did. And he understood that part, too. He had lost guys. Sometimes it was his fault. He understood the guilt that came with it.

Widow wasn't going to lose a member of the White family. That was for damn sure.

Widow wasn't a family man. He had no family himself, except a father who might or might not still be alive, out there somewhere. Family man or not, Widow used to be an undercover cop. Once a cop, always a cop. He would stop these guys no matter the cost.

Widow recalled in his mind what he could from seeing Pine Farms from a distance on the road and in the dark. He remembered seeing a barn with an open loft on top. He thought to himself that was a perfect spot to set up a sniper's nest. That's what he would've done if he had been on the Athenians' side.

Widow went out the back. Maggie slid the door shut behind him and locked it. She and Foster, with the help of both children, lifted the largest of their sofas and carried it over to the slider and set it down in front as a kind of barrier. They closed the blinds tight and scooted the sofa all the way back. It wouldn't stop anyone from surging through the glass, but it was an obstacle they might not suspect.

Widow was gone, and Abe was in charge. He sent the rest of the family to their posts to wait for further instructions, like his very own platoon. Maggie and the children went to Walter's bedroom and barricaded themselves in.

Abe stayed on the first floor. Everything seemed to go in their favor. If the bad guys had beaten Adonis and her guys and they were coming for the Whites next, then they probably thought they had the advantage of surprise. They probably thought they had the upper hand. But the Whites were expecting them. Now the element of surprise reversed, tipping the scales in their favor. Plus, they had guns of their own. And they had Widow.

Abe was worried about Walter. He would do anything for his only remaining son, but he wouldn't give up the rest of the family. He would die before he would allow Abel to come into his home and threaten all their lives.

He felt confident. The rifle in his hand and diligence on his side. He knew they were as prepared for anything as they could be. But maybe the bad guys wouldn't even come. Maybe Widow would get to them and bring his son back in one piece. Maybe.

Right then, the power went out, and the house went dark and cold. Everything but the living room was dark. The fire in the fireplace burned on and crackled, providing low light to the family room.

He heard screams from upstairs.

It was the kids and Maggie.

Abe turned, abandoned his post, and ran to the stairs and bounded up them as fast as he could. He attempted to take two steps at a time but couldn't. On top of being short, his age and the stress of the day were impacting him.

On the second floor, he turned the corner and ran down the hallway to Walter's bedroom, where the screams and shouts were coming from.

He tried the door handle. It was locked.

He knocked on it.

"Maggie, everything okay in there? Something happen?"

He heard the fragile inside lock turn, and the knob followed. The door opened. Maggie stood there with Dylan, hugging her tightly. Lauren was behind her, holding her almost as tightly.

"Everything okay? Is this about the power?" Abe asked.

Lauren said, "Not just the power."

Dylan said, "Tell him, Mom."

Maggie said, "The phones. They're out. I was on the landline. I finally got through to the sheriff's office. They said Henry left to come out here more than an hour ago. They said no one's answering his phone or his radio. And then the phone went dead."

Maggie paused a quick beat.

She said, "It went dead at the same time as the power."

42

Widow moved slowly, starting at the back of the Whites' farmhouse. He walked for about a football field until he was in the north section of Christmas trees. They were tall, but not quite ready for harvesting. He figured they were one of the older sections. Their year might be the next or the one after that.

He turned west and threaded between the trees until he made it into a new section. He glanced back at the White's farmhouse and barn to maintain his bearings and direction, as well as to see what he could see. Going slowly, it took him seven minutes before he crossed over from the last section of trees out to some dead brush before the road.

He walked through the snow and dead brush and thick oak trees with countless branches verging off in numerous directions.

Widow came to a ditch right before the road. He paused and knelt down. He looked right and north, tracing the road, looking out for any oncoming traffic. A passerby might be of help. He could wave the driver down and see if they had a cell phone and ask them to keep trying the police as they went on their way south. Or he could get them to drive to the nearest sheriff's office or roadblock and tell someone what was happening. But he saw no one.

He looked left and south, down the winding main road. He could see the beginning of the Whites' driveway and the big, metal mailbox. He studied the mouth of the drive closely. He figured that if the bad guys were any good, they wouldn't have posted someone at the end of the drive, where they would be visible from the main road. Plus, whoever might be there would want to see the main house, and it wasn't visible from the road.

He saw no one and nothing, so he got up and crossed over the road.

Once Widow was on the road, he picked up his pace and fired across, and over a new ditch, and into the brush. This time he had to hop the Pines' dilapidated, wood-railing fence. He took it slower once he made it over.

The Pines' farmhouse wasn't visible from where he was. But he could see bits of red paint from the top of the barn in the distance. He crept at the same westward angle as best he could. He knew he would be off because he didn't have the Whites' farmhouse to use as a landmark any longer, and the sky seemed to get more overcast.

Thunder rolled again, deep and heavy. He figured rain or heavy snow would follow, or both. Winter thunderstorms during snow-fall are called thundersnow or thundersnowstorms. Both were terminologies he didn't hear used very often. But he had been through the phenomena before. The snow gets heavy and hard. In bad ones, the snow can turn as hard as baseballs.

Knowing this, he hoped for one. Widow knew Abe was armed and ready to protect his family. But they were just civilians, not military-trained special forces. Not like Abel and his guys were. They wouldn't stand a chance in a firefight. He doubted they could even hold off a siege for more than a couple of minutes.

Widow crept through the trees and brush and over the snow until he came to a long empty field of more snow. From there, he saw the barn and the back of the farmhouse. He wished he had access to field glasses. He realized he should've opted for one of the scoped hunting rifles instead of the Winchester rifle. He could've used the scope to recon the farm. Or he could've opted to take out the sniper from there. Maybe. But that wasn't an option, so he leaned in and narrowed his eyes, trying to focus on the open shutter doors of the loft.

Widow couldn't make out any detail, not enough sunlight out to reflect a glimmer of light from the sniper's scope glass. Luckily, that didn't matter, because he saw proof of the sniper in the loft. The guy wasn't hiding too well. The barrel of the rifle stuck out. It pointed northeast, skewed from the direction Widow had come.

Widow stayed crouched in the snow and tall, wintry grass. He watched the sniper for a long minute, taking mental notes of the guy's movements. Basically, there were none. Widow stayed focused on the approach to the barn, watching the ground ahead, checking the terrain, and staying low.

Suddenly, Widow noticed a small, slow movement from the sniper's nest. He stopped and dropped to his haunches. He watched. The sniper moved as if he was tracing a target through the scope.

But Widow wasn't the target. The sniper rifle was trained elsewhere.

Widow kept his body facing forward, but twisted slightly at the hips and craned his neck and looked in the scope's directional view. He looked to see if the sniper was pointed toward the Whites' farm. But there was no way he could see it from there. Too many trees, distance, and geological interferences. Besides, if the sniper could see that far, then Widow would've been spotted and dead already.

What was he looking at? Widow wondered.

It hit Widow he was probably watching and providing cover for a scout. Widow encountered no one on his way over, but they wouldn't cover the long way around that he took. They would have someone watching the driveway. They must've figured that the White family heard the gunshot, which they might've ignored except that Abel had Walter.

Widow pressed on but took it slowly. His gut told him to run, to turn back because snipers worked in pairs. There could've been two in that nest right then. The other one could've been using binoculars, scanning the terrain for targets. But there weren't two. He knew that because, again, he would be dead already. No way would they've let him get this close without putting a bullet in his head. He had been in an open field for a good minute. Widow wasn't wearing bright orange, but he wasn't dressed in winter camo either. He wore plain, dark street clothes, and he was surrounded by snow. He would've been spotted by now, for sure. But there was no second man up there in the loft.

Widow moved toward the back of the farmhouse. He creeped slowly. He wanted to get there as fast as he could, but he didn't want to register in the sniper's peripherals.

He still had a hundred yards of distance to cover when he heard a thump behind him. He turned and saw what looked like a potential lightning strike over the trees near the Whites' driveway. But it wasn't a lightning strike.

It was Brooks taking out the transformer on the power line pole.

43

BEING OUT HERE on his own came with certain advantages, sure, but it came with more disadvantages. Mainly, he had no backup. No intel, except what he had gotten about Abel from the internet. And he had zero support.

A significant disadvantage to committing to a takedown-rescue mission like this on his own was that going up against an unknown number of special forces cult guys was risky as all hell. With everything going on, he had no chance of guessing where any of them would be onsite. He knew one was posted in the barn's loft. And he knew one was scouting the Whites' place. He also knew there was one highway patrol officer, Adonis, and an unknown number of ATF agents in the helicopter.

Every few minutes, he glanced at the sky, but there was no sign of the bird, only more gray clouds that filtered the sunlight to a dim white. He figured Abel's guys already had possession of it. He had no idea where it was. He didn't know if it was just parked somewhere on the property or if they had taken off it.

Widow's choices for his follow-up actions were pretty limited. He figured the best thing to do was to stay quiet as long as he could and take them down one by one.

His priority was to locate and rescue Adonis, Walter, and the others—if they were still alive. He guessed Walter was still alive. The others—he wasn't so sure about.

Widow started with the Pines' farmhouse. He tried the back door. It was locked. He didn't have the equipment to pick it, and he couldn't risk kicking it down. Too much noise. So, he left it and walked the length of the house, peeking in each window to see if any of them were unlatched. No luck there.

He made it to the last window before the corner of the house. So far, he had seen no one, no movement. No sounds came from inside the house.

Widow traced the back exterior wall to the corner and stopped. He peeked around the brick and saw no one there. All he saw was the barn.

Widow stepped out, rifle stock in his shoulder, his right eye over the Buckhorn rear sight, gazing through the ivory bead front sight. Widow's left eye stayed open. A common mistake that amateur shooters make is closing one eye when aiming. They close one eye when aiming. Widow was no amateur shooter.

He stalked the side of the house, close, nearly hugging the wall. He could hear noises and voices from the driveway. He continued.

At the front corner of the farmhouse, Widow stopped, pulling the rifle up, so the barrel didn't give him away at the corner.

The voices chattered on like busy people doing busy things. It almost sounded like workers on a dock, loading crates, working equipment, and shooting the breeze; only he heard no sounds of machinery like rigs and cranes and forklifts. He heard engines fire up. He counted three: one car engine and two trucks.

Widow put his back to the wall and slid down until his knees were up and his butt was on the heels of his boots. He flattened himself down to waist-height and minimized his profile. He twisted and peeked around the corner.

He saw the side of the barn. It was a little over fifty yards away, past the driveway and a single large oak tree. Behind it, Widow saw the helicopter. It was parked a hundred feet back from the rear of the barn.

He stretched his neck and headed out to see the driveway better. He saw two trucks and one car, as he had thought. The car was a South Carolina patrol car. It was out front, engine running, no one at the wheel, but the driver's door was wide open. Next, he saw the Spartan County sheriff's truck. He knew it was the sheriff's truck because it had a light bar on the roof and the Spartan County sheriff's decals on the doors. The last vehicle was Walter's truck.

Both the trucks, like the police car, had no one in the driver's seat. But there were two passengers, one in each truck, seated in the passenger seat.

The sheriff's truck had an old guy that Widow had never laid eyes on before. But Walter was in his own truck. He sat on the passenger side, quiet because a dirty car rag was stuffed in his mouth.

Widow figured if he was gagged, then his hands were restrained as well. Why gag a person and not restrain their hands?

Walter didn't look back at Widow. He just stared forward, as if his life depended on it. The old guy wasn't gagged, but he also had the same hopeless look on his face. He must've also been restrained with handcuffs or duct tape.

The thing that was obvious, without a doubt, was the old guy was a prisoner, like Walter. It was obvious because the guy had a black eye swelling up on one side of his face. And a couple of bruises on his cheeks and chin, like he had been roughed up. Not too badly. Not fatally. But someone delivered several good punches to the guy's face.

Suddenly, Widow saw something he hadn't expected. Two ATF agents exited the barn, and a third one came out after.

They wore ATF gear he had seen in newspapers before—all-black gear like SWAT. They were armed with only sidearms in holsters.

Widow stayed where he was. He wasn't sure what was going on. These agents weren't acting the way cops acted at crime scenes. They weren't on edge or arresting bad guys. They were casual, which made no sense.

Widow never knew a cop anywhere to act nonchalant and blasé around cop-killing terrorists before.

Widow watched as the third one skipped out in front of the first two quickly. He got to Walter's truck and lowered the tailgate. The following two carried packages—wrapped up, addressed, and stamped like post office mail. The two guys carried as many packages as they could hold, but they were careful with them. The third guy climbed up into the truck's bed and took the stacks of packages from the tailgate, and stacked them close to the cabin. After the other two finished with a stack of packages, they returned into the barn and came out again with another stack. This went on for three trips each.

The ATF agent in the truck's bed carefully set each package down, toward the back of the truck, near the cabin. He stacked them neatly, as if they might explode. After the last of the packages were arranged and stacked orderly, the ATF agent in the truck's rear secured them down, using Walter's hauling cables and bungee cords that were in the back of the truck. The same ones Widow had removed from the lumber and shingles, hours ago in Abe's barn.

The final ATF agent exited the back of the truck and closed the tailgate. Widow had counted the packages loaded onto the truck as forty-one. Each was equal in size, equal in volume. They were probably equal in contents.

Widow stayed where he was—baffled, but not by the packages. He figured those were something sinister, but why were Adonis's guys loading them onto Walter's truck?

Like a ghost that had walked through a wall, Widow saw a face he knew. It was a man dressed in all white—white clothing and a heavy white winter coat. He stepped out of the barn behind the ATF agents.

It was Joseph Abel, the crazed cult leader behind the whole Athenian explosion, and Adonis's hell-bent obsession.

Widow crouch-walked all the way to the corner and stopped and stepped out three inches from the wall. He lifted the Winchester and aimed it straight at Abel.

He waited. His finger slipped into the trigger housing. He squeezed. He could've killed Abel right then. He had a clear headshot. One bullet would do it. He could take him down right there. But he didn't, because Abel held onto Agent Adonis by the collar. Tears streamed down her face. Blood seeped out her nose from being punched in the face.

Unlike the sheriff and Walter, she didn't have an expression of hopelessness on her face. She expressed nothing but fear.

Widow thought of POWs he had seen over his career. The ones who never gave up, never gave in to the torture, only to break years later. That's the same look he saw on her face.

Widow still had the shot. He could squeeze the trigger and blow Abel's head clean off. But then Adonis was dead if he did.

Widow retracted the rifle and ducked back behind the corner.

Abel suddenly felt the hairs on his arms stand up. He felt that tingle that follows the suspicious feeling that you're being watched.

He looked around. He glanced in at the corner of the farmhouse where Widow had just been aiming a rifle at him. But he saw no one. No one was there.

He couldn't shake the feeling that there had been someone standing there, staring at him.

44

LIGHTNING STRUCK on the outer edge of the Whites' property line, and thunder rolled. Abe and Abby looked out different windows on different floors in the direction of the lightning strike. Foster glanced back to a wall with no window. It was a simple reaction to the thunderclap. She returned her focus forward. She looked out the front of the house, from the second floor, using the hunting rifle.

Dark gray clouds rolled in overhead, fast. They streamed over and covered the sky like a dark presence. The farm was covered in gray, shadowy darkness.

They had no working phones, and the cell phones were useless, so they had to yell out to communicate.

Right when the power went out, Abe headed back out to the shed and uncovered a power generator. He cranked it up, and the lights in the house came back on, as did the clocks on the oven and microwave. After he went back inside and locked the slider behind him, he moved from room to room, switching off lights and unplugging things they didn't need sucking up gas from the generator.

Abe called out.

"Foster, everything okay?"

"Yes, Dad. Still no sign of anything coming down the drive."

Abe called out to Abby.

"Abigail, you see anything?"

Abby went to the master bedroom door and opened it, and called back out. She left the door open behind her so she could hear better.

"I'm fine. Nothing to see from the back."

"Okay. Everyone, just hold your positions till we hear from Widow."

Abby stayed quiet.

Foster shouted back.

"Okay, Dad."

Abe paced from window to window, from room to room. He checked out the front, the sides, and the back. He saw and heard nothing.

* * *

BROOKS LEANED AGAINST A TREE, out of sight and comfortable. He had been on many, many stakeouts and recon missions. This was a cakewalk by comparison, and it was better than sitting up in the loft with Jargo, who constantly mumbled to himself.

It was only five more minutes until he heard trucks coming up behind him. He turned and walked back uphill and stepped behind some brush. He saw Walter's truck pulling into the drive, heading toward him. Behind it was the sheriff's truck, and behind that was Shep's police cruiser. Adonis was at the wheel with Abel in the passenger seat; his Glock was pointed at the side of her head. The muzzle was in her ear.

Abel didn't have a suppressor on his weapon.

Brooks backed out of the brush and stepped onto the driveway. He crept back down toward the entrance, back toward Abel and the vehicles. He crouched, staying out of sight of the house windows until he was sure he was completely over the hill and not visible to them.

Walter's truck rolled up first, kicking up snow.

Flack drove with Walter in the next seat. He was handcuffed, using cuffs from one of the ATF agents. The same hopeless fear painted his face a ghastly white. Brooks noticed and chuckled at the thought of a white guy named White, who was white with fear. Brooks didn't consider himself sadistic, not compared to Abel, but he enjoyed what they were doing.

The vehicles took it slowly and pulled up alongside Brooks. Flack rolled down the window.

"Everything good?" he asked.

"They're in there. Power came back on. They must be running a generator."

"See any weapons?"

"I can't see anything from here, but I'd bet on rifles, at least."

Brooks stepped back and smacked the door with the palm of his hand, twice.

He said, "Keep going. See you there."

Flack smiled, rolled up the window, and pressed on. Walter's Tundra bounced and drove away, up the hill following the drive to the house.

Brooks saw the packaged pipe bombs, stacked and fastened down in the truck's bed.

He called out behind Flack.

"Be careful!"

Weapons expert, my ass, he thought.

Brooks waited on the side of the long drive in the snow. Thunder clapped again in the distance, way up in the sky. Then he saw a lightning crack to the south.

It *boomed!* Once. Twice. Thunder rolled far above.

The sheriff's truck came next, with Cucci at the wheel, the sheriff handcuffed with his own cuffs in the middle of the front bench. Tanis sat next to him in the passenger seat. There was no weapon pointed at the sheriff because what was he going to do? Nothing.

The truck drove past Brooks, slowly, like they were staying back from Walter's truck in case one of the pipe bombs exploded from the bumpy drive, which was a valid concern. If one pipe bomb exploded, while stacked on top of forty other pipe bombs, there would be a huge explosion. It would probably kill several of them.

Cucci stared at Brooks as they passed. Brooks gave him a quick nod but stayed quiet.

The third car was the South Carolina Highway Patrol car. Adonis looked both terrified and angry.

The cruiser came to a complete stop. Abel barked an order that must've been, "Roll down the window," because Adonis rolled the window down.

Abel leaned forward over her lap, close to her face. He kept the Glock in her ear. His cheek was in biting distance, which crossed her mind.

He said, "Anything to worry about?"

Brooks said, "They know something's up. But I've seen no movement. Nothing to show they know who we are. I suspect there're guns on the premises."

"They expecting us or the cops to come back?"

"Not sure."

"Okay. Get in."

Brooks sidestepped to the back of the car and opened the back door and slipped in. He adjusted his M4 to rest in his lap with the muzzle pointed to the driver's side of the car.

He sat back, no seatbelt.

"Keep going," Abel barked.

Adonis slipped her foot off the brake and gassed, slowly. She followed behind the sheriff's truck.

She asked, "Why're we coming here?"

Abel said nothing.

She said, "These people know nothing. We don't need to come here."

Abel said, "We took their son. They probably heard your dead friend shoot his shotgun. This shotgun."

Abel patted Shep's Mossberg like it was a trophy. It rested against his thigh, and between his legs in the passenger side footwell.

"You don't need them. What difference does it make if they heard anything? The whole FBI and ATF are looking for you. It makes no difference what some backwoods family saw."

Abel smiled.

"Agent Adonis, that Quantico psychobabble, reverse psychology bullshit won't work on me. All the book-learning you got won't match up to me. Just save it. These people're a liability right now. And if you don't watch your mouth, you could end up one too. Like your friends."

Adonis stayed quiet. She kept her head forward and drove on.

Just before reaching the house and the barn, Abel gave Adonis one more command.

"Switch on the light bar. No sirens."

She didn't protest. She reached up to the roof and flipped a switch. The light bar came on, flashing blue lights over the terrain. It wasn't as pronounced as it would've been at night, but right then, snow started falling hard again. Within seconds, it mounded on the roof of the car. Abel thought that if they hadn't been in a polar vortex and it was just a normal South Carolina winter, then the snow might've been hail.

* * *

FOSTER CALLED out to her father while staring through the hunting rifle's scope. She watched an entourage of vehicles come up the drive.

"Dad! They're coming back! On the driveway! Walter's truck is first!"

Abe was already at the front door. He had the Winchester ready. He tried peering through the peephole in the door but saw nothing but gray beyond the porch.

He squinted. He could make out movement coming up the drive, but saw no details. He stepped back. Suddenly, blue lights from a police light bar strobed around outside. He saw them through a set of stained-glass windows next to the door. The blue lights strobed through the front foyer casting shadows of approaching doom.

Abe's skin crawled.

He opened the front door to take a better look. He stepped out onto the porch against his best judgment. But he needed to know if his son was alive. The force drawing him to know if Walter was dead or not was undeniable, unavoidable.

He watched the vehicles pull up the drive onto the circle in front of his house.

Headlights beamed out in cones of bright white lights like the high beams had been left on. Abe threw up a hand to block the light shining in his face. Then he put it above his eyes like a visor.

First, Walter's Tundra pulled up and circled around the tree in Abe's front yard. Abe saw two men in the front cabin. He couldn't make out their faces beyond the bright headlamps. The driver turned the wheel, circled the drive, pulled the Tundra's nose way up toward the barn, and slowed and stopped in front of the doors.

The next truck to ride up was Henry's Spartan County Sheriff truck. Abe watched it and saw three men crammed in the front seat. Henry's truck didn't ride with the high beams on, but the light bar strobed on top.

Abe saw Henry stuffed in the center of the front bench just under the rearview mirror and in front of where his radio would be. His hair was disheveled. It looked like he had a bruised eye, almost like a black eye forming. But Abe only got a glimpse of

Henry because the truck stopped out in front of his house. And Henry's face fell under a dark shadow.

He saw both the other two men and their faces, but didn't recognize them. They were both white; both had facial hair. One had a beard—the other stubble.

The last car was the same South Carolina Highway Patrol car that Shep and Adonis had arrived in. The blue lights streamed from the light bar on top, just like Henry's truck.

Abe stepped left on the porch, leaving the front door wide open behind him. He squinted and struggled to make out who was in the patrol car. He saw nothing but figures in dark shadows. The driver was a short woman. He could see that. Her hair was wild and disheveled like Henry's. The driver might've been Adonis. Only when he had seen her twenty minutes ago, her hair had been neat and pulled back out of her face. Now, it was a mess. It looked so wild he first thought she wore a wig probably titled: *Jungle Woman*.

There were two other figures in the patrol cruiser. Abe saw one in the backseat and one in the passenger seat. The one in the back was a big guy. The outline of his head disappeared into the ceiling. The guy in the passenger seat was also tall, but gangly and bony-looking.

All three drivers threw their vehicles into park. Abe heard emergency brakes being pushed down all the way and clicked into place. He glanced back at Walter's truck. He saw the driver park it, kill the engine, open his door, and step out. Abe couldn't see his face. The driver walked around the tail of the Tundra to the passenger door and stopped. He turned and faced Abe.

The driver of Henry's truck also stepped out, leaving his door open and the engine running and the blue lights flashing. He threaded around the nose of Henry's truck. The snow on the driveway must've been plowed aside from the vehicles because Abe heard footsteps on gravel.

The driver of Henry's truck stopped on the passenger side and stayed there, facing Abe. The passenger door opened next, and the other guy he didn't recognize stepped out.

Both truck drivers stood by, carrying military or law enforcement weapons. Abe was no gun expert, but he recognized one as an M4 Carbine, military-grade. The other was a tactical combat shotgun. He didn't recognize the brand. He didn't recognize the model. But he knew expensive military weapons when he saw them.

Abe stayed where he was on the porch. He lowered his hand back to the front stock of the rifle. He slipped his trigger finger into the housing, ready to squeeze it. But he didn't point the weapon at them. He kept it up near his chest.

The patrol cruiser's doors all opened at the same time. The driver with the wild hair got up and out in a downhearted, forlorn way. The tall guy in the backseat got out behind her. He was tall, like Widow. At first, Abe thought it might be Widow, but then he saw it was a black man.

The tall black man shut his door behind him and stepped up close behind the woman with the wild hair. It looked like he whispered something to her. Then he shoved her forward. She plummeted past the open driver's door. The tall black man slammed the driver's door shut and walked past it. He came up behind the woman again and kicked her in the butt—not hard, just enough to shove her forward again.

The woman with the wild hair lunged forward, rolled down the hood of the car, and slammed into the snow and gravel. She stopped on her hands and knees, her face down. She was about thirty feet from the porch steps. She sat back on her heels and looked up at Abe.

He saw her wrists were handcuffed together. The short chain rattled as she moved. Her hair was wild. Her face was dark, partially from being punched in the face and partially from tears.

He instantly knew who she was. Her head bandage was gone, ripped away, but it was her. It was Agent Adonis.

The bony guy in the passenger seat got out after the tall black man and Adonis. He casually shut his door and stepped out toward them. He came up side-by-side with the tall black man.

It was Joseph Abel. Abe recognized him from his picture on the internet.

The tall black man was the same guy who had come to their house earlier, telling the lie about a broken-down car.

The thing that was different about him now, different about all of them, Abe supposed, was that they were all dressed in stolen ATF uniforms. Except for the tall black man. He wore most of a South Carolina Highway Patrol uniform that was a little too small and a little too snug in some places.

Abe realized the South Carolina Highway Patrol uniform belonged to the patrolman he'd met earlier with Adonis. He never saw the other agents. They were up in the helicopter. But he knew none of them were legit. Only Adonis was the real agent.

Abe said, "What the hell is this?"

Abel stepped up two long paces in front of the black guy, but behind Adonis.

He said, "What's your name, sir?"

"Abe White."

"Abraham. What a great, Biblical name. Well, Mr. White, my name's Joseph Abel."

"I know who you are!"

"Oh, good. Then this can be easy. I prefer to do this the easy way and not the hard way. You know what the hard way is?"

Abe raised his rifle and pointed it at Abel.

"I don't much care for any way that's your way."

Brooks quickly raised his M4, pointed it at Abe, followed by the two guys dressed as ATF agents by Henry's truck and the one from Abe's right, standing at Walter's truck.

Abel said, "Mr. White, you don't have a choice. Why not put down that peashooter, before someone gets hurt?"

Abe stayed where he was. His cheeks slowly turned red in the snow and the cold.

The snow fell rapidly, climbing in speed, showering a white, translucent curtain between all of them.

Abel said, "Brooks."

Brooks nodded and slowly lowered the target of his M4 down to Adonis. He stepped closer to her and pointed the M4 right at the back of her head.

She looked up at Abe, made eye contact. She shook her head, slowly telling him no. Telling him to say no to whatever they demanded.

"No! Wait!" Abe shouted.

Brooks didn't fire, but Abe saw his finger on the trigger.

Abel said, "Do you want a dead ATF agent on your front lawn? On your conscience? Because it will be your fault."

Abe kept his rifle up.

He said, "I'm not letting you in my house."

"Mr. White, things aren't up to you."

Abe stayed where he was. From behind him, he heard footsteps slowly coming down the hall. It was Abby. She walked past the mudroom and the foyer and stopped in the doorway.

He heard his wife's voice.

"Abe, what's going on?"

"Stay back, Abby!"

"Is this the Missus?" Abel asked.

Abe turned at the waist to look back at Abby. She stared at him. Her rifle dangled and shivered by her side in one hand.

"Go back, Abby!"

"Abby, it's nice to meet you," Abel said. "Why don't you come out here and join us?"

Abe turned back to Abel, rifle still pointed at him.

"You leave her out of this!"

Abel asked, "Abe, where's Foster?"

Abe stared at him in disbelief.

"Where's Maggie and Dylan and Lauren?"

"What?"

Abby said, "How do you know their names?"

"Don't be surprised," Abel said. He raised his voice higher and shouted out at the house so the whole White family could hear him.

"I know all your names," he shouted. "I know everyone in your family. I know everyone in your house."

Both Abby and Abe stared at Abel in terror.

Abel shouted, "Maggie, Lauren, Foster, and little Dylan, why not come on out here?"

Abe's eyes lingered on Abel a little longer. Then he turned his head and looked at Walter sitting in the truck, shame on his face.

"Oh, don't be hard on your son, Abe. No one resists me. He's no military-trained, hardened combatant. He told me everything I asked in less than a minute. It only took a punch to the gut to get him to squeal like a pig."

The two guys at Henry's truck snickered.

Abel said, "Even the old man there."

He pointed at Henry.

"That old sheriff took more abuse, and he didn't tell us nothing."

Abel shrugged and walked forward, passing Brooks, passing Adonis. He closed in on the rifle in Abe's hands.

He said, "No one's ever resisted us. No one. The ones who try…"

Abel stepped up the driveway, into the snow, his hands out and up like he was giving himself over as an offering. He walked up the steps, slowly, and lowered his hands, palm out in front of Abe like he was waiting for Abe to hand over his weapon.

Abel said, "The ones who try, they die slow deaths."

He stared into Abe's eyes.

"You want your family to survive?"

Abe nodded, said nothing.

Abel said, "Give me the rifle. Hand over all your weapons and give us shelter through the storm. Then we'll leave you and your family in peace."

Abe's eyes flicked left to right like he was searching for something or someone. He looked at the drive, past the last car. He looked at the forest of planted Christmas trees to the north. He looked for Widow.

Abel said, "No one's coming to help you. The ATF isn't coming. This agent here..."

Abel twisted at the waist and pointed back at Adonis.

"She lied to you. She came alone. The ATF, the FBI, the local cops, none of them know where she is. There's no backup."

Abe looked deflated.

Abel said, "Give over the weapons, and Walter can join us all in the house. We can be civil."

Abe asked a question. His voice shuddered under the weight of it.

"No more bloodshed?"

"No more bloodshed," Abel said. He reached out and placed one hand on the rifle's barrel in Abe's hands. He pushed it down so that it no longer aimed at him.

Abe didn't fight back. He lowered the Winchester slowly.

He knew in his heart that they would all die if they resisted. They couldn't defend themselves against Abel and his guys. They were outgunned and out-experienced.

Through the open door behind him, Abby asked, "Are you sure?"

"Put down your gun, Abigail. This is the only way to ensure our survival."

Abby lowered her rifle as well.

Brooks signaled to the two guys standing at Henry's truck to get moving. Both men walked up past Abel and Abe and took Abby's rifle away from her.

Abel took Abe's Winchester and held it down by his side. He smiled.

"You made the right decision, Mr. White. Now, let's get in there and get any other guns you got. Mrs. White, would you be a dear and put on some coffee? Think you can scrounge together some lunch for my boys and me?"

Abe said, "The power went out. We're on a generator."

"What's that got to do with it?"

"The oven may not work."

"Of course, it'll work. Don't worry about it. Powering key appliances is what generators are for."

Abby said nothing.

The two guys from Henry's truck walked up to her. One pushed her aside and passed her and entered the house. The other jerked the rifle out of her hand and moved to stand directly behind her, towering over her.

Abby stared past Abe at Abel.

"I think so. What would you like to eat?"

"Oh, surprise us. But something special. You know what? Go into the kitchen and look for your finest dish. The kind you save for when the president comes to visit and cook that up for us. Take your time now. I want it to be the best meal ever. Got it?"

Abby nodded and turned. The big guy behind her was Tanis. He stayed there like a tree trunk.

"I've got to go to the kitchen," she pleaded.

Tanis grinned and stepped aside. She went past him, past the mudroom, and off toward the kitchen.

He followed behind her, pairing his steps to match hers mockingly.

Abel took the lever on the Winchester and racked it, over and over, quickly ejecting every bullet out the top until the gun ran empty. He took the rifle and walked back to Brooks, handed it to him.

"Hide it behind the seat in the Tundra. Do the same with the rest after they collect them all. Lock it up. Do the same for the car and the sheriff's truck and keep the keys handy."

Brooks nodded and looked down at Adonis. She was still on her knees in the snow.

He asked, "What about her?"

"Take her up to one of the bedrooms. The master bedroom. Handcuff her to the bed. I'll check in on her later on. Maybe after lunch."

Abel cracked a grin.

Adonis protested and shouted. Abel reared his foot back and kicked her in the stomach with a heavy boot.

"Shut up! You're lucky to be alive."

He turned back to Brooks and gave him one more order.

"Gag her. I don't want to hear her voice again."

Brooks nodded. He went to the cruiser's trunk to find an extra car rag. He found one that was in a pack of clean rags. He returned to Adonis and shoved it in her mouth, forcibly.

He went to the Tundra and leaned the rear bench forward and laid out Abe's rifle. He left the seat forward for Tanis and Cucci to return with any other weapons they found.

Abel walked up to Abe and threw an arm around his neck as if they were grade school friends.

"Come on, Abe. Show me around your house. I'm especially interested in how you became a Christmas tree farmer. Tell me about it."

The two men walked into the house together. Sounds of arguing and fighting and loud voices came from the upstairs, but no gunshots.

A long minute went by. Then the rest of the White family came down the stairs and joined Abe and Abel in the living room near the fireplace.

Abel saw the sofa against the sliders. He pointed at it and barked an order at Tanis and Cucci.

"Now, how did that get there? Do the Whites a favor, boys, and move that sofa back over here away from the slider."

Tanis and Cucci did as ordered.

They all sat, trying to crowd onto the same couch. The children both sat on the floor at Maggie's feet.

None of them spoke. None of them dared to speak. They just all stared at Abel.

Abe stayed standing, and Abel sat at an armchair.

"Got any cigars, Abe?"

"I do."

"Bring out your best. Make it one for me and one for you."

Abel drew his Glock out and kept it in his hand, but resting on his knee. He stared at Abe, who walked to the mantel above the fireplace and opened a cigar box, took out a couple of Fuente cigars still in plastic wrappers. He also came out with a silver Zippo.

He unwrapped the first cigar and tried to give it to Abel.

Abel didn't take it with his hand. Instead, he opened his mouth and leaned forward. Abe slid it into his mouth, like a slave from another time. He whipped out the Zippo and lit the cigar. Abel kept his eyes locked on Abe's the whole time. It was some sort of twisted power trip.

Abel smoked the cigar.

He said, "Abe, my man, that one's for you. Why don't you take a seat there, near me?"

Abe sat on one of the arms of a sofa just across from Abel.

"What about my son?"

"Oh, right," Abel said. He looked back at the front door.

Brooks was hauling Adonis in. She was kicking and mumbling against the car rag stuffed in her mouth. Brooks had her in a bear hug. His M4 was strapped across his back.

Adonis's feet were clear off the ground. Brooks didn't seem to be fazed by her kicks.

Abel called over to him.

"When you're done with her, tell Flack to bring Walter and the sheriff in here. They can join us."

Brooks didn't answer. He just nodded.

Abel leaned back in the armchair.

"You got a nice place here, Abe. Nice life. I bet you really enjoy it. It'll be hard for me to leave later. But don't worry. A deal is a deal. As long as your family cooperates."

Abel glanced over at Foster.

He repeated, "As long as everyone cooperates. Does as I ask. We'll have no problems."

45

WIDOW HEARD the storm revving up. He saw the gray clouds sweep overhead, covering the sky. He waited till all the vehicles drove out of Pine Farms and stayed out of sight. He knew where they were going. They were going over to the Whites' place. There wasn't much other explanation for keeping Walter alive. They didn't need him as a hostage. They had Adonis. She would make a more valuable bargaining chip than Walter. But they'd kept Walter alive, which indicated they were stopping at the Whites' place next—probably to take cover until nightfall. They had cargo that Widow could only guess contained explosives or drugs or something of value. Explosives made the most sense. Why else package everything and stamp and address it all so meticulously, as well as stack it and transport it under armed guard?

Widow compartmentalized this new information and focused on one thing at a time. He'd watched three ATF agents load up the cargo and counted one other guy, who was Joseph Abel. The three ATF agents were obviously not ATF agents. They had stolen the uniforms from Adonis's crew. He knew that for sure. What he didn't know was if the others were still alive or dead.

This was his chance to find out. The other agents hadn't left with Abel and his guys, but they had come over here with Adonis. They must still be here. Maybe he would get lucky and find them all tied up somewhere on the property, or maybe not. Maybe they were dead.

The other opportunity that presented itself was that they'd left the sniper behind, probably for road cover, probably to watch the surrounding backroads and the skies for incoming law enforcement, in case Abe or his family had heard the shotgun blast from earlier and gotten through to the cops or FBI.

Widow knew they didn't. He knew that when he saw the telephone pole's transformer explode earlier, which meant that there was another guy in Abel's crew. That must've been the black guy that came by earlier and took Walter with him on a lie about a vehicle breakdown. Widow figured the guy was sent over to recon the family and take the truck, which meant Walter was along for the ride. But now he was a liability, along with Abe and the rest of his family.

Right now, Widow couldn't risk following the crew over to the Whites' farm, not while the sniper was perched in his nest. If he snuck back the way he had come, it would take too long. He would have to go slow, so the sniper wouldn't notice him. It wasn't fast enough. If he wanted to get back over there in time to stop anything bad from happening to the Whites, he would have to take out the sniper first.

Widow waited for the last of the vehicles to roll out, so he was sure that he was alone with the sniper. He wasn't sure how long they would keep the guy up there, so he wanted to move fast.

He walked out to the front of the farmhouse, staying low, hugging the exterior walls where he could. He kept one eye on the view from the barn loft to make sure that the sniper couldn't see him.

He saw the suppressor on the end of the rifle turn slowly. He froze and waited. The rifle stopped facing northeast, his direction. It faced way over his head at the road.

Widow turned and came to the farmhouse front window. He glanced in and saw nothing but darkness. He leaned over and put an ear to the glass. He listened but heard nothing except the farmhouse's old creaking bones.

He wasn't one hundred percent sure the farmhouse was empty, not without clearing it. But he was satisfied enough. He didn't want to go far and risk the sniper catching him. However, he saw none of Adonis's men when Abel's guys left. He only saw Abel's guys in stolen uniforms. Therefore, Adonis's agents were still there somewhere. Widow would've put them in the house if he were Abel. Probably locked them in the basement. He would have to come back to see if he could find them after he took out the sniper.

Widow turned and faced the barn. He raised the Winchester, pointed it at the loft.

He crept back along the farmhouse wall to the corner, until he was back in the sniper's blind spot. Then he slow-scrambled the twenty-plus yards to the barn, keeping his steps big and long. He put all his weight on each without stomping down on the snow.

At the barn, he backed off the wall and pointed the rifle at the doors. He sidestepped left and covered the doors. No movement. No sign that the sniper knew he was there.

Widow reached out and grabbed one of the door handles. He pulled it and stepped back with the turn to keep the door between him and any bullets that might come his way.

The door raked up gravel and snow, giving out a loud scratching sound. He pulled the door halfway open, big enough for him to squeeze through. Then he paused and listened. He looked up at the bottom of the loft window.

The sniper rifle didn't move. He heard creaking, low enough to be dismissed as a wind. Then the rifle barrel and suppressor rotated again, slowly to the southwest. He watched it stop there. Then he heard coughing. A second later, he heard shuffling, light, not like the sniper had jumped up to see what the noise from the barn door was. They were just slow, non-threatening shuffles on wooden planks, like the sniper slid himself into a better sitting position. But Widow wasn't born yesterday, so he stayed where he was, Winchester pointed at the wall just under the window, where he pictured the sniper to be seated.

He waited, keeping his aim up, ready to flick his wrist up and lean back and fire at the open window if the guy stuck his head out. But he didn't. Instead, Widow heard a sound known all over the globe, except for people of remote parts of the world who still hunted by bow and arrow and just discovered fire.

He heard the *Psshhhhhhh* of a beer can being popped open, followed by the sound of a man taking a swig from it. He even burped after.

The sniper didn't know Widow was there, which was good.

Widow lowered his rifle and moved through the half-open barn door. He didn't linger in the doorway. He stepped through and rotated and pointed the Winchester to where the sniper was seated. He sidled to the center of the barn. He was forced to stop when he nearly walked into a parked van. It was all black. The rear doors were closed, and the engine was cold.

Widow took cover behind it as a precaution. He scanned the first floor of the barn. There were several horse stalls and old bales of hay—so dusted over they looked ancient. The barn's woodwork was old but looked stable. There were no tools anywhere in sight. The previous owners had taken everything that mattered.

On the furthest set of horse stalls, near the feeding trough, Widow saw a ladder that went up into the loft. He crept toward it. It was nearly fifty feet away. At the ladder, he stopped because of what he saw next.

In the horse trough, stuffed in like garbage, was a corpse. It was a guy, white, and dressed all in black. Widow lowered his rifle and turned it. He used the barrel to turn the head so he could see the dead guy's face.

The bones in the guy's neck *cracked* as if they had turned brittle. There were dark, deep cuts and bruises around his throat. He had been strangled to death, no doubt about that. The weapon used was a garrote. No doubt about that either.

Widow looked over the face. The eyes were rolled back in the head. But it didn't matter. He had never seen the dead guy before. And he was pretty sure the guy wasn't one of Adonis's men.

The corpse's clothes were all wrong. He wore black, but none of it looked like official ATF.

Widow removed the barrel of the rifle from the guy's dead face. He glanced beyond the trough and the corpse and saw Adonis's men. He had found them. They were all dead. Four dead bodies were stacked haphazardly in one of the horse stalls. He abandoned the ladder and went into the trough. He saw three of the men had been executed, double-tapped—one in the center of the forehead, dead-on, and the second bullet in the heart, or vice versa. Without forensics, Widow couldn't be sure which bullet came first. If he had to guess, they were all shot with a nine-millimeter handgun, probably the same handgun.

All four men were half-naked.

On the bottom of the pile, Widow saw a face he recognized. It was the only one without a bullet hole in the center of the forehead. It was the South Carolina highway patrolman he had seen with Adonis.

Widow grabbed the top corpse by the foot and gently pulled him off the pile, and dragged him to the side. He did the same with the second and the same with the third one, dragging each corpse to a different side, so they weren't piled on top of each other. He came back to the one he recognized and stared down at him. It looked like the man was killed by a major bullet, heavy grain, heavy caliber.

The bullet had exploded straight through the guy at a downward angle.

Sniper killed him, Widow thought. *Had to be, because of the bullet's caliber.*

The dead highway patrolman had a jarhead haircut. He looked like a former Marine. Widow didn't know for sure, but he whispered to him.

"Oorah, brother."

Widow got back up and looked up to the loft. He couldn't see anything over the railings from the first floor. He stepped back to the ladder and looked up again. He listened. He heard the sniper readjusting his sitting position again, and he heard what he figured was the last swig of the beer can because then there was a crushing sound. After, the crushed beer can came flying over the railing near the loft window. It clanked on the ground at the rear of the van.

The sniper burped again, loud and vulgar, like a drunk at a party.

Widow now faced a problem. The Winchester didn't come with a shoulder strap, and he needed both hands to climb the ladder if he was going to avoid making noise. He set the Winchester out of sight, back in the horse stall with the dead agents, leaned it against a wall.

He returned to the ladder and used both hands to test the rungs, checking for squeak level. They were all right. Not too loud.

He began climbing, slow and steady. One hand in front of the other. One foot at a time. Halfway up, one of the rungs squeaked as loud as if he'd stepped on a bird.

He froze and looked up and behind him toward the loft window. He saw no one. No movement. He waited a long, long beat, holding his breath. Then he heard another cough and another set of creaks from the sniper moving around. He heard another beer can pop open, followed by a loud gulp and another burp.

The guy settled and was back to watching the road.

Widow thought if he had more time, he could just wait for the sniper to get completely hammered. Then it would be easy to take him down.

But he didn't wait. He couldn't wait. There was no time. He moved on, ascending the ladder until he was over the lip of the second floor. Once he got to the top rung, he rolled onto the second floor and found himself on a catwalk that tunneled to his left with two routes splitting in opposite directions, one to the right and the other to the left—where the sniper was perched.

Widow stayed low to keep himself out of sight. He crawled on hands and knees, staying as close to the deck as he could. The railing next to him covered enough to keep him hidden. The boards under him squeaked quietly. It wasn't loud enough to give him away. He made it to the corner and stopped. He sat back against the railing and took out the Beretta M9.

The wind blew in from the open barn door. It whistled loudly.

Widow rotated out on one foot and pointed the M9 at the sniper's nest. The nest was dark from lots of shadows, but he saw the sniper laid out, not sitting. The guy was short and stumpy-looking. He wore a ball cap backward on his head.

Widow crept slowly down the walkway to the loft window. He saw the rifle still pointed out toward the southwest.

Widow was nearly ten feet away when he stopped and froze. The sniper looked strange. He looked almost like a crash test dummy. There was nothing lifelike about him. Nothing animated. Nothing real.

Suddenly, Widow heard a board creak behind him from the opposite way. He didn't turn around. He leaped forward off his feet, landing in the middle of the sniper's perch and hitting the wooden floorboards hard. Dust kicked up into the air. He rolled to the left.

Alongside him, the sniper on the ground exploded in bursts of dust and chicken feed. The surrounding air clouded up dust. The explosions were small holes from a nine-millimeter gun. Someone behind him was firing a suppressed gun at him.

Widow scooted all the way back to the railing. He was inches from the edge that turned into the catwalk, back the way he came.

The wood exploded next to him and then above him and then behind him. Wood splintered and dusted up all around him. He felt the bullets hit the other side of the wood, directly behind his back. He was suddenly very grateful that the loft's skeleton was constructed with solid wood.

Dust clouds from the wood and the chicken feed bags used as a decoy sniper filled the air. Widow couldn't fire back. If he got up into the dust cloud, he would be blind. He stayed where he was.

The gunshots stopped.

A voice from beyond called out.

"You still alive, buddy?"

Widow stayed quiet.

"You know you're pretty dumb. I can't believe you fell for the beer cans. I just poured them out the window and then crushed them so you'd think you were fine."

Widow said nothing. In his brain, he heard himself shouting. He felt utterly stupid.

Silence fell between them.

The sniper shouted out again.

"Hey, buddy. You still with me?"

Widow hadn't even counted the shots from the guy's gun. He couldn't. It all happened too fast, and the gun's silencer made it especially difficult. But he knew the sniper was using a handgun. He knew the guy had reloaded because he heard a magazine fall and bounce off the floorboards. Any standard, modern handgun that will take a silencer will hold around fifteen bullets. Some hold more. Some hold less. But fifteen was a good average.

Had this guy fired fifteen?

Widow didn't think he did, but he wouldn't swear to it. Plus, the guy may have fired half the magazine before this encounter. What he could rule out was a typical 1911 model that many guys preferred because a 1911 holds seven bullets, and the sniper had fired more than seven. He could also rule out any revolvers for the same reason. No revolver he ever heard of could hold as many bullets as he had counted.

Widow struggled to think of what to do.

The sniper shot several more bullets, all of them hammered on the other side of the railing, pounding into the wood at Widow's back. He couldn't stay there for long.

The way he saw it, he had two options. Neither of them was ideal. He could make a run for it and jump out the loft window, which led to a long drop to the ground below. He couldn't remember how far it was, but it was survivable. He remembered skydiving training in the SEALs. He knew that a man in good shape could survive a fall from about three floors if he landed and rolled and if he fell on the ground and not concrete or some other hard surface.

The good news, with this option, was the ground was covered in snow. The bad news was it was still a long distance down.

More bullets fired, and the boards behind him cracked and splintered. His back muscles fired red alerts in his brain. He had to move.

Widow opted for the second option, a slight twist on the first.

He spun around, faced the loft's railing and reached his hand up over the railing, and fired the Beretta blindly at the sniper. He fired several rounds, providing cover fire.

With his other hand, Widow grabbed the top of the railing and heaved himself up and leaped over it into the interior of the barn. He hoped the van was parked where he remembered it.

Luckily, it was.

Widow landed on the roof of the van, on his side. It hurt, but not as much as a sprained ankle or a broken chin from hitting the driveway in front of the barn would have.

As soon as his right arm hit the van's metal roof, he rolled in the opposite direction of the sniper.

Widow rolled off the back of the van and landed on his feet. His right bicep hurt from banging on the van's roof, but hurt was better than broken.

He whipped around and planted his back into the van's rear doors. He got low and threaded the van's corner until he saw the nearest horse stall, under the walkway. He scrambled to it and went in and turned right and climbed the wall to the next one. He scrambled to the next wall and climbed over and repeated the run and wall climb two more times, scrambling through two more horse stalls until he was back at the stall with the dead bodies and the Winchester rifle. He pocketed the Beretta M9 and took up the rifle. He stopped at the ladder and waited.

Silence.

Widow came out beside the ladder, aimed at the railing above, and waited.

The sniper said, "You still alive, buddy? Come on, say something."

Widow was at a loss. He wasn't sure what to do next. He couldn't climb the ladder again. He would never make it to the top. No question.

Then he heard a sound that changed his mind.

A static voice *crackled* above and back to the front of the barn from the sniper's nest.

It was a radio. The sniper had a radio. He'd left it in the sniper's nest with his rifle and the old chicken feed bags he had set up as a decoy.

The voice on the radio said, "Jargo, status report. See anything out there?"

Silence.

"Jargo, come in."

Jargo? Widow thought. *What a stupid name.*

The sniper said, "Oh, shit. I need to get that. You wanna step out so I can kill you, buddy?"

Outside the barn, thunder boomed heavy and loud, full of dense weight like a giant clobbering another giant to death with a club.

Widow stepped out and aimed at the only exposed part of the walkway between Jargo and the walk back to his radio. He squeezed the trigger, once—fast, and levered the action.

The gunshot blasted and echoed through the barn like they were inside an acoustical sound stage.

The bullet ripped into the barn wall.

Jargo called out.

"Whoa, buddy! You almost got me. Here I thought you were dumb, but I gotta admit, I'm the one who left the radio over there."

Widow stayed quiet.

The radio hissed, and the static voice returned.

"Jargo, come in?"

Silence.

The voice ordered, "Come in!"

Jargo said, "If I don't answer, they'll send some guys back here. You can take off now. That's what I'd do. Start running before they get here and kill you. Let me tell you, buddy, if they catch you, they'll kill you slow."

Widow had fired a lot of guns in his life, including a Winchester lever-action rifle. And he'd fired a lot of different bullets with a lot of different calibers and a lot of different grains. A thirty-thirty bullet was surely one of them, but he couldn't remember. No one used them anymore. Not in his Navy circles, anyway. They were normally found in Granddad's gun, which was the Winchester rifle.

Off the top of his head, Widow didn't know if a thirty-thirty bullet with a hundred-fifty grain would punch through the wooden floorboards. Even if a bullet punched through, would it punch all the way through, maintain velocity, and hit Jargo?

Probably not. But staying in low ground and trying to outwait a trained sniper was about as stupid as staying up in a tree and hoping a hungry bear would leave. Bears climb, and they're damn good climbers.

Widow wasn't going to sit around and wait for Jargo to make a break for the radio. He had to make a move.

Silently, trying to keep his position unknown to Jargo, he left the ladder and threaded around the van to the rear, near the barn doors. He returned to the rear of the van, behind its rear cargo doors. He stepped up on the bumper, stowed the rifle on the roof, and scrambled up. He moved as fast as he could. For a second, he thought of Hell Week in the SEALs. They made him do crazy things that week. Some of them, he'd never had to do since, not on a mission, nowhere. Some of them were exactly things he had to do over and over. But they were all useful.

One thing they made him do was scramble up a stack of giant truck tires, and they timed it. Every time he successfully climbed a stack and stood straight up on top, they would use a crane to place another giant tire on top of the pile and make him climb that, also timed. Every new tire, they shortened the allotted time, making it shorter and shorter.

Widow had climbed the tires over and over. He had done this for hours. To his knowledge, he still held the record for the most tires, and the highest stack climbed. But Widow failed this exercise, as did all the other guys who've ever taken it. That was the point. The whole endeavor was like stacking rocks in a prison yard and then being told to re-stack them somewhere else over and over. The purpose of climbing the stack of giant tires wasn't to be the fastest or climb the highest stack. The purpose was to teach him to fail and to learn to accept it, embrace it, and learn from it.

Widow's record in this exercise wasn't a thing to brag about. It meant that he was the idiot that kept going like the definition of insanity, repeating the same thing over and over while expecting different results.

Still, the tire-climbing exercise proved to him he could scramble up a stack of giant tires pretty fast. He did the same with the van.

Widow climbed the back of the van fast and got up on the roof and stood straight up. He aimed down the barrel of the Winchester. He waited. Suddenly, he glimpsed the top of Jargo's head.

Widow called out.

"Jargo!"

The sniper stood up tall and looked over the railing. He looked right at Widow standing six-foot-four, stretching out as tall as he could on the top of the van.

Widow squeezed the trigger and racked the lever, forcing out the fired cartridge and chambering another fresh bullet.

Jargo's head exploded in the time between the cartridge ejection and the new bullet chambering. It was so fast, Widow missed it, but he saw blood and bone fragments and probably brain matter, all sprayed on the barn ceiling behind where Jargo had been standing just a second before.

Widow kept the rifle aimed at the kill spot and called out again.

"Jargo?"

Silence and wind.

Widow said, "Jargo? Buddy? You still alive?"

No answer.

Widow walked the length of the van's roof toward the ladder. He hopped onto the van's hood and climbed down off the grille. He set the rifle down by the base of the ladder and climbed the ladder as fast as he had the rear of the van. He stopped at the top, Beretta out, and pointed at the back of the catwalk, where a shadowy heap was sprawled out.

The heap used to be a sniper named Jargo.

Widow kept the Winchester pointed at the heap until he confirmed the guy was dead, a precaution. You never know. But there was no need. The sniper named Jargo was dead.

Widow pocketed the Beretta and looked over the body. He checked the pockets but found nothing of interest, just a wallet and an ID from the great state of Kentucky. The guy's real name was Jargo—Vincent Jargo.

Widow thought nothing of it. He tossed the wallet and ID back on top of the dead body and left it there. He went back to the loft and picked up the sniper rifle. He looked through the scope. He looked both ways, up and down the road. The snow was getting heavy. He couldn't see much farther than a quarter-mile in both directions. He stepped back from the rifle and ejected the magazine and the bullet in the chamber. He took them with him. He picked up the radio and climbed back down the ladder. He picked up the Winchester off the roof of the van and stared at the vehicle.

He opened the doors to search it.

The first thing he saw, which he couldn't help seeing, was a roll of duct tape stuffed into a cup holder, which made him think that one of these clowns had paid attention in Special Forces training. Duct tape was a Special Forces operator's best friend—a universal tool. It was up there with fire and the invention of the wheel, more useful than bullets.

Widow got inside, dumped himself down in the driver's seat. He thought there might've been a small chance these guys had left the key under the visor. But they didn't; at least he didn't check because the keys were dangling right there in the ignition. They never took them out.

He put the rifle down on the passenger seat and pushed a foot down on the brake. He grabbed the key and tried to start the engine. It cranked and whizzed, but didn't start. He turned it back to the starting position, paused, and tried again. It was a hard start, but it fired up. The dashboard flickered for a second, but the engine ran. He gassed it up and closed the driver's door. He reversed the van, hitting the gas hard. The van's rear bumper slammed into the barn doors and shot them straight open.

He spun the wheel all the way and backed up away from the farmhouse. He ended up spun all the way around one hundred and eighty degrees, facing the right way back down the driveway and back to the road.

Widow punched the gas. The van peeled out, back tires kicking up snow and gravel. He drove back to the road.

46

AT THE WHITE'S FARM, Abel smoked one of Abe's cigars and drank coffee out of a family mug. The mug rested on an end table next to his armchair.

Abe moved off the sofa arm and was, now, at the chair across from Abel, which wasn't his favorite chair, but it might be from now on because Abel sat in his favorite chair.

Right then, he was thinking of burning that one as soon as this was all over, if this was ever over.

The White family members were all clustered together on the other furniture. Walter was with them. He sat on the sofa with his wife on one side and his two children on the other. He hugged all of them together. They grabbed onto him like a family riding out a hurricane in the dark, hoping to survive the night.

Foster sat on the other side of Maggie. She stayed strong, at least trying to put on the facade that she wasn't scared. Abby was in the kitchen, preparing a big meal for everyone. It was a big lunch, as Abel had called it. Flack was in there with her, watching everything she did, every step she took, from taking out a frozen pack of T-Bone steaks to peeling potatoes, and every step in between.

Every time she pulled a sharp kitchen knife out of the knife block, he planted a heavy, gloved hand on her shoulder and stood behind her, panting. It forced her to shiver.

Sheriff Rourke was in the downstairs bathroom, handcuffed to the pipe behind the toilet. He didn't beg to be freed or left in the family room because he knew the less he spoke, the better they would treat him. The one who punched him repeatedly at Pine Farms had made that clear.

Abe watched Abel's men put all his guns back in the shed outside. They took the key from him and locked it.

Abel finally spoke.

"Guess we didn't need to cut the power after all. We can all do stupid things. People aren't perfect, you know?"

No one spoke. Abel smoked the cigar and sipped his coffee.

"Got anything stronger?"

Abe said, "We don't drink."

"Really? Nothing? Your wife doesn't have a stash somewhere? Something you don't know about?"

Abe's face turned red like he was going to explode.

Abel puffed out smoke rings and stared at the end of his cigar.

"Something you wanna say, Abe?"

Foster interrupted.

"Leave him alone. He's just an old man. He told you we don't have any liquor."

Abel glanced at her.

"Oh, good. Some balls in this family. I like that."

Tanis, who had been standing by at the bottom of the stairs, walked up slowly. He stopped behind Foster and looked at Abel, waiting for a sign to do something.

Foster felt him standing there behind her. She could see the wheels in Abel's twisted mind turning.

Maggie spoke up first.

"I've got bourbon."

Everyone turned to her.

Abel asked, "You do?"

"Yes. It's in my purse. Over there. On that table."

Abel nodded to Tanis, who stepped away from Foster and went to the purse and picked it up. It was a big white bag.

Tanis unzipped the main compartment and fished through it.

"Try the bottom," Maggie said.

He pushed down farther and finally pulled out a small bottle of Kentucky bourbon.

He tossed the purse back onto the table and brought the bottle over to Abel.

Abel said, "Jargo would like this. What's keeping him?"

Just then, Brooks came walking down the stairs from the upper floor. When he got to the bottom, the front door opened, and Cucci walked in.

Abel twisted the cap off the bourbon bottle and dumped half into his coffee. The rest he didn't offer to anyone. He just set it aside for a second round in the future.

He turned to Brooks at the stairs and asked a question, followed by a long pull of his bourbon coffee.

"How's Agent Adonis?"

"In the master bedroom. Handcuffed to the bed."

Abel smiled wide.

Cucci interrupted.

"I can't get Jargo to answer."

Abel's smile shrank to nothing.

"Why not?"

Cucci shrugged but didn't answer.

Abel asked, "The weather?"

Brooks said, "Could be. It's getting bad out there."

Abel stayed quiet.

Brooks asked, "Want me to go back?"

"No. Cucci, you go. Take the police car."

Brooks asked, "By himself? Sure you don't want me to go with him?"

"No. What for? Cucci can handle Jargo. Right?"

Cucci thought about watching Abel strangle Dobson to death with the garrote earlier.

He swallowed and answered.

"Yeah. I got it."

Abel said, "He's probably taking a piss break. But if he's napping, you tell me. Don't cover for him. Got it?"

The same image of Dobson dying stayed in his mind. This time Cucci remembered seeing the guy's eyes bulging out of his head.

He swallowed again.

"Got it. Be back."

Cucci spun back around and headed out the front door.

Brooks called out behind him.

"Wait."

Cucci stopped.

Brooks dug in his pocket and fished out the keys to the cruiser. He realized they were on the same keyring as the handcuffs he'd used on Adonis, but he didn't care. He handed them over to Cucci. No reason to hold on to the handcuff keys. She wasn't coming out of those cuffs. Not alive.

Cucci took the keys and headed out the front door. He fired up the cruiser, backed it up to face the road, and drove the long, bumpy drive back to the road, back to Pine Farms.

47

THE SNOWFALL PICKED UP, falling fast in what could only be called snow bombs. It was coming down hard by the time Cucci drove Shep's cruiser down to the main road, just outside the Whites' large mailbox. Cucci had to stop dead right there because he couldn't drive onto the main road. Something was blocking the driveway entrance.

He saw it through the windshield. He switched the wipers up to full-blast. They sped up and scraped across the windshield, kicking off snow as fast as they could. He heard the snow battering the roof of the cruiser.

The wind gusted, and thunder rolled and rolled above and all around.

Cucci slowed and approached the obstruction carefully. He leaned forward in the driver's seat, his chest pressed against the steering wheel so hard that he honked the horn. He went back upright. He continued to stare. He knew it was a vehicle. He could see the lights. The headlamps were switched on brightly, but the vehicle was facing north on the road and parked sideways right at the mouth of the driveway, acting as a roadblock.

He stopped the cruiser and put it in park. He kicked down the emergency brake and clicked on the high beams. He stayed ten yards back.

He picked up his radio and clicked the talk button, but stopped because he recognized the vehicle. It was the black panel van they'd escaped the Athenian compound in, hours earlier. What the hell was it doing there? It should've been stowed away in the barn at the abandoned farm.

It was parked, engine running, and the driver's side door had been left wide open like someone just hopped out and took off running.

He craned his head and stared at the ground around the van. There were no footprints in the snow, but there should've been.

"What the hell?" he muttered.

He clicked the radio, but someone else did first. He listened, thinking it was Brooks or Abel, but no one spoke. Whoever was pressing the talk button held it down because the radio continued a long hiss and crackle. And nothing else. It didn't stop.

Cucci waited, but there was no one. No one spoke. No voice. Nothing.

He held it up to his ear, wondering if this weather could disrupt their radios. He wasn't sure. Dobson had been their mechanic and their equipment guy. Cucci knew nothing of radios. He was more apt at fixing two tin cans connected by a string than electronics.

He thought of Dobson again. That look on his face while being strangled to death would haunt him forever, and he knew it.

He held the radio close to his ear, pushing it right up against his head. Suddenly, he realized he wasn't hearing static. He was hearing rain—no, not rain. He heard the hard snow. It pounded on the other end of the radio like it was falling on the roof of the cruiser.

The radio was in the open air, near a vehicle.

Cucci grabbed the M4 and opened the driver's door, setting the radio down in a cup holder. He left the door open and threaded around it. He pointed his weapon at the van and approached it slowly, staying loose, keeping his head on a swivel.

The snow hammered all around him. It pummeled his shoulders. One ball of snow hit him dead on the top of the head. It was hard and ruggedly packed, but not as hard as hail. He looked left and scanned all the way to the right as he approached the abandoned van.

The van's headlights flickered. The interior lights flickered. The sound from the open-door alert hissed and dinged. Then, when he was five yards away, the van coughed once and died. The power went off as it had when they were driving it several hours ago. And the engine died. He stopped and stared at it. Now it was just dead weight, blocking the road.

He called out.

"Jargo? You idiot! This isn't funny!"

No answer.

"Jargo? How the hell are we gonna move this piece of shit now? Dobson can't fix it. He's dead," Cucci said. He stepped forward slowly.

A big step forward later, he called out.

"Jargo?"

Cucci got three yards from the front tire and stopped and scanned the area in front of him, around him, and behind him. He saw no one.

"Jargo? Where the hell are you?"

Cucci walked around the van to the back. He sidestepped far enough out to give him room to scan and shoot. He was also consciously fighting his shoot-first instincts because he didn't want to shoot Jargo, in case the guy jumped out at him.

But Jargo didn't jump out at him.

He circled around the van to the open driver's door and looked flabbergasted. He lowered the M4 and stared at the seat, which he had expected to be empty, but it wasn't.

On the seat, he saw Jargo's radio. A long strand of duct tape was wrapped all around it, holding the talk button down.

Suddenly, he heard footsteps on the snowy road and tree branches shuffling around behind him. He spun around, M4 still pointed down. A mistake, because right then, a large man with a gun faced him from the tree line next to the Whites' mailbox.

The man was Widow.

Widow stomped across the road and the snow. He pointed the Winchester right in Cucci's face and barked at him.

"DROP IT!"

Cucci was embarrassingly stunned. He should've reacted and raised the M4 and shot at the stranger, but he didn't.

Widow stopped charging toward him and stayed about ten feet away.

He shouted, "DROP IT!"

Cucci dropped the M4 and raised his hands. He stared at Widow as if he was some kind of monster rising out of the gray and the gloom.

Widow asked, "How many?"

"What?"

"HOW MANY MORE OF YOU ARE THERE?"

"There's six. Six of us."

"Including Jargo?"

"How do you know his name?"

"Take a guess, genius."

"You. You're the reason we can't get him to answer the radio."

"No shit! You must be the brains of the outfit."

"General Abel is our leader."

Widow stood there, frozen for a moment out of disbelief.

How dumb was this guy? he thought.

He asked, "General? You just told me his rank."

"Yeah? What about it?"

"Whatever happened to only giving your own name and rank?"

Cucci said, "I'm not in the Army anymore."

"Surprise. I wonder why you got kicked out."

"I didn't get kicked out. I mustered out."

Widow shook his head and said, "You're not up there with the IQ score, are you?"

Cucci said nothing to that.

Widow asked, "The dead ATF agents in the barn, how much of that is you?"

"Are you a cop?"

Widow took a big step closer, putting the barrel of the Winchester inches below Cucci's chin.

He half-shouted, "DON'T change the subject!"

"I had nothing to do with it. That was the others. Not me. I like cops," Cucci lied.

He followed his lie with a grin that seemed involuntary, as if he'd just thought of the look on the face of whichever of Adonis's men he'd shot and killed.

Widow stayed put. He nodded at Cucci and made another demand.

"That a Glock on your hip?"

Cucci kept his hands above his head and nodded.

Widow said, "Take it out. Slow. Pinch the butt. If I see three fingers touch the weapon, I'll put a bullet under your chin. Got it?"

Cucci nodded and did as he was told. He used his right hand and slowly reached down to the Glock. There was no safety strap on his holster. He pinched the weapon with his thumb and index finger, nearly fumbling with it, at first. In the end, he pulled it out. He didn't throw it away because Widow hadn't given him any instructions yet. He didn't flip it around and fire it at Widow, which Widow knew he wouldn't. He knew it because this guy was no kind of risk-taker. He wasn't the kind of guy to think for himself. He was a follower.

Widow shoved the barrel forward, all the way into Cucci's neck. Then he stepped left and, one-handed, he swiped the Glock out of Cucci's hand, sending it flying into the gloom. Before Cucci knew it, Widow was back in his original position. The Winchester gripped two-handed, ready to fire.

"Now, what's your name?"

"Thomas Cucci."

"Cucci?"

"Cucci."

"Where do you boys get these dumbass names?"

Cucci said, "It's Italian."

"It was a rhetorical question."

Cucci said nothing.

Widow moved the barrel from under Cucci's chin and backed away three feet. He trained his aim on Cucci's center mass.

He asked, "You got any other weapons on you?"

"A knife."

"Where?"

Cucci moved his right hand again, down, dropping it from the surrender position. He pointed at his foot.

"It's in my boot."

Widow glanced quickly, in case it was a trick. He saw nothing, which meant it was a folding blade, probably tucked into the boot and not on an ankle sheath.

Widow said, "Kick the boots off! That way!"

"They're boots. I'll need to use my hands."

"No. Figure it out."

After he said it, he regretted it because of the thought that this guy was so dumb that it might take him all night to take off the large boots without his hands. But he figured it out, and it only took him about a minute.

Cucci turned to the side and kicked off the right boot, using the left to pinch down the heel. He repeated the process by holding down the left boot's heel with his right foot. After he kicked off both boots, he turned back, hands still raised.

He asked, "You going to kill me?"

"Kill you? What makes you think that?"

"You don't look like a prisoner-taking kind of guy."

"How you know that? Because that's who you are? That's how you and your boys do it? You shoot unarmed prisoners?"

Cucci paused a beat, and then he said, "You should join us."

"What?"

"Yeah. You took out Jargo. You're basically one of us."

Widow stayed quiet, but his trigger finger itched.

Cucci said, "What were you? Ranger? Green Beret?"

"Empty your pockets. Slow! Use your left hand first. Dump the contents on the road right there!"

Cucci nodded and moved his hand down, emptied his front pockets, coat, and pants. He turned around so Widow could see the back, and he dug in there. He repeated the process with the right pockets.

"Take the coat off and drop it."

Cucci removed it and dropped it.

He shivered and complained.

"It's cold."

"Get comfortable, being uncomfortable."

Cucci stared at him.

"SEAL? You're a SEAL?"

Widow stayed quiet.

Cucci said, "I knew a guy who used to say that. He was a frogman."

Widow asked, "That a pair of handcuffs on your belt? Well, on one of the dead ATF agents' belts?"

"Yes."

"Where're the keys?"

"Right there."

He didn't point down, but he was talking about a small ring with two keys on it. It was on the ground in the snow. They had fallen out with the pocket lint when he turned out his pockets.

For no explainable reason, just another sign that Cucci wasn't very smart. He said, "There's another set of handcuff keys on the ring. In the ignition."

"What about them? Where do they go?"

"They're not for these cuffs. They're for the ones on the woman, I guess."

"The woman?" Widow asked. He raised an eyebrow.

"A black chick. She's some kinda big shit with the ATF."

Cucci grinned another involuntary reaction like he was thinking back to shooting the dead agents. He was relishing it.

Widow felt trigger itch again. He was tempted to kill him. But he didn't. He barked an order at him instead.

"Put the cuffs on!"

Cucci took the cuffs out and started to clip them behind his back.

Widow barked, "In the front!"

Cucci stopped and moved his hands to the front. He did as he was asked.

Widow said, "Tight! All the way down to the wrist."

Cucci racked the cuffs till they wouldn't go any farther.

"Good. Now, I've got a question for you."

"What's that?"

"How much do you weigh?"

"I don't know. Two hundred pounds?"

Widow smirked and nodded.

"Good," he said. He stomped up to Cucci, fast, and wrenched his torso to the right like a major-league baseball pitcher throwing the hardest, fastest fastball ever thrown in his entire career. He used the force and momentum and speed to wrench back hard; only he wasn't throwing a fastball. He was swinging the Winchester. He swung hard. The butt of the rifle slammed into Cucci's jaw, almost as hard as Widow could swing it. A fraction more turning of the screw, and he would've broken Cucci's neck.

The butt slammed so hard into Cucci's jaw that there was an instant *crack!* It was loud. It echoed over the snowfall and the running engine of the police cruiser. It bounced off the trees like a plank being slammed into the side of a rock.

Several of Cucci's front teeth flew out of his mouth. His jaw broke. The bones in his left cheek dangled in his face. Later, when being seen by a doctor—if he was going to be seen by a doctor—someone would think he'd been hit in the mouth with a wrecking ball.

Cucci flew off his feet into the air. The force of the blow was so hard that his consciousness checked out the second of impact. He landed with his eyes half-open.

Widow lowered the Winchester. No reason to point it at a half-dead guy who wasn't going anywhere.

Blood seeped out of Cucci's mouth.

Widow set the rifle down against the police cruiser and returned to the keys on the ground. There was also a cell phone and a wallet and some folded cash in a clip, separate from the wallet. Widow had no idea why, and didn't care. He scooped it all up and pocketed the keys and the money. He popped the cruiser's trunk and tossed the wallet and money clip in. He tried the phone for a signal and got nothing. It was useless, so he left it in the passenger seat of the cruiser.

He went back to Cucci and lifted the guy up and dragged him across the snow to the trunk. He heaved him up and rolled him into the trunk. Cucci fit, but it was a little tight. Widow propped the guy's head up so he wouldn't choke on his own blood or possibly other broken teeth fragments he might swallow.

The gesture was merciful. But if he choked to death, Widow wasn't going to cry about it.

Widow returned to the van and got out the radio. He tore the duct tape off it, stuffed it into his pocket, and listened. He didn't want the others to get suspicious.

He heard nothing but static. Then, after a moment, a new voice came over the air.

"Cucci? Cucci? Come in? What the hell was that? Who held the talk button down like that? Hello?"

Widow had to answer. He had to keep them feeling safe and unaware of him as long as possible, so he answered, keeping his voice low, putting his lips right up to the receiver, and using his best smoky radio disk jockey impression. And he added paused breaks to make it seem like the weather was bad enough to disrupt their radio communication. He did this by pressing and depressing the talk button while saying complete sentences—an old, cheap trick he didn't learn in the SEALs. He'd learned it as a kid, using his mom's police radio, despite knowing he would later be punished for it.

To anyone listening, it would sound like he was breaking up, like bad weather ruined the radio signal.

He said, "I'm here. Sorry. Weather bad."

The voice said, "What was with the talk button being held down?"

"Sorry. You're breaking up."

The voice asked, "What was with the talk button?"

"Weather bad out here. I don't know."

"Where's Jargo? You find him?"

"I found him. He's fine. He dropped the radio off the roof. Dumbass."

Silence.

Widow hoped his impression of the guy in the trunk was believable enough.

The voice came back on.

"Okay. Get back here. Bring Jargo with you. This weather might get worse before it gets better. No reason for him to stay out there."

"Affirmative."

That was the end of the transmission. He wasn't sure if they bought it or not. He thought so. He hoped so.

Widow switched off the radio and left it in the van. He didn't suppose he would have use for it again. Then he went back to Cucci's boots on the road. He looked in both and found the folding knife. It wasn't like the one Abe had. It was only a three-inch blade, but a good one. He pocketed it in his coat and looked at the boots. He could pick them up. But what for? He left them on the road, as well as Cucci's coat, and returned to the car.

Widow slammed the trunk lid closed. He scooped up Cucci's Glock and the M4 and his Winchester. He laid them across the backseat of the cruiser and shut all the doors; after that, he dumped himself down in the driver's seat. He K-turned the car around, put it back into drive, and peeled out, up the mouth of the Whites' drive. He switched the headlamps off and used only the fog lights. He drove as fast as he could, bumping and racking around in the seat. At one point, he had to slam on the brakes because of a huge oak tree that forced the driveway to half-fork to the right before the largest hill.

48

Widow sped until he was close to the farmhouse. He slowed Shep's cruiser all the way to a crawl about fifty yards from where the Whites' drive opened to the circular driveway.

At the beginning of the circle, he stopped and killed all the lights. He scanned the terrain. He saw the parked trucks, all with the engines off. He looked around for outside patrol.

The wind and snow pounded on the exterior of the car. He saw no one. He scanned the upstairs windows and didn't see Foster. He didn't see Abe. He saw none of the White family at their posts, which he already figured, being that Abel's men were there.

The lights in the house differed from when he left. The lights downstairs were on, but they were low.

They cut the power, he thought. *They forced Abel to use a backup generator.*

Widow thought the whole move was stupid. It was overkill. He supposed that's how they operated. Everything they did was overkill.

Widow pulled the cruiser up behind the sheriff's truck and parked it. He took out the keys and pocketed them. He looked around one more time and saw no one. He opened the door and slipped out, opened the rear door, and looked at the Winchester and then at the M4. The Winchester was a good rifle. It had served him well so far, and he had more ammo for it in his pockets. But sometimes, you find better ordinance in the field.

He picked up the M4 and checked it. The bad side of the M4 was it only had one magazine.

The Glock was a different story. It had been fired—twice. Cucci had lied about shooting the ATF agents. He must've helped kill at least one of them. The thought made Widow hope the guy died in the trunk.

The M4 had one other component to consider. It had a sound suppressor on the end. That was the deciding factor; he scooped it up.

Lightning cracked overhead, and thunder rolled. He looked up. The snowfall beat down on his shoulders and face.

He left the Glock and the Winchester and took the M4 and kept the borrowed Beretta. He closed the car doors and locked it behind him.

He kept the M4 up, switched the firing selector from SAFE to AUTO. He had four bad guys left, and the M4 came standard with a thirty-round box magazine. There were twenty-nine rounds in the magazine and one in the chamber.

Widow walked along the side of the sheriff's truck, keeping his eye on the front door to the house.

The wind gusted around him. The barn door flapped open in the distance, which startled him. He almost shot at it. Then he remembered the huge hole in the back of the barn. The wind must've been blustering through it.

He ignored the barn doors and looked back at the house, expecting the sounds of the barn door flapping and banging on the wood to get Abel and his guys on their toes and outside.

He didn't know all of them or what branch of the military they were from, but he remembered reading enough about Abel's Special Forces career to know they were good. He probably stood little chance with one on four, which made him glad that none of them came outside to check it out.

He continued moving alongside the truck. He passed the tires and stopped at the door. He tried the handle. It was unlocked. He opened it. The door squeaked loudly on rusted hinges, but not loud enough to out-blast the barn door's banging. He opened the truck door and looked inside. He saw what he was looking for. It was the sheriff's radio. It was an old-fashioned thing, bolted under the dash, like a CB radio.

He had hoped there would be one, so he could call for help from the sheriff's department. Cops don't operate on cell phones and telephone lines. A police radio would work. There hadn't been one in Shep's car. Not surprising because it was probably on his body, once. It wasn't there when Widow saw him. Nothing was there. Someone was walking around in his uniform. Whoever had it had probably tossed the body radio.

Widow set the M4 down across the bench and scooped up the radio receiver. He switched the knobs on and turned the volume all the way up, hoping it was already on the right police channel. And maybe it was. He didn't know because the damn thing didn't come on at all. He clicked the receiver back down on the radio and lowered himself down to the footwell to get a better look at the radio. The wires out of the back were completely ripped out, haphazardly and recklessly like someone had done it with their feet from the driver's seat, not caring what damage was done.

Widow cursed under his breath and slid back out of the truck and took the M4. He shut the door and moved on to Walter's truck.

There was nothing of value for him inside the Tundra's cabin. He already knew that. But there were the packages, stockpiled in the cargo bed. That part was of interest. If he had to guess, that part was the most interesting part, at least to Abel, which made it valuable. And one thing that Widow loved to do was destroy things that guys like Abel thought were valuable.

The little pleasures in life, he thought.

Widow set the M4 down, leaned it against the back tire, and lowered the tailgate to the Tundra. He reached in and ripped up a heavy tarp they had strapped down over the packages. He unhooked two cables, holding it all down.

Underneath were the same forty-one packages he had seen them loading. He picked one up, read the name and the address of it.

James Wallace. Nashville, Tennessee.

He read the next one.

Shaun Kimerson. Dallas, Texas.

He read the next one.

Steven Scott. Seattle, Washington.

He read one more.

John Omaha. Norfolk, Virginia.

He looked up, scanned the yard, and the front door to the house. He saw no one. Then, suddenly, there was movement in one of the front windows. It was the dining room, where he'd eaten a big breakfast with coffee only hours ago.

The curtain moved, and the blinds ripped back. He saw an unfamiliar face looking out the window. He ducked down behind the truck and stayed quiet for a long moment.

The barn door flapped again, hard, slamming into the side of the barn and then swinging all the way back and slamming back shut.

He peeked up over the side of the truck, hoping whoever was looking out was only checking out the noise from the barn door, and didn't linger too much on the Tundra and the tailgate that was now down.

He got lucky. The unfamiliar face was gone. The blinds were back in place. And the curtain was pulled shut.

Widow paused a beat, kept his eye on the window, and then glanced at the front door, just in case.

No one came out.

Widow stood back up and looked at the package in his hand. It was heavy and bulky. They were all the same size, about the size of a kids' shoebox.

Each was the same weight, as best as he could guess. The only difference between them was that some had more stamps than others.

He came out from behind the truck and stood over the tailgate. He set down the package he had in hand and tore it open. Under the manila wrapping was a plain black shoebox-size box. Not a shoebox, although it could've been one from the factory, before they put all the labels and pictures all over it.

Widow tore through a second, protective layer of brown, industrial packing tape—easy enough to rip through.

He stopped at the tape on the lid. He left one last tape in place. He froze and stared at a small coil of wires taped right under the lip of the box. It just barely stuck out.

He almost missed it. He felt utterly stupid. The wire, the weight, the packages being so valuable to the Athenians—they were all rigged to explode. They were bombs. They planned to mail them all out, blowing people up, like the Unabomber—Ted Kaczynski.

The names were targets.

Widow stared at them, tried to figure the connection. Why these names?

He had no idea who they were. But whoever they were, they were all going to die if they opened these package bombs as carelessly as he almost had.

Widow put a hand in his coat pocket and took out the folding knife from Cucci's boot. He whipped the blade out and flipped the package over. He felt around the corners, pinching each one, searching for a weak spot. He found one not rigged with the wires—he hoped.

Usually, bomb makers will pack these kinds of devices, rig them to blow when opened or tampered with, but they'll leave a single corner alone in case they need to reenter the device.

Warily, he sliced into the box with the knife. He cut all the way down nearly to the edge. Then he cut two slits on both ends of the slice. He folded the knife closed and pocketed it.

He pried at both edges of the slits at the same time and folded the corners back and down and out, making two equal flaps. Then he bent the hole open wide enough to look in.

The first thing he found was packing. The box was packed full of shrapnel pieces. There was broken, jagged glass, broken nails, and screw ends.

The shrapnel added to the devastation of the explosions. If there were other people in the room when someone opened the package bomb, and the explosion didn't kill them, then the shrapnel would.

Carefully, he used the blade to sift through the nails and glass. Then he found what he was looking for. He dug down until he found a homemade pipe bomb with crude metal pieces and wires sticking out of it.

Devastating, he thought.

He left the package right there and inspected the others from the same stack. He pulled one out at a time, reading each, reading the addresses and the names, hoping something would click in his head.

Finally, he came to a name he recognized.

It was a guy named William Buckley, a name he remembered for two reasons. First, he'd met the guy once. It was an assignment where a SEAL team was sent into enemy territory to rescue some POWs in Afghanistan.

Widow was a part of the team.

The second reason he recognized the name was also because Buckley shared the name of a famous English convict sent to Australia during a whole period when England sent more than a hundred fifty thousand of their worst inmates to the island nation. Only Buckley escaped prison and went to live among the Aborigines. He became a legend in his own right.

That's the only reason Widow remembered the name, because the William Buckley he knew wasn't memorable. Not for him.

The Buckley he knew had one more title to his name. He was General William Buckley in the US Army.

There were forty-one package bombs with forty-one addresses across the US. And there were exactly forty-one still-living, retired generals from the US Army.

Abel packed these pipe bombs as one last act of terrorism. At least that's what he probably told his followers. Widow could imagine the lunatic selling them on fighting a fake, crazy revolution. Telling them all their sacrifice was worth it. Targeting retired military generals was unheard of. It would send a clear message to the government, to the military, to the world.

All the while, Widow was sure that Abel was emptying their bank accounts, using the money of gullible, lost souls looking for new lives, searching for meaning.

It was nothing more than petty revenge for what they'd done to him. And, now, dozens of innocent people were dead. Widow imagined Abel was probably plotting an escape from the country, with one last stop somewhere to hand over the packages to someone he trusted to mail them out. Then he would get on a plane or a boat and disappear with bank accounts full of stolen money.

49

THEY HEARD THE THUNDERCLAPS, the lightning strikes, snowfall, and the wind outside the farmhouse. Inside, Abel smoked the last of his cigars, asking Abe questions about Christmas trees and farming and the times. When Abe mentioned the nearby farms closing because of the financial crash over a decade earlier, Abel took it upon himself to give Abe, and the terrified family, a lecture on government and corporate corruption.

Brooks stayed near the front of the family room. He angled himself at the bottom of the stairs so he could cover the front hall, the mudroom, and the front door while staying aware of Abel and the main room. An M4 rested in his hands, across his chest, muzzle down. Flack leaned on an island counter right behind Abby in the kitchen, out of sight of the others.

Occasionally, he grunted at her, making her uncomfortable.

Tanis patrolled the house. He went from room to room, slowly and methodically, like he was a potential buyer looking at every crown molding and every stick of furniture for reasons to criticize the house in order to negotiate a lower price.

After checking out the downstairs, he ventured up the stairs and went room to room there. He stopped to check in on Adonis in the master bedroom. She was handcuffed to the bed, still gagged. Her clothes were still on, everything but her boots and coat, which were nowhere to be found.

She wasn't crying, not like others he remembered, but tears had left streams of black mascara on her face. She looked blank and empty and desolate, as if she knew Abel was going to kill her, and her mind had already moved on. Except for her breathing and occasional movement from side to side, she looked like nothing more than a human husk.

Tanis stayed at the door for a long while, staring at her.

She stayed quiet.

He entered the room carrying one of the combat shotguns. He slowly walked across the carpet and stopped dead center in the room. He turned to an open hallway that passed a walk-in closet and led to a master bathroom with a huge rectangular mirror over double vanity sinks.

He looked at himself in the mirror. Then his eyes panned down to Adonis behind him on the bed. She stared back at him.

"Honey, you look so good! I mean, the general takes a lot of brides. I've seen all kinds. I've seen him take Muslim whores in Iraq. I've seen fathers hand over their daughters here in the US.."

Tanis paused a beat, looked back at his own reflection, and opened his mouth. He stared at his teeth and then his beard. He held the shotgun one-handed and brushed down his beard with the other hand. Then he looked at her reflection in the mirror.

He said, "Yeah, I've seen him take all kinds of whores. But never, ever—not once—have I seen him take a cop."

He looked back at his own reflection, turned his head from side to side, inspecting the rest of his face.

"Then again. Those towelheads don't let their women become cops. They don't let them become much of anything over there."

He turned slowly and approached her. He passed the center point of the room and came right up to the foot of the bed.

Adonis stayed still, stayed frozen. She only turned her head to keep him in her line of sight.

Please, God, don't come any closer, she thought.

And for a moment, she thought he wouldn't. But he did.

Tanis walked down the side of the bed and stopped at her stomach. He peered down at her.

"You are a fine-looking thing," he said.

He reached a gloved hand out, and rubbed over her stomach, over her clothes. His gun hand crept up her torso and over her breasts. It was light at first. But then he grabbed one, cupped it, squeezed it.

Adonis squeezed her eyes shut. She bit down hard over the rag, nearly hard enough to bite her tongue through it.

Suddenly, she couldn't take it anymore, and her desolate, hopeless feelings vanished from her completely. She came back to life and kicked and wriggled around like a fish on the deck of a boat.

Tanis retracted his hand like she might bite it.

"Whoa!" he said, "Guess you're still with us."

She muttered and shouted at him, but no words came out. She made little sound. The rag stuffed in her mouth nearly muted her completely.

Adonis stopped squirming around, stopped kicking, and quieted down.

He said, "I'm not supposed to touch you before the general. It's a rule. Sort of SOP. That's Standard Operating Procedure for you civilians."

"That's why I keep my gloves on. You see. It's a loophole. I'm not physically touching you. No skin on skin."

Adonis found no comfort in that. But she stayed still.

Tanis said, "I'm not supposed to touch. No tasting either. No sampling. Not before. But after he's done, we can all have our way with you."

She looked at him in utter terror.

Tanis said, "You know, you should be grateful. Know why?"

Adonis said nothing.

"DO YOU KNOW WHY?" he yelled.

She shook her head. Another tear streamed down her face.

He leaned down to her, returning his hand to her breast. He got right to her face and stared into her eyes.

He whispered, "Because once we're through with you, we have no more need of you. We don't keep you alive. What for? So, the longer we take with you, the longer you live."

Tanis took his hand off her breast. He got back up, retreated, but only a foot. He stayed there for a long moment, staring at her.

He said, "You know what, though? I guess no one will know if I get a taste right now. I mean, you won't tell the general. Know how I know that? Because then I won't get you after. Then you'll die sooner. You don't want to die, do you?"

50

Widow walked around the farmhouse, past the parked vehicles, past Foster's covered vehicle. He started from the north side and walked to the back, along the wall.

Snow battered around him, making little puff sounds as it slammed into the yard and into the house. Luckily, he was mostly sheltered by the eaves and gutters on the roof. They hung out far enough to keep him from getting slammed in the head.

He hugged the wall, staying tight, staying close to the brick.

Widow didn't figure that the weather outside classified as any kind of blizzard or anything, but a brewing snowstorm? Sure. That was reasonable. The sky was gray enough to be called near dark, but not light enough to be called overcast. It was gray gloom, pure and simple.

He didn't expect all the exterior lights to be switched on, but some were sporadic like they were picked to be turned on when using the generator. Or it was just random, with no rhyme or reason. Knowing Abe as well as he did, either thing was possible.

The dark grayness of it all was disorienting. The human body knows night from day and vice versa. It's a seemingly natural affair. But the dark grayness that surrounded him, plus his being up all night, plus taking a mid-morning nap, plus all the coffee sent mixed signals to Widow's brain. It made it hard to tell the time of day. He knew it was midday, but his senses kept trying to convince him it was night.

The terrain around the farm had lights posted high on metal poles overlooking the Christmas trees. These lights were all completely off, which made the farm look like something out of a horror movie. It was dark and creepy. He saw the dark shadows of Christmas trees everywhere, combined with the gusts of wind and the snow. That old Stephen King movie came to mind— The Shining. He liked that movie, but it had terrified him as a kid. It was the atmosphere—that and the naked, dead zombie woman in room 237.

Thinking about the part where she turned old and decayed still gave him the shivers.

He glanced up at each window on the second floor, every couple of yards. Most of the house was dark.

Widow traced along the house wall until he reached the back corner, just near the fireplace. He skirted around the brick, pointing the M4 ahead, ready to shoot anything that moved. But nothing did.

He came to a trellis that he had not seen before. There were rose bushes all along it, climbing up the sides to the roof. There were no roses on it, only the stems with thorns. The rose petals had fallen off weeks ago.

Widow stopped at the end of the trellis and saw the wooden protrusion that was the shed with the rifles he and Abe had gone into earlier. He knew the back slider door was beyond that.

The Whites had a big family, not a world record or anything, but they had several members. He figured there were several options to keeping them hostage, but the best one was to let them all sit around their own family room, lumping them together, keeping them at gunpoint.

In the living room, seated on their own furniture, they would feel safe and be docile. They were less likely to rebel if they were treated civilly. It was a false sense of safety. Widow knew that. But that was his guess. He didn't think it was likely any of them would be upstairs, which made it his best point of entry.

He let the M4 hang by its strap and scrambled up the trellis, hoping not to make a sound, hoping it would hold his weight.

He made it up to a second-floor window and stopped on the roof above the shed. He paused and glanced in the window. It must've been Dylan's room because he saw a bunk bed and a TV with a gaming system linked up to it, not to mention the posters of rap groups he'd never heard of, on the walls. He didn't know any of them. There was also a poster on the wall that was probably controversial with Maggie. It was a female singer, half-dressed, showing her jeans-covered butt to the camera. It was alluring for an eight-year-old boy. It was a little more than Widow was allowed at that age.

He couldn't remember being into girls when he was so young. He remembered thinking they had cooties. Now, cooties or not, he thought they were worth the risk.

Widow sat down on his haunches and lifted the M4, slipped the strap off himself, to give him more range of motion, and reversed the M4, reared it back, ready to break the glass. He hoped the sound wasn't loud, but these things were like Band-Aids. Better to rip fast.

He slammed the rifle forward, but stopped an inch from the glass. He paused because he thought back to his eight-year-old self. He may not have had posters of half-naked girls on his walls, but he remembered being rebellious. He remembered not liking to follow the rules. He liked to take risks. One of those risks was sneaking out of his bedroom at night.

He used to meet up with his friends and play Squish-Squash, down by the train tracks. They would place coins and marbles and rocks and anything else they found on the train tracks. Then they would sneak a couple of beers and pass them around while they waited to see the train pass through at midnight to squish whatever the object was.

They used a ball-bearing once. They thought it might fire off into two different directions. But it didn't. It got squashed like everything else.

Widow stopped from bashing in the glass and looked at the locks on the window. They weren't latched.

Amateur mistake, he thought.

Dylan was risking getting caught by being so careless. Widow's own mother would've busted him for sure.

Overall, Dylan had the perfect setup for sneaking out. He probably climbed out his bedroom window, onto the roof, and down the trellis, same as Widow had come up.

Widow let the rifle hang by the strap and slid the window up, slowly, using both hands. He grabbed the rifle and climbed into Dylan's room. He shut the window behind him. He scanned the room and the door, in case it suddenly opened. It didn't.

Widow went through the room to the door to the hallway.

He remembered that Dylan's room was near his grandparents' master and Walter's room. Foster's and A.M.W.'s, the dead son, were on the other side, nearer to the guest room he had napped in earlier.

Widow opened the door all the way and stepped out into the hall. It was showtime.

He moved across the hall, stepping lightly, but also thinking about Abby reacting to his wearing dirty, snowy boots on her clean floors.

Widow planted his back to the wall and held the rifle ready to shoot. The muzzle was at eye level.

He walked forward toward the direction of the stairs until he heard voices behind him in the master bedroom. He also heard what sounded like someone jumping on a bed, or like a kid pounding his fists and feet on the mattress, throwing a tantrum.

He spun around and headed that way first. He had expected no one to be upstairs, not any of the hostages. And he was half-right because, in the open doorway, he saw one of the Athenians— had to be. The guy stood over one of the agents he met earlier. It was Toni Adonis.

She was handcuffed to the bed's headboard. She was laid out at the start of a horrifying rape scene. Rape was the intent. That was obvious.

Widow breathed a sigh of relief because he wasn't too late. She was still clothed. Her pants were still on. Her top was still on. But her coat and boots and Glock and shoulder holster rig were all gone. He didn't see the Glock or the holster anywhere in the room, which made him wonder if he'd missed them back at Pine Farms. They were probably stripped from her and tossed in the barn somewhere.

Adonis stared at the Athenian standing above her. Widow saw sweat on her face. She had been the one making the tantrum noises. She had been struggling to get free or get away. The voices he had heard were only one voice—the Athenian's.

He talked out loud like it was half to himself and half to taunt Adonis.

Widow caught the end of whatever the Athenian said, and the groping that just took place.

The guy stood over her, saying more. Widow couldn't make it out. It was low, like a whisper.

The guy had a vicious shotgun in his hands. Widow didn't recognize the model. It had all kinds of aftermarket features on it. It wasn't a weapon Widow wanted fired at him, or fired at all. The blast would tell the whole house he was there, like Shep's shotgun had warned them earlier, only worse.

But Widow made a mistake. He paused too long in the doorway, and the Athenian saw him in his peripherals.

Both the Athenian and Adonis saw him.

The Athenian raised his head and looked right at Widow. Adonis turned her head and looked at him. They both stared at him.

The expression on Adonis's face shifted dramatically, as dramatically as anyone's face had ever turned. She went from utter terror to extreme hope and then unbelievable exhilaration. It was the adrenaline spiking in her brain from seeing him standing there. It was the kind of emotion that rescuers saw every day when they saved someone from certain death.

The Athenian's face was the opposite. Now terror reflected in his expression.

The Athenian's brain was overloaded with questions.

Hadn't they swept the whole house? How could they miss this large guy? Who the hell was he?

The Athenian reacted and raised the combat shotgun to kill the guy in the doorway. Unfortunately for him, Widow already had the M4 ready and pointed straight at him.

Widow squeezed the trigger.

Bullets blasted out of the muzzle, through the sound suppressor, and through the Athenian. The gun was suppressed, but a suppressor on a weapon like that didn't silence the noise. It wasn't dead quiet. It rattled loud like the sound of ten rattlesnakes.

The bullets sprayed out and gutted Tanis straight through his abdomen, tearing through flesh and bone and organs. Blood sprayed out—first, from the front of his gut and then from behind him, through the exit wounds. Blood sprayed out all over the wall behind him, part of the glass on the window, and across Adonis on the bed.

Widow took his finger off the trigger and watched the Athenian crumple backward and forward, which folded his knees back and underneath him like a paper-mâché man.

Blood seeped and squirted and spilled out of multiple bullet holes in his gut. It turned black within seconds, as gut shots often do.

Widow walked into the room, keeping the M4 pointed at the Athenian. He shut the door behind him. In case someone came up the rear, at least the door would be between them. He glanced at the bathroom to make sure no one was there. The room was empty except for the two other people, but then the Athenian uttered one last question, and died, leaving only Adonis and Widow left.

The Athenian asked, "Who are you?"

Widow stayed quiet.

The Athenian's eyes went blank. Someone was there, and then he wasn't.

Adonis started saying something, but it was all gagged utterances.

Widow lowered the M4 and went over to her. He pulled the gag out of her mouth.

She said, "Get me out of these!"

"Where's the key?"

"They were on Shep. Brooks has them."

Widow looked at her dumbfounded.

"I don't know these names."

"Uh! Brooks is the black guy with Abel. Shep was with Highway Patrol. You met him earlier."

Widow fished a set of keys out of his pocket.

"Here are the keys to the Highway Patrol car."

"Yes! That's them, on the end. The little ring."

Widow took the small handcuff key and unlocked her.

She sat straight up.

"Is he dead?" she asked, glancing at the body beyond Widow's waist.

"He's not sending out any Christmas cards this year."

Adonis sat up, taking the handcuffs off her wrists as fast as she could. She rubbed her wrists, which were legitimately bruised from her trying to wriggle out of the cuffs.

"They took my boots," she said.

"Where are they?"

She shrugged.

Widow asked, "Can you walk okay?"

"I'm not dead."

She stood up off the bed. Without the boots, she was an entire foot-and-change shorter than him. She could stand behind him in a police lineup and be completely invisible.

Widow glanced down at her feet.

"At least you still have your socks on."

"Yeah. At least."

Adonis went over to Tanis and cursed at his corpse. For a moment, Widow thought she might either spit on it or kick it. He wouldn't have blamed her. But she did neither. Instead, she sidestepped to the left and scooped up the combat shotgun. She turned and pumped it, ejecting a perfectly good shell that was chambered. He didn't know why. Maybe she was making sure it was loaded and ready to go. Or maybe she was venting her anger, making a dramatic statement. Pumping a shotgun was good for dramatic statements.

Adonis said, "Thank you for saving my life, Cousin Jack."

"Call me Widow. I'm not their cousin. I'm nobody's cousin."

"No shit!" she said, ironically, "Okay. Widow. What now? There're still five of them left. And they're ex-Special Forces."

"Former Special Forces. We don't say ex. We prefer former. It's an honor thing."

"These assholes don't got no honor."

"True."

"So, what now?"

"We can't call for help. They've seen to that. They probably took out a cell phone tower. I know they took out the local transformer."

"There's a radio in the sheriff's truck?"

"Already checked it. Nothing. Not in this weather."

Adonis asked, "So what, then? We go down guns blazing?"

Widow shook his head with a big: *No! That's not a good idea!*

Adonis asked, "What? Why not?"

"My concern is saving the White family."

"They killed my guys. They killed them in cold blood. Right in front of me. First, they blew up half my friends. Then they murdered Shep, Ramirez, James, and Swan."

"I'm sorry for that, but that's not this family's fault. They don't deserve to die so you can have revenge. Our responsibility is for their safety. Not your vendetta."

Adonis was silent for a long moment. But then she nodded and spoke. Her voice was raspy. Maybe from the gag, maybe from the truth.

"You're right."

Suddenly, a deep voice called out from downstairs.

"Tanis? What's that racket?"

Adonis said, "They heard the shots."

Of course they did, Widow thought.

An M4 on full auto is a loud weapon; a sound suppressor just turns loud gunshots into loud rattles. It'll still be heard all over the house.

"There goes the element of surprise," he said.

"What do we do? There's at least five more of them."

"There're only three left."

"You killed the others?"

"I killed a sniper in a barn. I stuffed one in the cruiser's trunk. And I killed that one," Widow said, pointing at the dead one on the floor.

Adonis looked at the dead one on the floor again.

Widow said, "We'd better keep the others on their toes."

"What do you have in mind?"

"Follow me."

They heard the same voice call out again.

"Tanis? Answer!"

Before they left the room, Widow looked over the corpse one last time, thinking there might be a radio on him, but there wasn't. The radios were limited, apparently. You had to be in the top tier to get one.

Widow returned to the hallway.

"Come on," he told her.

She followed him. They threaded the hall, hugging the wall opposite the stairs. She kept the shotgun trained on the stairwell opening, expecting to shoot one of Abel's guys, but no one came up.

The voice called out again, louder because they were closer to the stairs. It sounded like he was right at the foot of the stairs.

"Tanis?"

Widow whispered to Adonis.

"This way."

They passed the stairs and went through an open bedroom door, back into Dylan's room. Widow led her to Dylan's sneaking out window and opened it.

"Down the trellis."

She went first, climbed through the window. He held the shotgun for her. She scrambled down. She was glad not to be completely barefoot, but as soon as her socks touched the snow, she felt it. Shivers crawled up her toes, feet, and legs.

The wind blew on her, and the snow blasted her shoulders and head. It didn't help her feel any less cold.

Widow tossed the shotgun down to her. She caught it; then, he removed the strap and dropped the M4 down to her. She caught it as well. He climbed out the window after her, but not till after he heard the voice again. Only this time, it was on the second floor, right on their trail.

"Tanis? What's going on in there?"

Widow made it down after her.

"We'd better move," he said.

51

DYLAN SAT NEXT to his father and his sister, but he eyeballed the sliding doors. He was only eight years old, and he was scared, as they all were. He kept thinking about the sliders. He bet he could make a run for it. Maybe he could get away. Maybe they wouldn't even shoot at him.

Who would shoot a kid? he thought.

In movies, no one ever shoots children. It just wasn't likely. He had seen R-rated action movies before. His dad let him watch the old ones, the ones from the eighties, which his dad said were significantly better than the action movies they make today.

Dylan looked at Abel. Then he looked at the slider.

He figured that if he ran to the slider, unlocked it, slid the door open, and then made a run for the Christmas tree fields, he could get away. He could run all the way through them to the road. He could flag down a car.

Cars would stop for a kid—especially one his age with no winter coat on and no winter boots. Adults are more likely to stop their cars for a kid than for adults. He knew that. He had seen it in movies.

And if he didn't run to the road, maybe he could find Mr. Widow. He looked tough. He remembered Widow and his grandpa had gone outside together. Widow never came back. He must be out there somewhere.

Dylan could find him. Mr. Widow would help.

But he had to get past Abel first.

His thoughts were interrupted when the black guy, Brooks, called up the stairs to the other one.

"Tanis? What's the racket?" Brooks called out.

Dylan looked at the slider doors again.

I could run for it, he thought. *I could be a hero like in the eighties movies. Mr. Widow is like one of those action guys. We could fight these guys ourselves.*

Brooks faced the stairs, looking up them to the second floor.

He called up again.

"Tanis? Answer!"

Dylan looked at Abel, who stared at Brooks and the stairwell. Dylan gazed around the room. Everyone was looking at the stairs. He could slip down off the sofa and sneak over to the slider.

How long would it take him to snap the button to unlock it? A second?

The Charlie bar was left off already. He could see that.

Brooks shouted, "Tanis?"

Dylan started edging off the sofa.

52

ON THE GROUND, Widow and Adonis snuck back the way he'd come, to get out of sight from the master bedroom's window and Dylan's window, in case the Athenians had figured out where they escaped to.

They paused on the far side of the house between the backyard and the driveway.

Adonis asked, "What now?"

Widow edged on toward the driveway. He stopped at the corner and hugged the wall and peeked around to the front. He saw the same grayness, the same parked vehicles from before. No change. No one was out front, not yet.

"Okay. Follow me."

He took off running, away from the house to a line of leafless oaks and brush. Adonis followed behind him. At the oaks, he paused behind the larger one and looked back at the house. They were about a hundred feet away from the porch.

He looked at the windows in the front and saw no one. He knew they must've found the dead guy called Tanis by now.

"Come on," he said.

He took off running, not at a full sprint, more of a jog because Adonis was barefoot and probably couldn't keep up running that fast in the snow. But she kept up just fine.

He led her to the side of the barn. Then he followed the wall north to the back of the structure.

At the back, he showed her the big hole in the wall, which Abe had told him a storm took off the year before. They climbed through it.

They walked over to stacks of various pieces of lumber and construction equipment and the shingles he had set down with Abe.

They propped their long guns up against a pile of lumber.

Widow grabbed Adonis by the waist from the front, like they were going to do a slow dance, and lifted her up and set her down on a pile of the roof shingles.

She didn't complain.

She gathered her breath and asked, "What now?"

"You stay here. I'll go try to figure something out."

"No way! You're not shutting me out!"

"But…"

She cut him off with a hand to his face.

"Don't give me that loner, hero bullshit! I'm the ATF agent! We're doing something together or not at all."

Widow waited for her to stop before speaking.

She stared at him.

He said, "Okay. I'm just going to look."

"Oh. Okay. Sorry."

He left her there and went to the barn doors. He cracked one side open and peeked out at the front of the house. No one came out, but he could hear yelling from inside the house, over the wind and snow. He saw the shadow of a head pass the kitchen window. It was a man's, but he passed too quickly for him to figure out which man.

Widow shut the door and came back to Adonis.

"They've discovered the dead one."

"What now?"

"We have to go in. We can't wait around for them. Knowing Abel, he'll start shooting them until we give ourselves up."

"You know Abel?"

Widow shook his head.

"I googled him earlier. After you left. I've never met him, but I know the type."

"He killed dozens of my agents. My friends."

"I know."

"He deserves to die."

"I know."

She started tearing up again. It was nothing at first, but then she just burst into tears like a levee breaking.

She turned away from him like she was ashamed. She began sobbing. It was bad, about as bad as anyone he ever heard cry before. She had held it in all morning until now.

In a sobbing, broken up voice, she said, "I'm sorry."

"Don't be. I've seen full-grown Navy SEALs cry. You've been through something traumatic and emotional. I get it."

"It's all my fault."

"No, it's not. They're the ones who strapped you to a bed. They're the ones who were going to rape you. That's not your fault."

She wiped her face and stayed facing the other way.

Widow glanced back over his shoulder to the barn doors, listening to see if they had come out front yet. He knew that once they combed the house for Adonis, they would eventually figure out she'd escaped through an upstairs window. At any moment, he expected them to come out in a hunting party of at least two.

But there was nothing so far.

Adonis said, "You don't understand. It's all my fault. They killed my guys, and that's my fault. It was my operation."

"You're talking about the compound exploding?"

She said nothing to that.

Widow said, "Look, Ops go bad. No plan survives first contact with the enemy."

She turned back and looked at him. Her face and mascara were worse than before.

She half-smiled.

"Is that an Army motto or something?"

It was a SEAL proverb. His head was full of them, as were all SEALs' heads. It couldn't be helped. Everything he learned back then was hammered and stamped and plugged into his head like a tattoo on the brain.

But he didn't tell her that part.

He said, "I saw it on a bumper sticker somewhere."

"You still don't understand. This is more than false guilt. I mean, my guys are dead because I took them along on my own personal vendetta."

He stared at her.

She said, "Shep, Ramirez, Swan, and James. They were killed down the road from here because I took them with me to hunt Abel. I was ordered off the case this morning. After the Op went bad."

Widow nodded. He understood. She felt guilty for the Athenians blowing themselves up and killing half her agents. But she was bullheaded and defied orders and took the men she mentioned with her to hunt Abel down. Only now they were dead, too.

Widow said, "I'm not going to tell you that you're wrong. That's up to you to decide for yourself. But look, Abel's alive. His guys are alive. And they've got an innocent family hostage. There's a sheriff in there too. We can save them. We can save them all. You can make it right."

She nodded.

Widow said, "I need you to pull it together."

"Okay. You're right. What do we do?"

He looked around the barn.

"We need a distraction."

"What do you suggest?" she asked.

He had an idea, but it wasn't one that Abe or Walter or Abby would like.

53

BROOKS STOOD at the foot of the Whites' staircase leading up to the second floor, where Adonis had been strapped to the bed, where Tanis had been patrolling. Only everyone downstairs had all heard a ruckus coming from the master bedroom. It sounded as if some kind of heavy machinery had been set off. It sounded like an industrial sewing machine had been kicked on and was working tirelessly.

Abel said, "What the hell was that?"

He stared at Abe with the question, like he had the answer.

Abe, not wanting to look like he was guilty in a coup attempt, offered a possible explanation.

"Maybe the heater's finally giving way. That damn old thing has needed to be replaced for twenty years now."

Abe glanced at Walter. They locked eyes as if they were both thinking the same thing, like a psychic connection.

Widow is still out there.

Walter said, "That might've been it kicking off for the last time."

But Brooks wasn't buying it.

He said, "Sounded like automatic fire to me."

Abel looked at him.

"Autofire?"

"One of our silenced M4s, maybe.

Abel stood up from the armchair. He put the cigar out on one of Abby's end tables. The whole White family, minus Abby, noticed and cringed.

Abel stormed over to the stairs, stayed behind Brooks. He called up.

"Tanis!"

Nothing.

"Tanis!"

Silence.

Flack came in from the kitchen with Abby. He pulled her around by her collar like a pet. The White family noticed that too. Especially Abe, who stood up like he was going to protest, but Abel turned back to him.

"Sit down!" he said. Abe sat back down.

Abel said, "Flack, get your ass up there and see what's going on. Brooks, go with him."

Flack released Abby from his grip and walked into the living room, toward the stairs. Abel stopped him before he got there with a long, bony hand on his chest.

Abel said, "Hold up. Give me the M4."

Flack nodded and handed over his M4 and took a Glock out of his hip holster. It was also silenced.

Abel took the M4 and swept the muzzle over the family once, reminding them he was in charge.

Flack joined Brooks at the bottom of the stairs. Brooks held up his hand.

"I'll go first," he said. He aimed his M4 up the stairs, and together they both ascended.

On the second floor, they headed straight toward the master bedroom. They went right in, not checking the room with their weapons, which they both immediately knew they should've done. Because the first things they stared at were the empty bed and the handcuffs opened and lying on top of the covers. Then they saw the blood across the covers and the wall and the window across from the bed. They walked around the bed and found their friend dead.

Tanis's corpse was crammed into the wall awkwardly, as if he had been catapulted into it like a rag doll.

Tanis's eyes were still open. They stared at the floor, completely lifeless and hollow. He was nothing more than a husk.

He was up against the far wall, near a window overlooking the backyard.

Flack took a knee down beside his dead friend and reached out and checked for a pulse on Tanis's neck. There wasn't one.

Brooks said, "What the hell're you doin'?"

"He's dead."

"No shit, he's dead! His blood is all over the carpet. Come on!"

Flack got up and followed Brooks. They checked the rest of the room, the closet, the bathroom. Then they moved to the next bedroom on that floor and the next and the next until they had checked them all.

Brooks checked all the windows. Finally, they ended up in Dylan's room, where they found an unlocked window.

Brooks held the M4 in one hand and used the other hand to palm the window all the way up. He looked out of it. A cold wind gusted into the room and over his face. He stuck his head out the window, fast, and scanned the back of the house. He saw nothing but grayness and tall, snow-covered Christmas trees everywhere.

Even though they were Christmas trees, it was all rather spooky.

Brooks looked down at the side of the house and saw the rose trellis. And then he saw the footprints. There were two sets. They ran off around the side of the house, around the corner, and vanished.

He ducked his head back in and grabbed Flack by the collar, same as Flack had done to Abby, and jerked him with it, pulling him alongside for the journey. They stormed out of the room and back to the staircase.

They went down it.

On the stairs, Brooks stopped and stared at Abel, who looked back at him impatiently, waiting for an answer.

He said, "Well?"

Flack said, "Tanis is dead."

Brooks said, "The girl's gone."

"What?"

Brooks said, "There're footprints behind the house. Two sets. It looks like we missed somebody."

Abel's face turned red. He raised the M4 and pointed it at the two of them like he was going to shoot them both dead. If Brooks was honest with himself, he thought for a moment that Abel would squeeze the trigger.

Abel said, "Get Cucci on the radio!"

Brooks pulled out his radio and tried it.

"Cucci. Come in. Over?"

They listened and heard nothing but static.

"Cucci? Come in?"

"Try Jargo!"

Brooks clicked the button and put the receiver up to his mouth.

"Jargo? Come in. Over?"

Nothing.

"Cucci, Jargo, answer. Over!"

Nothing.

They waited for an answer, but they didn't get one, just more silence.

"We should follow the footprints," Flack said.

No one answered. There was no time because suddenly, outside, a stone's throw from the front of the barn, less than fifty yards from the Whites' front door, something exploded! And then it exploded again. And again. And again.

The explosions *boomed* in the cold, grayness like a gas main exploding, but it was over and over.

The Whites all stared at the wall in that direction. Walter covered his family and huddled them into him, pulling them down to the floor. He feared the worst. They all did. Abe scrambled to Abby and grabbed her, pulling her in and away from the explosions with a bear hug. Foster joined her parents. She turned her back to the fireplace.

Flack hit the ground like someone had thrown a grenade into the house. It was automatic, as if PTSD had kicked in and caused him to react. Brooks stayed standing, unfazed by the explosion.

Abel faced the front door. Rage spilled across his face, but he also didn't move.

They all saw the light from the flames of multiple rushing fireballs that erupted straight into the air. The orange light was bright and fierce. It shone through the front windows and into the house.

They heard shrapnel exploding outward, slamming into the sides of the barn, the vehicles, and the front of the house.

The windows of the vehicles, and some on the house blew out completely, shattering into thousands of fragments. The windows that shattered in the house exploded inward. All the ones in the kitchen went. They heard the glass rake across the kitchen tile.

The fireball erupted into the sky, like a car bomb concentrated upward. Several old oak trees ignited in flames and burned and burned. They brightened the gray sky into a twisted medieval painting.

The thing that none of them knew yet was that Walter's Tundra was engulfed in flames. All the pipe bombs in the bed had exploded in rapid succession.

Walter's Tundra burned bright red. The flames leaped off the bed and onto the barn, setting it on fire. The cabin in the truck wasn't on fire yet, but it would be in a matter of minutes. As of now, the interior of the truck was covered in broken glass and embedded fragments of metal from the pipes and packed shrapnel encased around the pipe bombs.

Flack jumped back up to his feet, embarrassed that he had hit the deck so quickly.

Brooks said, "What the hell was that?"

Flack said, "It's the pipe bombs."

"All of them?"

Nobody spoke.

* * *

DYLAN HELD HIS HEAD DOWN, next to his sister and his father. Maggie was across from him on the other side of the huddle. After the explosion ended, he saw his chance.

They all stood back up, staring toward the front of the house at the bright orange and red hues dancing in their front yard.

Dylan jerked on Walter's shirt.

"Come on! Come on!" he whispered to them.

He pulled away and ran to the slider. He unlocked it and slid it open and took off, running straight through it, leaving it open behind him, hoping his family would follow.

As Brooks, Flack, and Abel stared at the front door; the White family took off running behind Dylan, all but Abby and Abe and Foster.

Maggie took off after her son, followed by Lauren, holding her father's hand. They all made it through the open slider.

Abe pulled at Abby's hand.

"Let's go!" he whispered.

"No! I can't! I can't run! You go!"

"No! I'm not leaving without you!"

Flack was the first to react to the Whites' escape. He stormed over behind them, blocking their way to the doors. He shoved his Glock into Abe's face.

"You're not going anywhere!" he said.

Brooks walked behind his boss and planted a slow hand on Abel's shoulder.

Abel turned around. His pale face was flush with rage.

Brooks had never seen him so angry before.

Abel stayed quiet. The anger, the rage boiled in his face. They all saw it.

Brooks asked, "What do we do now?"

"Kill them! Kill them all!"

54

RIGHT BEFORE THE EXPLOSION, Widow had taken Adonis out of the barn and to the bed of the Tundra. He lowered the tailgate.

She said, "I saw them loading this at the abandoned farm down the street. What are they?"

"It's mail."

"I see that. But what's in them? Anthrax? Drugs? Money?"

Widow said, "Pipe bombs."

Her mouth gasped open.

"Like the Unabomber?"

"Yeah. Just like that."

She picked one up, carefully, and read the name and address off the label. Then she picked up another and read that name and address of the label.

"I don't know these names? Who're they?"

Widow didn't have time to help her figure it out on her own, so he just came out with it.

"These are all the names of still-living retired Army generals."

She nodded in agreement. He was right. She knew it instantly.

"Abel's planning to send a message by blowing up all the Army's retired generals?"

"It's not a message. It's petty revenge. Plain and simple. He blames them for ruining his career, I guess. Or some such bullshit."

"All of them?"

"I guess. He's twisted. Who cares? Right now, we're going to use these to foul them up inside."

"How?"

"Abel went through a lot of trouble to protect these. They blew up their own compound just to get these out. He abandoned his life and whatever else he had in there. This was the thing he chose to save. It must be important to him."

"So, what do we do with it?"

Widow looked at her. He cracked a slow smile. She saw mischief in his eyes like she would imagine on the devil's face.

He said, "We blow them up."

"All of them?"

"Yes."

She said, "But. This is evidence."

"We're past that, Adonis. We're past evidence-collecting. He's gotta go down. We need to do this. It'll distract him long enough to make a difference."

"Okay. You're right. How? Won't that blow us all up too? That's what happened in Carbine."

"No. The bombs in Carbine weren't pipe bombs. Couldn't have been. They were probably pressure-cooker bombs or C4. Either way, these bombs will explode upward because of the truck's bed."

"There're a lot of bombs here. Won't setting them all off at once cause a huge explosion?"

"Forty-one bombs. There're forty-one."

She nodded and looked at them.

She said, "One for each retired general. Forty-one names. Forty-one retired generals."

"Forty-two, if you count Abel."

She repeated her question.

"Okay. Won't the explosion be huge?"

"It definitely will. The fireball will be big. The real danger is in the force behind the shrapnel. But pipe bombs don't have internal shrapnel jammed into them. No room. Still, these are dangerous. What they did here was pack glass and metal pieces around the bomb inside the package."

"That sounds like it'll kill all of us."

"It won't. Trust me. They're safe in the house."

"What about us?"

"We'll be behind cover. We'll be safe. The vehicles are a different story."

"Let's do it then. How do we do it?"

He explained his idea to Adonis in all its crude simplicity. He explained what they would have to do. She listened and got it and agreed.

They left the packages stacked where they were. Widow closed the tailgate, and they ran back into the barn, pulling the doors closed.

Adonis took the shotgun and crawled back through the hole in the barn, and ran back to the Whites' house. She went around to the back, the same way they had run from, tracing over their footprints.

She turned the corner and was gone from sight.

Widow watched and waited for her to vanish behind the back of the house. He listened to the shouting from inside. He tried to imagine and time the Athenians running upstairs, checking out the bedroom, finding their dead friend, and then clearing all the upstairs bedrooms until they realized Adonis had escaped through Dylan's unlocked bedroom window and climbed down the trellis. He imagined them returning to Abel and the Whites in the main room.

Widow climbed a ladder in the barn up to a loft, not unlike the one he'd killed Jargo on.

He walked to the loft's window and stood close to the wall, as close as he could to provide some protection. He aimed the M4 at the back of the truck, and then he sidestepped completely behind the barn's wall, keeping the rifle out, one-handed. He squeezed the trigger, firing blind.

The bullets hit home.

The pipe bomb packages exploded in a fiery heap. The packed shrapnel and the bomb's casing all exploded. The pressure wave swept up the front of the barn and slammed Widow's location a fraction of a second after the heat and the boom from the explosion.

The force expanded up and out from the Tundra. It slammed into the barn wall. Widow went flying back and away from the wall like a wave of boards had catapulted him off his feet. He dropped the M4.

He fell back into the barn, landing on the floorboards of the loft. He hit his head hard and blacked out.

55

ADONIS WATCHED from the back corner of the house. She flinched from the pressure wave and the boom and the bright fireball, but it was a reaction held over from earlier. Her muscle memory from watching her friends and colleagues explode around her in Carbine set off the chain reaction in her body that caused her to flinch.

She was too far away from the explosion to feel it the way Widow must've felt it.

She saw him fire from the window of the barn's loft. She saw the M4 rip from his hand from the explosion, and she saw his hand vanish back into the interior of the barn. She waited for a long minute for him to come out, maybe stick his head out the window, but he didn't. She watched the rear of the barn, expecting to see him scramble out from behind.

But he didn't.

"Where're you, Widow?" she muttered.

He didn't come out.

From behind her, she heard the door at the back of the house slide open on tracks. And then she heard voices, scrambling and frantic. She heard someone shouting after someone else.

"Dylan! Dylan! Wait!"

Adonis looked back at the barn, one last time, hoping Widow was alive. But then she saw the front of the barn, the barn doors, the loft window, and the front part of the roof flame up from spitfire popping off the fire in the back of the Tundra. Then the Tundra itself exploded. The fire from the bombs had reached the gas tank. The whole thing went up into a fiery mess.

The barn was burning, and burning fast. She paused, thought about running back to see if Widow was all right, but then she heard the voices again.

"Dylan! Come back!"

She turned and watched a boy running off into the grayness, into a section of huge Christmas trees, bunched and growing so close together it was like a maze.

She watched the White family running behind him. All of them vanishing into the gloom. The adults turned the wrong way and disappeared into a different section of trees. The boy was off alone, running for his life.

They all ran for their lives.

Widow came to mind one last time. Then she saw two of Abel's guys dragging the elder Whites out of their own house. They dropped them down to their knees. Abel stood over them.

She thought he was going to execute them, but he didn't. He argued with his men for a moment. Then they took the Whites and locked them into a shed at the back of the house. Abel locked them in with a padlock and pocketed the key.

The three Athenians took off, running into the maze of trees after the Whites. The only thing was, all three men went the same direction as the kid.

Adonis ran to the shed first.

"Mr. White," she called out.

"Agent Adonis?" he said.

Abby said, "Oh, thank God!"

"Let us out of here."

She studied the padlock.

"I don't have the key."

"Please, let us out!" Abe said.

"I'll get you out. Just hold on."

She stepped back, aimed the combat shotgun at the door, but she stopped. She thought about the ammo. She only had what was in the weapon—no extra shells. And there were still three armed and dangerous Athenians out there.

The elder Whites were safe, for now. The others were in danger.

She pounded on the door with a fist.

"Don't worry now. I'll come back for you. I'm going after them."

"No! Wait!" Abe shouted.

"Get us out!" Abby shouted.

They both pounded on the inside of the door and begged for her to let them out, but Adonis had already taken off running by then, after Abel, into the maze of trees.

56

DYLAN RAN AND RAN. He ran until he was out of breath, and then he ran some more. Finally, when he thought he was relatively safe, he stopped and put his hands down on his knees, faced the ground, and breathed.

His breaths came in waves of exhaustion. He panted and huffed and panted some more, letting his body catch up to his breathing. He sucked the cold oxygen into his lungs and pushed it back out in steamy exhalations.

He knew their farm well, but the snow and the wind and the lightning scattered him, confused him, turned him around. Now, he wasn't sure where the hell he was or where he was going.

The grayness in the sky and the dark clouds made it impossible to gauge direction. North, east, west, and south were all spinning in his head.

Which way? he thought.

He was still in the trees. He knew which section of trees because of their heights. He was lost in the nine-year-old trees, the ones just before the section to be cut and sold the next year. The second problem was that they had large sections of trees. Knowing the section where he was lost did little if he couldn't figure out where the edge was. He was right smack in the middle of the nine-year-old section, or "The Niners" as his dad called them.

Dylan's problems didn't stop at just two. He had another issue. He wasn't allowed to play in the sections over seven years in age because they grew larger, making it harder to find his way around. Abe and his father liked for him to stay out of the trees closer to being ready to harvest and sell. Even though he had broken this rule and had snuck in the Niners before, it was the section he knew the least about. He could've gotten lost in them in broad daylight.

Suddenly, he heard voices around him; only he couldn't tell which direction they came from. One seemed behind him, on his trail, and another seemed right in front of him.

He didn't know where to run, so he took off east, thinking he was going north. He ran and ran and slammed right into something that felt like a tree.

He looked up and faced a black man staring down at him in the gloom. It was Brooks.

Brooks bent over, took a hand off his M4, and bunched up the boy's collar. He scooped him up like a light backpack. He held him up in the air off his feet.

Brooks said, "Where're you running off to?"

Dylan couldn't answer. He was out of breath and frozen in terror.

Brooks called out.

"I got the boy."

Flack came running up from behind, and Abel walked in through the gloom. He walked right up to Brooks and stared into the boy's eyes.

"Goodie. We got bait. Let's take him back to the grandparents. The others will come out of hiding."

Flack said, "They took off to the north. I think. What if they kept on running?"

"They'll turn around when they realize they lost this one."

"Then what? They've blown up the pipe bombs."

"I told you already. We kill them."

Brooks lowered Dylan to his feet but kept a big hand around his neck. Dylan squirmed and struggled, but it was like being in a vise grip.

Brooks loosened his grip enough so Dylan could breathe again, but that was all the slack Dylan got.

Brooks said, "Maybe we should just get out of here now. You know? While we can."

Abel turned and stared at his longtime number two.

"Not you too?"

"I just think that our operation is over. Why stick around?"

"I call the shots, Brooks! Or have you forgotten your place?"

Brooks stared into Abel's eyes. He had seen the general snap before. He had seen him with crazy looks in his eyes and on his face, but he had never seen the man make irrational decisions, not the kind of tactically ignorant kind, not like this.

Brooks said, "The Whites are gone. The bombs are destroyed. The compound is gone. There's an ATF agent loose."

Abel turned slow and paced back and forth, shaking his head, repeating the same word over and over.

"Tsk. Tsk. Tsk."

He stopped dead center between Flack and Brooks.

"You disappoint me, Brooks. I never thought I would live to see the day that you'd give up like this."

"General, I'm not giving up. I'm just saying that right now, we've lost everything. And there's a helicopter back at that other farm. We can get away clean before the FBI figures out we're still in their dragnet."

Silence.

Brooks said, "Flack, you can fly the bird, right?"

Flack said, "Yeah. Sure."

Brooks said, "We've got a pilot right here."

Abel looked like he was thinking it over.

Brooks said, "General, we can get out now. Clean. We can rebuild somewhere else."

"Rebuild? You want me to rebuild?"

Flack said, "I can go get the bird right now. I can circle around back here and pick you up."

Abel thought for a moment.

Brooks said, "Just let him get the helo. We can still tear this family apart."

Abel stopped and stared straight up to the sky. He breathed in and breathed out like a psychotic mental patient doing his treatments to help him come back from the edge of darkness.

Abel quieted down the noise in his head and turned back to his men.

"You're right. You're both right. You're a good soldier, Brooks."

Brooks nodded.

Abel said, "Okay. Go get the bird. Meet us at the back of the house."

Flack nodded and turned and ran back the way they came, thinking once he got closer to the farmhouse, he could just follow the fire to it and find his way to the bird from there. But he didn't make it ten feet.

Fast, Abel raised the M4, turned toward Flack, aimed, and squeezed the trigger. The weapon purred like a silent jackhammer in the stillness. He fired several rounds at Flack. The bullets riddled through his back and neck. Red mist erupted out in front of him as the bullets exited.

Blood sprayed out of him and splashed across a big, snow-covered Christmas tree. Flack fell forward and died, staring at the bottom of that same tree. He watched blood drip from the needles until he took his last breath.

Abel swung around and pointed the M4 at Brooks, who raised his weapon one-handed and aimed back at Abel.

"What the hell did you do?" Brooks shouted.

"I'm in command here! Not you! Not him! Not anyone else!"

For the first time in his life, Brooks flashed fear across his face, not worry, not concern, but utter, real fear. He was looking into the eyes of a madman, and he finally realized it.

"You've lost your mind!"

"I'm in command! Lower your weapon, soldier!"

Brooks didn't lower his weapon. He kept it pointed at Abel. They circled each other, with Dylan in tow.

57

ADONIS STOPPED RUNNING when she heard shouting just behind her. She had passed them somehow. She circled back and headed toward the voices. She kept low, creeping through the vast rows of trees. They all looked the same to her.

Occasionally, she stopped near one and had to glance at it twice to make sure it wasn't a giant creature lying in wait for her to get too close before it swooped her up in its branches. But the trees never moved except for swaying in the wind, which caused a whole other scary effect.

The wind gusted and blew, and the branches on the trees swayed back and forth, up and down. Staring down the rows made it look like hundreds of swaying arms moving up and down, like an elaborate, choreographed dance of hundreds of giant beasts.

She kept going, staying close to the trees for extra cover, but also keeping one eye on them. Finally, she made it within proximity of the voices, or so she thought, but then, she heard loud purrs to her left like mechanical sounds, like thumping. She knew instantly it was one of the silenced M4s. She recognized the sound because she just heard Widow shoot his, back in the master bedroom.

She picked up the pace and came to a scene she hadn't expected.

Abel had shot one of his guys in the back, and now he was arguing with Brooks. She remembered from their files that Brooks had been second to none in Abel's eyes for more than fourteen years. They were ten years together on tour in Baghdad and then four years together at the Athenian compound. Now they were at each other's throats. It was the opportunity she would never get again.

She crept up closer, staying three rows of trees away.

They kept arguing. She kept drifting. She didn't want to get their attention. She came right up to one tree row away. She tried to move once more, to be right alongside them, but she froze. She knelt, taking a good shooting position.

They had the boy. She saw him squirming around in Brooks's grasp. He was fighting to get away.

Brooks held him out front, between himself and Abel, like he might snatch the kid up as a human shield if he needed to.

Adonis saw the kid, but then she looked over to Abel.

She aimed the combat shotgun. Abel was right there in her sights. She stared down the barrel at him.

This was her chance. She could shoot him right here and be done with it.

She glanced back at the kid. She couldn't help him anyway, not really. She had a shotgun, not a rifle. If she fired at Brooks with it, she would hit him, no question. But she would also hit the kid. Probably. She would probably kill him.

The best way to save him would be to convince Brooks to let him go. She could kill Abel now and then deal with Brooks. He seemed like he wanted to live, to escape. She could probably make a deal with him.

Let the kid go, and I'll forget I saw you, she could say. He would probably go for it. Or some version of it.

She could kill Abel now and save the boy after.

She stared at Abel again over the shotgun's barrel.

Dorsch's face flashed across her mind, then Shep's, then Ramirez's, followed by James' and Swan's, followed by Clip's face. Then she remembered the fire and smoke at the Athenian compound. She remembered all the dead. It was all her fault. It was all his fault. Then she remembered her Timex, the one that her dad had given her. A final present before she went off to the Marine Corps. It was the last time they spoke of her going into a career that he disapproved of. But he gave it to her like an apology without words. That's how he was.

Suddenly, she thought of Widow. She thought of what he would do, like one of those rubber bracelets people wear that say WWJD, What Would Jesus Do?

Those bracelets weren't religious things to her. It was a way of forcing you to ask yourself: *What's the right thing to do?*

She glanced at the boy again, and she thought, *What Would Widow Do?*

And she knew what he would do. He would rescue the boy at all costs.

"Shit," she muttered.

She scooted close to a line of trees for cover, and dropped to a knee, and lifted the shotgun and fired a warning shot in the air, hoping to scatter Abel and Brooks, which it did.

The shotgun blast rang out like a bomb going off. It echoed up into the grayness and the gloom and the treetops.

After she squeezed the trigger, she pulled her body close to the tree to keep herself out of sight.

Both Abel and Brooks turned and fired without aiming, without thinking, in her direction. They fired from automatic Special Forces reflexes.

She folded over, staying as low as she could to the ground and a row of trees.

Abel blind-fired the M4 on full auto. The bullets sprayed all around her, cutting off tree limbs and the top of the tree across from her. She felt the bullets cutting and slamming into trees all around her. She pulled herself in tight, balling herself up, trying to stay low as best she could.

Christmas trees aren't very thick. They're not good for cover. She had to stay low; staying out of sight was her best hope of survival.

Brooks released Dylan from his grasp so he could shoot his M4. He pulled it up and shot it alongside Abel. Both blind-fired in the shotgun's blast direction. They fired into the gloom and trees and snow.

Both weapons purred in the dead silence, killing the quiet, filling the air with echoing sounds of rattling bullets, shredding tree limbs, and toppling over treetops.

They fired until both guns went empty.

Brooks reloaded his M4 with an extra magazine. Abel didn't have an extra magazine. He fired it empty, and then he jerked his Glock out and aimed it through the smoke and gloom, waiting for another shotgun blast to be fired in their direction.

* * *

DYLAN LANDED IN THE SNOW, out of breath from nearly being strangled. But he knew it was his chance. He coughed and gasped, but kept it to just a few seconds. The M4 purred next to him. He crawled away from Brooks, and once he was three feet behind the man, he jumped to his feet and scrambled away. Beyond the first row of trees, he darted into full sprints, heading northwest.

He ran and ran and didn't look back.

58

WIDOW CAME TO, realizing that he had hit his head and blacked out. It was only seconds later, but it felt like he had taken a long power nap. He felt dazed, but not confused. He knew exactly where he was and how he had gotten there. He pulled himself up to his feet. Sparks of fire fell from the barn's ceiling. The explosion had caught part of the barn on fire.

His first thought, before his own safety, was: *Sorry, Abe.*

Widow looked around. His head started pounding. He had hit it pretty hard. He turned to see what he hit it on. It was a low beam from the roof.

The blast wave must've slammed into the outer barn wall hard enough to send him flying back into it.

He felt the back of his head and found a bump right off. It hurt under his touch. He looked at his hands. There was blood, but not that much. It wasn't gushing, and he seemed fine, minus the bump on his head.

He would live.

He glanced around for the M4 he'd shot the bombs with, but it was nowhere to be seen. It might've been sent way up onto the roof of the barn for all he knew.

He still had the Beretta, luckily.

Widow looked down from the loft to see if everything was on fire around him. He felt the heat from the fire on the roof. Smoldering embers fell around him. He felt the heat from the fire outside, too.

Walter's Tundra was on fire. He felt bad about that.

But the barn floor seemed okay. He scrambled down the ladder and went to the barn doors, automatically. He stopped at the doors when he saw smoke fuming in under the crack at the bottom of the doors.

He turned and headed for the hole in the back wall. He climbed through it and took off running to the front of the Whites' house. He moved up to the wall of the house, staying back from the heat of the blaze.

He saw that he had been wrong about one thing. The fire wasn't just consuming the Tundra. It had leaped onto the sheriff's truck. It wasn't completely engulfed in flames like the Tundra, but it wasn't far behind.

Widow moved around the front of the house, passing Foster's covered car. And Abe's older model Tundra, neither on fire yet.

He went up to the porch and to the front door and pushed it open, fast. He pointed the Beretta up and scanned the downstairs. He saw the slider left wide open. A cold wind blew in through it, nearly extinguishing the fire in the fireplace.

He looked around fast and saw no one.

He called out.

"Whites! Adonis! Anyone here?"

He was half ready to shoot anyone who appeared. But no one did. He heard muffled noise off to his right. He turned and threaded a short hallway that he hadn't been down before. The muffled noise came from behind a door. He pushed it open and found the sheriff, handcuffed to the back of a downstairs toilet. His mouth was gagged. He had a swollen black eye, but all-in-all, he was fine.

Widow didn't have the keys to unlock him.

He said, "Stretch out your hands."

The sheriff muttered a question that Widow couldn't understand.

Widow said, "Pull them apart wide and close your eyes."

He pointed the Beretta at the toilet pipe and handcuffs.

The sheriff closed his eyes tight.

Widow shot two bullets at the handcuff chain and the toilet pipe. Water sprayed out everywhere all over the sheriff's face. But he was free. The chain broke.

Widow helped him sit up and ripped the gag out of his mouth.

"You okay?"

The sheriff coughed and coughed like water had sprayed up his nose.

"Yes. Yes."

"Stay here. In the house. I've got to go for the others."

The sheriff clawed at Widow's pants leg like a beggar.

He asked, "Who are you?"

Widow pulled away and stopped in the doorway.

He couldn't help himself, but he told him, sort of.

"I'm Cousin Jack."

Widow smiled and vanished from the doorway and ran through the open slider to the backyard. He paused, looking for signs of anyone, when he heard voices coming from Abe's shed.

He went over to it and saw the padlock back on it. He banged a hand on the door.

"Abe? You in there?"

"Widow! Yes! We're here!"

"Stand back from the door!" Widow said.

He stepped back and shot off the padlock. It took four bullets in rapid succession. Padlocks are tough. The padlock sparked and crumbled inward from the bullet. The door jerked open, and Abe and Abby both clambered out.

They hugged him at the same time.

"Where're the others?"

Abe said, "Dylan. You have to get Dylan. He ran off that way!"

Abe pointed.

"What about the others?"

Abby said, "We don't know. But our grandson is that way."

"Okay. Okay."

Widow stepped back and looked out over the back of the farm. He saw vast grayness and rows of tall Christmas trees and hard white snowfall.

Then he heard something. It was a loud gunshot to the north. He looked up into the gloom and heard crows squawking and taking to flight. He could barely see them. They scattered, terrified of the noise, and flew off in different directions.

The gunshot was from a shotgun, like the one he'd heard when they murdered Shep. It was Adonis, had to be. She fired only once. He didn't hear another gunshot, which scared him because Abel and Brooks had silenced M4s like the one he'd killed the guy upstairs with.

Widow needed to get out there, and fast. He needed to see. He had an idea. He thought back to the huge tractor and heavy equipment that he had seen out in the field. He thought if tractors could maneuver out there between the trees, then why couldn't a car? He still had Shep's cruiser keys in his pocket.

Widow waved a hand out to the Whites.

"Stay here. The sheriff's inside. I'll be back."

"Where you going?"

Widow didn't answer that. He just took off running at full speed, as fast as he could go.

Widow ran around the side of the house, passing Abe's Tundra, Foster's covered car, and the kitchen's shattered window. He threaded and weaved around numerous fires to the police cruiser, which was fine. He hopped in and fired up the engine. But then, he heard muffled shouts from the trunk.

He'd forgotten about the guy in there.

He hit the trunk button and got out of the car. He went around to the trunk and opened it, scooped Cucci up and carried him to the porch, and dropped him there.

"Don't you go anywhere," he said.

He could see Cucci nodding along, but he didn't trust him.

Widow reared back and punched the guy square in the face.

He watched a second longer as Cucci went out cold.

He felt a little bad because he had already clocked the guy with the butt of the Winchester. But there was no time to feel bad.

Widow hopped back up and dumped himself back into the cruiser and slammed the door. He slid the gear into reverse and gassed and backed it up and flung it back to drive and drove around the front of the house, back the way he had run, re-passing the fiery trucks and the barn and all the broken glass.

He drove around the back, knocking over Abby's bushes, which made him cringe.

He stopped at the backyard, facing the trees in the distance.

He left the car's lights off. They wouldn't have helped. The head-lamps would've just reflected off the gray gloom.

He saw a section in the snow on the ground that looked different from the rest. It was snow-covered, but there were clear tire tracks underneath. That must be where the Whites drove trac-tors and the heavy equipment out into the fields. Then he real-ized they must drive the trucks out there too. Christmas trees don't move themselves to be shipped.

Widow hit the gas and floored it toward Adonis's shotgun blast.

59

ADONIS CLUNG to the shotgun like it was her salvation. She kept her eyes shut tight as gunfire ripped the bark and branches and needles and twigs off the trees lined up behind her. It reminded her of a Marine she'd gun-trained with a lifetime ago.

He used to call machine guns: *weed cutters*. She saw why.

The bullets sprayed around her. One of the M4s ran empty. The other stopped for a moment and she heard the magazine eject. One of her assailants was reloading it.

She squatted down and glanced around the tree. Snow pounded on her back.

She saw Abel in the gloom. He'd ditched his M4 and maneuvered several feet to his right. Brooks reloaded his M4 and took aim in her direction.

Adonis saw Dylan wasn't there. He had run off and was clear from the line of fire. She raised the shotgun and opened fire. She pumped once and fired. She pumped twice and fired again.

She pumped and fired. Pumped and fired.

Brooks ducked and dodged to his left, and Abel went further right. They scattered.

Adonis hopped to her feet and walked in their direction, pumping and shooting. She made her way to another cluster of trees and stopped. She waited. Smoke and gloom and puffs of snow filled the air.

She squatted low in case one of them fired back. She heard nothing but wintry farm sounds, like wind blowing over the hills.

She trekked through the snow toward where the two Athenians had been standing.

She knew Abel had gone in the direction she was walking. She looked down and saw his boot prints. She followed them. Every few paces, she glanced back over her shoulder to make sure Brooks wasn't sneaking up behind her. No one was there.

She turned back and saw Abel. At first, he looked away. He looked west and then turned north like he was lost. He had a Glock in his hand.

She came up behind him, stopped at arm's length. She shoved the shotgun in his back.

"Turn around!" she ordered.

He swung around.

"Slow!" she barked.

He slowed and finally swung all the way around, facing her. He looked down at her eyes over the barrel of the shotgun.

"You going to shoot me now, Special Agent Adonis?"

"I should, you son of a bitch! You deserve to die!"

"Do it then."

She stayed quiet and stared into his hollow, soulless eyes.

She paused a long beat. Her finger was inside the shotgun's trigger housing. She squeezed the trigger, slow. She put enough pounds of pressure on it to pull it back a fraction of the way. All she had to do was squeeze a little harder, and he would be dead.

She lingered on the thought. But she didn't shoot. She spoke instead.

"Joseph Abel. You're under arrest for terrorism and murder. Toss the gun."

He looked at her, stunned.

He said, "I gotta say that's disappointing, Agent Adonis. I thought you were better than that. You're just gonna arrest me like some common criminal?"

She stayed quiet.

He said, "I'm not going to prison. I'll die first."

"Drop the weapon!" she barked.

Abel stepped back away from the shotgun's muzzle. He held the Glock still. It was muzzle up, pointing into the air.

He said, "You're going to have to shoot me! I'm not going in!"

He lowered the Glock, slowly like the minute hand on a clock.

"DROP IT!" she shouted.

He kept moving the Glock down.

"DROP IT!" she shouted again.

He kept lowering it.

She squeezed the trigger of the combat shotgun. But it didn't fire.

The weapon *clicked!*

It was deafening in the snowy silence. They both heard it.

He lowered the Glock all the way and pointed it right in her face.

She pumped and clicked it again. Pumped and clicked again. Pumped and clicked.

Nothing.

She stared at him.

Abel slapped the shotgun out of her hand. It went flying off into the snow. He walked toward her, forcing her to stumble back. She fell back onto the ground.

He smiled at her.

"Maybe we can have that fun time now, and then I'll kill you."

She back-crawled away. He followed her. She crawled away through the row of trees and out to a clearing that seemed like a manmade track.

Abel followed, gun pointed at her. He had a terrifying, wild man look on his face.

Abruptly, they both heard a noise. It was sudden and loud, like a train barreling down tracks.

Shep's police cruiser came straight out of the gloom and slammed Abel into a cluster of Christmas trees. The trees broke under the force and weight and impact of the speeding car. The police car went up off the front wheels. The radiator burst from the impact. Hot steam exploded and smoked out of the engine.

The accelerator gassed and whined until Widow took his foot off the pedal. The airbag deployed, hitting him right in the face.

He popped open the driver's door and fell out of the car.

Adonis jumped to her feet and ran around the tail of the car over to him. She helped fish him out of the seat.

Widow now had bumps on the back and front of his head. His nose bled from being punched in the face by the airbag. There was a gash over his left eyebrow, but otherwise, he was fine.

He slinked out of the car and slung one arm across Adonis's shoulders to help him stand straight up.

She said, "You saved my life. Again."

"Where's the boy?"

"He was here, but he took off when the shooting started."

Widow looked around and saw Flack's dead body.

"There's one of them. Did you do that?"

She said, "No. They turned on each other. Abel shot him in the back."

"Just like rats," he said.

She helped him walk to the rear of the car and leaned him against it. He stayed there for a moment. He felt like his brain was in a fishbowl. Between getting exploded into a wooden beam and then clocked by an airbag, he was more dazed than before. But still not confused.

He asked, "What about Abel?"

She left him sitting there for a moment and went to the front of the car. She looked.

Adonis had seen a lot of dead people in her law enforcement career. But she had never seen someone plastered half into a tree and half into the grille of a car before. She felt sadistic, but it made her smile.

She returned to Widow.

"You killed him."

"That's too bad. I was just trying to knock him over."

"Yeah, right," she said.

"How many are left?"

"Just one. Brooks. The tall black dude."

"Not sure I've met him yet."

Widow got up and stood tall.

"You should take it easy," she said.

"Not yet. I'll take it easy when we find Dylan."

She didn't argue with him. She had learned by this point.

He asked, "Where's the last place you saw the kid?"

She said, "Brooks is armed. We need weapons."

Widow paused and looked in the car's backseat. He wrenched the back door open and dipped down into the rear bench. He came back out with the Winchester rifle. It had fallen down into the footwell on impact with the tree.

"What's that, a gun from the Old West?"

"It's an 1894 lever-action rifle. So, yeah. It's from the end of the Old West."

"Does it work?"

He pointed it at the sky and fired it, levering the action and replacing an old cartridge with a fresh bullet.

The rifle *boomed!*

"Good old-fashioned American-made. It works."

He handed it to her.

"Me?" she asked.

"Unless you want this?"

He took out the M9 Beretta.

"How many bullets are in the rifle?"

"Left?" He asked and started counting in front of her on his fingers. She watched him as he mouthed, "Carry the one."

"Never mind. Give me the nine-millimeter."

He handed it to her. She ejected the magazine and checked how many were left. Then she put the magazine back in.

"There's one chambered?" she asked.

"Yes."

"Good. You take the popgun."

"Suit yourself. But don't lose that gun. It belonged to Abe's dead son. He was a Marine."

She nodded.

"Now, where was the last place you saw the kid?" he asked.

Adonis looked around, saw the tree that she had been hiding behind, and pointed at where Abel and Brooks had been standing and shooting at her.

Widow walked that direction, away from the car. It wouldn't be helpful anymore. The airbags had deployed, and the engine was basically a ticking time bomb waiting to catch fire.

He led Adonis away from the wreckage and the dead cult leader.

They made their way to the position she remembered last seeing them.

"What're you looking for?" she asked.

"It's snowing, isn't it?"

"Yeah."

"Footprints."

They looked at the ground.

"There," she said and pointed to a set of child-size footprints.

Widow saw them too and nodded.

"This way, then!"

They took off running, chasing after Dylan.

60

DYLAN RAN AGAIN like he had before, only this time, his heart pounded in his chest like it was beating to fight its way out. He couldn't go on anymore. He had to stop.

He stopped in the gray, near the tree line to a big opening to the next section of trees, which was the good news. He knew he was almost in the ten-year-old trees.

He dropped to the ground, sat down on his butt in the snow, and laid back. He stared up at the sky and tried to catch his breath. He saw a bird flapping its wings overhead, lost, as if it were separated from the flock, and he recognized it. It was a blackbird. No. It was a crow. They had a lot of them around. He wondered if someone would say it was separated from the flock or separated from the murder?

He smiled at the thought. But that smile was short-lived when he heard boots on snow, running. He sat up and looked back the way he'd come. He saw nothing but gray and trees.

He stood up and breathed in heavily, taking deep breaths so he could take off again. He turned and ran right into a brick wall, for the second time.

Dylan fell back on his butt, making an imprint in the snow right next to the one he'd just left.

He looked up, his eyes traced up the brick wall all the way from his boots, up his torso, past the M4, to Brooks's face.

Sweat covered Brooks's forehead. His eyes bulged like anger festered underneath.

"Get the hell up!" he said, and he scooped Dylan up by the arm. Dylan started kicking at him and screaming.

Brooks lifted him to his feet and dropped and reared back, and punched him square in the face.

"Shut up!" he shouted.

The punch didn't break any bones; it wasn't meant to. But it dazed the boy. He stood on his feet, rocked a bit as if he might pass out.

"Snap out of it!" Brooks shouted.

He jerked Dylan by the collar, dragging him back into the tree line. They stopped at the edge. Brooks looked in every direction for any more speeding cars he didn't expect. There was nothing.

He said, "Which way?"

"What?" Dylan asked.

"Which way to the road?"

Dylan looked around like he was trying to figure it out.

Brooks shook him and showed him another fist.

"Want another one? Because I'm holding back on you, kid! This time, I'll break your nose!"

Dylan threw his hands up in self-defense.

"Okay! Okay! It's that way!"

He pointed back to the farmhouse.

"You think I'm a fool?"

"No!"

Brooks slapped him across the cheek, not as hard as the punch. It was just shock and awe.

"I'm not lying! I swear!" Dylan said.

"That's going back to the house!"

"Yeah. You asked which way to the road."

"Where's another road?"

"There is no other road. That's the only one. Every other direction is nothing but forest for miles and miles."

"How many miles?"

"It could be fifty or more. I don't know."

Brooks stared at him; then he looked in all directions other than the one leading back to the farmhouse.

He had no intention of wandering around South Carolinian woods for days. He thought about it. He could still fly the helicopter away. He was no pilot, but he was smart enough to figure it out. Better to take his chances with the bird and get as far away as he could from the FBI's dragnet than to linger around there for any more time.

He shoved the boy to his feet. He kept one big hand on Dylan's shoulder.

He said, "You lead the way, boy."

Dylan started to walk, but the big hand on his shoulder held him in place. He glanced back at Brooks.

"You try to run, and I'll shoot you in the back. Got it?"

"Got it."

"No funny business!"

Dylan nodded.

Brooks released him, and they walked back toward the house.

61

Widow led Adonis through the snow, moving as fast as they could without running full-speed. They moved at a rate somewhere between first-time joggers and a gazelle's top running speed.

They tore through two rows of trees. Widow put a hand up like he was signaling STOP to a SEAL team in enemy territory. Adonis saw it and stopped next to him.

"What? Do you see them?"

Widow pointed up ahead in the clearing at two figures.

"There," he said.

"I see them."

"It could be them, or it could be someone else."

"Who else could it be?"

"I don't know, but why would he just stop and stand out in the open like that? He knows we're on his trail."

"Is it a trap?"

"Probably."

"Are we still going in?"

"What choice we got?"

"True."

Widow said, "You go around that way."

He pointed left.

He said, "Circle all the way behind. Stay a good twenty yards away. Maybe the gloom will give you some cover."

"What about you?"

"I'm going right up the middle."

"Will he be expecting that?"

"Of course."

"Won't he be expecting me to come up from behind?"

"I'm counting on it."

Adonis looked at him sideways.

She asked, "So, won't he shoot me?"

"Probably."

She slapped him in the arm. He didn't budge.

"You're making jokes? Now?"

Widow said, "A sense of humor is a strength beyond all measure."

"What's that, some more of your Army mumbo-jumbo?"

"I was never in the Army."

"What were you in?"

"What makes you think I was in anything?"

"Look at you. I'm not stupid. I was a Marine, you know?"

"I knew you were a jarhead!"

"How?"

"Because you can't shoot straight."

"Hey!" she said and smacked him again on the arm.

"Okay. Okay. No time to argue about it. We gotta get the kid."

"So then, what the hell is your plan? We've only got the two guns."

He paused and stared at the figure. And like a light bulb went off over his head, he smiled at her.

"What?" she asked.

"You like Christmas movies, Adonis?"

"What?"

"Know what my favorite Christmas movie is?"

"What the hell are you blabbing about?"

Widow said, "Die Hard. Ever seen that one?"

"Of course. Who hasn't?"

"Greatest Christmas movie ever made."

"What the hell're you talking about, Widow? Did you bump your head?"

Widow rubbed the back of his head and felt the bump.

"Actually. I did. But that's not relevant."

He dug into his coat pocket and pulled out a bunch of duct tape taken off the roll from the van. It was bunched together. It was the piece he had wrapped around the radio earlier.

She arched an eyebrow and stared at him. And she realized exactly what he was thinking of doing.

"No. No. You're nuts."

"It'll work. Trust me."

He told her his plan, and she listened.

"That's the most idiotic plan I've ever heard in my life," Adonis said.

"And that's why it'll work."

She shook her head but didn't argue. They took the necessary steps to go through with it. He took off his coat and shirt and undershirt, and he kicked off his boots. He left them on the snow, and he gave her the duct tape. She did her part and then she scooped up one of his boots. A moment later, Adonis took off running west, away from Widow and the figures up ahead. She circled around, staying twenty yards away at a minimum, as Widow had instructed.

Widow imagined her circling around, and he waited, calculating the time it would take her to get into position. Once he figured she was there, he disheveled his hair, pulled off his socks, and started walking completely barefoot through the trees, toward the figures in the clearing.

62

BROOKS clung tight to the back of Dylan's collar and held the boy out in front of him. They stood in the middle of a clearing. He held the M4 out in front of them, but he also kept his Glock loose in its holster for a quick draw.

"How long are we standing here?" Dylan asked.

He was uncomfortable being that close to Brooks, and he also needed to pee. The whole afternoon being held hostage, being jerked around by these bad guys had taken a toll on him. He was afraid to tell Brooks, but he couldn't hold it forever.

He tried to focus on his bladder problem, which seemed counter-intuitive, under most circumstances, but not this one. Concentrating on holding it distracted him from the fear of being shot once Brooks had whatever it was he wanted from him.

Brooks tugged at his collar, choking him momentarily.

"Shut up!" he said.

Dylan shut up.

Brooks turned, pushing the kid along, keeping him out front. They turned like a lighthouse beam swinging around three hundred and sixty degrees.

Brooks knew there was someone coming after them. He figured they would split up and come at him from two sides, or more if they were more than just two people. He knew one of them was Adonis, but he had no idea who the one, or more than one, was in the car that ran over Abel. He prepared himself for the unexpected.

They rotated, checking all directions until he saw something.

There was something coming at them, slow from out of the gloom. It was a man—one lone man. He came up from out of the trees, the way they had come, from behind him.

Brooks faced the man coming toward him. He pointed the M4 right at him, but also kept himself loose, ready to flip around and shoot whoever came up behind him, which he assumed would be Adonis.

The guy walked closer and closer. He started out as a gray silhouette at about thirty yards away.

Brooks yelled out.

"I see you."

The man stayed quiet, but kept approaching. The guy had a rifle of some sort in his hands. Brooks could see the outline.

The man continued coming at him.

Twenty yards.

Brooks jerked the kid in closer.

"I'll shoot you!" he shouted, but the man kept coming.

Fifteen yards.

Now Brooks could see him, but it wasn't anyone he had ever seen before. It wasn't Walter. It wasn't Abe. It wasn't anyone he recognized.

"Who the hell are you?" he shouted.

The man kept walking. Now, he was ten yards away, out of the gray and the gloom and past the trees. He was right at the edge of the clearing.

The man stopped.

Brooks looked him over. The guy was tall, maybe as tall or taller than Brooks. His hair was a mess. He was barefoot. And he was shirtless. He looked like a crazy man, like a guy raised by wolves, having left a cave for the first time.

Every time the guy exhaled, Brooks saw his breath.

Brooks lowered the M4 down to hipshot level. The weight was heavy to keep holding one-handed, and he was as good at this range with a hipshot as he was any other way.

The man rambled out of the trees' edge and into the open clearing. He walked until he was five yards away.

Brooks said, "That's enough! One more step and I'll kill him. I'll snap his little neck like a twig."

Brooks jerked Dylan back, moving his hand from Dylan's collar to his neck. He pulled him in close.

"I'll do it."

The man stopped moving.

Brooks repeated, "Who the hell are you?"

"Jack Widow."

"Who the hell are you in relation to this kid? Where the hell did you come from?"

"I'm Cousin Jack. I was asleep upstairs. Your boys missed me."

"I doubt that."

"Why don't you toss the rifle?"

Widow held the Winchester in both hands like John McClane at the end of Die Hard. He tried to make his best impression. He even dragged his feet in the snow like he had also cut them up by running through broken glass.

Brooks wasn't picking up on the impression.

Widow said, "Okay."

He tossed the rifle down and raised his hands in the universal *don't shoot me* way that everyone knows.

"Now, where's the other one?"

"I'm right behind you," Adonis said.

Brooks turned fast and pointed the M4 toward Adonis's voice.

He couldn't see her, but her voice had come from where he was staring.

He flipped back around, quick, thinking it was a trap. He pointed the M4 back at Widow, who hadn't moved. He stood in the same place, with his hands up.

"Come around," Brooks ordered him, and he flicked the M4's muzzle in the direction he wanted Widow to circle around to.

Widow said, "Okay. Okay. Don't shoot."

He circled around Brooks and Dylan, keeping his front facing them.

"Stop there!" Brooks ordered.

Widow had hoped that Brooks wouldn't have him come all the way around to stand right next to Adonis, which he didn't. He ordered Widow to stop where he was in Brooks's line of sight, but Adonis was still ten feet to Widow's left. It was a big enough gap between them, as Widow had hoped for.

"Come out!" Brooks called out to Adonis.

She did nothing.

"Come out, or I'll kill this kid!" he shouted.

"Okay. Okay. Don't hurt him!" Adonis called back.

Slowly, she came out from behind a tree. He saw a dark object in her hand. She held it like a gun.

"Stop there!" Brooks ordered.

She stopped.

"Toss the gun!"

Adonis paused a long moment, like giving up her weapon wasn't an option. Certainly, she had been trained not to give it up.

Brooks jerked the kid closer and repeated himself.

"Toss the gun!"

"Okay. Stop hurting him!"

She threw the gun off in the distance, farther than he had expected. Widow thought it was overkill. It might give them away, but it didn't.

"Come closer," Brooks ordered.

Adonis walked closer. She did like Widow and stuck her hands straight up in the air. She stepped out of the shadows. She was not in line with Widow, but stayed ten feet away, as he'd told her to do.

Brooks said, "Well. Well. We meet again. It looks like I'll be the last man standing this time."

Adonis said, "Widow?"

Widow eyeballed Dylan. He was too close to Brooks. So, Widow called an audible and started laughing hysterically like a madman.

Brooks stared at him, dumbfounded.

Adonis turned, looked at him sideways, her hands still up in the air.

This isn't working, she thought.

Widow wanted Dylan to pick up on what he was doing, but he didn't. Widow thought about Maggie, his mother. She was a bit stern, a bit strict. She probably didn't let him watch R-rated movies. He may not even have known what happened in Die Hard. He probably wasn't even allowed to watch it on TV, edited.

Widow shifted gears.

He said to Brooks.

"What's your name, by the way?"

Brooks stared at him like he was trying to figure out what Widow was up to. He had them both dead to rights. They'd tossed their weapons. What would be the harm in playing along?

He said, "Brooks."

"Brooks, I got a question for you."

Brooks stared at the insane-looking Widow.

"I'm all ears."

Widow said, "Know what a dead fish is?"

"What the hell is a dead fish?"

Widow glanced at Dylan. The boy's eyes widened and stared back at Widow.

Adonis was a little lost, but she knew something clicked with the kid when she saw his eyes.

She shouted, "Now!"

Time slowed.

Brooks looked at Adonis, flicked the M4 in her direction like he was waiting for her to make a move.

Dylan pulled his feet up off the ground and let his body go completely limp, which started a chain reaction.

His body went limp, causing more weight on Brooks's arm. Brooks wasn't prepared to hold a kid up with one hand and the M4 with the other. His arm slunk, and Dylan slipped down and completely out of it. The barrel of the M4 wavered and moved away from Adonis.

Widow reached back with his right hand over his shoulder to where the Beretta M9 was duct-taped between his shoulder blades. He jerked it off his back and shot Brooks four times in the chest.

Blood exploded out the front and misted in the air. Brooks released his grip on both the rifle and the kid.

Dylan rolled away from Brooks.

Adonis went for the M4 and scooped it up and pointed it at Brooks in case he got back up. But he wasn't getting back up.

Widow walked over to him, stopped, and stood over him, pointing the M9 at his face.

Brooks stared up at him. He gurgled blood. His teeth were red with it.

"Who. Are. You?" he struggled to ask.

Widow lowered the weapon. Brooks wasn't going to fight back. He wasn't going to do much of anything.

"Me? I'm nobody."

Widow watched Brooks take his last breath, and then he stepped away from the corpse. Dylan ran over to him and hugged him like he really was a long-lost cousin.

Adonis dropped the M4 in the snow. She was tired of guns.

She walked over to Widow and Dylan and wrapped her arms around them, joining them for a big bear hug.

They stayed like that for a long time until Widow finally said something, breaking the silence.

"It's cold out here. Let me get my clothes back."

They laughed together.

Adonis went back to get the gun she'd tossed away and came back with one of Widow's boots. She never had a gun. She used his boot as a prop.

They all walked together, still half-hugging, back to his shirt and socks and coat and other boot.

On the way, Adonis said something that Widow understood.

"I'm surprised you didn't say, 'Happy Trails, Hans,' after you shot him."

Widow laughed, but Dylan didn't.

He said, "What? I don't get it?"

"It's from Die Hard, kid," Widow said.

"Oh, Die Hard. That's that old movie. With that actor that died."

"You're talking about Alan Rickman," Adonis said.

Widow glanced at her.

She said, "What? I like the movies."

Dylan said, "No. I never heard that name. I'm talking about the dead guy from the Six Sense."

Widow said, "That's Bruce Willis. And he's not dead."

"He's not?" Dylan asked. "He must be ancient, then. Like sixty?"

"Sixty's not ancient," Widow said.

"Oh. Sorry. Are you sixty? I didn't mean to offend you."

Widow stayed quiet. He had no comment.

63

Two days later, in both the town of Carbine and in Spartan County, South Carolina was swarming with FBI agents. They came in from all over the region, more than a hundred agents. They took statements and investigated all over Cherokee Hill.

Abe was upset about his barn burning to the ground more than anything else. But he was thrilled to have his family back in one piece. They told Widow he could come back any time to visit. He was always welcome to come back for that Christmas dinner. He promised that if he was ever in the area, he would stop in.

They ended up keeping him out of the police and FBI reports. Sheriff Henry Rourke took credit for saving everyone. He was happy to do it. Being handcuffed to a toilet was something he didn't want getting out.

Agent Adonis was fired from the ATF, which she had expected. She viewed it as a fresh start for her. She was lucky not to be facing any charges, considering she'd disobeyed orders. At least, that's what the reps from the FBI kept reminding her.

After Widow reunited the Whites, the first thing they did was move the White's other vehicles away from the fiery trucks and barn. The sheriff called in a ride from one of his deputies. He took Widow and Adonis with him back to the station. He radioed everyone at the fire department to get out to Cherokee Hill.

Former ATF Agent Adonis asked Widow to stick around, to meet with her in Charleston. She gave him the address of a little café she liked there. She said she'd be there on Christmas eve. The café would be one of the few things open. It was open every year on Christmas Eve, until eight o'clock at night.

Widow thanked her for the offer, but said he'd have to think about it. In the end, he went his own way.

From the sheriff's station, Widow took a bus south.

On Christmas eve, Widow sat in a roadside diner, locally owned. He ordered eggs and bacon. He drank his second cup of coffee, waiting for his order and chatting with a lonely waitress. She'd drawn the short straw and had to work Christmas eve. But she got to be home in the morning when her kids woke up. It was a yearly tradition for Widow. He finished the second cup of coffee and watched as the waitress went to get a refill for him. He stared out the window at the empty highway. He stared past the Christmas lights hanging from the restaurant's window. He watched as a light snow fell around the diner.

For a moment, he contemplated what it was like to spend Christmas eve with a family, as most people do. But he was alone. By now, he preferred it this way.

Another thought entered his mind. It was a simple but fundamental question.

Where would he go next?

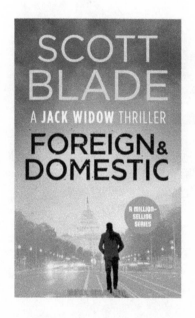

Out Now!

FOREIGN & DOMESTIC: A BLURB

What does the Secret Service want with Jack Widow?

A mistaken arrest puts Widow into the Miami criminal system. A mysterious phone call from the US Secret Service and Widow is on his way to D.C. to face a covert emergency.

The emergency: someone kidnapped the Secret Service Director's daughter.

Their demands: 1: Tell no one. 2: Assassinate the President.

Widow races against time to save an innocent girl and keep the President alive from enemies, both foreign and domestic.

Readers are saying...

★★★★★ Danger! This book series is highly addictive!

★★★★★ The best author next to Lee Child!

CHAPTER 1

ONE THING LEADS TO ANOTHER.

Cause and effect.

A bullet leads to a target, and a democratically-elected president dies. A fragile country is thrown into upheaval, and the world changes, and somebody benefits.

Simple. Cause and effect.

A son shoots his father in front of an entire nation, and the entire world sees it, and politics shift. Power struggles happen, and a country's destiny changes forever.

On this occasion, the equation equaled three bullets fired—two center mass and one miss, with one trigger pulled, three times, and one father killed by one son, his eldest. The son had no choice.

Three bullets. That's all it took.

One thing leads to another: cause and effect.

Moments before he was assassinated, in the small African country of West Ganbola, President-elect George Biyena stood offstage in a freshly pressed suit with a black and gold tie—his country's colors.

Not just on his tie, but the same colors were ahead of him on the stage, sewn into a large West Ganbola flag that waved proudly in the wind, standing next to and at equal footing with the flag of the African Union.

The African Union's flag also waved.

A big part of Biyena's platform had been to move West Ganbola more in line with the rest of the union's humanitarian and democratic policies.

He was a champion of his country's poor and impoverished.

His wife stood on a provisional platform, built the day before in preparation for his first speech as West Ganbola's president-elect. She faced out toward his constituents. He gazed over them through a black and white curtain, surveying the crowd of hundreds of supporters, non-supporters, and the media, both foreign and domestic.

Biyena had just emerged from a vicious election cycle, fraught with back-and-forth political character assassination ads and propaganda. Some true, most lies. He had almost lost the election, but not because the other guy was more popular—or even popular at all—and not because the other guy was the sitting president. It was only because the people of his country were terrified of the other guy. He had been an extreme dictator, a warlord, categorically.

The other guy wasn't a legitimately elected official, not in the sense of what an elected official was supposed to be. The other guy was a dictator, a military leader who overthrew a democratically-elected government fifteen years ago and then installed a fake democratic one over it. He installed what a lot of strongman-types did. They would hold elections, make it all look real, make it all look legitimate, but under the surface, the votes weren't counted. The whole thing was staged to make it look like the other guy was mandated by his population.

It was all a scam.

The other guy was nothing more than a criminal.

Not this time. Part of Biyena's campaign was to get the votes counted by a new third-party institution. This time, Biyena had made enough friends in government, and the other guy had made enough enemies, that the vote was counted, and Biyena had won.

He was proud of his political victory, a road fraught with more than just potential political defeat. It had been dangerous for him and his family. His path to leadership had led him through treacherous waters and political acrimony. Where so many others had failed, forced out of the previous presidential races against the incumbent socialist dictator, or were simply the other guy's patsies, Biyena had succeeded.

Any of his close, personal friends would attest to his patriotism. He believed his country deserved a fresh start, a new beginning. It was truly a great day for democracy and a great day for West Ganbola.

He had not appeared publicly in the three days leading up to the election because of concerns from his head of security. Death threats against him had risen the week before, and it looked as though he would legitimately win the election. This meant he had to be under close guard. He waited in secret, in a secret location, until the ballots were counted—and he won. Now he was about to give the speech that would move his country into a new era of peace.

He had rehearsed the process many times in his head. Walk up the steps. Cross the raised platform. Go over to the podium and hug his wife. Stand and recite his speech, eyes locked on his people.

Don't show fear.

Biyena had stayed up the entire night before, practicing his speech in front of his two most trusted advisors. When they had run out of energy, he had practiced it in front of a mirror at the Royal Hotel on Webiga Street, the street with the hospital that he was born in fifty-three years ago. It was not on purpose, just one of life's coincidences, like dying on the same street.

English was the official language of West Ganbola, but over eighty languages were used in the region. Languages other than English were especially common in the more rural areas, which were almost everywhere.

Near the craggy mountain ranges and olive jungles to the east, you could walk into a village, hear a regional language that had originated there, and then travel a few miles inland only to hear a completely different vernacular and see completely different jungles and mountains.

He loved his country.

Biyena waited for his wife to announce him to the crowd. He heard her voice. He heard her rehearsed annunciation paying off.

She said, "I'm so proud to announce my husband as President George Biyena."

Biyena took a deep breath and held it, and another, and held it. He felt the air go in through his mouth and expand his chest, and then he released it. He repeated the whole thing and then stepped through the curtain, releasing his breath as he did.

The crowd was already standing and chanting his name.

"BI-YE-NA! BI-YE-NA!"

It grew louder and louder as he stepped onto the stage.

"BI-YE-NA! BI-YE-NA!"

He was overwhelmed by the chants and the distant sounds of beating drums and blasting trumpets to mark his arrival, by the sea of faces, and the rows of children brought out to see him. They waved little black and gold flags to show their support. He watched as the flags swayed in the air, not knowing it would be his last time seeing them.

The children in the crowd were dressed like the adults, most of whom were dirt poor. They couldn't afford the kinds of clothes that the richer citizens could, the ones who stood closer to the front of the crowd and on the balconies of the two- and three-story buildings lining downtown.

Even though most the onlookers couldn't afford suits or ties or decent shoes, they were dressed in the finest clothes that they owned. Many of the children wore threadbare, button-down shirts that didn't fit them, with long ties that belonged to their fathers. Many of them were barefoot, toes digging into the gritty dirt. They weren't barefoot because they couldn't afford dress shoes for the occasion, but because they couldn't afford shoes at all. Many of them didn't own a single pair—not all of them, but many.

Biyena noticed. There were far too many children who lived wretched lives because of how poor they were. This was one of the reasons that he'd joined the presidential race in the first place —no matter the risk, no matter the chance of losing his life. In a country filled with the oppressed and the poor, ethics mattered. Honesty mattered. That was why winning was Biyena's only option. He had to change things.

It called to him like God called to him.

Biyena walked out onto the stage and held his arms out and open in a gesture of embrace as if to say: *I'm here, my friends. I'm your new president.*

The crowd never stopped chanting his name. Instead, they upped the ante and roared on.

"BI-YE-NA! BI-YE-NA!"

They repeated it over and over.

They grew louder and louder. They too had felt the rush of hope. Hope for a new future for their war-torn country —freedom from the political corruption and the fallacy of a government that had enslaved them into poverty instead of freeing them to enjoy a better economy and a better life. Parents hoped for a better life for their children. Grandparents hoped for a better future for their grandchildren. Wives hoped their husbands could go to work and return home with a decent wage. Husbands hoped they could pay for clothing for their children and food for the entire family.

To them, George Biyena was a beacon of hope. They wanted a nation without terrorism. Without war. Without fear. Without overwhelming crime. Without brutal poverty. Without instability.

Biyena was what they had longed for. He would change their lives and alleviate their struggles.

Biyena sauntered to the center of the stage like he was taking a stroll. He wanted to savor the moment. He earned it. He had worked hard for this victory.

The months of moving secretly from one location to the next had taken its toll on his wife and four grown boys—especially his firstborn son, Nikita.

Nikita was his pride and joy. He had grown into a successful man in his own right. He was the father of three children. He was a good husband to a good wife.

Biyena couldn't be prouder of Nikita.

President Biyena looked across the stage and saw that, near the bottom of the steps, his son Nikita was passing through the capital police. He was waving frantically at his father.

He wasn't supposed to come up on stage, but the policemen recognized him and let him pass. What were they supposed to do? He was the new president's firstborn son.

Nikita wore an intense look of concern on his face. He was normally the only one of his sons who always kept his cool—nothing ever fazed him.

Whatever was worrying him must've been something urgent, something that couldn't wait. Or maybe Nikita was so proud of his father's victory that he just wanted to share the stage with him in a show of support. Perhaps he wanted to hug him tight and was worried he wouldn't make it. Perhaps.

After all, Biyena had been so busy for months that the two had barely had any time to speak.

Biyena reached the podium and leaned in toward an old, worn-out microphone, the kind with the steel vented face that an old-timey radio station might have. It was a vintage Shure microphone, but Biyena didn't know that, and it didn't matter. He knew that his country had modern equipment. Just because they were a third-world nation didn't mean they were lost in the nineteen fifties.

He wondered whose idea it had been to set up the old-style microphone. Maybe it came from his campaign manager. Maybe it was supposed to represent a more traditional appearance to his constituents and countrymen. Maybe the microphone would make him look like a mid-nineteenth-century revolutionary who had just won a similar election battle, or maybe it made him resemble an American leader like Martin Luther King Jr., giving a speech that would change a nation. Perhaps his people were waiting for him to give a groundbreaking, game-changing speech that would inform his enemies that the people of West Ganbola were no longer afraid. Or perhaps it was because there was an international news crew there covering his speech. Whatever the reason, Biyena liked to be included in all decisions, no matter how small. He believed that every little detail about his televised appearance was crucial. He believed people remembered the details.

He dismissed his concern and stared at the microphone.

A black wire ran down the front of the wooden podium and offstage like a long, thin snake, disappearing below gray cedar boards that made up the platform.

Biyena leaned forward to the microphone and spoke.

"Good morning!"

His voice *boomed* across the crowds and city streets.

The crowd went crazy—chanting and hooraying, waving their flags, and stomping their feet as if they were at a sporting event.

The smallest sons were picked up by their fathers and held high on their shoulders. Mothers hugged their daughters. Brash cheers filled the square, echoing past the low buildings, carrying over the corrugated iron roofs, and dipping down the other side to fill the ears of people standing farther away.

Biyena asked, "How are you doing today?"

The crowd roared, repeating all the same chants and waves and stomps as before.

The capital police stood in front of the stage in a tight perimeter, preventing overzealous citizens from rushing the stage.

The cops directly in front of the stage wore body armor and antiriot gear: helmets and vests, but no guns. They had only batons and stun guns, as they weren't allowed to carry guns—Biyena's orders.

He had clarified that this was an unwavering policy. He strongly believed in it. It was his opinion that guns created a temptation for violence, and the last thing that Biyena wanted was for his police force to be tempted to fire their guns.

The days of cops haphazardly shooting off their guns were over, as far as he was concerned.

Shooting guns into a crowd of civilians was the kind of measure his predecessor would've taken, and had taken many times before. It was not the kind of image Biyena wanted to project for the new direction of his country. He had forbidden guns for most of the police. The only guys with guns were the snipers, Biyena's personal bodyguards who stood in the wings offstage, and the soldiers who stood guard on the outskirts of the capital in case of an external threat.

Unfortunately, the armed soldiers were necessary.

Biyena's predecessor was nowhere to be found. It seemed he was hiding out in one of the many presidential houses—some of which were secret from the public.

No one knew how he would respond to being beaten by Biyena. In fact, no one had seen him in almost seventeen hours, ever since it looked as if Biyena would win.

The soldiers were a precaution, but Biyena had no fear of the old leader returning because he had been told by his advisors that the old dictator had already fled across the border and would probably never be seen again.

So far, transferring power seemed to go off without a hitch, which made sense. Biyena's predecessor was old. He had no children of his own. There were no sons to follow in his footsteps.

He had ruled over West Ganbola so viciously that he never allowed one person to rise to second in command. No one would follow him.

Biyena concluded that the old guy saw the writing on the wall and just ran. He was too old to fight a civil war. And he didn't want to go to prison.

Likely, the new president would have him executed. Why not just run?

The old guy could retire somewhere warm, like the coast of Brazil or Venezuela, countries he had strong relations with, allies.

Biyena and his advisors figured the old guy would most likely spend the rest of his life on a beach rather than in a jail cell, where he belonged, but that was fine with Biyena. He could live with it if the old dictator never again showed his face in West Ganbola.

Biyena looked out across the crowd and then over his shoulder at his son.

Nikita was fighting with two of his father's personal guards, who had stepped in after the police allowed him up the stairs to the stage.

Biyena could see the guards trying to frisk his son, which annoyed Nikita.

Biyena turned back to the crowd and held his hands up high and spoke into the microphone.

"This...this is because of you. All of you. We deserve a better country. We are on our way."

Cheers roared.

He repeated slowly, "This is because of you. All of you."

The crowd cheered again, and people continued to wave the little flags with West Ganbola's colors, more and more, harder and harder. A sea of black and gold flowed across his sightline.

The spectacle kindled a sense of patriotism deep down in Biyena's bones, igniting that sense of nationalism a man feels at his core. He felt like he was dreaming.

Suddenly, he heard his son call out to him over the roars, from behind him.

"Father!"

Biyena turned and looked at Nikita. He looked into his eyes. They were laden with emotion and a look that seemed to be regret and panic all at once.

Perhaps his son was overwhelmed with pride, and that was the look he was seeing. He wasn't sure.

Biyena waved at the guards to allow his son on stage. Then he turned back to the microphone.

"This is because of my family. This is because of my wife. My sons."

He glanced back at the spectators and then at his wife and his son, again.

Nikita walked toward him, and Biyena saw in his eyes that something was off.

Suddenly, fear shot through Biyena. He didn't know why. It was deep down in his bones.

Nikita said, "Father."

There was a tear in his eye.

Biyena didn't step back from the podium or the microphone, but simply turned halfway.

The crowd quieted to a murmur.

Biyena said, "What's wrong, son?"

His voice was low and deep. It fired into the microphone and echoed over the crowd in a low boom from the speakers near the foot of the stage. The crowd fell silent in a cohesive hush, as if they were listening to a sermon. A hiss from the speakers resonated over them in the dead silence. Whispers could be heard wafting through the air.

Nikita walked past his mother without looking at her. Not a glance. Not a nod. Not a flicker of his fingers in a partial wave. Not a single acknowledgment.

As he closed in on his father, the tears multiplied. They filled his eyes.

Biyena knew it was bad news. No—it was the worst kind of news. He had seen nothing rattle his eldest son, and he would never again because right there, Nikita pulled a Colt 1911 handgun from under his jacket. It had been stuffed in the inside left pocket of his suit jacket.

Now it was out and visible, and gripped tightly in Nikita's right hand.

Biyena stared into the end of the barrel. It looked like a single, eyeless, black eye socket staring back at him.

The gun was matte black, but it appeared black and polished in the bright morning sunlight.

Nikita wielded the gun, pointed it at his father's center mass, and, in three quick strides, he closed the gap between them.

Biyena froze in utter terror.

His son was pointing a gun at him.

Confusion filled his mind at first, but then he had a split second of absolute clarity. He was going to die, and his oldest son would be the one to deliver his death to him.

The worst thing a parent can witness is the death of his own child, but the reverse is also true.

With tear-filled eyes, Nikita pulled the trigger, as he had been instructed.

Once. Twice. Three times.

Boom! Boom! Boom!

The sounds were deafening in the silence. The flashes were all bright, fiery orange sprays, small explosions thrust out of the muzzle.

With each shot, the muzzle climbed like Nikita was pulling the trigger recklessly and not squeezing it, which he was.

He had never fired a gun before, not once, but the bullets hit where Nikita aimed. That was what usually happened at close range.

The first bullet ripped through Biyena's upper chest. Red mist burst out and colored the short distance between them.

By the time the second bullet fired, Mrs. Biyena had gone off into a howl of frantic screaming, the shrieks of a banshee.

The second bullet blasted upward and to the left, sending it on a trajectory that ripped through Biyena's right upper side, where the shoulder joins the neck.

The third followed but deviated on a slightly higher path and barely missed Biyena's head. It fired off into the air over the crowd of spectators and rocketed another sixty-four yards before crashing through an office window and embedding itself into the back of a thick wooden bookshelf.

Nikita never got the chance to fire a fourth bullet because Biyena's personal guards had drawn their own weapons and shot him dead.

Two guards fired a pair of classic M9 Berettas and killed the son of the president. They fired nine-millimeter parabellums straight through Nikita's back, rupturing his pancreas and collapsing his lungs and severing his spinal cord.

The guards were well trained and overzealous. They knew how to shoot their weapons, and they didn't miss. They fired into Nikita until he fell, face forward—dead. It was overkill, but the job was done.

Biyena died before his son, but both were lying on the same stage, dying, bleeding out.

Biyena's wife dropped to her knees. Between them, almost perfectly centered, perfectly framed, like a morbid painting of a scene right out of a Shakespearean play.

She watched, her head moving back and forth between them.

First, she saw her husband gasp his final breath. Then she watched the light from her son's eyes die away to nothing.

She wailed and screamed, never uttering a single word.

Only once did she glance up at the crowd. That was when she saw the news cameras. Her eyes fell on them, and she stared as if she was staring at a train barreling down.

All the major stations from West Ganbola and the neighboring nations were there.

Al Jazeera was there, and one crew from an American-owned network was there. It was *CNN International*.

She never spoke.

A WORD FROM SCOTT

I hope you enjoyed reading The Standoff. You got this far—I'm guessing that you like Widow.

The story continues...

To find out more sign up for the Scott Blade Book Club to get exclusive content and notified of upcoming new releases.

THE SCOTT BLADE BOOK CLUB

Building a relationship with my readers is the very best thing about writing. I occasionally send newsletters with details on new releases, special offers and other bits of news relating to the Jack Widow Series.

If you are new to the series, you can join the Scott Blade Book Club and get the starter kit.

Sign up for exclusive free stories, special offers, access to bonus content, and info on the latest releases, and coming soon Jack Widow novels. Sign up at www.scottblade.com.

THE NOMADVELIST
NOMAD + NOVELIST = NOMADVELIST

Scott Blade is a Nomadvelist, a drifter and author of the breakout Jack Widow series. Scott travels the world, hitchhiking, drinking coffee, and writing.

Jack Widow has sold over a million copies.

Visit @: ScottBlade.com

Contact @: scott@scottblade.com

Follow @:

Facebook.com/ScottBladeAuthor

Bookbub.com/profile/scott-blade

Amazon.com/Scott-Blade/e/B00AU7ZRS8

Printed in the USA
CPSIA information can be obtained
at www.ICGtesting.com
CBHW022027071024
15514CB00030B/75